THE BIG STICK

THE
BIG STICK

Lawrence Alexander

DOUBLEDAY & COMPANY, INC.
GARDEN CITY, NEW YORK   1986

Author's Note

Every fact, date and event herein depicted is based on historical record, save for those few instances in which discretion and a damn good story make the better part of accuracy.

Acknowledgements

For the time, advice, support and friendship: Gene Kirkwood and Barry Rosenbush of the Kanter-Kirkwood Company . . . Adrian Zackheim, Mary Ellen Curley and Elaine Chubb at Doubleday . . . Esther Newberg in the New York office of I.C.M., and Mr. Howard Brandy, who was there when it wasn't even Page One. For the room and the music and the Ridge, Eric Bauer in Los Angeles . . . Peter and Joan Dichter, ex of the Bennett Avenue Hilton.

Library of Congress Cataloging-in-Publication Data
Alexander, Lawrence.
    The big stick.
    I. Title.
PS3551.L35696B5   1986   813'.54   85-16118
ISBN 0-385-23131-8

For Brad Marer

On May 6, 1895, Theodore Roosevelt, future Governor of New York State, Rough Rider in the forthcoming Spanish-American War, and twenty-sixth President of the United States, took office as Police Commissioner, the City of New York. He served in this post until April 17, 1897. The city never saw his like before. Or since.

Customer's Order No.				Date	8-23	19 92	
Name		Joy					
Address							

SOLD BY	CASH	C. O. D.	CHARGE	ON ACCT.	MDSE. RETD.	PAID OUT	R

QUAN.	DESCRIPTION	PRICE	AMOUNT
NJW-	Book- war ches		1 60
NJW-	Book- mystery		2 40
NJW	Book- ayres		2 40
NJW-	Book- stick		2 40
NJW	Book- Beacon Hill		1 60
NJW	Book R.F.D.		1 60
			12 00
		TAX	60
		TOTAL	12 60

0019512 Rec'd by

GS-201-2 PRINTED IN U.S.A.

Thank You

BOOK ONE

"Dear Old Beloved Brother"

1 FRICK

■ At 11 P.M. on the twenty-fourth of that May, Theodore Roosevelt was standing in the foyer of Mrs. Edwina Smith's West Twenty-second Street whorehouse, his massive white teeth glinting beneath the brush on his upper lip, bright as the wire frames of his *pince-nez*. Was she telling him that that coat on that hook there, the one with the badge, didn't belong to one of his men?

Was she?

"Of course it belongs to one of your men, dearie," she finally replied, pausing first to light a cigarette as insouciantly as possible, fluffing her carrot-colored curls and lowering her painted lids. " 'Bad boy,' I said, 'coming in here while you're supposed to be out patrolling the beat.' But what could I do, Commissioner . . . ?"

Her hand reached out for him, the hint of intimacy implicit on contact. T.R. removed it, resolute. "It is hardly necessary to compromise me, madam," he warned, "in order to make your point."

Edwina Smith shrugged, coquettish still. The smile. "He was so much bigger than me—so determined to have his way. You can't blame me for thinking it'd be better all around if I let him spend a half hour derelicting his duty instead of causing a scene."

"Was he drunk?"

" 'Was he drunk,' what a question." The caked-on rouge that

covered the sagging cheeks seemed to redden. "Certainly he was drunk. Like I told you: you got a bad one there."

"Not anymore I don't." Roosevelt confiscated the potsy and pocketed it, the clinking of metal against metal audible within the confines of his own coat: several other shields were already in custody. "Good night, madam."

"Good night?" Didn't Teddy want to go on up to room 19 and barge in on his fornicating officer?

"Not necessary," he confided, turning to take his leave. "When number 3419 comes down you can tell him he can begin the appeal process first thing in the morning . . . if he likes."

A cocking of the Leghornesque head. "And me?" Was Mrs. Smith's shut down?

T.R. put his teeth on display again, more rictus than grin. "*Ab*-solutely. Do give Judge Cockran my regards when you get him up out of the bed in room 23."

Laughter erupted from her, hard and real. "You bastard," she said, coughing him away, closing the curtained door between them. She'd seen the two uniformed patrolmen the Commissioner had stationed on the sidewalk in front of her establishment and she had to give him his due: life in Hell's Kitchen was going to be much more evenly matched from here on out.

The prospect was not entirely unappealing.

▪ Something was moving in Henry Clay Frick's garden at 11 P.M. on the twenty-fourth of that May, just outside the beveled glass in the French doors.

Squirrels?

The park on the other side of Fifth Avenue was infested with them, venturesome little rodents Patrick MacFarland thought useful only as targets. If it weren't almost midnight, the Pinkerton thought, he might remove the weapon from the holster on his hip and go hunting. How many of the cheeky, bushy-tailed rats could he mow down within the space of, oh, thirty seconds? Fifteen?

Enough to make goddamned Lieutenant Meeghan sorry that he had kicked Officer MacFarland off the New York City Police?

Enough to convince the Pinkertons of his potential as a team leader, giving him plainclothes responsibility on the Chicago and Northwestern?

Confidential from L. T. Davies, District Supervisor, subject: Patrick MacFarland, promotion. Not only did operative MacFarland rid the client's garden of innumerable squirrels, he did it without damage to any of the treasures in the adjacent drawing room. Vases, porcelain figurines, silver candlesticks, all intact.

Crystal lamps.

Cedar cigar box, mosaic lid.

"Watch this, everybody," the uniformed guard muttered to himself as he stepped through the portal into the balmy night air, squinting, expecting squirrels.

He found men, a pair of them standing in front of a rhododendron in lavender bloom. Tall, fierce-looking figures, one with a face like a death mask sundered by a jagged scar on the cheek; the other younger, perhaps too handsome, arrogant. Confident.

They were waiting for MacFarland to come out. The noises had been deliberately made, a lure. Before the guard could do more than gape acknowledgment of the fact, a third intruder moved in the darkness behind him, the blade of his knife slicing horizontally through the back of the neck, just above the collar. One single expert slash: it bisected the flesh and the muscle beneath, it severed the vertebrae, the spinal cord encased within, cleaving the carotid artery.

Patrick MacFarland's face drained to corpse white even as he crumpled, a welter of blood fountaining, pulsing, splattering crimson on the flagstones. Tiny flowers, ragged petals.

Tiny flowers.

"Schnell," the most youthful of the invaders hissed, gesturing his companions through the open door, impatient, preceding them.

Quick, hurried glances at the bric-a-brac. The crystal lamps, the Dresden plates edged in gold. Tempting stuff, were they common burglars.

Were they anyone. Was it fair that one man, one single family, should hoard this treasure? *Nein,* not fair at all. But they were art thieves tonight, art thieves only, and what they came for was not in this drawing room, it was in the rear of the place, in the reception hall, in that grand and ornate wing of the mansion used by the Fricks for their galas, their debutante and charity balls.

The Hals hung there, a portrait from the artist's later years when his magical brush leaped the centuries, presaging impressionism itself. *Ausgezeichnet*, perhaps even more so in the flickering yellow light of the twin oil-burning lamps they brought with them. *Schönheit*, like the Vermeer across the parquet.

Interior, Delft. Rectangles within rectangles depicting a room so spare as to be Spartan, save for the stained-glass window in the background. Seated behind a trestle table, a woman with a downcast mien, small mongrel at her feet. Standing some significant distance away, a man with a broad-brimmed hat, grim, steadfast in his refusal to look anything but straight ahead.

Man and wife?

Lovers estranged?

Landlord and tenant?

Sweat unexpected in the palm of the beholder caused him to bobble his end of the oil as it was lowered alongside the Hals already on the floor. The corner of the hand-carved frame glanced off the waxed oak, reverberating.

"Sorgfältig!" he was warned, the whisper as loud as the impact, the echoes ascending. Two stories overhead, Augustus Lennert awoke in his bed. Something was . . . different. The breathing of the house itself had . . . changed.

Sixty-seven. Ill. Aching. "Stay in bed," that was the last order Henry Clay Frick had given his servant before he'd entrained for Saratoga. But the walls were speaking to him, asking him to make sure that nothing was wrong.

Duty.

Augustus Lennert fumbled for a wooden match in the box beside the lamp, rising, ignoring the electrical switch to ignite the wick. Part of the reason the house was calling out to him now might very well be the holes that Edison's crew had drilled in the walls, respecting neither the polished old English oak nor the smooth rose marble. Oh, they'd been as good as their word in that they'd covered up the gashes with metal plates but Augustus knew the damage could never really be repaired, and the house knew, too.

The rape of the virgin: one of the Rubens in the reception hall. He suddenly wanted to look at it again, to make sure it was safe. To make sure they all were safe, the Rubens, the Titians, the Holbeins.

Two stories down, and an exercise in futility, of course. What else could the Old Masters be but safe, Mr. Frick having so carefully contracted for twenty-four-hour-a-day guard service?

And, indeed, there they were where they always were, the Rubens, the Titians—

—And yet the old man found himself pivoting in the center of the hall, blinking. *Interior, Delft* wasn't on its hook, nor the Hals portrait. Nor the Gainsborough. Three paintings, on the floor, leaning against the side of the *causeuse.*

Those oil lamps. Who did they belong to?

Augustus Lennert knew the answers even as he posed the questions. He knew that Patrick MacFarland was crumpled dead in the garden; he knew that the shadow looming up from behind the settee held an already bloodied dagger and that the blade was descending in an arc from a high angle, at a virulent rate of speed.

His spirit slipped out of his body just in time, just before the pain would have made him scream. Wasn't it a fantastic thing, he thought at the end, seeing how the steel pierced the sternum and severed the aorta. Wasn't it a fantastic thing, the way the heart continued to pump even though the purpling blood was gushing outward, soaking the clean white nightshirt.

Wasn't . . .

■ Murphy's Saloon on Ninth Avenue was only nominally Murphy's, its real owner being a thug named Estes Hanrahan. Roosevelt was not surprised to see him there.

But in the company of a young police officer? Right out in the open? "By Godfrey," the Commissioner exploded, lashing out at the door with the flat of his hand. "The only intercourse any man of mine *ever* has with scum like this is at the point of a gun! With the handcuffs out!"

T.R.'s voice ricocheted off the plated tin ceiling, cutting
through the conversational din like a lumberjack's saw, striking
Officer Richard Kerner directly through the heart. It couldn't be
the new bossman himself striding toward the table, backed up by
a pair of senior officers. It couldn't be.

And yet there was no mistaking that barreling figure, the bull-
dog face, the bristling complexion. "Commissioner," Kerner
squeaked, swallowing, aphasic.

"Yes?" It was as cold a "what can I do for you" as the youth
had ever heard. No explanation would suffice. None.

"Really, sir," Estes Hanrahan interjected, sweet reason all over
his genteel voice: Teddy was not the intimitable proprietor of a
Ninth Avenue produce stand soliciting protection. He neither
bought nor sold stolen goods, soft or hard. "Officer Kerner is here
only because he is doing his job."

"Is he."

"Informing me that some stolen merchandise of mine has been
returned? Yes: I think so." The thug looked across the table. What
time did Richard say he could pick it up at the station—"nine?"

A cue, but Richard was hesitant and Roosevelt beat him to the
punch. What exactly was the "it" which Hanrahan had reported
stolen?

"Office equipment. A pen and inkwell set, a lamp—one rather
expensive typewriter."

"For which you still retain a bill of sale?"

"Naturally." Hanrahan brazened a look directly into T.R.'s
eyes. "I'll be bringing it along with me when I come to claim
everything, tomorrow."

The Commissioner was sure the paperwork would be very neat,
hooking his thumb through the air: would Officer Kerner join him
outside?

"Sir?"

"Outside." If the young cop had anything to say for himself
perhaps he'd feel more free in the privacy of the open air. "Just so
long as you don't stick to that cock-and-bull story about stolen
property."

"No," Richard agreed. "Mr. Hanrahan made that all up to get me off the hook with you."

"You being one of his valuable connections on the inside of my department." Roosevelt's voice was razor thin, deliberately, the object of his ire wincing.

"That's the impression I've been trying to give him, yes, sir."

Impression.

"Infiltrating his gang was the only way we were ever going to get enough to send Hanrahan up the river, or maybe even to the end of a rope. I've been working on it for some time now, and—"

"Under whose authority?" T.R. was not quite sure he liked the way the rookie was twisting things around. What had been incontrovertibly corrupt was suddenly the opposite, an endeavor of high moral purpose, possibly splendid.

Possibly Kerner was playing him for fool.

"My own authority," the patrolman was saying in response to the Commissioner's question. "I know it's not according to the rules, but if anything didn't come out right it'd be me taking the blame, not the department. Also, there've been rumors around the station: maybe some of the other officers are already on Hanrahan's payroll. I figured I'd be better off trusting nobody there."

"You expect me to believe that."

"The only way you could find out would be to let me go ahead and see if I turn up any proof." He examined Roosevelt's face, imagining that T.R. would be hardly likely to grant him so much carte blanche on so brief an acquaintance. "Even though I think Hanrahan is just about to take me up on my offer."

"Indeed!"

"There aren't any guarantees, sir. But—"

T.R. cut him off. "By George!" he boomed. "No one could just make up a story like that: it *has* to be true. And I say bully!"

To his senior officers he said more than bully.

"Individual initiative: we could do with a lot more of it, gentlemen. A whole lot more!"

They yessed him while Kerner waited for the final disposition of the case. "Does this mean I'm not on report anymore?"

"It means, Officer, that we will go into it in detail tomorrow morning at my office on Mulberry Street, eight A.M. sharp."

Unless Richard didn't want to talk about being the Commissioner's new aide?

▪ Two hours before 8 A.M., after barely three hours' sleep, Theodore Roosevelt could be found wide awake at the top of the steps in front of the home he leased from his sister Bamie at the corner of Sixty-second Street and Madison, hand extended with enthusiasm. His visitor was right on time, right on time, a wide-faced gent dressed in a Chesterfield and a bowler, and everything was ready in the downstairs parlor. "My sons have been up for an hour, pushing the furniture aside; we should have plenty of room."

The boys said "wow" several times, watching their father and his guest strip down to boxing trunks and strap-shouldered undershirts, seeing the brand-new regulation-weight gloves come fresh out of the box.

"Are you sure you wouldn't want gloves with extra padding? I did bring some," the visitor wanted him to know. "Just in case."

Six-year-old Kermit shook his head. "Father says beating 'Gentleman' Jim Corbett with extra padding isn't beating him at all—isn't that right, Father?"

" 'Beating' is not what I said," T.R. wanted it understood. " 'Standing up to'—that's how it was put." He grinned at the champ, unembarrassed. "Which is precisely what I expect to do, for six three-minute rounds, at least. Ted will keep the time."

The clang of a flat brass bell followed, the commissioner's eldest son, proud as any eight-year-old could possibly be, pleased to tell the pugilist that "Father borrowed it from the timekeeper at Madison Square Garden, just for this fight."

"Then *I* hold the watch. If you're going to ring the bell, it's only fair." Alice Lee Roosevelt, eleven, swept into the parlor, another girl trailing in her wake: Anna Eleanor Roosevelt, Alice's cousin Nell, mouselike in contrast to Alice Lee's breathtaking looks and mercurial charm. Ringlets of flaxen hair highlighted the perfection of Alice's bones and Alice's skin; Anna Eleanor's face was primarily teeth. No wonder she clutched so at the shredding old rag doll her late father, Teddy's younger brother Elliott, had given her, a memento of his final European trip. One had to clutch at something when one's appearance alone endangered mirrors everywhere.

Alice confiscated the timepiece.

"Daddy," Ted complained, abused.

"Children." His fellow commissioners on the Police Board, the City Council, Democrats of Tammany Hall, none of these would accept so adenoidal a warning. Neither would any of his offspring, certainly not the heir apparent, on whom the watch had originally been bestowed.

"You gave it to *me,* tell her."

"He gave it to you because I wasn't here," Alice was sure. "I'm here now."

All right. "Kermit gets the watch."

"Kermit can't tell time, Father."

Ah. Well. True. He could ring the bell, though. So. "Alice will hold the watch. Ted will *read* the watch. And, when they both call 'time' at the end of each three-minute round . . . ?"

". . . I ring the bell, oh, boy!" Kermit was *de*lighted.

"Very good." Corbett directed his approval at the elder Roosevelt.

"Not quite yet," the Commissioner's quiet tone suggested, his eyes focusing on Anna Eleanor. The child was standing slightly removed from her cousins, her head bowed as though its weight were too heavy to bear, her fingers unconsciously kneading the belly of the threadbare little doll, making it sag in the center. She, too, had to participate in the event this morning, it was only proper, and perhaps she would play the most important part of all. "You know what that is, Nell?"

"No."

"The audience," her burly, bristle-lipped uncle cheerily informed her, personally seating her in an overstuffed armchair at the edge of the makeshift ring. "You and your friend here. Has he got a name?"

Eleanor shook her head, saying not that her "friend" didn't

have a name, but that it was private, between the two of them. Roosevelt knew better than to press.

"I was shy, too, when I was his age." And it was not necessary to give a name in order to be an audience. "All you have to do is keep your eyes open."

"What's so important about that?" Alice sniffed.

The heartiness in her father's voice did not completely obscure the intended reproach. What was so important about that would come afterward, "when your cousin is going to tell me whether I kept my guard up properly, whether my footwork was all it was supposed to be, whether my jab wasn't sharp enough, or close enough to the body." As he said, "a very important part."

"We'll keep our eyes very open," Eleanor promised him. "Baby Joss and me, both." Her fingers manipulated the doll's hand, extending it. The Commissioner automatically reached out to shake the little pink member.

"Pleased to meet you." And if the little man had any comment on whether T.R. was able to get any good right hooks off, "they would be welcome, too."

" 'Gentleman' Jim wouldn't mind some comment on how he did, either." Roosevelt's sparring partner shadowboxed as he spoke. Was Teddy ready to dance?

"Ready, willing and able!" The gloved hand gestured in Kermit's direction. "Bell!"

Bell. "Sock 'im, Dad!"

"Partisan." The President of the Police Board circled his opponent, beginning the bout with a series of feints and jabs, he and Corbett exchanging small bubbles of laughter in mutual appreciation, style and technique.

"Who's been giving you lessons behind my back?" the champ wanted to know. "Sullivan?" The phone rang in the hallway outside the parlor.

"John L. and I have gone at it once or twice." T.R. blocked a Corbett cross with an upraised forearm, getting back at the professional with a punch to the ribs strong enough to elicit an oof. "He said if I really wanted to test my mettle you were the man."

"He's pestering me for a return match, you know." Corbett's

voice was conversational, matter-of-fact, even as he unleashed a
series of rights and lefts, retaliation for the surprise the Commissioner had just given him. The telephone rang again in the hall.

"I'd look forward to that," said his host, backing away from the
prizefighter's onslaught, forearms up again, an ineffective shield in
front of his face. "You and John L. toe-to-toe again: magnificent!"
He uncorked a powerhouse which caught Corbett's cheekbone
square, bruising it as surely as it would have been had the great
John L.'s fist been in the glove.

"Hey." Corbett was impressed, shaking his head to clear his
vision. "I think I underestimated you."

A third ring of the bell in the telephone directed Roosevelt's
attention away from the business at hand. "Edith," he found himself calling. "Isn't anyone going to answer that telephone—
whoop—!"

"Pay attention," Corbett advised, almost knocking the wind
out of Teddy's sails with a good strong one to the midriff.
"There's still time left in the round."

"Fifteen seconds," Alice announced. "Hit him back, Father!"

"Yeah," Ted and Kermit concurred. Out in the hall Edith
Carow Roosevelt, thirty-three, came up to the phone, lifting the
horn off the hook.

"Hello?"

The voice was musical, generous, filled with thirty years of
memory as far as Roosevelt was concerned, pictures of childhood
picnics and outings in the Long Island snow suddenly flooding
through his mind. The stunned look on her face the morning he'd
come back from Harvard to tell her that he would not be marrying her, after all; that a blond girl from Massachusetts had
stolen his heart—the stunned look on that very same face the
afternoon four years later when the young widower had come
back early from a political meeting and found her on the stairs
bidding his sister Bamie a casual good-bye: one single "hello"
triggering all of that in him, as always.

As a result, he did not see the beautiful uppercut that "Gentleman" Jim steamrollered into his nose.

"Can you come to the telephone, Theodore?" Edith appeared

beneath the arch that separated the parlor from the hall, slender, well-proportioned, secure, not at all perturbed to see her husband flat on his back on the rug, bleeding profusely from both nostrils.

"Time!" Kermit struck the bell as his brother and sister made the call, in unison. The count would have been ten had the champ not paused to reaffirm which corner was the neutral.

"Saved by the bell," Roosevelt remarked, rueful as he struggled up to a sitting position, several drops of bright red nose blood adding to the complexity of the pattern in the carpet.

"Can you please be a little more careful where you bleed?" Edith offered him her arm and a lace-edged handkerchief. "The carpet was just cleaned."

Better to avoid the subject. "Who's on the phone so early in the morning?" T.R. glanced at his watch keepers. "What time is it?"

"A quarter past six," his daughter replied. "Milkman's hours."

"Policeman's hours," the Commissioner wanted her to understand as he went to take the call. "The immigrants in the sweatshops downtown are no doubt chained to their sewing machines by now, too. The bargemen in the harbor."

Where else should they be, Alice's expression seemed to ask. If God hadn't brought the immigrants over from Europe to sew, who would make her dresses? As for the bargemen—

"Theodore Roosevelt here."

The voice in the earpiece was distant and tinny, and wrenching in its grief. "This is Henry Clay Frick, Commissioner," it said, on the verge of break. "My family and I just got back from Saratoga this morning and I'm calling to report a robbery and two murders."

▪ Milkman's hours.

The expression came back into Theodore Roosevelt's mind as he turned west on Sixty-ninth Street twenty minutes later, still fiddling with the buttons on the vest of his three-piece suit. The bout with Corbett had been rescheduled even as Edith had supplied the cotton wadding for his nose, handing him the brown tweed fresh from the closet on the second floor, but breakfast? Canceled. Not even thought of, not until his belly growled as the

Commissioner strode up Madison, as he rounded the corner and saw the Borden's wagon in front of 18, behind the whinnying bay.

"Teddy!" the milkman waved, loading a wooden carton filled with empties into the rear. "What's all the fuss?" His head indicated the commotion building at the corner of Fifth, two department vans already in place in front of the Frick house, a third coming aclang out of Central Park.

Spectators were gathering, curious.

"Robbery," that was the fuss. "Murder." Would a bottle of milk be available for sale?

Commissioner Roosevelt wanted to buy a bottle, from Nick Gibson? "Wait'll I tell the wife," the dairy company representative exclaimed, choosing the perfect wax paper–sealed carafe from a compartmentalized crate. "Could you write your name on, I dunno, how about the back of this order form? The missus won't believe it was you, you don't."

A fast scrawl—"although I really don't think it's quite the honor you make it out to be, selling milk to a civil servant." T.R. dug for change in the right-hand pocket of his trousers.

"On me, Commish." Gibson sprang up into the driver's seat of his gaily painted delivery wagon, grabbing the reins. "Consider it my contribution to good government." All Teddy had to do was go on keeping 'em on their toes downtown "and the two of us're even."

"By Godfrey!" Roosevelt exclaimed, saluting the departing deliveryman, with the bottle. "See if I don't, sir! See if I don't!"

Harrigan and Hart couldn't have covered the remaining distance to 5 East Sixty-ninth any more exuberantly, not and drink milk from a bottle at the same time.

■ "Who is the detective in charge?" The question was addressed to a young officer with apple cheeks so smooth the Commissioner was sure they'd yet to experience the sting of a morning razor.

"Lieutenant Meeghan, sir. He's inside with Mr. Frick."

"Not letting any grass grow under his feet, good," Roosevelt said, nodding. "I like that." He started past the youth, who didn't know whether to stop him with a word or with a word and a restraining hand.

"Excuse me, sir, they're coming down to meet you. I asked one of the other officers to tell them you were on your way." He'd seen T.R. up the street with the milkman and—

"*In*credible!" And his name was?

"Lindsay Hargate. They call me 'Lindy' for short."

"Well. Officer Hargate. 'Lindy.' " The teeth gleamed. "Would you have any objection if I were to commend you to your captain later on this afternoon?"

"Objection?" Followed by an immediate "sir?" The *tabula rasa* which was Lindsay Hargate's face made Theodore Roosevelt laugh: every once in a while he liked to be reminded of the faith he was supposed to have in humanity.

"Theodore!"

Henry Clay Frick was still on the other side of the threshold when he called out the name, preceding the thick-set Lieutenant Meeghan into the morning. "Thank you for getting here so quickly; a tragedy like this is something I just . . . I just . . . my God, Augustus practically raised me."

The collector's eyes couldn't seem to stop moving. Welling, rimmed, they darted this way and that over a set of pouches swollen with grief. Roosevelt took his hand. " 'Augustus'?"

"Mr. Frick's manservant," Meeghan explained. He spat: a loose piece of cigar leaf irritating his tongue, broadening the brogue. "One of the two deceased."

"Normally he would have gone with us to Saratoga, but he had a touch of the grippe. We all thought he'd be better off caring for it in his own bed."

Because they had prevailed, because they had prevailed . . .

"Stabbed several times," the lieutenant reported, the facts already down on the pad in his palm. "Front and back. I figure he walked in on the gang while they were taking the paintings down from the wall." The body was still in the ballroom, if the Commissioner cared to see.

"I didn't come here to listen to a report you could have just as easily given me in my office." T.R. bristled. "I expect to be shown both bodies and I expect to hear how you propose to solve the crime."

Meeghan's swallow was audible. "Whatever you like," he finally said, gesturing toward the garden alongside the house. "We could start with the Pinkerton, MacFarland: he's right over here."

"One moment." A shiver had broken through Frick's composure: the detective might not have been sensitive enough to notice it, but Roosevelt had. No need to experience the horror twice; perhaps the industrialist might prefer to linger behind, with Officer Hargate?

Pale, but with the shattered pieces of his equilibrium gathered around him again, Frick shook his head. "I can't imagine it being any worse than it was the first time," he murmured, grateful, waving them ahead. Drawn, in fact, to the crumpled body on the discolored flagstones, the flies feasting on the face, the eyes like eggs fried with broken yolks.

Was that a beetle crawling in the cavity?

"I used to know this guy back in Murray Hill," Meeghan was telling the Commissioner, pointing as he spoke to the scuff marks in the pine needles on the ground between the path and the wrought-iron gate. "The Pinks'll hire anyone, even if the department gave 'em the heave. Muscle is muscle."

T.R. found himself eyeing the French doors, half-open, the branches snapped on the bush to the left. "They lured him out to cut his throat; is that your theory, Lieutenant?"

"Something like that." It wouldn't be smart, arguing it either way, not with the most conspicuous of the commissioners. "Once they had him out of the way they could go on in and take what they wanted."

It didn't look to Roosevelt as though there was anything "wanted" in the drawing room.

"Guess not." Meeghan shrugged as he and Frick followed Teddy inside, watching him circumnavigate a table, fingering a gilded clock. A hand-tooled silver tea service on a matching tray.

"So many treasures." Jade carvings from China. Medieval tapestries on the walls. The finest examples of workmanship that unlimited money could buy.

Ignored.

"That's right," the lieutenant was pleased to agree. "These boys weren't your ordinary everyday housebreakers out for the fast snatch-and-run: they knew what they wanted." He would lead the tour from here, thank you, down the corridor to the reception room in the rear.

"The last place I thought of when we arrived home and Augustus didn't answer the doorbell," the millionaire recalled as they reached the double doors, one of Lindsay Hargate's fellow rookies standing watch. "The truth is I didn't come back here looking for him, either: I just had an urge to spend a little time with my new Vermeer."

A bundle of dirty clothes had been left in the middle of the floor. Why would Augustus have left a bundle of dirty old clothes out like that, in a formal setting like this, a man with his immaculate sense of order?

Frick leaned against the raised oak molding which framed the ballroom entry. "Funny, isn't it. How you interpret things on first glance?"

It did seem like a pile of discarded clothes, Teddy reflected, stepping up to the inanimate object which had up until two days before been Augustus Lennert. Julius Caesar must have looked like this after the storm was unleashed in the Roman Senate, that hurricane of knives.

"They made damn sure he wasn't going to be around to finger them." Meeghan's voice broke the silence: Roosevelt found himself startled.

"Yes," he said, feeling an irrational need to recoup. "But then why stop with only three paintings? Why didn't they just clean the place out?" No one else was likely to walk in.

"Honor," that was the detective's impression. The thieves had an order for those three specific canvases. They prided themselves on their professionalism. One Hals, one Vermeer, one Gainsborough, period.

Or else they spooked.

"These 'professionals,' as you call them." A contradiction in Meeghan's own terms?

"Maybe." On the other hand, if anyone else were to walk in, "hey: it could be the hangman. So three valuable artworks away on the milk wagon, that's a lot better than nothing."

A weight seemed to attach itself to the bottom of the half-consumed bottle in the Commissioner's hand, dragging it downward. What did Meeghan mean, three valuable artworks away on a milk wagon?

"Well, now," the lieutenant preened. "Of course they'd be disguising the thing they'd be using to get their loot away in, putting some kind of phony sign up on the panels. 'Flannigan's Bakery,' that was a favorite with the Barlow brothers down around Chelsea. Up in the Bronx there was a gang that always went with the likes of 'Paddy's Fine Furniture,' or 'Izzy and Mike, Junk Dealers to the Elite.' "

"Or 'Borden's Milk.' "

The gray eyes twinkled in the taurine face. "That's only in the Silk Stocking District, Commissioner."

T.R. threw his head back and laughed. "You know, Lieutenant," he remarked, "if we both didn't know this crime was committed some days ago, I'd have had to say, 'You're right—I could very well have just bought my breakfast from one of the gang.' "

"Forgive me, Theodore," a bitter voice interjected from in front of the J. M. W. Turner across the room. "Would that have been amusing, you buying milk from someone who killed a man I've known since childhood?"

"Henry." Roosevelt reached out for the man, coming up to grip the shoulder from behind, feeling the silent sobs welling up from within. "They'll be punished for this, I promise you."

When Frick spoke again the voice was so low as to be almost inaudible. "It will be a long time," he said, "before I'll enjoy one of these paintings again. A long, long time."

2 MINNIE KELLY

- "Hi yi yi!"

The Sioux war cry rang out from the corner of Sixty-ninth and Fifth, where Lieutenant Meeghan's bluecoats had set up the wooden barricades. "Hi yi *yi!*"

Teddy's head swiveled on his neck as he stepped out of the mansion. Who in New York would know that? East of the confluence of the Cheyenne and the Missouri it was only the Commissioner himself and perhaps a handful of Bill Sewalls. Wilmot Dows. Cowboys Roosevelt had originally recruited on hunting trips to the woods of Maine.

Sewall . . . Dow . . .

". . . Jake!"

"Hi yi yi!"

Of course Jacob Riis would be on the scene of a story like this: *The Evening Sun* would want the best reporter it had covering a murder at the house of a Frick. A personal friend of the new Commissioner—who'd taught the avuncular author how to shout in Sioux.

"Let that man through!" T.R. gestured as he dashed across the street, the officer assigned to the spectators angling the sawhorse outward only to ten degrees: barely enough to give the honoree access. "I need a favor, Jake."

"Name it." The *quid pro quo* had never yet failed to follow.

"Get Dana to play this down"—that was the request, made as Roosevelt ushered the reporter toward his carriage, arrived from Police Headquarters on Mulberry Street while the Commissioner had been inside. "I'm not saying don't print it, just don't scream it in twenty-four-point type."

"Better that than forty-eight." Which Hearst and Pulitzer would use even if Dana didn't, Riis felt obliged to observe, accepting Teddy's offer of a ride downtown. " 'Frick Mansion Robbed, Two Dead; T.R. Asks Press to Hush Up Crime.' "

"To keep the copycats quiet in the woodwork." Even the yellowest of the yellow journals wouldn't want to start a rash of similar atrocities.

"Charles Dana would commit them himself if he thought it would up the circulation," didn't Theodore know that? "And then he'd publish a front-page editorial, daily: 'Why isn't our city's celebrated new Commissioner of Police doing anything to stop this outbreak of barbarism?' "

"He would, too, wouldn't he." Roosevelt lapsed into silence, contemplating the worshipers on their way into St. Patrick's, the little black shoeshine boys lined up in front of Abercrombie and Fitch. Riis knew enough to let him think, all the way down past the Waldorf on Thirty-fourth, the "Garden" on Twenty-sixth.

Buffalo Bill's Wild West Show was due, opening next week.

"What if," T.R. finally said, "what if there was an even bigger story than the robbery at Frick's?"

"It would have to be *very* big. Very shocking. Another Custer massacre. A new Pullman strike. One of our battleships blown up in a foreign harbor while it's making a state visit. Otherwise"— Jake started to shrug—but then he noticed the smile blooming on Theodore's face.

"It doesn't have to be anything like that at all," the Commissioner was convinced. "Close to home, that's where the money is. The closer, the better."

■ "Home" was Police Headquarters on Mulberry Street, sulphuric yellow, four stories high, corniced green at the top. Teddy was going to go inside and personally fire the men he'd found with the Edwina Smiths and the Estes Hanrahans: was that the story he thought would relegate the crime on Sixty-ninth Street to the lower left-hand corner of page one or, even more preferable, to the police blotter in section two? " 'Haroun-al-Roosevelt Holds His Own Departmental Hearings; Drops—it'd have to be at least a two-digit number, Commissioner."

" 'Haroun-al-Roosevelt.' " T.R. always liked the sound of that, from its first appearance in print two weeks before, after Riis had accompanied him on the first of his midnight tours. What he was doing was very much in the style of his Bagdadian predecessor, the sultan Haroun-al-Raschid, going out to see the corruption for himself. Very much indeed.

Departmental hearings chaired by the President of the Police Board: a thought. A damn good thought. But not a big enough story to take real precedence with Joe Pulitzer and Bill Hearst; that'd have to be something else.

"Teddy, hey! Teddy!"

Children and adults both called out his name as the carriage pulled up to the curb on the east side of Mulberry Street, games of hopscotch and ring-around-rosie momentarily set aside. Old men and mothers waved from the windows of the tenements facing the police department, from the clotheslines strung across the roofs above. "Commissioner!"

"Mrs. O'Herlihy, hello! Mr. Silverstein!" And, not ever forgotten, the little ones. "Boys and girls." Studying hard for their exams, were they?

Giggles, the games resuming. Roosevelt dashed up the stone steps of the stoop, which took him to the main entrance of the old headquarters building, barred basement windows fanning out on either side. The ambulance chasers and Tammany hangers-on cleared an instantaneous path.

"Theodore." Riis had trouble keeping pace, T.R. already halfway up the stairs to the second floor. "If it isn't a mass firing, what is it? Byrnes?"

Byrnes. New York City's incumbent police chief. A crook, pure and simple: the new Board President would have him out, fast. Headlines when he finally rammed the ouster through the three other commissioners on the panel, but not today. Not the story Raschid-al-Roosevelt had in mind for today.

"What then?" Frustration raised the reporter's voice almost an octave, constricting it.

"That."

That. A gathering of officers and officials, all crowding around the door to the Commissioner's office at the end of the hall, their breathless murmurings underscored by the machine gunning of a typewriter.

"I thought it was just talk," someone was saying, awed.

"Who'd have believed," from another. A third man gave it no more than two weeks, whatever "it" was.

"Two weeks, are you crazy? Three days, tops!" The speaker wasn't merely adamant, he was outraged, sensibilities offended.

"Gentlemen." The unexpected sound of the office holder's voice made them turn in synchronization, the mutual movement reminding Jake of the flock of penguins newly installed in the Central Park Zoo. One, braver than the rest, stepped forward in challenge.

"Are you serious, sir?" The arm whipped out behind him, toward the open door. "Have you no shame?"

"Listen to that typewriter," Teddy snapped, pushing past. "Can any of your employees make it ring like that? Can they?" Ability was ability. Talent was talent. "And Miss Minnie Gertrude Kelly makes a far more attractive receptionist than any man"—as Miss Minnie Gertrude Kelly herself had said when she first came to apply for the position of secretary to Police Commissioner Theodore Roosevelt.

"Miss Kelly," said Mr. Riis, kicking himself forward to present himself. "Jacob Riis, at your service."

"From *The Evening Sun,* yes." Minnie's smile was soft and her pleasure genuine. "Mr. Roosevelt told me I could expect to make

your acquaintance; I came prepared." The volume which appeared in her hand was a copy of *How the Other Half Lives,* an
exposé of immigrant life in the slums of the Lower East Side and
Brooklyn, by Jacob Riis.

"Minnie is as much of an admirer of your work as I am," T.R.
advised, passing the book on to the author. "Your autograph on
the frontispiece would probably get you the kind of inside department information other reporters on the police beat would give
their eyeteeth for." What did Jake think, was this breach of the
all-male bastion the kind of sensation that the Commissioner anticipated? "Yes? No?"

"A girl secretary?" Riis ceremoniously returned *How the Other
Half Lives* to its owner, autographed. "One who looks like Miss
Kelly? Scandalous. I doubt Mr. Dana will have room for anything
else on the front page this evening." Assuming there'd be a photograph they could feature across the six middle columns of newsprint, just over the fold?

"In fact." The sepia-toned portrait was already up in Teddy's
hand.

"I might have known." Jake grinned, accepting the enlarge-
ment. How, by the way, would Roosevelt feel about an interview
with Edith? "A companion piece. How she reacted when you told
her there was going to be a beautiful young woman working with
you at the office."

"Actually," the Commissioner revealed, somewhat uncomfortable, "she doesn't know yet. Edith." He'd intended to fill her in at
the breakfast table following the bout with Corbett, the plan pi-
geonholed when the call came in from Frick. "Not that Edith
would be anything but enthusiastic, I'm sure."

His wife might not have had the assertiveness of a Susan B.
Anthony, but she saw no reason for a woman of aptitude to be
confined to the kitchen and the bedroom. "They can teach, they
can nurse, write, they can do any number of things like that and
not be considered 'loose.' "

Minnie Gertrude Kelly could never be called loose: Theodore
Roosevelt wanted The *Sun* to emphasize that. This was a young
lady of high moral quality, "a parishioner at St. Francis, living at

home in Brooklyn Heights with her parents. She's engaged to be married—"

"To?" Riis's pencil found itself poised above his pad, professional sleight-of-hand which would have been the envy of almost any magician.

"Kenneth Boylan; he's a carpenter in Crown Heights. But," Minnie wanted it understood, "the banns aren't near ready to be posted, my mother and father notwithstanding."

"Interview them," T.R.'s editorial advice. "All three. Edith, too." His hand made a headline in the air. " 'Roosevelt Hires Girl as Secretary, Creates Sensation at Mulberry Street Police Headquarters'—right?"

"Right," the reporter replied, imbued. The troubles at Mr. Frick's really were going to be relegated to the back pages, they really were.

Luck. The kind you get only if you work at it.

The new Commissioner worked at it very hard.

▪ "Now, then, Miss Kelly."

Jake was gone. T.R.'s new secretary had an assignment of her own to get cracking on, her boss urgently needing the names of all the prominent art dealers in the city. "Art dealers, importers, curators—call and see if we can arrange a meeting, as many of them as can come. Early this evening. No later than first thing tomorrow."

"Here?"

"Yes." No. "Better on their own ground," Roosevelt said on second thought. "Some gallery they'll feel comfortable in. A room in one of the museums. Eight A.M."

Eight A.M.

"Sir?" The time seemed to jog something in the Commissioner's memory.

"I had an appointment with a young police officer this morning," he started to say, the awareness on Minnie's face stopping him.

"Richard Kerner; he was here when I arrived. I thought you

might want to have him wait in the inner office, just in case he wasn't supposed to be seen."

"You," Teddy wanted her to know, "are a pip." He turned toward the door marked "Private," hand on the knob. "They used to drown people for being so prescient, though."

"Not as much as all that." There were some messages she'd forgotten to give him—two calls, the first from a fellow member of the Board, Commissioner Andrew D. Parker. "He said if you were too busy to get back to him during the day, he'd expect to see you at *The Yeomen of the Guard* this evening. And the second call was from—"

"Why would Parker think I'd be 'too busy' to return his call?" The implications were irritating. Damn that thin-lipped son of a bitch. Whatever made the mayor think that he and Theodore Roosevelt wouldn't be oil and water?

"He didn't say," Minnie was telling him.

"No doubt." That other call?

A fast glance back at the record. "Mrs. Evans." The Commissioner was supposed to know the name and the reason for the call.

"Well, well." He'd been anticipating this one, ever since the day he took office. How many minutes would the lady wait, two? Ten? That she'd managed to hold off for two whole weeks bespoke volumes. Progress, at last. Restraint. "There's hope for us all."

His ironic laughter hung in the air behind him as he went into his office, closing the door. Minnie Gertrude Kelly stood there for a moment, listening to the echoes, telling herself it was none of her business.

She had art dealers to find.

■ "But wouldn't I be more useful doing what I was doing, sir?" It wasn't that Officer Kerner was ungrateful, he appreciated the opportunity, but he was—as Roosevelt was—an active individual. A cop who preferred to work out in the field, to fight the criminal element on its own turf. "Being your aide means I'd be spending most of my time here at Mulberry Street. Indoors."

His heart wouldn't be in it, trapped indoors.

"Of course it wouldn't," Teddy was pleased to agree. "I'm not

hiring you on as my secretary, Kerner—I have a secretary. You
may have noticed."

"Yes, sir." Richard had noticed, and had kicked himself for
noticing. He had plans in life, and she was Irish, dammit. Pretty,
yes, redheaded and voluptuous in her lace bodice and flowing
skirt, but Irish.

Catholic.

"What I have in mind," the Commissioner was saying, "isn't
the traditional aide's position. No one is going to know about this;
everybody's going to go on thinking you're just another officer on
the beat . . . open to 'suggestion.' "

Kerner's frown knotted his forehead. "Isn't that what I'm doing already?"

"Except," that sousaphone voice declared, "now you've got
someone to report to. Someone as official as they come." Theodore Roosevelt wasn't about to pull Richard off the streets, not
when the likes of Estes Hanrahan expected to stuff the young cop
smack dab into his dirty little pocket any minute now, no, sir. "I
want you in there; I want you to tell me who else is in there. What
schemes are being hatched."

Deal?

Deal, of course. But . . . "if Hanrahan finds out I was here,
talking to you, I dunno . . . we could be dead before we start."

"He's going to know," T.R. said, strutting. "And that is exactly
why we are not going to be 'dead'—because Estes H. is going to
think Commissioner R. had you in to give you the single worst
dressing-down of your entire miserable life. Had fun, raking you
over the coals."

A grin came slowly to Richard's face. "How much do I resent
you for doing it to me?" he wanted to know.

" 'Resent'?" Not even close. *Hate:* that's what you're made of
from now on. Teddy Roosevelt is a sanctimonious hypocrite with
a mansion out on Long Island and a fortune in the stock market.
'What does he know about having to make ends meet?' "

"Nothing. 'I'll show him.' " How the rogue cop would talk in
front of the leader of the West Side gangs.

"You think so, do you." The door was kicked open, the Commissioner raising his voice, aiming it down the length of the corridor. "Listen to me, you abject excuse for a flatfoot, go on the pad again and I promise you: I'll slam the door on your jail cell myself!"

"Sure," the officer snarled, defiant. "That'd really make you feel like a big man, wouldn't it, jugging some innocent guy so you can get your picture in the paper again." Roosevelt could go to hell.

Minnie Kelly at her desk—and the people in the hallway beyond, cops and civilians alike—gasped, shying away from Richard as he stalked past them, lips compressed, jaw like the prow of a ship. "Don't push it, boy," T.R. warned him, loud. "I mean it."

He thumbed Minnie back to her work, aware of her dismay. Officer Kerner had seemed so nice.

"Officer Kerner is nice. Very nice. Very brave."

"I don't understand." How could he and the Commissioner say those things to each other if Roosevelt thought so highly of him?

The explanation filled her with relief, renewing her faith in the job. In her employer. It was a pleasure to tell him that she had, as instructed, arranged a meeting of gallery owners, importers and museum curators. "You don't have to wait till tonight or tomorrow, either, they were available this afternoon."

At *La Galerie des Artistes,* 4 West Twenty-third.

"Give the little lady a box of cigars!" Teddy whooped, whirling at the last minute because if he didn't, the flat of his hand would have connected with her decidedly unmasculine shoulder, his overweening exuberance knocking her clear across the room.

■ Four West Twenty-third was a fashionable brick building which could have passed for the home of a family of quality, which was, of course, the effect intended. Only a polished brass plaque alongside the unpretentious entry identified the structure as a place of business, not really open to casual customers off the street.

"It's primarily by appointment only," Maurice Harbinger said as he led the Commissioner through the showrooms, a maze of furniture and accessories, chandeliers overhead profuse and haphazard as the stalactites in an ancient cave. "Most of the Four

Hundred shop here for their art. Lawyers, doctors: professional
people." The sculptured goatee wagged. "You wouldn't be considering a new decor for your home, by any chance? A public official
does have to keep appearances up, I should think."

Undoubtedly. "But that isn't the reason I asked you gentlemen
to meet with me."

"Even so." Roosevelt just *had* to see the dealer's latest and
most unique acquisition, a full-length mantelpiece unlike any
other, with snakelike tendrils twining out of gnarled roots on either side of the firebox, writhing upward around clusters of broad
leaves in purple and green, closing in on the mirror above. *"Art
nouveau;* it's all the rage on the Continent." Perfect for someone
of T.R.'s prominence, "a leader in style as well as in civic affairs.
You really can't afford to be out of step."

"I'll risk it," Teddy assured him. There were more immediate
things to talk about.

"A traditionalist." Harbinger accepted the no-sale with con-
summate grace, gesturing him forward: his colleagues were waiting in the adjacent room. Unless, of course, the Commissioner
was attracted to this moderately sized painting by the door, the
nightmare landscape with the fiery trees bowing in a wind which
seemed to swirl out of a screaming sky . . . ?

"Who would paint something like this?" A madman?

"Who killed himself in an asylum; you're very astute," the collector confirmed, nodding as he presented Roosevelt to the men
gathered at his request. "I'm told he cut his ear off in a fit sometime earlier."

"Is that what we're selling as art these days?" T.R. felt a shudder violate his backbone. "The effusions of the insane?"

"What did I tell you?" Vindication and antipathy mixed on the
face of the curator speaking, a short man in his bald forties. "He
called us here to lay down the law, what's 'obscene,' what's sacri-
lege. . . ."

"There's nothing obscene in Van Gogh." This from a large,
unexpectedly coarse-featured man, someone Teddy would have
categorized as a laborer or, worse, one of Estes Hanrahan's thugs.
"Not a nipple in sight."

The teeth went on display, enigmatic. "Nudes per se," Roosevelt announced, deadpan, "aren't obscene. It's only in conjunction with other nudes that they begin to break the blue laws. Depending on position and proximity, of course."

Laughter. The Commissioner hadn't brought them together to restrict their businesses, and they were all ears. What could they do for him, sir?

He told them what happened at Frick's. Listed the paintings, named the artists. Asked for their cooperation should the thieves approach them, "in need of a middleman."

"It's more likely they'd contact Frick himself," the opinion of the gallery's owner. "Hals, Vermeer, Gainsborough: these aren't exactly obscurities. People in our profession are very careful; they want everything properly pedigreed."

"These hooligans might not know that."

"Common sense would tell them," the bald curator ventured. "Who would they expect a dealer'd be able to sell the canvases to, crooked or not? No museum would touch anything so tainted, and most private collectors—"

Most. Not all. The shock of his own unexpected logic silenced the speaker.

"Mr. Goosens has a point," Harbinger agreed, settling back against the pillows of a brocaded chair. "The paintings may have been stolen 'on order.' "

"On whose 'order,' " that was what Roosevelt wanted to know.

"Would it surprise you if I said it was probably one of Mr. Frick's fellow robber barons?" A Mellon or a Morris—a Whitney —anyone who would logically have been in attendance at a select *soirée* on Sixty-ninth Street. Anyone obsessed with the finer things, with the money to buy a break-in, indifferent to the possibility of injury.

Indifferent to death.

T.R. "just might want to ask Henry Clay if any of his socially prominent guests made a real fuss over those acquisitions, going back to them all evening. 'One last look.' "

"I wouldn't be surprised if whoever it is even offered to take them off his hands," Goosens was willing to bet. "Making some kind of innocuous little joke of it."

"Henry would have laughed, especially if the price were high enough." Teddy knew his man, and theft would become the only viable alternative. The Commissioner would indeed ask him who he dined with these past few weeks, oh, yes.

"You might also want to check into who bid against him when the pictures were first put up on the European art market," the coarse-featured importer advised, glancing at the proprietor of *La Galerie des Artistes*. "Wouldn't it be ironic if it turns out to be someone like your old friend Thackery?"

"Thackery." A moue twisting Harbinger's face, goatee and all.

"Daniel Thackery, you mean?" An industrialist along the lines of an Andrew Carnegie, if Roosevelt's memory served, with none of the Pittsburgh tycoon's philanthropic impulses. Reclusive, secretive, scientifically oriented—not at all artistic—"I didn't know he collected Old Masters."

"He doesn't. It's much more lucrative stealing inventions from people."

What inventions was the collector referring to? Whose? "You aren't a scientist."

"Nevertheless," Goosens wanted the Commissioner to know, "Maurice is good enough to get interest from people like Edison. If he knew as much about patent law as he does about great art, he might be just as famous and I think you ought to look into it."

"I think I ought to look into it, too." If Harbinger would fill him in on the specifics?

A streak of polished light slashed horizontally through the air, released by the stone in the ring on the dealer's pinky. "Ancient history," he insisted, palm up. "No one died." Theodore would do better concentrating his efforts on the crime at Frick's.

"Injustice is injustice as far as the President of this Police Board is concerned; I don't care if it's robbery, murder—or a swindle." Calling cards appeared in his hand, passed to Harbinger and the others. They could telephone him anytime, day or night, "the minute one of those paintings turns up."

Or, in Maurice's case, whenever he felt like unburdening himself: T.R. wouldn't mind if it were three in the morning.

Humbug, their faces said, but it wasn't humbug. Roosevelt was just as ready to go after corruption and evil at three in the morning as at three in the afternoon.

Maybe more so.

■ Not between six and seven in the evening, however. That was the children's hour, unless the Commissioner was out of town speaking on behalf of wildlife, or the Republican Party.

Tonight it was a relay race out on Sixty-second Street, from Madison to Fifth and back, twice, a cacophony of evanescent shrieks echoing off the brownstones on either side. Old records fell by the wayside every second minute, it seemed, Alice and Ted outdoing themselves as never before, Kermit hard on their heels. Even baby Archie participated, riding high on his father's shoulders while T.R. huffed like a tuba and leaned forward: the youngest was going to pass the baton to the next youngest, Ethel, four. Only Anna Eleanor was unable to keep up.

"It's the back brace," Ted would explain. "Her spine is crooked."

"Only a little," in Alice's opinion. "Some of us are naturally athletic and then there are the clumsy people, like Nell."

How could their cousin help it, her brother had to wonder. "There's nobody for her to play with, living down on Thirty-seventh Street with Mrs. Hall." Eleanor's grandmother, all that was left of that branch of the family beside the ten-year-old and her younger brother, Grace.

Once a twin.

"Practice has nothing to do with it." Alice led the pack into 689, flopping herself onto the nearest available sofa. She bounced up against the cushions, wanting the hair to billow up around her face, golden. Lush.

"Big sister's going to call Nell ugly again." Ethel Roosevelt, small and intuitive.

"What'd we say about that?" T.R. raised his *pince-nez,* using them to exaggerate the caution in his eyes. Careful, Alice.

The warning was disregarded. "God is making Nell pay for Uncle Elliott's drinking and everything. He does things like that when He's mad."

"Not true." When Roosevelt compressed his lips, the hairs of his mustache stood up like porcupine quills. "God does not punish someone else for your sins."

"But Ellie hasn't done anything." In which case Kermit thought that God was unjustifiably mean, "making her look like she does."

Edith entered the room, holding a strand of pearls, needing her husband's help with the clasp. "How many times do we have to tell you the story of the ugly duckling and the beautiful swan?"

"Mother," Alice sighed. If Anna Eleanor was ever going to turn into a beautiful swan, there'd have surely been some sign of it by now.

"I happen to think your cousin is very beautiful." If not on the outside, "all right, on the inside." Just as good.

Better.

Theodore's tuxedo was waiting for him, laid out on the bed in their master suite. Unless he changed into it now, they would be late for the curtain.

"On my way." One last word to the children first, about their late uncle, his brother. Elliott. Who was addicted to alcohol in his later years, yes—"but he wasn't always like that. He wasn't always like that."

"Theodore." His wife spoke softly but he was shaking his head, insistent. It was time they knew. High time.

Because Elliott was easily Teddy's equal. "He could ride faster, he could shoot straighter, and in school? He always got better grades than I did. Everyone liked him, especially the girls. By George, they loved him! Thought he was the handsomest thing they'd ever seen—and he was. He was. I used to wish I could look like him; wish I didn't have to go around wheezing all the time."

The asthma.

It was still with him even now, publicity notwithstanding. Strenuous life in the Wild West notwithstanding. The children were very familiar with the sound, scared by it more often than not, especially when it was loud enough to come through the bedroom door at three in the morning.

Alice found it safer to talk about Anna Eleanor's father, the drunk. How incomprehensible it was that such a paragon should ruin himself that way.

She wasn't the only one. "He had headaches in college," the Commissioner recalled. "Splitting headaches." The brandy alleviated them. Made everything gay. Rosy.

"Why don't you give us brandy, then?" Ethel was in favor of anything that made everything gay and rosy.

"Except it doesn't stay like that," T.R. wanted her to understand. "You don't even stay you. They call these things 'spirits' for a reason, children, because it gets into your system and when it does, it takes you over. Slowly. Insidiously. Before you know it, all that's left is a shell, crumbling away. Put yourself in your cousin's place."

Could they imagine how they'd feel, no mother and a father who, even though he'd be looking them right in the eye, wouldn't be able to recognize them?

"Think about what it'd be like if you weren't so good at games, if you weren't as good-looking as you are."

"If we had to wear a back brace," Kermit added, empathetic.

"Exactly."

"I don't have to wear it as much as I used to, Uncle Theodore." Nell's voice made them all pivot. She was standing there at the foot of the stairs clutching as always at Baby Joss, the fingers of her hand playing the threadbare abdomen as though it were an abacus.

"Of course not." Roosevelt spoke quickly, forcing a semblance of characteristic heartiness back into his voice. "It's done its job. Your back has gotten much straighter."

"That's what Grandmother says." Her eyes sought those of her contemporaries. Did anyone want to play checkers?

"Checkers is a *splendid* idea," Alice said, possessed of new, if temporary, insight. By morning it would be mostly forgotten but, for now, the effort was more than reward enough for the Commissioner and his wife.

"I thought Eleanor was going to cry, Alice made her so happy," Edith remarked when they settled back in their carriage, on their way down Madison toward Oscar Hammerstein's Manhattan Opera House on Thirty-fourth Street.

"Something I should have done a long time ago, talk to them about Elliott." His eyes were on the passing parade outside the beveled window. The sausage vendor on the corner of Fifty-first. The newsboy at Forty-third, selling a copy of Pulitzer's *World* to a man in a top hat and a Chesterfield. ROOSEVELT HIRES GIRL AS SECRETARY, CREATES SENSATION ON MULBERRY STREET.

"What made you decide to do it tonight?" If Edith remembered correctly, "this wasn't the first time Alice brought up her 'sins of the father' theory out loud."

Theodore?

"I got a call from Mrs. Evans today," he finally revealed, Edith's reaction the surprise of someone who wonders why she's surprised.

"How much did she want this time?"

"Ten thousand."

"Of course." Her eyes found his even in the dark. "You aren't giving it to her?"

"We're going to meet and 'discuss it.'" T.R. leaned heavily against the backrest, his shoulder blades in need of the sporadic massage supplied by the jostling of the coach. "I'm a fool, aren't I."

A possibility which Edith had to reject. All he was doing was trying to make it up to Elliott, having looked the other way. Having been "out" when the calls came in.

Right. "I didn't have to give up on him so easy."

"Easy?" Easy? Now she was angry with him, but he persisted.

"It's my fault he's dead."

"You don't believe that."

He did, though. He really did. Saying otherwise didn't make him feel any the less guilt-ridden as the winking lights on the marquee of the theater illuminated his face.

▪ Grant's son elbowed his way through the crowd, eager to intercept the Roosevelts. Freddie was in his forties; he looked like a fat Ulysses S. "It's the social event of the season," his incongruously high-pitched voice proclaimed, breathless with awe. "Everybody is here. The entire Four Hundred!"

Was Andrew Parker there, as their fellow police commissioner had threatened: that's what T.R. wanted to know.

"Behind you." Their abstemious colleague was pleased that Theodore had chosen *The Yeomen of the Guard* over yet another self-serving prowl through the back alleys of the Tenderloin. "Functions like this are very important, politically speaking." Followed by a flinty "Mrs. Roosevelt."

A perfunctory bow acknowledging the lady while her husband smiled and snarled. Andrew surely wasn't suggesting that the newly appointed members of the Police Board not live up to their promises when it came to reforming the department?

" 'Reform' does not mean a series of nocturnal raids on the saloons and bordellos of the West Side, especially," Parker added stiffly, "when they're accompanied by a Jacob Riis or a Lincoln Steffens, not to mention a photographer or two."

Or three.

"The only way to find out which of our men is being true to his oath and which is not is to get out there and see." Teddy would be *de*lighted, in fact, to have Parker come along. "Any night at your convenience."

"Accomplishing what? The rousting of some tired, thirsty officer who'd have the bad timing to take a ten-minute break from the dangers of the beat just as we'd happen along?" Andrew Parker thought that anathema. "I am also dead against the outright dismissal of these brave men for that kind of first-time infraction."

Brave?

"Since when does bravery have anything to do with whether a man wants to stop in for a drink or not?" The Commissioner's rival produced a small list from his inside jacket pocket. "Three of your detainees, had you taken the trouble to ask, have extremely impressive records. Arrests and rescues both, and I intend to bring these facts up at the next meeting of the Board."

Should its President be interested in attending, it was scheduled for the following Friday at three.

"P.M. or A.M.?" The minute he said it he knew it was a mistake. You don't throw a Parker a pitch like that, not when he is good at hitting them out of the park.

"You're the one who'd know more about three in the morning than me." A tip of the hat.

"Andrew."

Pain compressed the face. "We're going to miss the overture."

"When I took this job," T.R. persisted, "when I gave Bill Strong my acceptance, it was with the clear understanding that there was a cesspool to clean up in this city. We cannot have a police department in league with the very criminals it is sworn to arrest—and that means we have to root out every last bribe-taker, every last double-dealer, every last part-time policeman and send them packing. I don't know about you, Andrew, but I take a pledge like that very seriously. Very seriously indeed."

"As I am sure you will reiterate at length come Friday afternoon." Parker refused to let Roosevelt detain him further, sidestepping to join Commissioner Grant, already on his way down the aisle in search of his seat. Theodore had every intention of following: there was more to say. Had a scuffle not broken out in the lobby behind him at that exact moment he would have said it, too.

"Get your hands off me, Mr. Frick, I am warning you." The voice was raised at least an octave above its normal baritone, angry. Defensive. "I did not take your paintings."

"Not personally, perhaps." The steel magnate was glaring at a silver-haired patrician in white tie and tails, walking stick clutched protectively in his hand. "Dwight Morris wouldn't soil his own hands; why should he? Thugs and cutthroats are such a modest investment, a man of your means."

"Unconscionable!" Morris rasped, muttonchops quivering. "Retract that, sir: there are libel laws!"

"The Hals especially," an undaunted Frick shot back. "You

wanted the *Madwoman of Leyden* badly enough to rip it out of my hands when I outbid you for it in the Hague."

"Bid?" The bird's head which crowned the walking stick seemed to take as much umbrage as its owner. "That was no bid, Mr. Frick, that was collusion. Bald-faced collusion between you and the auctioneer. That oil by rights should have been mine. *Would* have been!"

A monosyllabic roar welled up out of the millionaire's throat. Before anyone could anticipate him he threw himself at Morris, wrestling the cane out of his opponent's hand, whacking him about the head and shoulders.

"Here now!" Roosevelt shouted, lunging forward to intercede before Morris was seriously hurt. "None of that!"

It was not easy to secure the weapon, the infuriated collector still attempting to bash Morris's skull with the brass beak. "Admit it," he was demanding. "Come on—ahhh!"

The "aahh!" was the result of the Commissioner's efforts, finally successful. Edith found herself in possession of the confiscated instrument, removed to a reasonable distance from the center of the storm.

"Did you see that? What this maniac did to me?" Morris was spluttering in disbelief, patting the bruises beneath his sleeve. "He could have fractured my arm."

With every justification, as far as Henry Clay Frick could see. No one else but Dwight Morris could have been the author of the break-in at his house. Hoodlums hired by Dwight Morris killed Patrick MacFarland and Augustus Lennert. "Search *his* premises, Commissioner, not only here but in Rhode Island. Newport."

Or did Dwight smuggle them over to his castle in Scotland?

"Search," snapped the accused. As many men as Roosevelt wanted. "My house here on Fifth Avenue, my estate in Newport. Have the British authorities go through my 'castle' in Scotland by all means."

They'd find nothing not his in any of those places.

"Then it's in one of his warehouses downtown," Frick contended. "His office on Wall Street."

"Be my guest there, too." While Theodore was at it, however,

he might also take a look at the properties owned by Andrew
Mellon. "Andrew Mellon, Robert Jerome and Solomon Carlyle,
just to cover all the contingencies."

"Carlyle?" Now Morris really was grasping at straws. Didn't
he know that Solomon was one of Henry's oldest friends? "We
shared rooms together at college."

"And still he bid against you for the same Hals as I did."

"As a gentleman. With a sense of good sportsmanship after it
was done." It wasn't Solomon Carlyle who behaved like a steve-
dore when Frick went up to the desk, checkbook in hand.

"I don't trust people who conceal their feelings, do you?" Morris had been straightening himself up, brushing himself off. He
wanted his walking stick back now.

"You're leaving?" Edith was genuinely startled. Why else
would Morris have come to Hammerstein's Opera House if not to
attend the performance?

"One opera a night is my limit." There was a twinkle in the
industrialist's eye as he repossessed his cane and started for the
exit. "Oh. Commissioner. You are going to descend on my places
all at the same time, I hope; unannounced? We wouldn't want
Henry to think I could shuffle his paintings one step ahead of your
squad."

"Henry wouldn't put it past you," Frick said, his faith in the
man's duplicity unimpaired even as Arthur Sullivan underscored
their parting. Jack Point, already on stage, had a song to sing, oh.

▪ Miss Minnie Gertrude Kelly left five lines between "yours very
truly" and "Theodore Roosevelt, President, New York City Police
Commission," carefully unspooling the paper from the platen of
the Underwood: the last of the letters T.R. had given her to type.
It was a quarter to nine and she was free to leave Mulberry Street.
A carriage was standing by on the Commissioner's order, ready to
take her across Mr. Roebling's bridge.

"Unless you'd allow me." The voice was male, warm, spoken
from a position just within the office door.

"Officer Kerner." Surprising, how happy she was to see him.

"Aren't you supposed to be consorting with known criminals in the vicinity of Thirty-fourth and Tenth?"

"After midnight," he said, smiling. "They get very suspicious if you try to consort with them before that." Which gave him plenty of time to escort her home, perhaps even to offer her a small supper on the way. "Gage and Tollner is still serving."

"I couldn't impose."

"The lobsters might call it an imposition. I'd call it an honor." Her wrap was up in his hands.

"Actually," Minnie had to admit as she slipped her arms through the sleeves, "I have been meaning to celebrate my luck in getting this job." Her carpenter, however, hadn't thought it cause for Joe's Bar, much less a Gage and Tollner.

Not Richard. "It's a bully position." The imitation of Roosevelt was uncanny.

"Yes. And I can handle it, too: some of the old-timers around here are in for a shock." On impulse, she took a neatly folded letter out from beneath the blotter on her desk. "Susan Anthony sent me this."

He read it aloud. " 'My dear Miss Kelly. It was with great enthusiasm and pride that I heard of your appointment as secretary to Commissioner Roosevelt. Please accept my heart-felt congratulations and my every wish for your success: the example you set will be inspiration to thousands of qualified young women in search of similar positions throughout the business world. . . .' "

" 'That it is an immense responsibility is undoubted. That you will be more than its equal is my sincerest hope.' " Minnie didn't have to have the page in front of her; she knew it by heart. " 'Yours most truly, Susan B. Anthony.' "

"You should frame that," the patrolman said. "It certainly doesn't belong underneath a blotter." Women were finally beginning to take their place in society—in business, industry, the arts —and she was in the vanguard. "Let 'em know."

"Well," Miss Kelly could only say as she carefully replaced the document beneath the blotter and accepted Richard's proffered arm. "Maybe champagne *is* in order tonight."

"Cordon rouge, at least."

They turned toward the door and then stopped. A gray-bearded man was standing there, blocking the way, unimposing in a suit he might very well have slept in. "Excuse me," he murmured deferentially, twisting the rim of the hat he held in his hands. "Is this the office of Police Commissioner Theodore Roosevelt, please?"

The accent was European. Austro-Hungarian or thereabouts.

"Yes," Commissioner Roosevelt's secretary acknowledged. Was there anything she could do for the gentleman in his absence?

An agitated shake of the shaggy head. "I must see Roosevelt," the caller insisted. "My name is Antonin Dvořák; I am president of the National Conservatory of Music. There has been a *terrible* robbery!"

3 DVOŘÁK

■ A child had been taken away from him. A precious infant, irreplaceable. Every minute that passed was more devastating than the previous; the pit of the composer's stomach clawed at him, pinching the lining.

Where was Roosevelt? "It has been over an hour," he noted, not only to Richard and Minnie but to the several uniformed officers who had been summoned to his home at 327 East Seventeenth. Surely it couldn't have taken so long to come from Mr. Hammerstein's Opera House.

Horses' hooves and carriage wheels clattered up from the cobblestones as he spoke, the Commissioner's conveyance appearing around the corner. T.R. was out on the running board, calling out as he jumped down onto the sidewalk. "Mr. Dvořák, forgive me: I thought it best I escort my wife home before I did anything else. This has the feel of an all-nighter."

"If only you could get it back to me in just one night, my symphony." The large, expressive hands clapped against each other, the Czech gesturing the company inside. "Nine in the morning the copyists are here, the manuscript is safe. Now?"

Now the only full score of Antonin Dvořák's new American symphony was God knows where, in the possession of God knows who.

"What kind of thief would be interested in such a thing?" the musician wanted to know, emotional. "It makes no sense."

"No, it doesn't," Teddy had to agree, "especially since all you have to do is sit and write it down again."

"In time for the premiere? Impossible!" Two months, it would take. Three. "And it would never be as good. Such wonderful details I had, so lovely for the orchestra. I couldn't remember half."

He sat at the piano, agitatedly searching for a cigar in the humidor alongside the rack.

"Just because it might be different doesn't mean it can't be even better," said Minnie, seeing how much he needed the encouragement. Dvořák regarded her as though she were mad.

"What is better than perfect?" Not a wasted note, not a single musical phrase that didn't belong. "Never has Antonin Dvořák written anything with so much, how you say, oomph!"

Seidl had thought so, too. The conductor of the New York Philharmonic.

"Listen."

Dvořák played it for them, some of it, a nostalgically beautiful theme which made Roosevelt think of the vast rolling plains, the prairie ablaze with the wildflowers of spring. Sweet pain lived in that melody, sweet and sweeping, as though the music were taking its leave of an entire era and simultaneously preserving it. Dried blossoms in the pages of a cherished diary.

"Is this not beautiful music?"

Dvořák's canaries thought so, awakened, their multiple voices harmonizing with the Bechstein. The music room was, in fact, decorated with a myriad of birdcages, all sizes and shapes, everything from Chinese pagodas to cathedral bells. In them, under the covers, an avian opera company, sopranos, altos, mezzos, singing on even after their master stopped.

"More," Richard found himself blurting. "Please."

A dissonance. "Even as it was, it was going to take right up to the first rehearsal to complete the parts. The concert is two weeks from tonight!"

"So each day that passes makes the manuscript more valuable, doesn't it." The Commissioner moved about the room, observing. The music stand, the antimacassared sofa and matching chair, the low table on which was a careless pile of music and several dog-eared periodicals in Slavic.

"More valuable to whom?" Was T.R. suggesting that someone would actually believe he could get money for a stolen symphony?

"You'd pay to get it back, wouldn't you?" If not Antonin Dvořák himself, what about Seidl? "The Philharmonic?"

Laughter, stark. Brief. "Why should the orchestra want to cough up one thin dime?" the onetime butcher's apprentice inquired, biting off the stub of his selected cigar. "They can substitute the Beethoven *Eroica* for nothing."

As for himself, perhaps Roosevelt might like to examine the red in his bankbook? Not that the Conservatory didn't pay its president, but there'd been previous debts. The hole was deep, still, less only with the new commissions. A string quartet, his twelfth. The symphony.

Payable on delivery. Only. "I suggest to you that ransom makes no sense."

"Maybe." A note might yet show up in the mailbox come morning, or arrive through the window attached to a brick. "Don't be startled if there's a phone call."

How like his expectations in the Frick case, Teddy suddenly realized.

"Commissioner?" Minnie couldn't help being struck by the shudder which passed through her employer's body, here and gone. Had something come to mind?

Yes. "Something irrelevant," however. "It has to be." Unless Dvořák's thief was intent on stealing cultural items from all the arts, which would make the composer the second in a series more recondite than rational.

"Another symphony has been stolen?"

"Paintings." Three rare Old Masters.

"Wouldn't that be an incredible coincidence," Richard had to wonder, "this crime having something to do with that?"

"Incredible," T.R. agreed, dismissing the thought. Where did Dvořák say he'd last seen his score?

"Over here." A jab with the now-ignited cigar. The low table with the periodicals. "I had it in my carrying case when I returned from my classes this afternoon." Dinner had been called; he'd dropped the grip between the music and the magazines and hurried to the table.

The *Bigos* was very good.

"But it almost came back up out of my stomach, the minute I stepped through that door again." The magazines were there. The other music.

Nothing else.

"Who was in the house besides yourself," Roosevelt was curious to learn. "Your wife . . ."

". . . my daughter . . . Mrs. Edelman . . ." The housekeeper. "A gem. She has been for years with us. Prague. London. Everywhere."

"And *her* financial condition?" It was Officer Kerner who asked, eliciting an ironic grunt. There were so many things in the house that the lady could take, so much quicker to cash.

"Pearls, earrings—a Guarneri. You know how much it's worth, a Guarneri?" A lot more than 227 pages of loose music paper in an old case with the leather rubbed raw. Had it not been a gift from Johannes Brahms he'd have replaced it years ago.

Years ago.

"They were not after the briefcase," Teddy was sure, his eye now on the window, glinting.

"You see something, sir?" His aide joined him at the sill, intrigued.

"What I don't see, that's what might crack this case." The room was going to be off-limits to one and all, even Dvořák. Sealed, till further notice. "We're going to find out if the New York City Police Department has a fingerprint expert worth his salt, by George!"

"Fingerprints?" Minnie was at a loss, and the composer. Officer Kerner wasn't.

"It's a new method of identifying criminals," he explained, pleased to see the approval on the Commissioner's face.

"Read Mark Twain's *Pudd'nhead Wilson,*" T.R. advised, passing a calling card to his host, a duplicate of those distributed to the gentlemen at *La Galerie des Artistes.* The Conservatory's president could call him at three in the morning, too. "The minute you're contacted."

If he was contacted.

"I'll be up, I think," Dvořák anticipated. For the next several nights, at least.

How else would one even start to recompose a masterpiece?

◘ At six the following morning the Commissioner was in his bed, Edith beside him, looking at him, reaching for him. They held each other for a long silent time, drawing comfort and strength from the warmth of their bodies and the duality of their breathing, and the telephone had the courtesy to wait until seven.

"For you, Father!" Ted had beaten Alice to the hallway.

"It was my turn," she complained, stamping a heavy foot into the carpet, plotting vengeance.

Dvořák wasn't on the line. Andrew Parker was. "What's all this nonsense about fingerprints?" he demanded.

"I could have a windowsill crawling with them, that's 'what.' " How did his fellow commissioner get the word so quickly?

"Thank that pretty little secretary of yours." Minnie had been down at Mulberry Street for almost an hour already, inquiring after the department's "fingerprint expert."

Judging from Parker's tone, the department didn't have one.

"Really, Theodore." How could a man of Roosevelt's intelligence and education actually believe that, out of all the millions of people in the world, no two ever (ever!) could have the same loops and whorls on their fingertips.

"None have, so far. Not one."

"Because those 'experts' you'd spend good taxpayer money on can't see straight, all those wrinkles they squint at all day." It boggled Andrew's logical mind, the ridiculous notion that the impressions could be "lifted" off surfaces such as windowsills with pieces of tape.

Balderdash. "I'm pulling the policemen you put on guard duty down there, Mister President. There are beats they could be out patrolling."

"No." Sharp and quick. Not until Roosevelt got that fingerprint expert in today.

"Didn't you hear what I said? The New York City Police Department does not have a fingerprint expert because the majority of its Board does not believe that you can solve a criminal case with mumbo jumbo." He didn't care how "scientific" it sounded to his colleague.

"Just because the department doesn't have an expert doesn't mean they don't exist."

"If you think this Board is going to contract out for one you are sadly mistaken," Parker advised.

"The Board won't have to contract out." Grim determination tempered Teddy's voice. "I'm doing it." And Andrew was going to keep those men on guard in that music room "or I'll have it all over the front page of every newspaper in town: 'Commissioner Parker Refuses Roosevelt Cooperation; Potential Solution to Dvořák Break-in Delayed.' "

Lovely reading on the Second Avenue El this evening, yes?

A pause so long T.R. began to think he'd been hung up on.

"Andrew?"

"You do like to govern through the press, don't you."

"Sometimes it seems it's necessary."

"Five o'clock," Parker snapped, resentment unconcealed. "You get your 'expert' in by then, Theodore, because that's when those officers are going to go back where they belong." Clear?

"As a bell," the Commissioner muttered, hooking his index finger around the cradle of the phone, clicking them off.

■ "I need a favor, Jake."

"Naturally," the reporter replied, genial in his bedroom halfway across town. "What took you so long to ask this morning? For a while there I was beginning to say to myself, 'Hey, Jake. It's all right to doze off, he's not going to call.' "

"Dvořák was robbed last night. The composer."

Riis knew who Dvořák was. He sat up in his bed. "What'd they take?"

Teddy told him. "I think they came in through the second-story window. There could be fingerprints on the sill; maybe one or two on the panes if we get lucky."

"What does your fingerprint guy tell you?"

"Rephrase that, why don't you."

"You don't have a fingerprint guy, right." And the *Sun* might be able to supply, that was the favor, wasn't it.

"Tell Dana it's your exclusive. 'Paper Provides Fingerprint Expert to Help Nab Culprit.' You know."

He knew. "How much time have we got?"

"Only till five," Roosevelt allowed, admiring the man's insight when it came to the workings of city government. "Parker's pulling my men off the premises at five. I know it's an imposition—"

"It's not. It's a pleasure." The Commissioner could expect a call before ten, perhaps even as early as nine-thirty.

"Ten is fine." This was one morning he wasn't going to be at his desk before then.

"Isn't that rather late for you?" Edith asked, feeling free to step forward now that her husband was off the call.

"Three-thirteen West 102nd Street, remember?" He preceded her into the dining room, bidding his children a hearty good day. "Is there bacon this morning? Pancakes? Isn't Nell joining us?" And where the devil was his New York *Times?*

"Right here, Uncle Theodore." It was Nell who delivered it to him. "The wagon was a little late and Cousin Alice asked me to wait for it out front."

"Without a wrap?" Edith was frankly dismayed, noting the feline expression on her stepdaughter's face. "Alice?"

A pout. "It's very nice outside," she claimed. "The sun is shining right on the stoop."

"I was fine," Anna Eleanor assured them all, squeezing Baby Joss and making him squeak.

"Are you all packed?" T.R. eyed her over the top of his *Times,* folded open to the editorial page, less interested at the moment in Adolph Ochs's opinion of the international repercussions of the

Dreyfus case than in the well-being of his niece. If memory served, wasn't this the morning that Mrs. Hall was to pick Eleanor up?

Yes. Nell would be back on Thirty-seventh Street by noon. She would miss playing with her cousins, even Alice. She would especially miss going with them to see Buffalo Bill's Wild West Show.

"Oh?" Were they going to see Buffalo Bill?

"You said." Naked horror made Kermit drop his fork. "The next time he was in New York, you said." The last time he was in New York.

"You said you would even take us back to meet him," Ted was quick to add, feverish. "It was going to be like it was when you rode together in the Dakotas."

It would be. "But only if your mother agrees that you can stay up late that one night."

The eyes all went to Edith. "Ganging up on me again, are you?"

"Begging," her husband amended. Much more apropos in view of the overlapping "please" 's which followed.

"We'll be good, we promise."

Please?

■ Three-thirteen West 102nd, a tenement, maintained well but dark inside despite the tiled walls in the stairwell and the red paint in the corridors above. Teddy had to squint to find the apartment marked 2A, knocking on the door.

"Mommy," a child was heard to say in response to the sound.

"Coming." Footsteps and then a pause. "Mr. Roosevelt?"

"Mrs. Evans."

She let him in. Elliott died here, hollow voices whispered in the back of his head. Here, in this flat.

It was neat, though, as Mrs. Evans was neat, with lace doilies on the arms of the chairs and a throw on the table, the weight of a bowl of fruit holding it down.

Cut glass. Sharp edges. Even empty it must have weighed a considerable amount. When Elliott fell over backward during that last alcoholic seizure, was that what he struck his head on? Or was it the metal cover sheathing the radiator over there by the window?

Elliott's son was playing on the floor, four years old, maybe a bit less. There was no question of the paternity: more Roosevelt was in those fledgling features than in either Anna Eleanor's or those of her brother Grace. With these and the inheritance from the Evans bloodline, the child was sure to grow up strapping and handsome, a conclusion the Commissioner reached as he compared the woman he remembered with the woman he saw.

She'd aged, yes, but just a little, and she still retained the simmering zest which first had drawn Elliott to her, in France. What more compelling reason to absent himself from the sanitarium at Suresnes, he'd said to Theodore over an aperitif in Paris, the newly erected Eiffel Tower casting a dappled shadow over their sidewalk table. "She is better for me than all your doctors, my dear old beloved brother."

"You are a married man."

"Am I?" Was his marriage to Anna Hall really a marriage anymore? "Have you any idea of how long it's been since we've even seen each other?"

"She is your wife." Vows exchanged in the sight of God were sacred. Adultery was something Theodore could neither condone nor comprehend, alien to his ethos, and Elliott was weak, succumbing to it.

Mrs. Evans was a homewrecker. The lady might cover his brother with as many blankets as he needed, she might sit up with him nights while he shook with *delirium tremens* and make him laugh afterward with silly, loving jokes. No matter. She was still taking unfair advantage of a man afflicted.

Proof? She brought it to Roosevelt in New York a year later, letting him know she was carrying Elliott's child, asking for financial assistance. Elliott certainly couldn't help her; she had no choice but to go to his brother.

If T.R. said no she would go to the papers. She would scandalize the city. She would.

"Oh," he'd responded. "T.R. will 'come through.' " But only if Mrs. Evans signed away any further claim to Roosevelt money.

Agreed, the quitclaim signed, witnessed and sealed.

There was nothing to talk about.

"I think there is." Her eyes directed his toward the boy, who'd greeted him as "Uncle Theodore," who was now playing with a number of tin cavalrymen and Indians on the rug. "Clothing costs more than it did four years ago. Food. A man of your means may not have noticed but, trust me, it's a fact."

He looked out the window, at the sight of the 125th Street ferry as it approached the Edgewater slips on the Jersey shore, forty-four-star flag whipping in the downdraft from the Fort Lee cliffs. "The settlement we negotiated was generous, Mrs. Evans, even by today's standards." Other families brought their children up on less. "On considerably less."

"Those children aren't Roosevelts." Her son was a bastard, yes. But he would not be deprived of his birthright. Choate would be in his future even if the private tutors Teddy's father once hired weren't. Harvard. "Roosevelts go to Harvard."

"Except your son is *not* a Roosevelt, madam. Not legally." Theodore was startled to find himself gnawing at the corners of his mustache. "Clause seventeen of our agreement?"

"When I signed that paper," she rasped, "I was alone, *pregnant,* broke—in no condition to refuse anything so long as I could have money coming in, regular." Hardly making their "agreement" fair.

"By God, it was more than fair!" Had Mrs. Evans talked to Elliott this way? So blunt? So tactless? Alcohol didn't merely attack a man's liver and brain in that case, it also destroyed his spine.

"Would you say that if the child were yours?"

"I'm not my brother." The Commissioner was not indiscriminate when it came to his seed.

"Who are you out to punish?" Mrs. Evans wanted to know. "Me? Elliott? It certainly can't be an innocent four-year-old; he didn't choose his parents."

"And I didn't make up the rules." He was bound by them, nonetheless. More, in fact, than she was.

"Very fine," she said, bitter. "Would you like to know what I'm

going to do, then—if I don't decide to go to the papers, after all?"
She was going to keep him informed of his nephew's condition as
he went on unaided through life, that's what. "I want you to
know if he makes a success of himself that it was without any help
from you. I want you to know that if he dies young and diseased,
or hungry, or swinging from the end of a rope, you could have
seen to it it didn't have to end that way. I want you to have real
trouble looking at yourself in the mirror in the morning, that's
what I want, Mr. Roosevelt."

Had he a hat she'd have thrust it into his hand and shown him
the door: T.R. was being dismissed. And for the first time he knew
what Elliott had seen in her.

"Mrs. Evans." He was on one side of the threshold, she on the
other. "I know you consider me a pompous, unbending, dogmatic
martinet. Possibly I am. 'Progressives' are often a lot more con-
servative than they'd care to admit—sometimes they have to be
thrown into a pool before they can learn how to swim."

Her breath seemed to catch in her throat. "Does this mean—"

"It's too soon for me to know what it means." He was going to
have to think about it.

Good enough, the cock of her head replied.

"The answer might still be no." It was important she understand that.

"One step at a time." One little step at a time.

A clatter behind her bustle. Elliott's son rushed up, clutching at
the hem of his mother's dress with one hand, waving with the
other. "Good-bye, Uncle Theodore," he called. "Good-bye!"

■ "No," he'd wanted to say. "The law does not obligate me to be
your uncle. Not if I don't want to be."

But Mrs. Evans was right, damn her. The blood that flowed in
his veins came from the same original source as the blood in the
veins of that child, that *nullius filius* who'd given offense only for
having been born.

"Commissioner!"

"Excuse me," Roosevelt apologized, dancing with the figure in the vestibule of the tenement until recognition came. "Officer Hargate?"

"Yes, sir." One of Mr. Frick's stolen paintings had been found. "Lieutenant Meeghan sent me to find you."

▪ It was the Gainsborough: *Sir William Pensionner and Family.* Located, if the note in the rookie's pad was correct, in a pawnshop beneath the el on Ninth Avenue. One more piece of junk among the racks of ragged old overcoats and the bicycle built for two, the stacks of water-damaged books, with spines and without.

"Have you seen it? Is it intact?" They were traveling south on the West Side Express, no faster, more modern way to get downtown in the opinion of the Police Board President, steam engine puffing two stories above the street.

"I only got a quick glimpse of the painting before the lieutenant had me hop to: it looked a little beat up around the edges."

"Ripped?"

"No, sir, just tacked down sloppy. If it'd still been in the frame I don't think I'd even have noticed it."

The express pulled into the Fourteenth Street Station and stopped. Even from the platform two stories above the sidewalk, T.R. could see their destination, a dingy merchandise-and-loan. "That is the place, isn't it?" he asked as he and Hargate descended the stairs. "Clinton's?"

"This is the place, all right." Lieutenant Meeghan appeared in the open door, gesturing, ubiquitous cigar between his yellowing teeth. "Ready to meet one of the thieves from the Frick job?"

"You've captured one? Mag*ni*ficent!" Certainly Roosevelt wanted to meet the knave. "Did he put up a fight?"

"That slime?" The detective led Teddy into the dust-saturated establishment, a narrow rectangle dripping faded dresses and work pants, the heraldry of the industrial age hanging from iron rods attached to the ceiling. "Delbert W. Clinton: some 'fighter.' "

Delbert W. Clinton, a weepy-eyed wraith with fluttering hands and billowing sleeves, incongruously colored garters banding the attenuated biceps. "How could I know it was stolen," the pawnshop owner was keening, directing the querulous question to a figure bent behind the counter which formed the front of the cage. "There was nothing about it in the papers. Nothing."

"Page twenty-three of the *Times,*" a familiar voice said, correcting Clinton from where he knelt, magnifying glass in hand. "The *Sun* also had it, in the back by the funnies, and the *Journal.* Not front page, I grant you, but not the 'nothing' you just decided to call it."

Interjection completed, Maurice Harbinger returned to his close-up examination of *Sir William Pensionner* and his family. Frameless, Lindy was right; propped up at the same slant as several other dusty canvases of similar size. A formal study of an English country gentleman, his wife, his son, their retriever. All were posed against the backdrop of a Gothic cathedral in a mid-eighteenth-century landscape, and Roosevelt could easily see why a collector like Frick would find the work irresistible. Composition, perspective, the use of color—the all-too-accurate condescension on Pensionner's face. The bored look the boy probably wore as a matter of habit.

Art.

"Indeed." The proprietor of *La Galerie des Artistes* rose to shake the Commissioner's hand. "It's a superb example of what a talent like Gainsborough could do even when he wasn't at his peak. Although, subjects like these, what might an El Greco?"

T.R. regarded the hapless Clinton. "How does a masterpiece like this happen to turn up in your store?" he wanted to know. How, incidentally, did Maurice find out about it? Did Meeghan call him in?

An airy wave of the importer's hand. "I was the one who called Meeghan, after Mr. Clinton here called me. 'I think I have a Gainsborough, Mr. Harbinger,' he said. 'Do you know someone who could authenticate it for me?' Meaning, how would I like to make a Gainsborough available to one of my clients, with the proceeds of the sale split, I don't know, eighty-twenty?"

"For a painting you ordinarily wouldn't have been able to offer at all?" There was froth at the corners of Clinton's mouth. "Twenty percent was more than fair."

"You still haven't told me how you came by it in the first place," Teddy pointed out, caustic.

"Am I going to have to go through it again?" The complaint was directed at the lieutenant, glowering because of the self-pity all over the pawnshop owner's voice. "Once isn't good enough for you people, ten times isn't good enough: why do you think that I'm going to tell you something different on the eleventh?"

"This time it's not me asking the question, pal." The reply was emphasized by a swat to the shoulder. A love tap. Nothing near Meeghan's full capability. "None'a your cheek in front of the Commissioner now, he wants it from the top." How Clinton got his mitts on the stolen property.

"The way I get all my merchandise. Somebody brings it in."

"Tell me about this particular 'somebody,' " Roosevelt urged. "What did he look like?" It was a he, was it not?

"Yeah, a he." Meeghan was the one who answered, speaking from the notes down in his pad. " 'A good-looking young fella in his twenties. Brown hair, brown eyes, six feet, maybe. Tweed jacket.' "

"He wanted twenty dollars for the picture," Clinton added, wanting to please. "I got him down to fifteen."

"Fifteen dollars for a genuine Gainsborough, can you imagine?" Harbinger could only shake his head in awe as T.R. addressed the detective. He had, of course, confiscated the pawn ticket receipt?

"As soon as we started going around the mulberry bush with Delbert here," Meeghan confirmed, looking as though he might actually put his arm around the bony shoulder in a gesture of mock friendship. The expression on the Commissioner's face made him think better of it.

Roosevelt wouldn't like the name written down.

"Another Smith? A Jones?"

"I had no reason to challenge that," the pawnbroker whined.

"Because you didn't want to know." Teddy's finger jabbed the air. "Or else you know only too well." Which was it? "Speak up, man, there's blood on that canvas. Two men murdered." Two good men.

"If I knew anything more don't you think I'd say so?" Clinton was pathetically trying to protect himself with his forearms. Pity for him surged in the Commissioner, a surprise.

Meeghan was not so empathetic. "Let me take him over to the precinct house," he requested of his superior. "A couple of minutes in the basement with me, he'll spill his guts."

"No, please." The suspect crouched, a fetus on its feet. "He's talking about the rubber hose." The fingers clawed at T.R.'s lapel. "I thought you were an enlightened man!"

"Come on, you." The lieutenant's hand came down on Clinton's arm, concealing the garter.

"Would I be here if I'd been in on a break-in like this, people dead? Would I be trying to sell part of the loot to a certified dealer like Maurice Harbinger?"

"Crooks like you," Meeghan sneered, "think they can get away with anything, they do it quick enough." He glanced at Roosevelt. "Ain't that right, Commissioner?"

"Let him be, Meeghan." Not for a moment had Teddy considered the little man guilty of being anything more than the receiver of stolen goods. Clinton would never have stayed put in his Ninth Avenue shop had he been part of such a gang, nor would he have had a Maurice Harbinger in to authenticate this Gainsborough.

"Wait a minute." Was T.R. telling the detective the suspect wasn't even going to be taken in for questioning, normal procedure in a case like this?

"Gaining us what?" Was there anything Meeghan could think of not yet covered?

Bluster. The sidestep. "I'm telling you, Mr. Roosevelt—"

"No, Lieutenant, Mr. Roosevelt is telling *you*. This man is nothing more than a two-bit scavenger picking at bones somebody else left behind."

Bones? *"Sir William Pensionner?"* Harbinger's eyebrows headed in the direction of his hairline.

"In more ways than one," the Commissioner was beginning to suspect. "The thieves who killed to get this painting went to a great deal of effort and then what? They dump it in a sleazy little Tenderloin pawnshop? Throw it away for fifteen dollars?"

Did that add up?

"Perhaps it was a spur-of-the-moment addition to the original order," the collector suggested, reminding Teddy of the hypothesis, that one of Frick's fellow magnates might have been behind the piracy. As Frick himself believed, particularly when it came to the likes of Dwight Morris.

"Queer lot, collectors," Maurice went on. "They'll move heaven and earth to get precisely what they want. Should something else fall into their laps, though, even something astonishingly beautiful—valuable—they'll turn their noses up."

Ergo: no sale.

"All right, you sell it to another collector. You ransom it back to the owner. You make a lot more than fifteen dollars." T.R. had no doubt that Henry Clay Frick would be willing to pay the price, whatever it was.

"I don't get it." Meeghan was scratching at his scalp. Was the Commissioner thinking the paintings were just incidental? "The burglars only took them on the way out?"

An afterthought?

"Or a cover." Had Frick made an inventory following the break-in, Roosevelt wondered suddenly, going outside. Could something else be missing from the house on Sixty-ninth?

Where could he find a phone?

"The candy store," a kid in a porkpie said, pointing as a shower of sparks cascaded down from the tracks above. Another steam engine pulling into the Fourteenth Street Station.

"Good man." A quarter tip for the urchin, who cartwheeled back to his friends, displaying the prize.

"Boy," they all whispered. "Boy." It was hard to suppress a grin, Teddy found, crossing in front of an oncoming trolley to reach the wooden newsstand which funneled customers into Benedict's Candy and Cigars, Optimos and Moxie.

"Hi yi yi!"

Riis. The reporter was descending from the el, the war cry more subdued than T.R. would have liked.

"We didn't do so well at Dvořák's, did we." *The Evening Sun*'s fingerprint man came up empty on that sill in the music room, he guessed.

"It was a long shot, Theodore. You knew that."

If he didn't, Meeghan did. "A case based on a lot of lines?" As Commissioner Parker would say, "there isn't a judge in the country who'd allow a conviction on that kind of 'evidence.' "

"How easily you dismiss an entire science you know nothing about." Harbinger was giving the detective a look of high-minded disdain, substantial enough to arouse Roosevelt's interest.

"Aren't fingerprints a bit out of your field of expertise, Maurice?"

Actually not. "My most recent invention is a classification system, in fact. We're hoping to do business with police departments all over the country by the beginning of next year."

" 'We'?" Jake was as intrigued as the President of New York City's Police Board.

"Mr. Edison and I." There had been a meeting scheduled between them on the subject that afternoon, "but when I received the call from Mr. Clinton, well, after our conversation at the gallery of course the Gainsborough took precedence."

"Bully for you. America needs all the public-spirited citizens it can get." Riis might want to write Maurice up, "the man is a genuine hero." T.R. stepped into the store; the telephone was boothed in the rear.

"Excuse me, madam: I must have the use of the phone. Police business."

"Dearie," Mrs. Edwina Smith grinned, turning. Not hanging up. "It's a conference with my lawyer, Mr. Dannemeyer. You know how they do go on." With what privilege. "We're discussing the charges you brought against my Home for Disadvantaged Young Women. What strategy we'll use to win out in court." Roosevelt would have to find himself another instrument.

"Your cooperation is duly noted," he assured her, reaching into the booth to depress the hook and disconnect the attorney.

"You can't do that!" Could he? "It's against the law, interrupting a private conversation."

"It's against the law, interfering with a police officer in the performance of his duty." Meeghan took her away and Teddy had Central place a call to Henry Clay Frick on Fifth Avenue at Sixty-ninth Street.

◼ He emerged unsmiling from Benedict's cleaning the lenses of his *pince-nez,* rubbing them with unnecessary vigor between the folds of his handkerchief.

Frick had made an inventory, all right. And the only things he could list as missing were three Old Master paintings. A Vermeer, a Hals, a Gainsborough.

Period.

4 BUFFALO BILL

■ The children knew the story by heart: how the intrepid Deputy Sheriff of Billings County, North Dakota, Theodore Roosevelt, had personally captured the notorious Redhead Finnegan, one of the worst of the badmen. But they were in the coach going to see Buffalo Bill's Wild West Show at Stanford White's Madison Square Garden; what better time to hear it all over again?

"All right," the Commissioner acquiesced, teeth opalescent in the glow of the landau lamps. It happened to be one of his favorite stories, too, in large measure because he didn't have to exaggerate about Finnegan: the man *was* as notorious as they came. A horse thief, a cattle rustler—"once he shot up the innocent little town of Medora with a buffalo gun just because someone played a minor little practical joke on him in the saloon."

"Why wasn't he arrested for that?" Kermit asked, on cue, the familiar ritual commencing as the coach rolled down Madison Avenue.

"Had I been in Medora when that happened you can be sure he would have been my guest in the pokey although, if memory

serves me right, Red did enjoy the sheriff's hospitality for a night
or two; I think so."

The twenty-seven-year-old Teddy Roosevelt had been at the
Elkhorn then, working his cattle ranch in the dead of winter.
Snow was in the air, a blizzard, perhaps.

"You could tell how bad it was going to be by how swollen the
river was." The Little Missouri. "Other times of the year you
could ford it on your horse but now? If you didn't have a boat you
weren't going anywhere."

Redhead Finnegan had stolen T.R.'s boat, he and his hench-
men. "Burnsted the halfbreed," Alice wanted to be the first to
say, "and Pfaffenbach the half-wit!" She loved the sound of "Pfaffenbach the half-wit," her slack-jawed moron look inevitably ac-
companying it.

Her father wouldn't ordinarily condone ridicule at the expense
of the afflicted but in the case of this brawler, this deviate, this
thug who'd made off with the Roosevelt boat?

He had it coming.

Teddy didn't care how much of a headstart the nefarious trio
had, "we were going up that river after them, on a homemade raft
if that was the best we could do."

A raft it was, three days in the making by the Commissioner's
ranch hands Sewall and Dow, their employer making use of the
time to begin a book on the life and work of Thomas Hart Benton.

"The wind started to howl. Snow came through the cracks in
the walls; the house creaked and shuddered; we all thought it
might even collapse!" The optical glass in T.R.'s *pince-nez* reflected the lights illuminating the entrance to the arena as the
conveyance approached their destination. Except that Alice, Ted
and Kermit saw only the scene on the Little Missouri nine years
before, Finnegan, Pfaffenbach and Burnsted holed up on the riverbank, their father about to pursue.

"Good evening, Commissioner," said the ticket taker at the
gate, gesturing them to their seats. "You're all in the front row."

Bill Cody had seen to that, personally. House seats for Theodore Roosevelt and family, no matter how hard to come by. No
matter how sold out. The Indian fighter turned showman was

inordinately proud of the set he'd had constructed in the arena—
trees, a few "hills" and even a watering hole of sorts; he didn't
want his old friend to miss an inch of it.

"Is that what the Badlands look like, Father?" Kermit was
mesmerized. All the outdoors had been brought indoors intact,
missing nothing but sky.

"It's a reasonable facsimile." More than reasonable, come to
think of it. "That shack there looks just like the shack Red and his
pals were in when we caught up with them after the storm."

Zero-degree weather. Ice floes on the water. All too often a limb
would crack off an overhanging tree and fall into the river, right
in front of their jerry-built raft.

Ice was heavy.

"Worse. We had no idea whether we were going in the right
direction or not. Those brigands could have traveled downriver
just as easily as up. They were almost ready to pack it in when—"

"—You saw the boat!" As Teddy, Sewall and Dow had seen the
boat at this point every time the story was told. "You came
around a bend in the river and," the eight-year-old recalled, "you
bumped right into it!"

And there was Pfaffenbach, a giant. "Mean. Dangerous—but
dozing. His gun was on the ground." Roosevelt's forces had him
safe before he knew what was what.

Luck was on their side. Finnegan and Burnsted were off hunting. There'd be quite a surprise for them when they returned.
Even so, the redhead was so ornery that at first he refused to drop
his pistol even though the Commissioner had him covered.

"We're talking about a cunning animal at bay. A wolf," T.R.
wanted his children to understand. "Never trust a man who has a
look like that in his eye, no matter how nicely he talks." Not just
out in the open, either. "There're wolves in business offices right
here in New York City, all over the place."

Roosevelt had the barrel of his gun pressed directly against
Finnegan's chest. Either Red put his hands up immediately or his
miserable outlaw existence would come to an end right then and
there, no matter what treachery he might have in mind.

The rustler did as he was told, his Colt clattering to the ground. But that wasn't the end of the tale, not by a long shot.

"Having these men was one thing. Bringing them in was another." They were 150 miles from the nearest town and they had no horses. "All that was left was the river."

The icy river.

"At least a week to Dickinson. At least." Could three fierce outlaws be managed for that length of time? Would it be worth it? "Nobody would have said boo if we had ourselves a necktie party and, believe me, children, the temptation was very strong."

"Father wouldn't hang anybody without due process, not even Redhead Finnegan." Axiomatic as far as Ted was concerned, if not Alice.

"Eight days down a river on a raft? With those dangerous criminals?" Her tone implied a last act considerably rewritten.

T.R. had done the honorable thing, though. He had taken the trio downstream on the raft, and then there were three more days of walking, behind a Conestoga borrowed from the C-Diamond Ranch. Even more of an ordeal. "The mud was ankle-deep. The wild roses had spines so sharp they slashed right through my clothes."

But he got them to the jailhouse in Dickinson, by George, blistered feet and all. Talk about earning the fifty-dollar deputy sheriff's arrest fee!

"After all that," Alice suddenly was curious to know, "how much time did Finnegan and the others actually get?" A new question, unexpected.

Potentially embarrassing.

"Well," her father said, equivocal, "a goodly number of years, I'm sure." The theft of a boat wasn't a hanging offense even in the Dakota Territory, after all.

Even so. Teddy was frankly relieved when a shout from the chute below the first tier of spectators ripped everyone's attention away from the foregoing exchange, particularly Alice's. "Runaway stagecoach, look out! Runaway stage!"

■ Screams. The clatter of hooves and harnesses moving at precipitous speed. Whinnies. Frightened whinnies.

The coach appeared like an apparition, shooting out onto the sawdust behind six maddened steeds, all charging blindly toward the teeterboard on the far side. A Wells Fargo wagon filled with terrified passengers, crying for help.

"Somebody do something!" a woman cried out from a seat two rows behind the Roosevelts, ashen. "Can't somebody do something?"

"Daddy," Alice gasped, aghast, cringing, clutching at her father's sleeve even as he stood, stripping off his jacket.

"Make room, children." He was all set to climb atop the railing in front of them and leap—but before he could do it Buffalo Bill was there holding him back and grinning. "Who's the star of this show, son, you or me?"

Yellow mane billowing in concert with the tan fringes of his buckskin jacket, Cody jumped, exactly as the screaming horses thundered beneath. The entire Garden was on its feet, wheezing with horror—Buffalo Bill had landed precariously, on the nearest of the lead team, grappling desperately with its bridle. The animal reared, unbalancing the already unbalanced. He'd fall—he'd be trampled—

But he didn't fall. He wasn't trampled. Both Bill and the horse knew what they were doing, and after a triumphant chord from the band, the audience knew it, too. Two thousand exhalations accompanied that exhilarating music, followed by a standing ovation.

Buffalo Bill's Wild West Show was under way.

■ "One hell of an opener, ain't it." Cody stood in the door of his dressing room beneath the stands and beamed at the President of New York City's Police Commission and his children, glad to have given them all so fine a thrill. "Works every time."

"I should say," Roosevelt enthused. "The glasses popped right off the bridge of my nose!" Here he'd been under the impression he'd seen it all, but this friend of his days in the Old West had happily proven him wrong. Dead wrong. Everything was eye-opening, from the cowboys on their ferociously bucking broncos to the full-feathered war dances of the proud Oglala Sioux—the very same that some of these very warriors had danced on the night of June 24, 1876, just before the battle of the Little Big Horn.

"*Wuh* wuh wuh wuh, *wuh* wuh wuh wuh . . ."

Gunfire. Smoke. A bugle call. U.S. Cavalrymen, blue tunics agleam, charged out into the arena as the Indians scrambled up onto their ponies. Huzzahs from the multitude as the horse soldiers chased the foe from the scene, especially when several of the savages seemed to have been shot off the backs of their fleeing mounts.

"Crackerjack!" Kermit had yelled, pointing, flush with excitement. "Look out behind you, Buffalo Bill!" A dastardly brave could be seen sneaking up on the Indian fighter from behind, tomahawk raised.

"Not this time, redskin!" It was a woman's voice, the voice of Annie Oakley herself, shooting the tomahawk right out of the redskin's hand. What choice did he have but to hightail it off, the last of his line, while Buffalo Bill held the lady's hand up over their heads in response to the percussive applause.

"Shooting a tomahawk out of an Indian's hand is only one of the tricks in Miss Oakley's repertoire," he wanted the people to know, announcing a demonstration to prove it. Marksmanship beyond belief, eliciting gasps at least twice, once when Annie's bullet split the apple which Bill had placed on top of his very own head.

Not frontward, either. Backward. Over her shoulder—using a mirror to aim.

And then Cody'd caught her next bullet between his teeth.

"How did you *do* that?" Ted had to ask now that he was face-to-face with the legend, his eyes saucering at the sight of all the cowboys, the Indians, the showgirls, up close. Live.

"Timing," Bill replied, giving the Commissioner a sideways grin. "If I bite down too late, the bullet'd go right through the back of my mouth and that would be very messy. If I bite down too soon, it'd bounce off my teeth and that wouldn't be any fun. Gotta be just right."

"Bullets bounce off your teeth." Do they. Do they really. Alice, ever the skeptic, even with an immortal such as Buffalo Bill.

"It's an old potion he got when he was with the Sioux," Annie Oakley said, coming up to join them. "Makes your front teeth iron." She was incredibly ugly, a little woman with braids and a broad-brimmed Western hat, rifle still in hand.

Her teeth, they saw, were rotting away. How come she hadn't gotten some of that Sioux stuff herself, the immediate question, tactless. Loud.

"Children," Roosevelt cautioned, frowning.

"That's okay, Commish, I'd ask me that if I was them." The Sioux, for their information, "they guard that potion of theirs something fierce. Fact is, ol' Cody here, he's about the only one outside of the tribe who ever was so honored; ain't that right, Bill?"

"Seem to be in a class by myself, all right."

Annie snickered. "Don't you go high-hat on me again, mister. Save it for the Queen."

"The Queen?" Alice's ears picked up. "Of England?"

"Big fan'a mine," the showman bragged. "The Prince of Wales, too." There'd been a Command Performance when the show was in London, two years before. "Gave His Highness a few lessons on how to twirl a lariat, in fact." They were going back for a return engagement in '97, not only England and France this time but Germany, Italy, Spain—"Hey! You! Where d'you think you're going with my saddle?"

Cody's shout was aimed at what looked like one of his cowboys, a large dude in a five-gallon hat, bandanna, leather vest and tooled boots. Silver spurs. The magnificently studded saddle which Teddy had last seen on Bill's prized palomino was perpendicular beneath the desperado's arm as his walk became a run, as he headed for the exit.

"My saddle, I don't believe it," the Indian scout spluttered, already in hot pursuit. T.R. was right behind him, yelling.

"Stop! You, there—stop!"

"Go get him, Father!" Kermit and Ted were leapfrogging in their excitement and even the porcelain face that Alice usually put on for the world was ablaze, fire in the eyes, fire on the cheeks.

"Don't let him escape!"

The piping of their voices made Roosevelt pivot. "Miss Oakley," he petitioned in his rush. "If you could keep the children with you for the moment—?"

Of course. "You just go catch that polecat!"

Teddy's "thank you" reached her ears long after he was out the door, keeping up with Buffalo Bill and the thief.

■ Carriages of all descriptions were lined up alongside the sidewalk outside the building. Landaus, hackneys, broughams, cabriolets and phaetons, into which elegant gentlemen in top hats were helping their ladies while a tide of the less wealthy streamed out of the Garden behind them, surging toward the Twenty-third Street Station of the Third Avenue El. Both groups of audience were buzzing with residual cheer, exchanging chaotic impressions of the production—and then screams, the scuffling sound of bodies knocked about in a crowd. One of the cowboys from the show seemed to erupt from the arena, the enormous western saddle in his hand used like a scythe, mowing people down, men and women—children.

"Are you crazy?" someone cried, but the fugitive paid no heed as he dashed across the sidewalk to the lineup of waiting vehicles, tearing one of the liveried drivers out of his seat. A squawk of monosyllabic complaint ripped out of the man, a similar protest emerging from the two-horse team attached to the front of his coach. Hooves flashed like axheads.

"Hup!" the usurper rasped, scrambling aboard and taking the reins, slapping leather against the flanks of the frightened creatures. Never had either been so maltreated; they bolted. Even closed in by the other carriages, the other mounts. They bolted.

"Grab that man!" Buffalo Bill raged, sprinting through the seething crowd, the President of New York City's Police Commission hard on his heels.

"I've got him," a husky young gentleman of society decreed, reaching for the harnesses.

"No—!" Teddy warned, not soon enough. The sharp *crack!* of a pistol shot echoed around the street, terrifying. A shriek burst from the tuxedoed samaritan hurled back by the impact, the pristine white of his studded piquot blackened by gunpowder and reddened with blood.

"Why, you low-down skunk!" Bill was ready to leap up at the criminal, all instinct and adrenaline; he even got so far as to clasp a hand around the brake shaft, leg half up in the air.

"Cody!" T.R. yanked at him as a second bullet exploded alongside the impresario's head, furrowing the skin at the temple. Buffalo Bill roared, more in anger than pain.

"He shot me, look!"

"Is there a doctor among you?" Roosevelt searched the crowd urgently even as the thief swung his commandeered carriage out into the middle of the street, free to pick up speed.

"I'm a doctor."

"Him first, Doc," Cody said to the physician who was squeezing through the six-deep circle of people, the showman pressing a handkerchief to his head, not nearly so wounded as the youth in the tux. For his part, the Commissioner was clambering aboard another of the coaches, prepared to continue the pursuit alone.

"You have that patched up, Bill; you hear?" His friend was not to do anything more, not in his condition. Theodore Roosevelt was on the job.

"Attaboy, Teddy, you show 'em!" It was the coachman whose rig T.R. had requisitioned, encouraging him to use the whip. His horses could take it: "Use the whip!"

"Damn right!" The Commissioner took the implement from the sheath at his foot, lashing out at the animals. His quarry was half a block ahead of them by now, aware that chase was being given. Firing over his shoulder, wildly. Anything to keep Roosevelt at bay, the hell with who got hit.

T.R. cursed him through clenched teeth. His horses flew over the cobblestones, the gap between the vehicles beginning to shorten.

"Hi! Hi!" The voice snapped with as much force as the whip, and by Third Avenue the coaches were abreast, near enough for Teddy to see the muzzle of the six-shooter aimed back at him. At this range a wild shot might not be so wild.

All he could do was follow his instincts. Duck. A shower of glass inundated him, scratching his face: the landau light beside his ear had been blown apart. "You lunatic—!"

This time the Commissioner flicked the cat not at the horses but at the man in the adjacent vehicle, extracting a cry and a clatter. The strike had glanced off the back of the fugitive's gun hand, splaying the fingers, releasing the weapon. It fell, pirouetting across the irregularly shaped cobblestones before it dropped through a curbside grate.

Alarm from the people on the sidewalk: the chariot in front seemed to go out of control, veering sharply to the right. Both wheels on its left side lifted off the ground as it skidded toward a girder supporting the elevated railroad above, missing the obstruction by what looked like less than an inch. Screams.

Scrambles.

Several of the men dropped where they stood, thinking only of their own skins. Others wheeled their women out of harm's way, shielding them with their bodies.

Mud splattered up. A spray of small stones. The carriages barreled past, careening down Third with increasing velocity, the wheels of both shrieking with anthropomorphic fury. If any of the spokes snapped, if the ring slipped off the hub, neither would survive, nor their horses.

Nor their drivers.

■ Madison Square Garden was well over a mile behind them now. Third Avenue had long since become the Bowery. Mr. Roebling's bridge loomed up ahead.

"Go there and I've got you," T.R. hissed into the dark space between himself and his prey, the churning carriages lurching out from under the el at last. For a moment it seemed the thief had heard him, continuing past the ramp that rose up from Park Row, as though the destination were the South Street waterfront. A thief could easily lose himself in the twisted alleys there, or become just another glaze-eyed customer in Shanghai Charlie's emporium, downstairs or up.

Smart. Roosevelt was giving him grudging credit when, at the last minute, the coach ahead of him veered. It was going to be the bridge, after all. Brooklyn. As if the counterfeit cowboy were accepting the Commissioner's dare. "You want it out in the open, do you, no pillars to run interference?"

Okay. Catch me if you can.

The brougham sped through the Gothic arches of the Manhattan tower, the vast cables reaching out from it, clutching at those descending from the Brooklyn side. A pair of Brobdingnagian arm wrestlers locked in eternal combat, Teddy thought as the wind whistled through the webbing and drove into his back, propelling him forward. Faster.

Faster.

Whipcracks. A foghorn, lowing down by the Battery. The wheels. The hooves.

Halfway across the river a leg snapped out from under one of the steeds in the fugitive's team, a splatter of red darkening the scream that flew from its mouth. A collision with its neighbor was inevitable, a tangle of horseflesh and hooves overturning everything.

Cracking wood—metal—popping glass: the cacophony of disaster.

"Whoa!" T.R. yanked back on the reins in his hands, braking, turning, bringing his own vehicle up to an abrupt stop alongside the broken brougham. "Whoa!" In one swift motion he secured the straps and leaped to the floor of the span, ready to face the thief.

Thin, sinewy—tall; he was European. Roosevelt was sure of it, western garb notwithstanding. The man with Buffalo Bill's saddle still in his hands was not a citizen of these United States.

"Stay back, Commissioner. Back!" Switzerland, the accent suggested. Austria, perhaps. Teddy could pinpoint it later. Right now he was dodging the swipes the criminal was taking at him, once again using the saddle as a weapon.

"This is useless, you know that—give up!" He was trying to memorize what he could see of the face as he spoke: the pock-marks on the brow, the scar on the cheek, livid even in the pen-umbral light from one of Mr. Edison's newly installed street lamps.

Laughter. High-pitched, derisive, exaggerated. Before Roose-velt could react, the saddle was suddenly jammed into his belly, the impact driving the wind from his lungs. It staggered him, yes, but he kept his footing, and he grabbed at the pommel and a stirrup, wrenching the *aparejo* to himself.

The thief let go. He jumped up onto the outer railing of the bridge, holding on to one of the wires, a human boom. "You can't touch me," the malevolent voice declared, its owner stepping out into midair, 135 feet above the East River.

"Not that, no—!" The Commissioner lunged forward, arm ex-tended, fingers straining outward toward the disembodied laugh which was all that was left of what once was a man. T.R. could only lean over the edge, blinking hard as he tried to discern the splash in the night, seeing nothing.

Nothing.

"By God." He turned away, leaning his back against the rail-ing, suddenly cold. Vision blurred. Unfocused.

What was that misshapen object over there on the bridge?

"The saddle." Buffalo Bill Cody's precious handmade saddle. Teddy hurried to reclaim it, inspecting it for damage, breathing a sigh of initial relief. All the studs were in place, the leather un-marred. The pommel was intact. The stirrups.

It had been worth it, at least. The pursuit.

And then Roosevelt turned the saddle over and saw what the marauder had done to the lining underneath.

■ "Why would anyone do something like this?" Bill said, over and over, his long thin fingers touching the slashes, smoothing the rents into place and separating them, smoothing and separating, as though the act itself could somehow knit the glossy fabric back into place.

It wasn't even good vandalism, the Commissioner had to agree.

That would have entailed the evisceration of the seat, the decapitation of the pommel and almost certainly the random removal of at least a third to a half of the jewels. As it was, the repairs were minimal. Cody could have his property back good as new by the end of the day.

"Because you were right there breathing down his neck." Cody was proud of his friend, almost as though Teddy were a protégé. "Can you imagine what it would've come out looking like if you weren't?"

A thief so doggedly determined to wreak havoc on the showman's pride and joy, chopping and hacking even as he hurtled around the stanchions which made Third Avenue an obstacle course—this was someone out for revenge. What else?

"I've made enemies in my time, son, some of whom would cut me up a lot quicker than my saddle." The old Cavalry scout might have gotten off light, come to think of it.

"Maybe." T.R. wasn't entirely convinced. Why would someone out for revenge confine his knife to the underside of Bill's saddle, rushed and buffeted though he might have been? Why wouldn't he at least have tried to deface the good leather? The polished silver ornamentation?

"Cutting through a piece of stretched cloth is a lot easier than cutting through cowhide and metal, especially when it's this thick." Almost a full inch in places. Never less than half.

"And you wouldn't have kept anything inside that saddle, would you."

The jaw dropped, and then the laughter exploded. "Now, there is an idea," Cody declared. "Better than a money belt, even." Who'd expect him to keep his savings under his derrière?

"Just a thought," Roosevelt muttered, looking up at the sound of his title, Lieutenant Meeghan calling from a department rig pulling up in front of the Garden.

"There'll be men on both sides of the river just south of the bridge, first light," he announced. "Just like you wanted."

"With a scow midstream," yes?

"Yes, sir. If there's a body in that water they'll fish it out."

Unless there was some credence to be put in a report which had just come in from the foot of Burling Slip, about half a mile down from the bridge. Could they believe a drunk sleeping it off on the pier, suddenly awakened by someone climbing out of the water a minute or two before midnight?

"Did the drunk describe this 'someone'?" Teddy's nose was twitching. "Pockmarked face? Scar?" It would be too much to hope that words might have been exchanged, that a European accent might have been noted.

"All the bum said was he saw this guy shimmy up a piling and run like crazy up Fulton Street. It could have been the alcohol, Commissioner."

But it wasn't. T.R. knew it, in his bones he knew it. The bum might have been inebriated, but that was no pink elephant he'd seen emerging from the river. That was a scar-faced man who could smirk at the stunned look on the face of a president of the New York City Police Board—because he was going to do what Steve Brodie had done nine years before, jumped from the center of the span and come out just as intact.

They'd dredge the riverbed in the morning, but nothing would be found. Andrew D. Parker would accuse his rival of being profligate with department money, and somewhere on the island of Manhattan a thief with a scar would be congratulating himself in a European accent. He had gotten away with . . .

. . . what?

5 RICHARD KERNER

■ ROOSEVELT TO THE RESCUE, the *Herald* said. TEDDY AND BUFFALO BILL IN WILD WEST CHASE THROUGH LOWER EAST SIDE, according to Pulitzer's *World.* Only the New York *Times* was muted. POLICE COMMISSIONER IN INCIDENT, it reported in a one-column-width paragraph at the bottom of page sixteen.

Edith made sure to fold the paper so that her husband wouldn't miss it once he got past the yellower journals, placing the stack on the bed along with his *pince-nez.* He adjusted them on the bridge of his nose and looked up to regard her through the lenses with as much reassurance as he could muster: an attempt to defuse the reproach all over her face.

"I really wasn't in any great danger." Those newspapers. She knew how they loved to exaggerate.

"It wasn't you." She sat beside him on the edge of the mattress. "You can take care of yourself." The children, though? He had left them alone in front of Madison Square Garden, alone in the middle of the night—"and over what, Theodore? A saddle?"

His hands reached out for her, both of them. "They were not left alone. Miss Oakley was keeping her eye out, all the time I was gone." Alice, Ted and Kermit were perfectly safe. Asleep in the carriage, in fact, well before their father's return.

"Out where they could catch a chill." Was the bedroom window open? It felt open. Edith went to close it.

"May nights are not chilly."

"This one was very warm, actually," Alice contended, preceding her appearance in the bedroom with only the briefest of knocks. Had her mother heard what happened? "How brave Father was?" Even though the thief was shooting real bullets at everyone on the street "he went after him. And when he came back with Buffalo Bill's saddle everybody jumped up and down, clapping and yelling, 'Teddy! Teddy!' It was wonderful."

"I'm sure." The sash was slammed down into the sill. Hadn't someone just told his wife the children were asleep in the carriage at the time of his return?

"Edith—"

"No." He could not appease her with a sheepish look, not this time. "For once I agree with your friend Andrew Parker," she wanted him to know, digging the *Times* out from under the *Sun* and the *Post,* quoting. " 'The physical apprehension of criminals is hardly the job of a Commissioner of Police.' Especially when there has to have been at least a dozen officers there in front of that building."

"Father has to set the example, though," that was Alice's opinion.

"Out of the mouths of babes," in case Edith might have forgotten. The fact was that her husband happened to be in tip-top condition, the best ever in all his life. After all the speeches, all the articles and books, "how would it look if Theodore Roosevelt acted like just one more desk-bound 'let Joe do it' appointee?"

"Awful," said Alice, her father nodding as he got up out of his bed, tendons complaining. Was he telling Edith anything she hadn't known long before they were married?

He wasn't, she had to admit. T.R. could no more let anyone make off with a stolen saddle than he could let a corrupt police officer accept a bribe from an Estes Hanrahan. It was the nature of the beast, what had set him apart even as a child, what had attracted her in the first place, when she was seven. When he was ten.

"That doesn't mean I can't get upset when you take chances like that, good cause or not." A side trip to the adjacent bathroom, for the bottle of Proctor's Liniment. Edith knew a wince when she saw it.

"I did not wince."

"Don't use it, then," she advised, escorting their daughter from the chamber. "But don't come to me when your back starts to ache, either."

"Shrew." For which he received a kiss through the air, returning it before the door was shut. Liniment. His muscles were not in need of liniment, not when there were all these front pages to read.

ROOSEVELT TO THE RESCUE. T.R. FOILS ROBBERY.

WILD WEST CHASE THROUGH LOWER EAST SIDE: *Death-Defying Leap from Brooklyn Bridge Described.*

God, his father would have been proud. The finest man Teedie'd ever known, dead so young so many years ago now. Let the Parkers call it "grandstanding," let them tut-tut because the physical apprehension of a criminal wasn't the proper business of a high-placed city official. They'd be on the bottom of page sixteen in a one-column-width postscript alongside some unimportant notices, civic and cultural, while Theodore Roosevelt dominated page one.

COMMISSIONER IN INCIDENT. TEDDY ACCEPTS PLAUDITS.

Something suddenly made him go back to those notices; what did that say there? Dvořák said what?

The newsprint rattled as he folded the sheets back to page sixteen again, using his finger to find the item POSTPONEMENT RESCINDED: *Symphony to Premiere on Schedule.*

With or without the score?

▪ The composer was seated at a table set up on the stage of Andrew Carnegie's Hall, just to the right of the podium. In one hand, his cigar; in the other, a pencil, both hovering over the multi-staved music paper spread open in front of him.

"C-sharp in bar forty-seven," he was advising, glancing up at the iron-haired conductor. "Seidl."

"C-sharp," came the reply, repeated for the players in the orchestra. "Six after letter *A*, gentlemen."

A downbeat. Music, even more beautiful here than it had been on Seventeenth Street, riveting Teddy halfway down the aisle.

"Can the trumpets play an octave higher between thirty-seven and forty-two?" Dvořák's voice stayed Seidl's baton, the Philharmonic reduced to undignified cacophony. The annotation of the parts gave Roosevelt his opportunity: he approached the apron. "Maestro."

"Commissioner!" The Bohemian countenance lit up. "Isn't it wonderful? Only in Vienna and Prague can the orchestras sight-read so well."

"Tell that to the orchestras in Prague and Vienna," T.R. recommended, pleased to hear Dvořák so unequivocal in his praise. Even more pleased that the Philharmonic had such eloquent music to sight-read.

"Ach, mein liebe Gott." Mortification. Chagrin. "I didn't call you. The first thing I said to myself: 'Tell the Commissioner. Pick up the phone.' But the copyists had to be called first," Roosevelt had to understand. "If we still wanted to make the concert date, I mean."

On top of which it began to rain questions. Everybody had a question. Was this to E-minor, this modulation at the end of the *allegro molto?* Did the trombones play this passage here with mutes, and what about the fingering on the crescendo at letter *F*, wasn't it going to be physically impossible in so short a time?

Days go by and so much for good intentions. "You must accept my apologies," Dvořák insisted. "And come tonight with your wife. Two tickets: it is a great symphony."

"Edith and I will be delighted; thank you." But first, how much had the composer paid for it, to get it back—that was the real question, not at all the afterthought that Roosevelt made it sound. " 'Bring in the police and your precious manuscript goes up in smoke,' is that what they told you?"

A shake of the shaggy head. "No one said 'boo.' The telephone did not ring, there was no brick through the window, nothing."

The piece was just . . . returned. Left on the doorstep, not a note missing. Nor a note attached. "Only the music," Dvořák declared, and then he had to laugh out loud. " 'Only': will you listen to me? 'Only.' "

Teddy was listening, listening more carefully, perhaps, than he himself even knew. "Does that mean it wasn't in its case?" That shabby leather carryall that Brahms had given him?

"It wasn't, in fact," the symphonist himself suddenly realized, the cigar bobbling in his mouth. "Just the stack of paper tied up with string." A tragedy in the making, had it rained.

"He kept the case." Teddy spoke to the ceiling of the auditorium. "He kept the case. . . ."

"More likely he sold it, the *ganef.*" Scratched and rubbed though it was, genuine leather had to fetch something on the open market, unlike a collection of used score sheets. "Once he saw there was no way my *New World* was going to make him one blessed *pfennig,* what else could he do but return it?"

"Throw it away?"

"A man who knows enough to steal a major work by Antonin Dvořák?" Antonin Dvořák did not think so. "This may be a thief, Commissioner, but that does not necessarily make him a Philistine."

"Maybe." Or maybe the Commissioner had been looking at the whole thing backward to begin with? "What if the *'ganef'* didn't break into your house to steal the symphony at all?"

What if he'd come to steal the case?

"Why?" The cigar became akin to chewing tobacco in the Czech's mouth. "It didn't even have Brahms's signature on it."

"I don't know why," T.R. could only growl as the brass blared behind him, Seidl humming almost as audibly. "If I did, I'd know everything."

▪ Frick was at the premiere that evening, in the company of Dwight Morris. The conversation was animated between them, all smiles and puffs of smoke. They were the oldest of friends.

"Theodore!" It was Henry who'd spotted the Roosevelts first, leading Morris over to the couple through a gap in the crowd. "A public official who gives his word and then actually lives up to it: the millennium has arrived!" In case his fellow collector wasn't aware, "this man is personally responsible for the return of my Gainsborough."

"And the restoration of an old friendship." Morris gesticulated with his stick. The bird seemed pleased that Frick no longer thought his owner a thief, or the employer of thieves.

"I did nothing, really." It was Maurice Harbinger who deserved the praise. "Speak to him."

"I have already." He would again, at the new unveiling the following week. Edith and Teddy just *had* to attend: Henry Clay was eager for their opinion of the replacement frame. "Whether it's even better for the painting than the original was." His opinion was that it was, of course—"but I'm prejudiced."

They laughed, all except the Commissioner. "Theodore?" Edith asked, on the verge of alarm.

"The frame," he whispered.

"Hand-carved," the millionaire was proud to reveal, blind to the crisis on T.R.'s face. "Gilded, filigreed—"

Was there a problem?

"Not anymore, I don't think!" Roosevelt was never more sure of anything in his life. He had it solved, part of it. The what if not the why. "Henry, they weren't stealing your paintings; they had no intention of stealing your paintings, not for sale on the underground art market they didn't."

"Theodore." There were still two blank spaces left on the wall of the reception room. Formerly occupied by two paintings.

"Surrounded by two *frames.*"

"Who steals frames?" Morris wanted to know, his faith in the Commissioner's intellect suddenly doing an Otis.

"Who steals an old case instead of the valuable one-of-a-kind symphony inside?" Teddy knew they didn't get it; he didn't care. *He* got it: a possible connection. Frick. Dvořák. Cody.

What was the "irrelevant" thing he'd said to the composer that night in the music room? That, who knows, Dvořák might be the second in a series?

Would that make Buffalo Bill the third? Could be. Damn well could be, unless . . .

. . . Unless Henry Clay Frick weren't really the first.

By George.

"The concert is about to commence, ladies and gentlemen." An usher, red uniform. Gold braid. "Please take your seats, the concert is about to commence."

Coincidental, Officer Kerner had called it. Officer Kerner was probably right. "But wouldn't it be interesting to see if there's been loot returned from any other recent burglaries." Without whatever cover it came in to begin with.

"Pardon?" Dwight Morris had to hurry to keep up as the President of the Police Board and his wife slipped through the crowd in the aisle of the auditorium.

"Frames, Mr. Morris. Saddles." Teddy beamed, seating Edith and beaming some more. "This is turning out to be one hell of a bully case!"

■ "Go through every file you can," he told Minnie at 7:48 A.M. the following Monday, having called her into his office even as he was striding in from the corridor, scrub-faced. Ebullient. The fingers of both hands delved into his vest pockets, spreading the wings of his suit jacket as he specified the kind of canceled robbery report he wanted to see. "The stolen property can't just have been returned, it has to have been returned without its box."

Whatever form that took. Roosevelt didn't care if it was a paper bag.

"How far back do you want me to go?"

"Three months at least." No. "Six." Seven, maybe.

"Manhattan only?" If Minnie had to call over to the independent city of Brooklyn "it could take a while."

"Manhattan primarily," the Commissioner replied. "Some Brooklyn; confine it to the Heights. Put it on a priority basis with the commanders if you're talking down at the precinct level; it's the personal request of the Police Board President, New York."

A knock on the open door turned their heads. "Is the Police Board President in to the press?" Jake Riis inquired, craning his neck around the jamb.

"The press, no. You, more often than not." He'd be with the reporter in just a moment. There was still one additional point he wanted his secretary to keep in mind while she was on the phone. "Well-known people," that was. All three victims fit in that category so far. "Don't be surprised if you run into more."

"That's right, isn't it." Riis hadn't exactly made a conscious note of the fact but it was there, nevertheless, an amorphous shadow in the back of his own mind—"although that could be because, after all is said and done, well-known people are usually rich, and rich people usually have a lot more for crooks to take, don't they."

"To take and fence. To ransom." Never to give back. "I'm starting to see a pattern here, Jake. Something bigger than any one individual heist." The reporter would be the first T.R. would call in, "as soon as I have something solid. *Pro quo* for all the *quid.*"

Riis nodded his appreciation, closing the door now that Minnie had excused herself, gone to her desk, telephone waiting. "After that I wish this particular *'quid'* could be better news."

There was going to be a rubout. Hanrahan's boys were ordered to do it sometime after dark, according to one of Jake's more reliable sources up in Hell's Kitchen.

"This 'source' tell you who Estes has in mind?" Teddy seated himself at his desk, his fingertips meeting in Gothic configuration.

"Richard Kerner."

The fingers separated. Curled. "Why?"

Why? Roosevelt didn't have to be told why, he knew.

"Hanrahan's found out that Richard is my undercover man." So soon. So easy. In spite of the big show the two of them had put on in the corridor. Listen to me, you abject excuse for a flatfoot, don't push it. Don't even try.

Sure. Go on. Jug an innocent guy and get your picture in the paper again, big shot.

"Dammit, Jake, where'd I go wrong? Dvořák's place?" He and

Richard could have been seen together there, yes, but that was *East* Seventeenth Street. Mike O'Bannion's turf. A Hanrahan boy would be taking his life in his hands.

Unlikely.

"Someone here at headquarters is in Hanrahan's pocket, that's what I think." Riis knew every wall in the building, which ones had the ears, which did not.

Very few did not.

"Except the only people who knew about Richard and me were you and Minnie." Neither of whom would ever give anything away: T.R. trusted them implicitly. Implicitly. "The walls can't hear what hasn't been said."

"True." But Estes Hanrahan wasn't the kind who needed definitive evidence to convict anyone. "He just doesn't take chances, even if all he has to go on is a rumor—you'd better get Kerner out of there, fast."

"I don't want to get him out of there!" The vehemence was unsettling, to the Commissioner as well as the reporter. "What I want is to figure some way to fix it, so Hanrahan doesn't suspect Richard of being in league with me or anybody else."

"Easier said than done," in Jake's opinion.

"Ten hours till dark." The pocket watch was out in Teddy's palm. "One of us can come up with something in ten hours. Minnie can cancel my appointments, we'll pace, think; we'll take care of the problem."

"Then you don't know about the board meeting this morning."

A stare, sudden. Blank. Uncharacteristic of Roosevelt. "What meeting?"

"The one originally scheduled for Friday afternoon. To vote on whether the officers you've suspended should stay suspended."

"Moved up five days." Courtesy of Andrew D. Parker, no doubt. Why should the reputation of those poor accused policemen have to suffer under a cloud any longer than necessary? "What time am I supposed to be there with my gavel?"

"Eight-thirty," the reporter said, mock amazement all over his voice. Surely Theodore had seen the notice Andrew'd been so careful to send!

"Right." T.R. led the way into the outer office. Minnie wouldn't have forgotten to tell him about any memo or telephone call from Commissioner Parker this morning, would she?

"Sir?"

"Exactly." He headed on through to the corridor. "Keep those legs up, Jake, you want to pace me."

Riis kept his legs up. Teddy was already halfway to the stairs, and one hell of a confrontation was in the wind. Headlines for two whole days. BATTLE OVER CROOKED COPS. MALFEASANCE ON THE BEAT. ROOSEVELT ACCUSES PARKER OF COMPLICITY.

Wonderful.

So wonderful that he didn't see that the Commissioner had stopped suddenly, at the head of the stairs. It was a near-miss.

"Theodore?"

What was that quirky little smile doing on T.R.'s face at a time like this?

The smile broadened. "Jake," he said, content, "you may not know it, but you just gave me what I need to save Richard Kerner's bacon."

■ Officer Ellis was cleared of all charges by the Board, three yeas, one abstention.

"Perhaps I was a little hasty the night I arrested him," Theodore Roosevelt allowed, bland in his chair. "Next?"

"Sergeant Aloysius Bova," Parker said, reading from a file. "Arrested the night of May seventeenth—"

"I withdraw my charges."

"What?"

"Charges withdrawn." Unless Parker, Grant and Andrews wanted to press them themselves?

An exchange of bewildered looks. Out among the spectators, sparse at this hour, Jacob Riis didn't know which to be more amused by, the muddled consternation on their faces or Teddy's dead pan.

"Next."

Officer Douglas Whyte. "The President of our Board has compiled quite a list of offenses here," Parker observed, glancing to-

ward his rival. "I assume this is one case you'd like us not to
drop?"

Roosevelt seemed more interested in his fingernail. "It's all
down on paper." He shrugged. "If you gentlemen think a suspension is in order, a suspension is in order."

If not, not.

Not.

"Majority rule." The fingernail was absolutely fascinating.

"Officer Richard Kerner," the next patrolman under the cloud.
"Accused," Grant read, "of consorting with known criminals on
the night of May thirteenth and again on the twentieth." If no one
had anything to say—

"Just a moment." T.R. had something to say. This time T.R.
had something to say.

"Really." Parker did not like the way the man with the mustache was straightening up in his chair, nor the way he chose to
echo Parker's "really."

"Ellis and the others so far, all they were were bribe-takers.
Cops who liked to walk their beat in a bar because a bar is a lot
more comfortable than a street, particularly when it's three in the
morning and twenty degrees out." Kerner, though, was another
can of worms.

Another thing entirely.

"How?" Parker demanded to know, skimming the report in his
hand. "I don't see anything more heinous here than elsewhere."

"Actually," the mild-mannered Commissioner Andrews felt,
"of all the cases we've reviewed this morning this one has to be
the weakest. Finding a man in a public place in a public conversation, even with a Bill Sikes: that is in and of itself not illegal."
Certainly not a firing offense.

"Perhaps not," Teddy was willing to agree. "What about armed
robbery? Is that a firing offense? Assault and battery?"

Extortion?

"This man Kerner has engaged in assault and battery? Extortion?" Andrew Parker leaned forward, sniffing, fully expecting to
smell a rat. "What proof do you have, Theodore?"

What witnesses?

Confidence made Roosevelt stand at his place, inhaling. "By three o'clock this afternoon I am going to have *three* witnesses, people who will not only point Officer Kerner out as their assailant, but who will be willing to say so in court."

"Pillars of society, no doubt." Parker had every doubt in the world.

"Shopkeepers, Andrew. Merchants." People with unblemished records, shaken down in their very own establishments by this criminal in uniform. "A protection racket, run by a cop. And when the store owner said no, it would be the billy club 'accidentally' breaking the glass in the display case." Or the bone in the arm.

As his fellow commissioners could see for themselves in his office at three.

"I'll be there," Freddie Grant piped, Avery Andrews me-too-ing.

According to Riis's notes, Andrew Parker "struggled to come up with a withering riposte. The best he could do was 'three it is,' on which he walked out of the room."

▪ By two-fifteen the telephone was ringing in Parker's office down the hall, Minnie Kelly on the line. If the Commissioner didn't want to wait another forty-five minutes, T.R. would be very happy to introduce him to those witnesses they talked about, now.

Five minutes later the entire Board convened in Theodore Roosevelt's private office, its occupant making the introductions. "Delbert W. Clinton, gentlemen, operator of Clinton's Pawnshop on Ninth Avenue . . . Harry Coopersmith, a pharmacist on West Thirty-third . . . Sidney Kyle, you might know his shoe repair stand on Chelsea Square."

Kyle had a shiner. His arm was in a sling.

"Was that done by Officer Kerner?" Commissioner Andrews, speaking for all, receiving a nod.

"In the alley behind my business." The voice wavered, the memory obviously as painful as the injuries themselves. " 'It's very dark back here,' he kept telling me. 'A man can get jumped by the worst kind of riffraff.' "

That was when the baton broke his arm.

"The arm—the face—just as Theodore said. If this isn't blatant sadism," Grant hawked, "I don't know what is."

"So it seems." Parker had turned his attention to Coopersmith, no emotion visible on his liturgic face. "Officer Kerner didn't do you any damage."

"Richard Kerner never hits people if hitting their display cases can get him his 'fee.' " Roosevelt had referred to that in the board room that morning, his associates might remember. "It took Mr. Coopersmith hours to clean up the glass, the syrups . . ."

". . . Pills, poultices . . ." There was an envelope filled with cash waiting for the officer the next time he returned to the pharmacy.

"We all paid him," Clinton asserted. "He was the one with the billy club, the gun—the uniform. What could we do?"

"Bleed." The shoemaker shook his damaged head. "Bleed until the veins went dry and then go to Theodore Roosevelt. Maybe he was as honest as the papers would have us believe."

"If we weren't we wouldn't be here with these fine gentlemen, would we." These fine members of the Board. The only question left being what they intended to do, "now that they have all the facts."

"Do?" Parker circled the witnesses, ceremonious. "Why, we're going to jail the miserable *ex*-policeman, as fast as we can."

"After we make sure he's fired from this department," Grant emphasized as Parker patted the shoemaker's shoulder and shook Clinton's hand. He shook the druggist's, too, before walking out, converted.

"Told you I could make a statue cry," Kyle beamed once the last of the commissioners had departed, leaving the witnesses alone with the President of the Board. "Aren't you glad me and that longhorn ran into each other at Madison Square Garden?"

Kyle wasn't a shoemaker. He was one of Buffalo Bill's best bulldoggers. Sometimes even the best comes a cropper.

"Sarah Bernhardt couldn't have been more moving." They were all magnificent, T.R. declared, and they helped save a brave young cop from unspeakable death, a tomb at the bottom of the Hudson River.

■ She was still at her desk at ten past seven, late sunshine streaming through the slats in the west-facing windows, highlighting the red strands of her hair.

"Shouldn't you have left to meet your fiancé by now?" Roosevelt asked, appearing in the door of his retreat. Minnie usually had dinner at the Boylan residence Monday evenings, corned beef and cabbage, kidney pie. She'd made a point of it during her interview, scared that the information would lead the Commissioner not to hire her, too beholden to keep it back.

"These files are more important." Files which might reveal more cases which fit the pattern of robbery-return, well-known individuals happy to be out only a box or a bag or a briefcase.

"It can hold one more night." Teddy did not want to be responsible for the cancellation of a wedding, imminent or not. "Go on."

"There's nothing to 'go on' to," his secretary confessed, inhaling first. This was hard for her. And yet there was an element of freedom in it, a sense of identity new and oddly invigorating.

"Oh, Minnie." He truly felt for her.

"I'm fine, Commissioner. Really." Making progress on the stack.

"Going cross-eyed over it, more likely." He pulled the girl up out of her chair, escorting her down the stairs to the carriage waiting at the curb in front of the building. His driver was going to take her to the home she shared with her parents, across the bridge.

"What about you, though?"

"I have my bicycle." Good, solid exercise, riding a bicycle four miles uptown. T.R. had another in Oyster Bay, using it to commute the distance between Sagamore Hill and the railroad station, even in the rain.

"Roosevelt!" someone was calling. Not "Teddy!" as the neighborhood kids did, and their parents. This was "Roosevelt!" and it was a curse.

"Look, it's Richard." Minnie's face brightened as he came up through the pedestrians on the sidewalk, brass buttons less than polished down the center of his uniform. That he had called the Commissioner by name was odd, that not all those buttons were buttoned was odder, but there was no time to register any of that. Officer Kerner was spitting fire and saliva, virulent.

Infuriated.

"You hypocrite," he snapped, enunciating every syllable individually. "I ought to wipe you all over the pavement, you know that? I ought to kill you outright, you sanctimonious fraud!"

His fist lashed out, wild. Roosevelt sidestepped, grabbing the flailing arm in both hands. Twisting. A guttural cry burst from the patrolman, slammed forward into the side of the waiting carriage.

"What are you doing?" Minnie gasped: Richard had pulled his revolver out of its holster. The dappled horse in front of the rig whinnied, fearful, the equine echo of her human dismay.

"Get out of the way," Teddy yelled, wrestling with Richard, wrenching the gun from the officer's grip. It went off skyward but the bystanders couldn't know that; they dropped to the ground or scrambled for cover behind whatever was nearest—a garbage can, a wagon, the steps leading down to a tenement basement.

"Isn't anyone here going to help Mr. Roosevelt?" His secretary saw no aid coming from anywhere. Even the cops in the station house door had gone for the deck.

"No help needed." T.R. could intercept Kerner's kick, he could use the villain's own foot to throw him off-balance once more. "We're almost finished."

The final punch landed square and loud, forceful enough to drive his would-be assassin backward, directly into the arms of the cops who, shamed by Minnie's outburst, had risen in time to receive the damaged goods.

"Inside, you," one of them ordered, tightening his hold on Richard's forearm as the disheveled renegade continued to struggle, hurling new abuse at his former boss.

"Who's more corrupt?" that's what he wanted to know. "Someone who leans on a bunch of lousy little shopkeepers or someone who leans on a whole damned city? At least I was giving them service for my cut; that's more than you can say."

His head glanced off the corner of the half-open door as his custodians hustled him inside, terminating the tirade. The sound of it made Minnie cringe, even with Roosevelt's arm paternal across her shoulders.

"Excuse me. Excuse me, please." It was a rotund attorney, emerging from his hiding place to snake through the cluster of ward heelers back at their posts in front of police headquarters, eyes like stones. A man who knew a potential client when he saw one, the Commissioner noted with grim satisfaction.

"Julius J. Dannemeyer, always on time." Hanrahan's legal counsel, should his secretary be unaware. Mrs. Smith's. "Punctual, gifted, and just as crooked as any of his clients."

Who would now include Richard Kerner.

"Mr. Hanrahan will be pleased," Minnie was sure, surprised by the bitterness in her voice.

"Hope that, my dear," Teddy advised. "Cross your fingers and knock on wood."

■ "Hope what? Officer Kerner is a thug? An extortionist?" She sank back against the bolster in Roosevelt's carriage as it went around the block, Mulberry to Bleeker to Mott.

"Only that that's what Hanrahan thinks."

The Kelly-green eyes flashed. Minnie suddenly remembered who Richard was. The job T.R. had recruited him to do.

"It was all an act." The curses, the punches. The gunshot.

"Edwin Booth might have looked to his laurels," her employer felt safe in saying, positively equestrian even in the rear of the coach.

"You could have told me."

"No. I couldn't." The reaction had to be real. "Julius J. Dannemeyer had to be convinced that Officer Kerner was so far gone he'd attack even Theodore Roosevelt." Commissioner of Police, President of the Board. "If Hanrahan's favorite barrister isn't on the phone right now, telling him how loudly you gasped before I managed to get my hands on that gun, we're all in trouble."

But Teddy was confident. They were on the phone. They were talking about bail, yes or no, which.

"If it's yes, Richard ought to be coming out that door any minute now." The brougham was pulling up at the mouth of a narrow east-west alley, the back way out of 300 Mulberry Street framed by sagging drainpipes and tumbledown fire escapes, mostly ladderless. Minnie studied them, feeling qualms.

"They could bail him out to kill him, couldn't they?"

"After I went to so much trouble, putting the mark of Cain on his forehead?" T.R. couldn't see it. "Hanrahan will wait to see if we're really going to put Richard on trial, at least."

Not that the case would ever come to court, of course. "I have every intention of jumping bail," the discredited cop wanted Minnie to know as soon as he emerged from the yellow brick building, grinning ear to ear.

"Quickly, dammit," Teddy hissed, giving the officer a hand into the carriage. The last thing they needed was for Dannemeyer to see them together here, or anywhere.

"He's in there conferring with the client he came to confer with in the first place." But Roosevelt was right even so, the aide had to agree. The faster they moved, the better—especially since their primary destination was Gage and Tollner.

"The restaurant?" Minnie felt lost again, the disorder on her face filling Richard with amusement.

"Our mutual superior is treating the two of us to those lobsters we missed three weeks ago."

"To make up for the deception this evening," the Commissioner explained, expansive now that they were rolling south on Mott Street. It felt good, he told Edith later, watching the way the young people kept stealing little looks at each other when they got out of the carriage in front of the place.

"Are you sure you don't want to join us, sir?"

A shake of the head and the merest hint of a smile. "You and Minnie are all the company you're going to need."

She kissed him on the cheek impulsively, and T.R. went home blushing.

6 ISRAEL BALINE

■ "It's the deer's head," Edith said to Minnie as she let her husband's secretary into 689, her wrinkling nose saying everything her voice wouldn't dare. "Theodore's been boiling the meat off the bones so he can stuff it."

"Another hour or so and I can set the antlers onto the form and be three days ahead of myself when it comes to the mounting." The Commissioner spoke from the head of the stairs, full of pep. Not only had he done a superb job on this particular buck—if he did say so himself—but the healthy stink emanating from the stove had inspired him to write even more at his desk than usual. Almost one whole chapter of *The Winning of the West,* Volume Four, and a critique of Mr. Henry James for the *Sewanee Review.*

It was not a complimentary critique. As far as Roosevelt was concerned, the novelist was an undersized "man of letters" who'd fled the United States of America "because he, with his delicate, effeminate sensitiveness," found conditions on this side of the water too "crude and raw."

"In other words, Henry James cannot play a man's part among

men." What, T.R. was suddenly curious to know, would the prissy expatriate think of the smell of good honest taxidermy?

No doubt he'd call it "symbolic."

Minnie, on the other hand, was not as repelled as either Teddy or Edith had anticipated. "You really do stuff them yourself," she said, fascinated as she regarded the animals already plaqued on the walls, the decor of the Commissioner's office downtown just as much in her mind, the moose and the tusked boar which stared down on his desk, the full-sized grizzly which stood in the corner pawing the air.

"A man's got to do something with his spare time." What news was she bringing him? "Those are department files, yes?"

Yes. "Both from Manhattan. Midtown and the Lower East Side."

Where?

"Two twenty-three Monroe Street. Mrs. Moses Baline." Not the well-known person her employer was expecting, but all the other details fit. "She reported a satchel stolen just last week."

"In which was what? Pearls? Candlesticks?" Immigrants from the Old Country often brought their savings over in durables rather than in cash. Silverware was much too bulky for the fast snatch and grab man, shipboard. Dockside.

"A wedding dress." Pearls brocaded in the bodice, mingled with a select number of diamonds. "It was returned the next day."

"But not in the satchel," Teddy inferred. "Excellent. Sharp. Most people would have overlooked a report like that—me, for example." He'd make a stop on Monroe Street on his way to headquarters, "after I see what you've come up with in midtown."

She handed him the report and let him take his own look at the name on the top of the file.

Lillian Russell. Diamond Lil.

"By Godfrey," the Commissioner said. "By George."

■ Miss Russell was not at home when Roosevelt came to call. She was touring in the western states, the housekeeper said, a small woman with a patch over her left eye. "We aren't expecting her back till autumn."

Was there anything she could do to help?

T.R. didn't know. "I came to ask her about a robbery she reported last month." A jewelry box filled with bracelets, earrings, lavalieres. Necklaces.

The housekeeper knew all about it. "Considering that it was me who they took it from, the scum." Two men, she meant, who had burst into Miss Russell's dressing room while the performer was on stage at Niblo's Garden, Prince Street at Broadway. "I was ironing the costumes and they threw me into the wall."

Not one minute later they were gone with Diamond Lil's jewels, box and all, and Diamond Lil's housekeeper was on her way to the hospital. Teddy was invited to examine the back of her arm.

"That's where the iron fell on me." Six weeks now and the burn was still not completely healed. "Neither is my head, the doctor says."

When the intruders had thrown her into the wall they made sure it was head first.

"The eye?"

"There was a hook in the wall."

"By God." By God. "A woman." Roosevelt wondered if that could have been a blessing. Had she been a man, the housekeeper might have suffered the fate of Augustus Lennert, mightn't she. "These people stop at nothing—and then they turn around and give it all back, as if it were only a practical joke!"

The jewels had been returned, that was correct, was it not?

"Oh, yes." In a paper bag.

"Was there value to the box?" Enough to make the thieves want to keep it?

"Let me tell you something, mister," she replied, almost amused. "If it was me who took that box and those diamonds, it wouldn't have been the diamonds I gave back."

"Me neither," the Commissioner had to agree. "Unless there were something else inside that thing worth a lot more than those stones."

"Like what?"

Ah.

■ Monroe Street, corner of Jefferson: it was as though Roosevelt
had stepped out of his carriage into the center of a city halfway
between Munich and Moscow. The street signs on the lampposts
were in everyday English, yes, but the Hebrew lettering ubiquitous on storefront after storefront attested to the origins of the
proprietors. Butchers, barbers, bakers, all spoke in a rapid-fire
Yiddish along with the vendors in the street, pushcarts like weeds
in clusters from sidewalk to sidewalk. The babble of so many
voices sounded to Teddy like an oratorio *a cappella,* even accompanied as it was by the creaking of wagon wheels and the rasp of a
grindstone, foot-pedal operated; the jangle of metal hangers from
which new and used fashions were on display.

Overhead, laundry flapped in the breeze, pinned to clotheslines
strung from pulleys imbedded in the weather-beaten wood of window frames and windowsills.

Now there really was song to be heard, T.R. glancing around to
locate the source. There: a small child of six with enormous
brown eyes, leading a blind man through the babushka'd shoppers
and the *payess*'d peddlers. *"Eli, eli,"* the boy was singing, the blind
man playing a squeeze box to which a tin cup had been appended.
Every so often there'd be the clink! of a coin, the generosity of the
poor for the destitute, rewarded by an *"alaichem sholem"* in return.

Theodore Roosevelt himself became a contributor, the dark-
hatted toy merchant beside him nodding serene approval. "Like
the gypsy plays the violin, this is how Izzy uses his vocal cords."
Were the ways of the Lord not magnificent?

"Magnificent." Who taught—Izzy, was it?—to sing so angeli-
cally so young?

"My father." The answer came directly, even though the youthful interest was more on the windup toys in clacking motion along
the edge of the vendor's cart.

"Your father is a performer? He sings?" In the Yiddish theater,
the Commissioner presumed, the presumption generating the superior smile on the blind man's face.

"Rabbi Baline a singer?" General laughter from those who

knew the beloved but tone-deaf teacher. Pious as the day was long, unquestionably. But carry a tune?

"Last *Rosh Hashanah*, when Cantor Fuchs caught laryngitis?" The rabbi had to carry the service all by himself, "and the terrible squawks that came out of his throat made us all fear for his life." Moses Baline was not a well man, as everyone knew.

"But still he taught me singing," insisted his eldest son, waiting for a signal from the toy man. "Did *Eli, Eli* earn me a toy, Mr. Gershowitz?"

"Two toys, a voice like that." He glanced up at Roosevelt. "Ten more years it is going to be such joy in the temple: the rabbi and his son together in front of the ark on *Shabbes,* can you imagine?"

"I think I can." Had he heard Gershowitz correctly? "This youngster here is the son of Moses Baline?"

A pulling back. An attempt to nevertheless display no alarm, only a partial success. "The Police Commissioner of New York City is interested in Moses Baline?"

"His wife, actually." Teddy double-checked the notes Minnie had given him. " 'Leah'?"

"My mommy's name is Leah," Izzy was too quick to confirm as far as the older man was concerned. "Teddy Roosevelt wants to see my mother, Mr. Gershowitz—Teddy Roosevelt!"

Honor. Glory. Fame . . . even if only in the neighborhood. Good enough. More.

"Not so fast, please." Just what kind of "honor" did T.R. have in mind? "Whatever you think she did I tell you she didn't. The *rebbitsin* is as upstanding a woman who ever walked the face of the earth."

"Don't worry," Roosevelt said. "Mrs. Baline didn't do anything." It was she who'd been victimized. A theft.

"And an important official such as yourself comes personally to Monroe Street, investigating?" Gershowitz began to curl and uncurl the hair dangling in front of his ear. "What a theft that must have been!"

The eyes went to Izzy.

"Chazzeh: everything you know about everyone except when it's *mishpocheh?*"

"Nobody said nothing to me," the child protested. "What'd they take?"

"Her wedding dress," T.R. advised.

"What 'wedding dress'?" Izzy didn't know what the Commissioner was talking about. "My mother didn't have any wedding dress—!"

■ "Not since Riga." A Cossack customs agent there had arbitrarily confiscated the carpetbag the dress had been packed in, one of the five the family had permission to take when they departed Temun in Russia.

She scrubbed harder, moving the rabbi's shirt up and down against the corrugated zinc washboard slanted into the soapy water which filled the oval tub at her feet. They were in the kitchen of a fourth-floor walk-up, and the varnish which once had protected the wooden floor had long since been eaten away by the soapy water overflowing on washday.

"Better my wedding dress than the *menorah.*" Two fingers to her lips.

"Then I don't understand." Teddy showed her the police report. "This is your writing, isn't it? 'Mrs. Moses Baline'?" The complaint described the stolen property as a carpetbag with metal corner stays and a horsehide handle, containing a white lace wedding gown embroidered with pearls.

"My writing but Mrs. Moskowitz's satchel," the *rebbitsin* admitted without hesitation, referring to the old woman who lived in the apartment across the hall.

Who got her dress back a week ago now.

"Why would you ask about it?" All's well that ended well, no?

"It's more than just the dress," Roosevelt allowed himself to reveal. "It's the carpetbag which wasn't returned."

"And this is important, this carpetbag?"

"Very important, yes." He thanked her for her help, turning. The rest was for Mrs. Moskowitz to say.

"I'd better take you," Mrs. Baline decided, rising from her wash, wiping her hands on her apron. Israel could peel the potatoes in the sink while she was gone.

"Maa." A sound just as common at 689 Madison as at 223 Monroe, the Commissioner was pleased to hear.

"Peel." Izzy was escorted to the sink and Theodore Roosevelt across the hall. "Ida is only now learning to speak English good enough to talk to policemen, even if they aren't wearing their uniform."

Reason for the chaperone, apparently. "But didn't she come to America because it wasn't Russia? Because the police department here doesn't arrest people with different religious beliefs?"

"The old ways die hard." Leah rapped on the green-painted door, number 43. " 'I'm only an old Jewish lady,' she said to me. 'Who's going to look for a widow's keepsake, even here in Manhattan?' " The wife of the rabbi, though, that might just make a difference. " 'An important woman in the community, maybe they'd do something if it were *her* wedding dress that was stolen.' "

"There'd be no difference either way," Teddy assured her, knowing it wasn't Mrs. Baline that needed the assurance.

"You think I never said that to her? If anybody can pass herself off as important, it isn't me who came across the ocean steerage like everybody else. It's Ida Moskowitz, who had herself a stateroom on the *Etruria,* no less."

A ship T.R. knew very well. Not the vessel he would have expected an immigrant like Ida Moskowitz even to try booking passage on, much less first class.

"I know what you're thinking," Izzy's mother nodded, acknowledging the look on her visitor's face. "Here's a poor lady from Yaroslav who trudges alongside an oxcart to get to a port on the Baltic; where does she come off acting like the grand duchess on an English boat?" Her knuckles struck against the panel again as she called through the door. *"Ida, dust bin ich, Leah. Vee bist du, in badrum, Ida?"*

"Here she comes." Roosevelt was sure he heard movement within.

"Ever since she twisted her ankle on the stairs, Ida walks very slow." At her age it wasn't good, living on the fourth floor, "but

where can the woman go? All the money was spent buying tickets
on the *Etruria.*"

What a wonderful concept, the Commissioner thought. Pov-
erty-stricken all her life, an aging widow decides to experience
how (to upend Jake Riis) the other half lives, even if that means
she will end up with nothing to exist on once the trip is finished.

So what? She is old as it is. How much more of life has she got
to look forward to, she asks herself. Would hoarding her nest egg
guarantee her more time?

Hardly.

Which would be sweeter, then, the memory of a steerage filled
with refugees smelling of vomit and sweat, or a stateroom on A
Deck filled with champagne and flowers?

"Ida?"

This time it was Roosevelt that knocked, the greater strength of
his arm angling the door inward, if only a hair. "It's open."

Cause for concern?

Leah shook her head, recognition in the synchronous sigh.
"This is the third day in a row. She goes out shopping, she forgets
to lock up—that's how the dress was lost in the first place." To be
expected, in a way, "a woman Ida's age."

"I still have to talk to her." Faulty as the memory might be it
hadn't gone completely blank, not yet. Even if the old woman
provided him merely a single disconnected piece of the puzzle,
Teddy'd come out ahead. One piece here, another piece there,
little by little it all adds up.

"Five minutes she's back, ten, she tells you everything you want
to know about the missing carpetbag. In the meantime," the *rebbitsin* said, unafraid to open the door wide, "I'll show you the
dress."

He'd want to see it: it was in the second of the two satchels Ida
had brought with her from Europe. A matching set.

"Lead on." T.R.'s nose wrinkled at the scent the moment he
stepped across the threshold, the ephemeral essence of Ida Moskowitz. Dried rose petals. Old lace handkerchiefs never really
used. The President of the Police Board found himself charmed,
the hospitable aroma making a stranger feel as though he were an

intimate, even in this alien world of claw-footed tables and Teutonic armoires.

"The man in the picture is her husband?" It was in a gilded cameo set out on the sideboard, the fading face of a man stifled by his collar, hair parted in the middle. Rheum in the eyes.

A nod. "Ida says he was a saint. The Czar's bully boys liked to use their sabers on Jewish saints." Leah Baline ducked through the fringed drapes tied back on either side of the Moorish arch which separated the parlor from the bedroom, a high-ceilinged affair with an overhead gas fixture, dominated by a mahogany wardrobe of imposing size. "Have a look," she invited, gesturing Roosevelt forward.

"Thank you," he said, stepping around the scroll-topped footboard of the bed to jiggle the curlicued handle on the closet. "You said the satchel in here was identical with the stolen one, detail for detail?"

Had she seen them both, together?

"Quite a few times," the rabbi's wife told him, and then she forgot the rest of what she was going to say and started to scream. In the kitchen across the hall Izzy dropped the potatoes into the sink and scrambled to his mother's assistance; in the stairwell Rabbi Moses Baline ignored the precarious state of his health and took the final flight two steps at a time.

"Leah—? Leah—?"

All the doors had burst open on the fourth floor, the residents spilling out into the hall as the screaming continued. Expressions of horror and nausea mirrored each other, face to face, as the rabbi pushed through to the Moskowitz apartment.

"What?" he asked, breathless from the upward rush. "What is it? Leah—?"

At first it was just the sight of his wife in the arms of another man which did him in, but then the pupils focused and Moses Baline saw who the man was. Realized that the embrace was not carnal but comforting.

Ida Moskowitz hung open-eyed on the inside of the wardrobe door, a hook jammed through the collar of her housecoat at the back. Blood, gouts of it, had spurted all over the front of her nightshirt, had splattered against the other garments in the closet, congealing from scarlet to black.

The knife that had slashed through her windpipe had sliced deep enough to almost sever the head from the neck.

■ "Is there a telephone?" Teddy was asking, voice sharp. "A telephone?"

"In Mr. Schnabel's downstairs," Izzy was finally able to say. "At the corner. The candy store."

"All right. Call the police department on Mulberry Street; tell them there's been a killing." The Commissioner dug into his pocket for change. "Give them the address and tell them I'm expecting them to be here in a jiffy."

A jiffy was less than five minutes: the boy was to make sure they understood that.

"I will!" He was already on his way to the stairwell, calling back over his shoulder.

"Good boy!" Was Mrs. Baline recovered enough to be placed into the arms of her waiting husband?

"Yes. Thank you."

As for everyone else, "it would be helpful if we could all stand outside in the hall—a crowd on the scene of a crime is the fastest way there is to obliterate evidence."

"What's the matter with you, the Commissioner is talking!" Moses Baline's voice had more strength in it than T.R. had been led to expect. Even high-pitched as it was, the sound of it made Roosevelt understand how this deceptive mouse of a man could have managed to get himself and his family out of Russia, frailty notwithstanding. "Move back, please. Back."

They retreated, enough so that the rabbi could close the door. He kept his arm tight around the trembling body of his wife and glanced past Teddy, from the parlor to the bedroom. "Poor woman. It was not supposed to be like this in the new land."

First evidence of *pogrom?* Here? Was that possible? America prided itself on being a country which had no *pogroms.*

Individuals with knives, though? Jew haters? Was there any country which didn't have these?

The Commissioner shook his head. "Ida Moskowitz wasn't the first victim in this case. Nor were any of the other victims Jewish." He wanted to see that satchel, if it was still there. If the wedding dress was in it.

There was no need for the Balines to return with him into Ida's bedroom, to peer over his shoulder as he looked past the blue-gray feet dangling above the open cabinet in the base of the wardrobe. There it was, the dress, white splotched with brownish, amoeba-like stains once red. A crumpled-up throwaway, it seemed, pulled from its protective sheath and dumped—after first being used as a towel, to wipe the blood from the hands.

A moan behind him made him focus back over his shoulder. Leah was there beneath the arch, fingers playing the fringes on the drape as though they were the keys of an accordion, her husband swallowing hard and stepping forward. "First they steal her dress, then they give it back, then they cut her throat? Where is the sense?"

"In the valise," T.R. told him. "I think they came back because the first satchel they took turned out to be the wrong one; don't ask me why." He rummaged as he spoke, not really knowing what he was looking for. Aside from the ravaged gown the only articles he saw in the niche were several pairs of shoes, and one single slipper. A left.

Hardly the clue he'd hoped to find. Whoever these murderers were, dammit, they covered their tracks beautifully. Roosevelt started to rise. Whatever cracked the case it wouldn't be slippers or shoes with stretch forms inside.

"Stretch forms." Labeled stretch forms for m'lady's good leather shoes. Compliments of Cunard White Star, the steamship company. Operators of the steamship *Etruria,* the site of Ida Moskowitz's last and only fling.

At least she had had that before death came. At least she had known what it was like to be one of the upper crust before—

"—By Godfrey!" He bolted upright as the oath exploded from his mouth, colliding with the corpse as he did. "Of course. Of *course!*" The hands reached out to steady its motion, to make everyone a promise. "We're going to find these killers; they're going to pay!"

"You found something? Commissioner?"

The tornado spun them around on its way to the door, calling back over the wind in its wake. "The key, I think! I found the key!"

He was already at the staircase, already on his way down to the lobby and the street, whipping himself past the midflight banister post and picking up speed. It sounded like a locomotive, Leah told her grandchildren years later, when her son Izzy was Irving Berlin and "God Bless America" was all over the radio, coast to coast.

■ Bells, sirens, shouts of "Coming through! Police! Make way!" The street vendors scattered in front of several sets of oncoming horses, trinkets and household goods making a racket while Sam Buxbaum's chickens squawked in their cages, beating at the mesh with their wings. Several official wagons came to a headlong halt in front of 223 just as Teddy emerged.

"Fourth floor," he told them, terse. "Rabbi Baline is waiting for you at the door."

"Who's dead, Commissioner?" The question was put not by one of the cops but by a journalist in the employ of *The Evening Sun,* one Jacob Riis.

It paid to hang around the front desk at Mulberry Street.

"Ida Moskowitz," T.R. said in reply, "an elderly immigrant who appears to have surprised a burglar in the act." Did any of the officers know whether Lieutenant Meeghan was going to be in charge of this investigation?

"If you want him, sir." A sergeant named Cullen, who wasn't about to challenge the President of the city's Police Board.

"I want him." A crooked finger for Jake, Roosevelt picking a footpath through the maze of pushcarts, peddlers and customers, returning to his own department-issue buggy. The reporter had trouble keeping up.

"This is part of the Frick-Dvořák-Cody thing, isn't it."

"Two and two are beginning to make four, yes." Which did

Jake think Mr. Dana would want more: his man on the scene of a homicide writing the eyewitness account of the body in the closet, or his man next to Teddy Roosevelt, certifying the link between this crime and all the others?

"A link is always bigger news." Besides, the Commissioner was going to give him all that eyewitness detail, probably with even more lexicological passion than a poor inarticulate journalist could ever come up with.

"How gruesome would you like it?" There was no levity in the tone. No irony. Riis felt a chill between his shoulder blades.

"Beginning to make Hanrahan look small-time, aren't they." The voice went low in the throat. "Servants and old ladies: real prizes."

"Anyone who gets in their way, Jake." Anyone.

"Tell me about this connection you've got."

"Potential connection." Depending on what boat Henry Frick came back from Europe on two years before, "him and his paintings."

▪ Now there was only one empty space on the wall in the ballroom, they saw when they walked into the house on Sixty-ninth Street. "My Vermeer is back, too; look." God was answering the prayers of an art lover, this time through the package mail.

"Did you save the wrapping?" Seeing the postmark would be of enormous help.

"Oh." Frick was full of apologies. "I swear, Theodore, I was so excited to rip that wrapping paper off I didn't think about anything else." The precious cancellation was long since in the trash, long since collected.

"Could you try remembering where it was sent from? Close your eyes, Henry: see if you can picture it."

The eyes closed for several seconds, but to no avail. "I don't see a damned thing." For a moment the industrialist had thought, "Long Island somewhere," but all that was was guesswork. "Pure guesswork, I'm afraid."

"If it does come to you . . ."

". . . I will call, you have my word." And because it was so much easier to go on than to live with the guilt, Henry Clay Frick beckoned them closer to the reinstated *Interior, Delft.* "Look. I had the framer add a new plaque."

In memoriam: Augustus Lennert, it read above a set of dates. *Loyal servant, faithful friend.*

"Augustus would have liked it, wouldn't he?" Didn't Roosevelt think? "I'd like to believe it, if nothing else."

"Believe it," Teddy advised, touched by Frick's gesture. His hand capped the sloping shoulder as the older man nodded his gratitude. "There's one other thing you might be able to help me with, Henry."

"Anything."

"The name of the ship you brought these acquisitions back on two years ago."

Everybody who knew Henry Clay Frick knew that, Theodore included. Theodore especially. "Hasn't the *Etruria* been your own favorite of all the liners?"

S.S. *Etruria.* His own favorite of all the liners.

"You were on board?"

"Six days and five nights." Frick, Gainsborough, Hals and Vermeer, all sharing a stateroom. Pay dirt. T.R. whirled and whooped at Riis.

"You hear that, Jake? The *Etruria:* I knew it. It had to be!"

"Excuse me, Commissioner," the reporter demurred. "How does it 'have to be'? Just because Mr. Frick here used that particular boat to cross the Atlantic on—"

He stopped. Roosevelt was giving him one of those expectant looks, the professor waiting for his brilliant student to spell it out, out loud. Of course Riis knew the answer, come on. Come on.

"They were *all* on it? That one single trip from Southampton to New York?"

"Every last one, I will bet my bottom dollar." Wouldn't Jake?

"Wait a minute," Frick interjected. If Teddy's suggestion were that the people who robbed him were aboard that vessel at the time, dogging his tracks all the way home, "it's not going to wash. Not when they could have stolen the paintings right then and there, right off the pier when they docked." At 3 A.M.

Why wait twenty-two months? Could Commissioner Roosevelt explain that? Henry Clay Frick didn't think so.

"I'm not talking about the thieves, Henry. I'm talking about your fellow victims." Yes, there were others. The collector was not the only one robbed, his people not the only ones butchered. "I can name at least one other first-class passenger from that same voyage whose home was broken into. Fact."

"Who?" Someone Frick knew? "A person of rank?"

Could anyone first-class on the *Etruria* be anything less than a person of rank?

"For the duration of the crossing," T.R. was pleased to affirm, "this woman was a person of rank."

A woman. "Lillian Russell?"

"Not Lillian Russell." But of all the names a man of society could drop! Lillian Russell. "Isn't it nice when the facts turn out to support the theory, Jake?" Henry had seen the entertainer with his own eyes, Teddy hoped.

"Indeed. I played several rounds of shuffleboard with her on deck, third day out. Fourth." And the last night at sea he was present in the dining room when Diamond Lil acceded to the captain's request and sang several songs, "one of which was 'Songs My Mother Taught Me.' And the most amazing thing, Theodore—Antonin Dvořák, the composer?"

"Was there." Not exactly the stab in the dark. Not anymore.

"Yes," Frick said, the memory reviving the excitement of the evening. "He came up and played the piano for her; it was quite a sensation."

"It's quite a sensation now," Riis assured him, judging from the look in the Commissioner's eyes. "William Cody wouldn't also have happened to have been there, would you know?"

"Cody . . . ?"

"Buffalo Bill." Roosevelt, prompting. Even a Frick would know that name, and remember someone saying the former Indian fighter was indeed on board.

"Never saw him myself, though." The same someone told him Buffalo Bill spent most of his time belowdecks. "The animals from the Wild West Show never did get all of their sea legs."

Who was it who told him that, dammit?

"Someone well known?" Every name like that was important as far as T.R. was concerned. These could be other victims, people who just hadn't bothered to report what seemed to be insignificant burglaries, or who got their property back even before they could go to the police.

"Someone well known, yes—oh." Henry knew who it was now.

"Tell me." The killings were continuing. The delay of even a minute could make a difference. "I have to get to the bottom of this thing, as fast as I can."

"You might not want to." Not since he had stumbled across the body of Augustus Lennert had Frick been so gripped by sudden despair.

"Why the hell not?"

"Because it was your brother, that's why not." A spray of words, regurgitated. The shipmate who'd told him about Buffalo Bill Cody was none other than Theodore's brother Elliott.

His younger brother Elliott.

7 MRS. EVANS

■ *"My dear old beloved brother,"* the telegram read when it reached Theodore in Washington that August of 1893. *"I will be returning to New York aboard S.S. Etruria, docking Thursday, one p.m. Please meet me; it is of the utmost importance we speak, a matter of considerable urgency."*

But Elliott was not coming back to America alone. Mrs. Evans would be there to disembark alongside Anna Hall's husband. For all the pull of family ties, Theodore couldn't face it. *"I cannot legitimize that relationship,"* he said to Edith that evening in their D.C. residence, 1820 Jefferson Place, NW. *"I just can't."*

A telegram was sent. *"Impossible to meet S.S. Etruria on Thursday. Administrative duties at the Civil Service Commission preclude. With all regret I remain . . ."*

It was not until later in the year that the brothers finally met, after Anna Hall had succumbed to her unmendable heart. The conversation between them was ostensibly convivial, not entirely concealing the tension, the awkwardness. T.R. did remember to ask Elliott what the urgent matter had been that previous August, and Elliott had replied with a sorry little smile on his face. *"Isn't it amazing how we can stand on our own two feet when we find ourselves left to our own devices?"*

*Teedie had mastered that lesson years before, in the West. That
Elliott was learning it now was a very good sign.*

Or so Teedie hoped.

*Deep in his heart he'd known otherwise; he'd known otherwise for
years. When the word came to him on the fourteenth of the August
following, when death by acute alcoholic seizure ended Elliott's life,
it was not really a surprise.*

The surprise was how deeply he grieved. How much he cried.

■ Acute alcoholic seizure.

Of course. " 'What else could it have been?' I said to Edith. 'If
ever anything was foreordained.' If ever anything was foreordained." He was rambling, describing it to Frick and Jake Riis; he
knew he was rambling there in the main vestibule of Frick's house
as they made ready to go. But he couldn't stop himself. If he
stopped, he wouldn't be able to breathe. Already he could hear
the first whistlings coming from the constriction of the bronchia:
it was vital that he talk on. Sense, nonsense, anything.

Was the Commissioner implying that his brother Elliott had not
died of alcohol poisoning after all? This question from the reporter, sounding as though he spoke through a hollow tube. A
metal tube.

"I don't know," Roosevelt cried, having trouble with the conso-
nants now. "That's what I've got to find out, that's why I've got
to go right up to 102nd Street. She'll know. Mrs. Evans. She'll—"

His chest was folding in on itself. Oh, Jesus Christ Almighty.
Oh, Jesus. Not since the night of February 14, 1884, when his
daughter was born and his wife had died. When his mother had
also died, within hours. Hours.

"Are you all right, Theodore?" Open concern was all over
Henry Clay's broad, sensitive face, and Riis's, too.

"I am fine," he was able to say, but he was not able to repeat it.
He had wanted to repeat it.

"Chandler!" the tycoon was calling, frightened. "Call a doctor,
Chandler, hurry."

Augustus wouldn't have had to be told.

"No. Henry. No doctor," Teddy managed to gasp. "Air—it clears up in the air. Jake, help me."

"I'll get him home," the reporter said to Frick, walking the Commissioner to the door. The carriage was waiting out front, the driver reacting with alarm to the sight of the man doubled over, *pince-nez* dangling as he hacked for a lungful of oxygen, spittle dampening the corners of his mustache.

"Mr. Roosevelt!" he blurted, the apprehension in his voice enough to goad Roosevelt's head up on his neck.

"Home," he ordered, inhaling as deeply as he could. "And not a word about this to anyone, either of you." His eyes fixed on Riis. "This isn't going to be a part of the story; I want your word."

The effort it took to say it almost wrecked him again, but T.R. refused to let them push him all the way into the cab unless they agreed. The driver nodded, and Jake?

"Hey." A cathartic laugh, forced. "You're the guy who overcame his asthma roughing it out in the Dakotas. And I'm the guy who wrote about how much courage that took. What d'you want to do, Theodore, make me a liar?"

Matching laughter hiccuped in bubbles out of the Commissioner's throat as he settled into his seat, the driver up front snapping the reins. "Cynic."

"Charlatan."

Now the laughter was stronger. Mutual. When it died away, Riis found Roosevelt regarding him with appreciation and respect. "Jake," he said softly. "I won't forget this."

One more favor owed.

"If I had a brother," the reporter said softly, "if I discovered that he didn't die the way it originally seemed, that somebody might have broken his head, I think I'd double over, too. I think I might still be doubled over."

A nod, because Roosevelt knew that Riis's next question would then be the same as his own. Why. Handsome, charming, shallow and sad though he was, was it possible that Elliott nevertheless met his death defending a souvenir of the steamship *Etruria*? Was there some way he could have known the real importance of that suitcase? That trunk?

That handbag?

"I have to go to 102nd Street. Driver," he started to call, stopping because he still couldn't catch enough air to both breathe and speak.

"Where you have to go is home"; 102nd Street would just have to wait.

"Don't you understand? Mrs. Evans probably has the answer to everything!" Even if she didn't know it herself.

"And it'll be a lot easier for her to give them to a man who isn't sitting there whistling like a teapot."

For a moment Jake thought he might have overstepped the bounds, that his friend would turn on him. But the image of Theodore Roosevelt as teapot tickled Theodore Roosevelt: he coughed up a new laugh and the newspaperman could exhale, relaxing as the carriage pulled up in front of 689 Madison Avenue.

"Would you be in need of a hand to the door, Commissioner?" The driver spoke over his shoulder, looking solicitously down at his stricken chief.

"Bite your tongue," T.R. said in cheerful reproach, summoning a smile as he smoothed the ruffled edge of his mustache and flattened the hair above his ears. "How do I look?"

Edith had sharp eyes.

"She won't notice a thing," Riis was sure.

"Not if I don't breathe too loud she won't." Teddy grinned and jumped the distance to the sidewalk, taking the stoop steps with what very much seemed to be his customary exuberance.

■ "How long, twenty minutes? Thirty?" An hour?

He'd splashed some surface color into his cheeks at the sink in the upstairs bathroom. The pallor beneath remained, and Edith, as he said, had sharp eyes.

"The smelling salts are in the medicine chest."

"I used them already." It was going away. Completely away. "Jake made sure I got back safe."

"It's the hours," there was little question of that in Edith's mind. "You never went all day and night when you were in the

Assembly; not even when Grover Cleveland had you running the Civil Service Commission."

"Work doesn't bring on an attack"; she knew that. Anxiety, tension, upsetting news—unexpected news—

It was suddenly cold in the bedroom. The children were all accounted for, weren't they?

"Not them." Elliott. The ten-months-dead Elliott. "I've gotten new information, Edie; it might not have been an accident." It might have been, how do the coroners call it? "At the hands of another?"

She fish-mouthed. "He had a fit. From drinking." He'd had a fit and he'd fallen in the apartment. "In Mrs. Evans's apartment."

Everybody said so.

"What boat did Elliott come back from France on," did his wife remember? Would Edith like to know who else was on that boat? "Frick. Buffalo Bill Cody. Antonín Dvořák."

"Lillian Russell?"

Lillian Russell. Ida Moskowitz. "Every last one of them so far." The whistling. The whistling. "He could damn well have been involved in something bad: Elliott. Or—"

"You stop it, you hear me?" Edith pushed him backward into the pillows on the bed. "I will not have you bringing it on again." She would do the talking.

"Edith—"

"No. The fact that Elliott was on that ship proves nothing." How many passengers were aboard at the time, did he know? "How many of those had anything stolen afterward? How many were killed?"

Hardly any.

"That man died because he was a lush. And Theodore Roosevelt is worrying himself sick trying to find some other reason."

"Unless," Theodore Roosevelt persisted, "unless Mrs. Evans tells me, 'yes, as a matter of fact. There *was* something missing from the apartment after Elliott's death. There was.' "

"For God's sake, what kind of chapter and verse is it going to take to convince you?" Sometimes Teddy drove her to distraction. To utter distraction. "Last February? When Elliott knocked a

kerosene lamp over and set himself on fire? Before that, when he
drove his carriage headlong into a lamppost? You yourself said he
wanted to die—he wanted to die in the worst way."

No one had to help him.

"Wouldn't it have been easy, though," T.R. felt honor-bound to
say, "if someone did come there to steal a valise." Could Elliott's
older brother rest without at least going to see Mrs. Evans?

Did Edith really expect to dissuade him?

Silence, and then an affectionate laugh. "I did," she confessed.
"I forgot who I was talking to. All these years and I actually
forgot."

Of course he was going to see Mrs. Evans. But he was going to
be well when he did, with air in his lungs. "Just in case I've had it
backward and it wasn't the crème de menthe."

"I don't want you to have it backward. I don't want to find out
that Elliott was mixed up with any of this." He was breathing
freely now, freely enough to be able to kiss his wife even as she
wondered why he wanted to bother with Mrs. Evans at all if he
felt that way.

"Do you really want to know?"

"I don't 'want to know,'" he told her. "I *have* to know."

▪ "That isn't what I came back to talk to you about today."

Mrs. Evans had naturally presumed the Commissioner had returned to give her his decision: whether the stipend for her son
would be increased or not.

What else was there to discuss?

"The circumstances surrounding my brother's death," better
late than never at all. His eyes were on the child, rolling a nine-
inch locomotive along a curving pair of parallel lines woven into
the rug, choo-chooing.

"Didn't we talk about it at the time, as much as you cared to
hear?"

Not an extensive exchange, as Mrs. Evans recalled. Had Elliott
been on horseback with saber in hand, banners afurl in the face of
withering enemy artillery, oh, how Theodore would have hung on

every glorious word. That one demise was as ultimately final as the other?

T.R. wouldn't think of that.

"Some new questions have come up since last summer." Some links to a number of other cases increasingly related.

" 'Links.' " Such as?

"Whether you might have noticed anything missing from the apartment after the funeral." Something which somehow just turned up again, as though simply misplaced. "But without its container—that's still 'misplaced.' "

"As a matter of fact," Mrs. Evans revealed, "I did happen to go through the closets and drawers, two days later. Three." To keep busy. To keep sorrow at arm's length.

"And?"

"Everything was exactly where it always was." Everything.

"It could have been something very small." So insignificant it could have been overlooked.

Something *had* to be gone, dammit!

"Nothing was, though." His brother's mistress seemed to take a modicum of comfort from the agitation on his face. What was he looking for? "What do you think Elliott was involved in?"

"I was hoping you might tell me." Were there something to tell.

Doors she had thought permanently closed were opening. Memories blinking, like reptiles suddenly exposed to the sun. There were some things she could talk about, yes.

"Splendid." Roosevelt waited for her as she collected her thoughts, her eyes fixing through the window on the Jersey shore. "Madam?"

"Commissioner," she said without turning, "the deadline for school registration is the end of this week."

"Is it." What dangerous ground the woman was on. What dangerous, dangerous ground. "If you think I'm so desperate I'll give in to blackmail, be advised. You are mistaken."

She wheeled. "Call it anything you like. I have a child to raise and you have a case to solve and if yours isn't as important as mine you can go out the way you came in."

"I can also," he snapped, "have you hauled up in front of a

judge as an unfit mother." The boy could very well be declared a ward of the court.

"And then neither of us gets anything but pain and Elliott's son gets the life of an orphan. Good for you, sir. Very good for you."

"Bah." He wasn't going to just stand there and let her heap abuse, not when he had the resources to make her regret ever having begun this little war.

"Uncle Theodore?" The little engine was silent in the four-year-old hand. "Why are you and Mommy so mad at each other?"

"Because—"

Because.

Because Uncle Theodore didn't want to accept the obvious, that this pretty woman here had been more wife to Elliott than the all-too-legal Anna Hall. That this boy was as much Elliott's child as Nell was. As Grace. He didn't want to acknowledge this one-bedroom flat as his brother's home, sixty-five blocks north of Thirty-seventh Street, on the wrong side of town.

Elliott was not a Hall, nor even the part of them that Nell and Grace were, protected by their grandmother. Mrs. Evans and her son, who'd be there for them if not himself?

Brother Teedie?

Teedie couldn't understand . . . not until it was finished for Elliott could the bile come out. The guilt. So what if it splattered all over the most innocent: did anyone really care what happened to an illegitimate bastard?

Theodore Roosevelt didn't. He had the family name to protect. The honor.

So why was he suddenly sweeping this child up into his arms, planting a kiss on top of the head, fitting it snugly into the hollow of his palm?

Why the water in his eyes?

"That tickles," said Elliott's son. Teddy's mustache.

"My little ones say that, too." They liked his bristly kisses, though; they always asked for more. "Before school, especially, the one I hear you want to sign up for. That true?"

"Can I, Uncle Theodore?"

A glance across to the woman who was his brother's widow. "It might be possible," he had to concede. "Might."

"Mr. Roosevelt." The held breath set free. "You are a good man."

Immaterial. "I am," she had to know, "just paying the price of the information. If it puts a stop to these atrocities, it'll be worth it." Mrs. Evans could skip the sentiment, thank you, and talk. "The details I wasn't ready to listen to last August."

"All right." Her hand directed his attention toward the carpet, not far from the "tracks" her son was riding his engine on. The death place, where they'd found the body. "We were coming home with the groceries and Elliott was . . . lying there."

"Warm? Cold?" Devastating questions for both. Unavoidable.

"Warm." So warm she'd thought she could save him. "I pumped his chest, I breathed into his throat—" She'd slapped his face, too, shaking his shoulders and shouting he had to wake up, dammit, they needed him. He had to wake up.

The hell with what the corner of the radiator cover might have done to the back of his head.

Of course, the whole situation would have been academic had Mrs. Evans insisted on his company at the store. She usually did, those last few months. "But he told me he wasn't going to be alone; he had 'a business meeting,' he said."

"At the apartment?" What sort of "business meeting" would that have been, T.R. wondered. "With whom?"

"I don't know." Her voice cracked in her larynx. "All he'd say was that if it went right it would mean a big change in our fortunes. He'd even be able to look his brother Teedie in the eye again."

"That major." If only his dear old beloved brother had given the lady even the smallest of hints, what this "business" was.

But she was turning her head back and forth on her neck, her lower lip trembling. "There was no 'business.' No meeting." Didn't the Commissioner get it? "It was just an excuse to get us out, so no one would be here to stop him from opening the window, climbing out onto the ledge—"

Had the alcohol not played havoc with his balance, Elliott

would have fallen forward as he'd intended, down to the sidewalk below. As it was, he had accomplished his objective, anyway, hadn't he? Dead was dead. Was dead. Was.

Did Roosevelt want to hear something funny? "For one real moment there I actually found myself believing him: it wasn't just a story. He did have a business meeting. We *were* going to have the good times again."

Wishful thinking? "Or did you have something specific to go on?"

"The two men we saw coming out of the building." She and the child were walking up 102nd from Broadway, packages in hand, and there they were. Neatly groomed. Nicely dressed. "Who else could they be but the people Elliott had just been meeting with, just like he said?"

If Theodore's brother was forming a partnership with go-getters like these, Mrs. Evans was convinced, then they were on their way back up to Easy Street.

"Did you mention these men to the police?" It would be very helpful, had someone from the department followed that up, finding out if it had been someone else at 313 West they'd come to see. If it hadn't—if their destination had been the "Evans" apartment —the worst fears would be true.

And Theodore Roosevelt would have the most personal of reasons to want these butchers caught.

"I didn't say anything." Why should she have? No "meeting" had taken place, as she had already emphasized. "What difference could it have made, who they'd been inside to see?"

It wasn't a question Mrs. Evans would even have thought to ask had she in fact remembered the pair at all. Up until just now, however, they'd been utterly out of her mind. Total nullities.

Teddy dug a folded old envelope up from the inside pocket of his jacket, and a pen. "Describe them to me," he said.

■ "The same two thugs Lillian Russell's housekeeper described, I'm positive," the Commissioner growled, pacing in front of Minnie's desk and rat-tatting the leading edge of his *pince-nez* against the open palm of his hand. "If the department had a library of 'mug' books worth anything, maybe we could close a few cases around here."

Damn Andrew Parker and his frugality, a good part of the reason it was taking so long to get the file on his brother's death up from the archives. Not that T.R. expected there'd be anything in the report adding to what he already knew, or presumed.

Elliott had been expecting company that afternoon. Those two men were not there blind: he had something they wanted.

"Wouldn't he take precautions, then?" Minnie expected that she would; wouldn't Roosevelt?

"Yes, but I don't drink." He doubted the duo had come with murder aforethought. As Elliott had implied earlier, a negotiation was in the offing. "Things could have heated up, that's my guess —Elliott had a tongue on him, particularly when he was in his cups. All he had to do was taunt them—tell them whatever it was they wanted was there right under their noses and they were so stupid they still couldn't see it. Couple that with a fine mist of brandy droplets spraying in front of their faces—Minnie—"

"Sir?"

"What's the one thing we can say for certain about this stuff they went there for?"

His question, his answer.

"Where it came from, right? S.S. *Etruria?*" Everything the killers were so hot to get had come to America aboard no other ship but that. "And I am a moron for not thinking of doing this the minute I found out."

"Doing this" meant snatching the phone up from Minnie's desk, index finger impatiently jiggling the hook. The diaphragm squawked inside the earpiece.

"Cunard White Star Steamship Lines, quickly. The main office." It was police business, urgent, and the connection was made accordingly.

"Cunard here." Upper-class accent. Oxford. "How might I be of service?"

"By telling me how I can get a passenger manifest for the *Etruria,*" T.R. responded, only then identifying himself. "The voyage took place two years ago, August, out of Southampton."

"You would want to speak to Mr. Witherspoon in Records."
Aplomb incarnate, as though the Commissioner's request were a
normal, everyday thing. "The gentleman is not in the office at the
moment, unfortunately."

In the middle of a workday morning? "Where is he?"

"Right behind you." The voice was Riis's, right behind him.
Roosevelt jerked around, finding the reporter in the company of a
slender young Brit who had yet to mature into harmony with the
muttonchops rampant on either side of his pale-skinned face. "I
had a feeling you might want to have a look at who had what on
the *Etruria* that trip."

Ergo: Mr. Witherspoon and the manifest.

"Exactly the man I wanted, exactly!" And Jake was a genius,
"beating me to the punch." Saving precious time.

Familiar names seemed to leap up from among the others
neatly inscribed on the pages passed into Teddy's eager hand.
Cody. Dvořák. Frick.

Moskowitz.

"Now maybe we can get ahead of these outlaws for a change."
He flipped through the pages, making them rattle. Witherspoon
winced.

"Please, Commissioner," he said. "Be careful." They were the
only copy left, a carbon. "I'm sure we'll eventually find the original, misfiled, but even so . . ."

" 'Misfiled.' " Or stolen?

"Who," Witherspoon asked, "would want to steal the manifest
of a transatlantic crossing almost two years past?"

"I don't know," T.R. said, knowing damn well. "Someone
other than me just as interested in who your passengers were and
what they were bringing home?"

There was the saddle, for example, under "Cody, William,"
topping a considerable catalog of equestrian equipment.

Three Old Master paintings, part of the itemization below
"Frick, Henry C."

Dvořák's leather manuscript case, with a purser's notation.
"Battered."

And Ida Moskowitz's carpetbags, Lillian Russell's jewelry box—

Without this documentation the thieves would have been lost, that much was now clear, explaining (perhaps) the long delay between the landfall and the first of the robberies. Once the list was in their possession, though, what could stop them? All they had to do was go from name to name, collecting.

Putting together.

"We'd know better one way or another if we could get our hands on one of these pieces before they do," Roosevelt was sure. "Every last individual indexed here has to be talked to, today. Abbot to Wycliff and everyone between."

Cooper, Jenkins, Maxwell, Roosevelt. Elliott Roosevelt.

Two steamer trunks, several garment bags. Hatbox. A host of personal belongings, everything from cuff links to stickpins. Gift items: one Eiffel Tower in copper miniature destined if memory served for Nell's brother Grace, and the lace shawl? For Anna, still alive.

Piaculum.

For Nell herself, a doll. "Baby Joss," T.R. said.

"Pardon?" Witherspoon couldn't recognize the reference, nor Jacob Riis. Roosevelt regarded them over the top of the manifest, horror mounting in his eyes.

"My niece's doll. 'Baby Joss,' that's her name for it. Little rag thing—Elliott bought it for her in Europe. Look."

Seventh item down.

"Is this meaningful?" The discovery was alarming to Witherspoon because it was alarming to everyone else present.

"We're dealing with people who've already killed three people to get what they want, one an old woman, one an old man." Did the innocent young man from Golders Green think a ten-year-old would be any more "meaningful" to them than that?

8 ANNA ELEANOR

■ When T.R. walked into Murphy's Saloon that evening, he did not have to look far to find the stigmatized Officer Kerner, his undercover aide exactly where he was supposed to be: at a table in the rear with Estes Hanrahan and several other subordinate mugs, sleeve rolled up. "Why I can't have an 'emblem' tattooed on my left arm," he was explaining, the space already preoccupied by a guardian eagle with ruffling feathers, talons clawing a spray of spears with dripping tips.

"Maybe we ought to use that instead of the *H,*" a suggestion of the henchman seated to Hanrahan's right, a barrel-shaped thug with brilliantined hair. "That is aces up, boss, I mean it."

"Can't say I'm not impressed myself," the boss agreed, winking approval at the newest member of his circle. "You must've been a holy terror when you were a kid." What did his former patron think of the artwork—"Mr. Theodore Roosevelt?"

"As if you don't know." Richard could imitate the Commissioner like nobody else, the caricature uncanny. "'Low-lifes despoil their bodies like that, Kerner, low-lifes and Indians.'"

"One more reason I'd have given you the boot, all right," Mr.

Theodore Roosevelt declared, stepping forward to kick the chair out from under the turncoat's thighs. Kerner had to stagger up backward, just barely managing to stay on his feet.

" 'Haroun-al-Roosevelt' strikes again," someone was heard to mutter at a table somewhere on the other side of the bar.

■ "Fascinating what you can find under rocks," Teddy was hissing, teeth prominent beneath his bristling mustache. "Back to tell your old pal Estes here that some more of his 'stolen' property is waiting for him at the recovery desk down at the station?"

"I don't have to answer to you," Richard retaliated, venom dripping. "Not anymore." He turned his back, the movement an insult in itself.

"You do when you've got answering to do." T.R.'s hand landed hard on the twenty-three-year-old shoulder, yanking him 180 degrees.

"Get your hand off me." White tendons pulsed beneath the skin of the neck, Roosevelt unintimidated by the sight.

"Do you really want to repeat what happened between us on Mulberry Street?" His free hand fisted.

"Except, Commissioner," Hanrahan felt obliged to observe, "this time it's Mr. Kerner who isn't alone." If Mulberry Street was Teddy territory, what was Ninth Avenue?

"A dung heap." The word, given from the door. Lieutenant Meeghan was standing there, several gruff Irish cops right behind him, batons tapping. Other batons began to tap antiphonally at the rear, cops there, too.

"To keep things one on one," T.R. said, "in the event that my eminent position doesn't impress you as much as that tattoo."

Richard rolled his sleeve down. "Just leave me alone." Backup or no backup, the Commissioner could only push him so far.

"Some of my files are missing. I immediately thought of you."

"How the hell would *I* know about your files?" Rasped.

"That is exactly what I came to find out." Teddy tugged at him. "What sewer are you living in these days?" Kerner was going to show him there, good boy that he was, wasn't he. A slap. Another. A shove backward propelling him toward the exit at the rear.

"Justice, Mr. Roosevelt?" Hanrahan was on his feet, scathing. "The back alley and the rubber hose? What do you think my attorney is going to say about that?"

"Mr. Dannemeyer?" T.R. thought he would understand it very well—"but not as well as you."

■ He kicked the door shut between themselves and the patrons of the bar, and then knocked a metal trash can over for good measure. Richard recognized the cue: he cried out, loudly. Partly because the edge of the can glanced off his shin.

"Sorry," the Commissioner apologized, gesturing the youth into a dark niche while his officers stood watch at the mouth of the alley, fifty feet from earshot.

No apology was needed. "I'm going to have to show them a couple of welts, anyway." What was up that Teddy had to resort to this kind of dramatics?

"It's the Frick-Dvořák thing." Roosevelt was going to need Richard on it for the next few days. "Hanrahan is going to have to be put in mothballs."

"That might not be so easy." Something was in the wind: a "job" for the new boy. Something to test the mettle. "Tomorrow night, it feels like."

"If you're not being given the third degree tomorrow night, that is." There was impishness in the Commissioner's eyes: improvisation could be fun.

"You're *that* mad at me?"

"Infuriated," Teddy said, beaming. "Especially since those 'missing files' weren't at your sewer when we went there. I figure three tough nights in the basement of the Forty-first precinct house, what do you think?"

"I think three nights isn't going to come close to making me talk about those files."

"That might make you even more of a hero to that big shot in there." Those welts Richard mentioned might have to be joined by an abundance of bruises, contusions and cuts, but the officer wasn't to worry: "the black and blue will all be courtesy of a theatrical makeup expert, Andrew Parker notwithstanding. When Hanrahan sees you, that little test of your mettle will be postponed a week, at least."

Fine with Roosevelt. They could use all the time they could get.

"Doing?"

T.R. pulled a thin sheaf of pages from his pocket. A duplicate manifest, S.S. *Etruria,* typed at record speed by Minnie Gertrude Kelly. "All the victims we know about so far, and probably all the others on the hit list." Elliott Roosevelt's daughter included.

"Your niece?" The patrolman reacted as though the Commissioner really had brutalized him. "What could she have they'd want?" And why was her uncle here if that was so? Why wasn't he downtown on Thirty-seventh Street?

"Eleanor's not there, that's why." She and her brother were with their grandmother on the train down from Mrs. Hall's summer house. They'd just departed for the railroad station at Tivoli on the Hudson, in fact, when Teddy'd put the call in from his office at headquarters. "I've still got almost forty minutes to be on the doorstep when they arrive."

He told Richard about Baby Joss.

"Baby Joss." Was that something to die for at the age of ten? "A worthless old rag doll?"

But of course it wasn't the "worthless old rag doll" at all, was it. No more than it was the silver reliquary the Reverend Mr. Timothy Pike declared upon the boarding of the steamship, or the two sets of surgical instruments, Leipzig manufacture, boxed, registered in all innocence by Dr. Louis Urbont, Deck A, Stateroom 12. "Some of these bundles are hiding pieces of a secret, Richard. The kind of secret some men don't mind killing little girls for."

Someone on that boat, realizing that—scared by that—decided early in the voyage that he'd be a lot safer smuggling the secret piecemeal into the United States, reassembling it afterward.

"Obviously he was prevented from doing that right away, but that doesn't change the fact," the Commissioner argued. "This man could break whatever it was down into parts while he was at sea—which means that we're probably talking about, I don't know, a collection of gemstones? Currency?"

"Incriminating photographs," the officer could imagine.

"Of the Mayerling kind—possible." It could very well be political, a confidential report if not pictures. "Governments fall when the dirty linen comes out; the same with trusts. Don't think there aren't monopolists who wouldn't stop at murder."

Whichever it turned out to be, they now had the means to at least enlighten themselves. The list. The manifest. What Teddy wanted his aide working on for the next days, as was Minnie already, and himself. "We're splitting the names up, *A* to *H*, *I* to *P*, *Q* to *Z*. We're going to call on these people, we're going to look at the bags they had with them on the *Etruria*, we're going to beat those galoots to one of these things and we're going to find out what it is exactly, once and for all."

He himself would waste no time, stopping off on Twenty-ninth Street before going on to Thirty-seventh. A traveler named Schaeffer lived there and Roosevelt thought it might be productive to spend thirty of the forty minutes available seeing what happened to the luggage listed, if anything.

Richard was equally imbued, promising to get right on the proffered *A* to *H*, "as soon as you give me my bloody nose and have the boys hustle me off to jail."

Hesitation. "You really want me to hit you that hard."

"Unless you brought that makeup artist with you tonight?" Officer Kerner ripped the sleeve of his shirt as he spoke, bending to scoop a handful of mud up from a puddle between the cobblestones at his feet. He smeared himself with it, cheeks and neck, wiping the excess on his trousers at the knee. "If you're worried about injuring me, don't. I've got the hardest nose you ever cracked a knuckle on, believe me."

"All right. Brace."

His fist connected dead center, compacting the vulnerable cartilage forming the nostrils. Richard careened, the back of his thighs colliding with another of the trash cans indigenous to the alley. It spun up, clattering, even as the officer slammed through the door behind him, staggering into Murphy's. "You son of a bitch, you broke my nose!" he screamed, the hand clapped up to his face thick with dark blood.

Patrons scrambled aside, a chorus of angry voices and shrieks. Guns were suddenly drawn, the officers at the front alarmed enough to cover the President of the Police Board as he shoved his prisoner into their custody. "Get this slime over to the Forty-first," he snapped. "I want a confession on my desk first thing tomorrow morning."

"My nose is broken, God damn it!"

"The man needs a doctor, sir," Hanrahan protested, the genuine shock on his face mirroring his new insight into Roosevelt's character, obviously more violent than most of the plug-uglies a gang chief could hire. "He could drown in his own blood."

"Couldn't he, though." The Commissioner couldn't have cared less, it seemed, heading out after the phalanx of uniforms. "If Mr. Kerner is interested in seeing a doctor, all he has to do is tell me what I want to know."

It was fun to feign smugness outside, to watch the cops toss the miscreant into the paddy wagon, headfirst. What a show Richard put on as well, all curses and a flash of tattoo. After all this was over, Teddy was going to have to ask him about that over dinner: just how much of a holy terror his aide had been in the sweet by-and-by.

■ "I took a bath this morning, Grandma."

"And you spent the last two hours sitting in a dirty railroad car." Mary Livingston Hall was adamant upon their arrival home: her grandson Grace was not going to bed covered with soot, and neither was Nell, standing there on the stoop with Baby Joss cradled in the crook of her arm.

"Bed?" Dismay. Despair. Didn't Grandma just tell them the train got in early?

"And you've had a hectic day." The quicker they washed and put on their nightshirts, the better off they'd be, she said as she propelled them forward into the house, unaware of the figures watching from the shadows across the street.

The door closed.

"You see it?" A hiss, a trace of the Teutonic in the accent. Even in the absence of light, the scar on the cheek was visible, an iridescent zigzag splitting the night.

"Yes." Amazing, wasn't it, how zealous the grip. "You may have to cut her throat just to loosen the fingers."

"Or if we don't want to wait till she's asleep." The flat of the thumb was testing the edge of the knife, and the blue-white serration grew longer as a smile cracked the cicatrized face.

■ Mr. Randall M. Boyar chugged up Seventh Avenue at a lively seventeen miles per hour, the boiler on his Stanley Steamer sending smoke signals up into the air. *"After the ball is over,"* he brayed. *"After the break of dawn . . ."*

A nip from the flask in his left hand, the steering stick loose in his right.

"After the dancers' leaving, after the stars are gone—" Then what? Oh, yes. *"Many a heart is aching, if you could something them something, something the hopes that vanish, after the ball!"*

That was West Thirty-seventh Street, wasn't it? Whoops. Mr. Boyar vaguely remembered that this was where he was supposed to make his turn, rectifying the near-mistake with a fast lateral whip of the stick. His horseless carriage swerved too quickly, bouncing up onto the sidewalk and lurching back over the curb at the far corner, heading directly into the path of an approaching coach and two.

"Look out," he could only call as he groped for the lever at his feet, braking the rear wheels too precipitously, spinning the car.

Galvanized, the driver of the oncoming carriage slapped viciously with the leather in his hands. His animals shrieked and veered while, inside the passenger compartment, Police Commission President Theodore Roosevelt forgot about the lack of information he'd come up with at Schaeffer's and went pitching into the bulkhead across from his tufted seat. Within seconds he was making the close acquaintance of the oscillating floorboards, fully expecting the sound of splintering wood and shattering glass to follow.

Great bodily damage. Ignominious death.

Wood did scrape, the glass in the coach window did rain down on his head and shoulders, but out-and-out disaster was averted. The vehicles sideswiped at an angle oblique enough to dissipate the shock.

When the dust above the still-rotating wheels began to clear, Teddy struggled up, bruised, whiplashed, and dropped out of the ruptured door onto feet not nearly as steady as he would have preferred. "Sweeney?"

"All in one piece, your honor," the driver assured him, seeing to the horses and looking daggers at Randall M. Boyar. "Yourself?"

"All in one piece." Confirmed even as T.R. went to check up on the motorist, breathing heavily in his machine, flask upended.

"Close call we had there, I'd say," he said, offering Roosevelt a swig. "Where *are* my manners?"

"By Godfrey," the Commissioner spluttered. "You're drunk!" Visions of Elliott and the lamppost formed and re-formed like hand-painted stereoptican transparencies in front of his eyes.

"It's okay, I've been blessed with two hollow legs." Boyar saw no relationship between the whiskey and the accident. How could there be? "The mind is totally unimpaired."

"Is that what you call 'unimpaired'?" The horseless might not have suffered much but the horse-drawn? Repair would take days, perhaps weeks, and Roosevelt was due at 11 West Thirty-seventh Street in minutes. "I swear, I am going to push for legislation: people should not be allowed to drive a motorcar if they've been out drinking!"

"My idea exactly." Randall M. Boyar tossed his emptied flask over his shoulder. Teddy had his vote—until Teddy yanked him out from behind the stick. "Hey."

"Maybe it's not on the books yet but you aren't driving this thing anywhere. No, sir."

"How do I get to my house, then, walk?"

"Where is it?" T.R. was regarding the automobile with a brand-new glint in his eye.

"Thirty-eighth. Five East." Around the corner from the Hall home.

"I'll drive you." The Commissioner seated himself behind the controls.

"You don't know how to drive." And this most precious of his possessions already had a crumpled fender as it was.

"Then you better be a damn good teacher," Roosevelt suggested, smiling grimly at the inebriate's newfound sobriety. "Hadn't you."

■ *"Now I lay me down to sleep,"* Anna Eleanor recited, kneeling at the side of the bed, her elbows resting on the edge of the mattress, her fingertips forming a cathedral. *"I pray the Lord my soul to keep. If I die before I wake, I pray the Lord my soul to take."*

Would He please bless her mommy in heaven, and her daddy? Her little lost baby brother, Ellie, Jr.?

"I know they're happy being together up there with You, and I know they're even happier because Grandma Hall is taking such good care of me and my other brother, Grace, down here on Earth."

Mary Livingston Hall had been privy to the prayer for almost two years now, ever since the decimation of the family. Even so, it still brought a stone to her throat, every time, and she never missed an evening if she could help it. Never.

"And God bless Uncle Theodore and Aunt Edith, and my cousins Ted and Kermit, Ethel and Archie . . ."

Prompting was sometimes required at this point. "Alice, too, dear."

"I was just getting to her, Grandmother." A devotional look upward through the ceiling: forgive us our uncharitable thoughts, dear Lord, please? "Bless Alice even though she's always so mean to me, and could you spare one more blessing for Baby Joss?"

"He'll need it," her guardian had to remark as she held the counterpane aloft so that Eleanor could crawl underneath with the doll. "I can't remember anyone in our family ever keeping anything so threadbare."

"Do you think he'll rip?"

"It's amazing he hasn't already." The old woman kissed her

granddaughter on the forehead and lowered the lamp. "Sweet dreams, my darling."

"Good night, Grandma."

Baby Joss said good night to Mrs. Hall, too, and even though it was soundless, Nell was sure the message got through: the expression on the woman's face grew bright enough to provide a residual glow well after the closing of the door.

"Your grandmother is a nice lady," the doll whispered as they made themselves comfortable on the pillow. "I like her."

"Me, too." Were it not for Mary Livingston Hall they'd all probably be stuck in some horrible old orphanage somewhere, "you, me and Grace."

The shrubs rustled beneath the bedroom window, outside in the night.

"What was that?" Baby Joss was so easily alarmed.

"The wind, silly." Eleanor adjusted the cover and patted his head. "You're a real scaredy-cat sometimes, aren't you," she said, the Sandman quick to weight her eyelids and terminate the exchange. After several minutes only the quiet sound of a little girl asleep could be heard in the room while, outside, the shrubs rustled again.

■ "I'm going to trust you to drive the rest of the way home unsupervised," Teddy stated as he halted the horseless carriage in front of 11 West Thirty-seventh Street, returning the stick to its owner. "And I'm going to hope you've learned your lesson: drinking and driving do not mix."

"Commissioner," Randall M. Boyar replied, "I think I might have learned my lesson when it comes to drinking, period." He slid behind the controls, delving down behind the driver's seat to retrieve the flask. "A souvenir."

A one-handed catch, midair.

"Theodore?"

Mrs. Hall was standing in the opened door of her house, atop the six steps of the stoop. He turned, face lighting up.

"You're here: bully." The delay on Seventh Avenue had concerned him more than he wanted to admit: every second was precious when it might mean the life of a child. "How are things in Tivoli this summer?"

She arched an eyebrow as he ascended, the puffing of the smokestack on the motorcar receding into the distance. "The President of the Police Commission doesn't just drop in unannounced to talk about conditions in the country." Related or not. "Not at this time of night."

"It's police business, Mary." He stepped through the open door, neither he nor Eleanor's grandmother cognizant of the men concealed across the street. "Does Nell have that doll with her? Baby Joss, she calls it?"

"Does Nell ever not have that doll with her?" Mrs. Hall closed the door and led the girl's uncle to the foot of the stairs. "What kind of 'police business' could you have with something like that?"

"I won't know until I examine it," Roosevelt replied. "Either way, I'm going to have a pair of patrolmen guarding this house before I leave." He was already heading up to the second floor.

"Just what kind of danger are we in?" She would have gone on to mention her right to know, but that was when Nell screamed in her bedroom. It was a ragged, terrified shriek, undulating. Breaking. Mary Livingston Hall went ashen as her unexpected guest raced up the remaining steps and lunged across the upstairs hall, his speed augmented by the sound of glass, shattering.

Upraised palms slammed flat against the door, shooting it open. It swung wide, impacting against the wall. "Nell—?"

"Uncle Teddy!" The child was standing on the bed, hair askew, face disfigured with shock and grief. Her finger pointed at the window, what was left of it. "He took Baby Joss! The man, he took my doll!"

"Not yet he hasn't." T.R. flung himself around the foot of her bed, leaping up onto the glass-covered windowsill, shards crunching under his heel. Hand supporting his weight and balance on the inside of the frame overhead, he leaned out, looking down.

There he was: the scar-faced man, about halfway down to the little garden between the homes of Thirty-seventh and Thirty-eighth, frantic. Trying desperately to extricate his cuff from a scissure in the wood of the trellis, Baby Joss horizontal under his arm.

"You!" Immediate recognition. Immediate. Roosevelt began to descend the trellis himself, closing in from above. As he reached out to tag his quarry, however, the thug ripped free, lurching backward, falling to the ground. The doll flew up into the air, dislodged, coming back down in a dogwood thicket.

A scramble, the thief plunging through the branches in search of the prize, cursing even before the Commissioner leaped onto him from ten feet above. "No, sir," he growled, yanking at the outstretched arm. "No, sir."

"Perhaps I should have killed you on the bridge?" He was all over his adversary, trying to knee him in the groin, trying to drive the lenses of his *pince-nez* directly through the whites of his eyes. If not that, then the knife, drawn with breathtaking skill. First the blade, then the doll.

It flashed in an arc designed to decapitate. Eviscerate. Teddy could only retreat before its fury, feeling the wind from every swipe, praying there were no hidden brambles beneath his legs. Trip and die. Fall and the knife cuts into your heart.

All he had to defend himself with was his jacket. He could slip it off, wad it up, use it as a shield to deflect—

No. Not a shield. This could be an *offensive* weapon, this jacket, thrust savagely enough. Thrust with a howl something Sioux. Something cougar.

And, indeed, the outcry alone was sufficient to make the scarface flinch: an opening. Coarse belted tweed lashed out at the scratches new to the already damaged face, eliciting another kind of howl. Pain.

Humiliation.

Another strike, this to the hand. The dagger. It dropped from the lacerated fingers, disappearing into an accumulation of fallen leaves. Inflamed, Roosevelt's antagonist charged, head down, claws extended. The war cry now torn from his throat was even more Sioux than Roosevelt's own: if bare hands was the call, then bare hands it would be.

Except the juggernaut came at the Commissioner only because

he stood between entrapment and escape, the desire no longer being to kill but merely to get away. Over the wall.

Why the split-second shift of tactic? Incomprehensible—and then T.R. heard the rumbling wheels, the clanging bells, the horses' hooves, all flooding up Thirty-seventh Street from Sixth, from the Chelsea precinct. Of course. Splendid. Mrs. Hall had obviously telephoned for help and here it was, arriving *en masse.* The fugitive would have no river to step off into, not this time, not with Teddy vaulting the wall behind him and all those officers converging in front.

He was in the middle of the cobblestoned street about ten feet from where Roosevelt landed, arms flapping as though he were a bird and flight were an actual alternative. "Stand where you are," the Commissioner called. Fumbling for his police whistle, he blew it as loudly as he could.

The first reinforcements came toward them at lather speed.

"That's your man, officers!"

But these were none of New York's Finest, T.R. was suddenly aware: these were the thief's own accomplices coming to snatch him away. One, tall and lithe, was leaning out from the body of the wagon, hand extended.

Contact.

"Stop!" Instinctive, impulsive, Teddy bolted forward in a reckless attempt to break the precarious grip, too late. The fingers closed, tightening; the scar-faced man was tumbled aboard the speeding cart, free.

Gone.

The horses thundered past, the rear of the vehicle fishtailing, forcing the Commissioner to dive aside or die trampled. He found himself horizontal in the gutter, directly in the path of the police units which were now reaching the scene. Only a precipitate roll sideways saved him, the distance between his head and the first of the flailing hooves infinitesimal.

Muddy, bruised, frustrated, Roosevelt tumbled up onto his feet at the curb, yelling, "After them, dammit!" even as he lurched forward to intercept one of the wagons pursuing. But his balance was off and his niece was suddenly tugging at his back. "Baby Joss," she cried. "Where is Baby Joss?"

"By Godfrey." He'd forgotten. He'd actually forgotten. The hell with the chase: much more important was the doll abandoned in the thicket on the other side of that wall.

Within moments he was back in the garden, braving the briers, grunting as he stretched out along the ground to grope, to poke, to find. The doll emerged smudged and scuffed, but theirs.

"You saved him," Eleanor wept, overjoyed as she came through the back door of the house, her grandmother hard pressed to keep up. "I love you, Uncle Theodore!" The little hands reached out for the beloved toy.

"Treat him gently," Roosevelt said softly, cradling the little rag head in the palm of the hand which wasn't supporting the little rag body. "Baby Joss is in need of repair."

"Can you fix him, Grandma?"

"I can do my best." Mary Hall examined the damage, a rip which reminded her son-in-law's brother of nothing less than the wound which had taken the life of Ida Moskowitz, only here the life spilling out was made of cotton wadding. White fuzzy balls of it, surrounding a folded paper. "What's this doing in here?"

"Hiding from those men," the Commissioner believed, withdrawing the sheet and carefully exposing it to the light.

A sketch. A sketch in blue ink.

Eleanor's grandmother adjusted the spectacles on the bridge of her nose. Did Theodore know what it was?

"Something scientific." Crisscross lines detailing a device identified as a rotor. T.R. tapped the word, hand-lettered between a set of parallel lines at the bottom of the sheet, centered. "If this is a page number here in the corner, we're looking at the fifteenth drawing in a set."

"Signed," Mrs. Hall indicated. " 'C. DeLacy,' it looks like."

" 'C. DeLacy' it is."

"Who is 'C. DeLacy'?" The obvious question, voiced by the little girl.

"That," declared the President of the Police Board, "is the next thing we have to find out."

9 EDISON

■ Monochromatic images moved on the wall: women at the seashore in ballooning bathing suits tempting the surf, fencing masters *en garde*. Racehorses tearing across a finish line.

And then the *pièce de résistance,* an enormous locomotive speeding directly at the audience. Quick intakes of breath came from all corners of the darkened room, and the scrape of chair legs shoved backward. Louis Lumière regarded his brother Auguste across the top of their *Cinématographe,* each pleased to mirror the satisfaction of the other.

When the "throw" was long enough, the velocity of that oncoming engine never failed to engender gasps—more, perhaps, in the unnatural soundlessness which made every last witness know what it was like to be deaf, if only for the nonce.

Applause inevitably followed, increasing as the house lights came up, underscored by shouts of "bravo!" and "bravi!" On this particular occasion these were augmented by a "bully!" or two: Police Commissioner Theodore Roosevelt was in attendance, guest of Maurice Harbinger, vice president of the sponsoring Society for Individual Accomplishment.

"Merci," Louis said, bowing, accent mellifluous. "It is so much the happiness for us, here in your Cooper Union. Not since we introduced our moving pictures at the exposition in Paris have we

received the reception so, how do you say, *superbe?*" Should anyone desire a closer look at the mechanisms, "step up, *s'il vous plaît.*" He and Auguste were eager that they examine each ingenious detail, everything from the way the successive images were placed on the filmstrip to the shutter which synchronously winked the light on and off, frame for frame. "This is what gives the illusion of continuity, you see."

First up to look was Maurice Harbinger's guest, bending and peering, the antique dealer behind his shoulder on the left and a professor named Lake opposite. "Ingenious indeed," the scientist declared after a quick probe. "Perhaps Mr. Edison is wrong. Perhaps there are commercial prospects for this sort of thing, after all."

Les frères Lumière had certainly improved upon the Menlo Park Kinetoscope, a bulky apparatus which could be used by only one person at a time. Edison had, in fact, given up on the project, visualizing no future for it. Not enough people could see it, not enough to make it pay.

"We're not in the business of sideshow attractions," the New York *Times* had him say, an odd position for a Thomas Alva Edison.

"Very odd," in Teddy's opinion. The mossbacks said "impossible"; the Edisons said "hogwash." The only limit was what the imagination could conceive. Nothing was beyond man, as the existence of this very Society attested—"one of the reasons I asked Mr. Harbinger if I could be here tonight, to see what you gentlemen might make of this."

The schematic executed by the unknown C. DeLacy appeared in the Commissioner's hand. Would anyone present be able to tell him what it was?

"An electrical circuit of some sort," the gallery owner ventured, regarding the cross-hatchings and squiggles with interest. "Part of one."

"Part of an engine," said Lake, as though correcting a pupil.

"What kind of an engine?" T.R. inquired. "This word here, 'rotor,' does that mean anything?"

"Something that turns, *n'est-ce pas?*" Auguste was as intrigued as his peers. Was this single page all the Commissioner had?

"Unfortunately." Teddy had come afraid it wouldn't be enough ". . . but if the members of this Society can't tell me what kind of a machine I'm dealing with here, who can?"

"*Monsieur* Verne, if we were at home." No irony intended: this diagram could very well be just a flight of someone's fancy. A fiction, no?

"No," Roosevelt thought not. "People wouldn't be dying over something like that." Whatever the device turned out to be, one thing was indisputable. It was real.

All too real.

What about the name? Did that ring any bells?

" 'DeLacy.' " Harbinger read it aloud for the benefit of those members too far away to see. " 'C. DeLacy.' "

Glances. Shrugs. "Wasn't there a DeLacy on Pasteur's staff?" A stab, made by an associate named Breen. Hooted down, by a patron named Fougère.

"I did the monograph on Pasteur," he declared, "including a complete list of all his associates, beginning to end." Not one DeLacy anywhere.

"He is not a member of *l'Académie,*" Louis could safely add, he and his brother in contact with most of the scientific community in France.

"What a shame," Maurice had to say. "I doubt there's anyone here who wouldn't like to meet this man." Were he half as original as his drawing implied, "Mr. Edison might find himself in a real run for the money."

"If you do locate him, Commissioner, please," Breen could only urge, "have him contact us."

"And if you suddenly remember where he might be, let *me* know." T.R. repossessed the rendering, replacing it in his pocket. Hands were shaken all around, and the coatroom revisited. It might not be too late to find Jacob Riis downtown at the *Sun.*

Harbinger knew the name from the by-line. "Isn't scientific inquiry somewhat out of his field, though?" Chronicling the activities of slum dwellers and Tammany hacks was one thing, getting to know who might be who in all the unsung laboratories from Pittsfield to Hoboken quite another. "Mutually exclusive, perhaps."

"It's a long shot," Teddy had to admit as he stepped through the door the collector held open for him. "I just don't know where else to turn." He set his foot on the running board of his waiting carriage, but before he could pull himself inside there was a halloo from the building, Professor Lake hurrying to catch up.

"The *C* stands for Charles," he piped. "I *knew* there was something about that name, I just couldn't remember from where."

"Charles DeLacy." Maurice tried it out on his tongue even as the President of the Police Board descended on Lake, all teeth.

"Out with it, Professor. Every second I lose could damn well mean another innocent person dead or in danger." Exactly where did he know this fellow from?

"He wasn't a 'fellow,' he was a boy." The reason the scientist had trouble placing him: who pays attention to children? "He *looked* fourteen, at any rate."

"Where did he look fourteen, sir? Where?" Roosevelt was prepared to shake it out of him, if need be.

"Oh. Right. Menlo Park."

Edison's Menlo Park?

"Edison's laboratory, yes." Lake sought confirmation from Harbinger. "You saw him when you were there."

"I did?"

"Last year. April, I think." Hadn't Maurice arrived for an appointment just as the old man was giving DeLacy a dressing down?

"That was the office boy."

"Since when," the professor wanted to know, "do 'office boys' tell Thomas Alva Edison he's too stuck in the mud when it comes to the kind of compounds he uses in the cylinders for his talking machines?"

A brilliant mind, DeLacy's. Intuitive. Conceptual. Tactless.

T.R. was not surprised. Prodigies were often too smart for their own good. "Would he still be there, with Edison?"

"After that?" The heretic was gone that day, well over a year ago now.

"Well over *two* years ago now." It had been April, yes, the gallery owner recalled, but April 1893, not April 1894.

"This is July 1895," the Commissioner didn't have to remind them. Where would DeLacy be now—"who would know?"

Edison?

■ "Why would I care?"

The Wizard of Menlo Park had agreed to see Roosevelt, but only with great reluctance. There were many more important things to think about than insubordinate protégés. Tesla, Weyburn, DeLacy, all the young upstarts, cutting off their noses to spite their presumptuous faces: it made no difference to him what they made of their lives once they went out by themselves. The only name which would go down in the books would be his own.

Edison was seated at his cluttered rolltop when Teddy was shown in, his Waterman pen scratching notes onto the ruled pages of a schoolbook. The filament burning in the electric lamp behind him haloed the hair on his head, prematurely whitened. He was an old forty-eight.

"Your former apprentice," T.R. told him, "may have invented some device that people are being killed over; that's why you might care."

Scratch. Scratch. The ink was brownish, the handwriting cramped.

"Sir?" Roosevelt moved between Edison and the bulb. The man was deaf in one ear, according to an article in *Murray's Magazine,* although perhaps not quite so deaf as all that. It was a very nice way for him to ignore problems, some of which actually would die of neglect.

Roosevelt would not be ignored, his eclipse of the light giving his host no choice but to look up, lip curled. "I find it hard to believe that that arrogant young mediocrity could have 'invented' anything anyone would even be interested in, much less kill for."

"See this and say that." The Commissioner handed him the diagram. Edison glanced at it: it was worth nothing more.

"Part of the design for an engine, that's all. A rather conventional engine, if you don't mind my saying."

"Not part of a project started here, then?" The shot had to be chanced, even though Teddy knew the odds had to be millions to one.

"If it was started here, it wasn't something I asked him to do. Of course," Edison had to add, "Charles always had a problem with what *I* asked him to do."

"He was rebellious, I heard."

"You could say that." The entrepreneur rose, returning the drawing. "For the first time in my life I began to see what my boss at the telegraph company must have gone through before he boxed my ears."

History would have repeated itself on DeLacy's ears, but Edison held back.

"I wasn't sure it would do the job," he recalled. "And if there's one thing this sorry old world doesn't need it's two semideaf inventors."

Sudden warmth transformed his voice, contradicting his own previously negative attitude toward the prodigal. What was happening here, T.R. wondered. Did the aging *wunderkind* of American science hate his impetuous pupil or didn't he? Was Charles a mediocrity as described, or not?

"Maybe I exaggerated." Annoyance, directed at the weakening of the emotional shield so assiduously maintained. It was none of Roosevelt's business if old Tom Edison felt like a father whose favorite son had run away from home.

None.

Better just to walk from the room, forcing his guest to follow him into the long wooden shed which jutted out from the main house. The place reeked of chemicals, fuming acids and ozone, all boiling and smoking in a forest of glass tubes branching above a root system made up of beakers, basins and vats. A hum permeated the walls and made the dust dance on the floorboards, registering on the rows of meters standing in dark banks between the windows and the stone-topped workbenches.

"Mr. Edison," the Commissioner said. "I didn't come here to

find out how you feel about Charles DeLacy. All I need is the man's current address; it's imperative I speak to him. If you have that, or if you know someone who does—"

"This is his table." A non sequitur. Deliberate. "One of these days I'll be able to assign it to someone else." As the inventor spoke, he opened the drawer beneath the slab and removed an address book from the clutter within, making Roosevelt catch it on the fly.

"The current address?"

Edison's tongue clicked against the roof of his mouth. "How many people do you know who put their own addresses in their own address book?" He headed back to his office, leaving Teddy behind to do his own research, flipping the dog-eared pages *A* to *C, D* to—

D.

Two entries, both with the same last name as DeLacy's own. William. West Seventy-second Street, Manhattan, a house number just off Central Park. Eugene, Cos Cob, Connecticut.

"Which is the father," T.R. asked when he reentered the office, "William?"

"Biologically speaking." The pen went scratch, scratch, more notes in the rulered book.

Understood. "If I am put on to his whereabouts, is there anything you might want me to tell him for you?"

"Can't think of a thing."

"Bully." Not exuberant, not this bully. "I thank you for your help."

A grunt. Whatever. Scratch.

■ The Commissioner went outside. The buggy he'd hired at the station was standing there in the shade of an elm, its driver, a slow-witted sixteen, regarding him from under the unraveling brim of his daddy's straw hat. "Didn't think you'd be back so soon," he drawled. "We push the old hayburner here you just might be able to catch the three forty-three instead of the four twenty-one."

"Push it." The voice was gravel as Teddy swung himself up into the bench alongside the youth.

"Hang on." A barely perceptible flick of the wrist and the mare in the harness in front of them trotted out, unexpected spring in her stride.

"Roosevelt, wait."

Theodore placed a restraining hand lightly on the driver's shoulder, the vehicle coming to a halt as Edison stepped off the veranda. There was something to say to Charles, after all.

"Splendid." T.R. would be *de*lighted to deliver the message. He really would.

Even so the inventor hesitated, shuffling his feet as he approached the side of the rig, stirring up the looser grains of dirt with shoes already scuffed, incongruous on a man of his fame and stature. "Just," he began, and then began again, "just tell him he was right. The thermoplastic disc is a vast improvement over the metal cylinder."

"Thermoplastic." Roosevelt made the note. "Cylinder." Were those tears he saw in Edison's eyes?

"Tell him I've had a prototype constructed and . . . and I would be pleased if he could see his way clear to . . ."

". . . come see it."

"No," with great vehemence. "To come *hear* it. If."

If Charles were still interested, he meant, clutching at the elastic of his suspenders as he wheeled and, head high, walked back into the house.

▪ William DeLacy's West Seventy-second Street address turned out to be a gabled, turreted, eight-story Gothic apartment building named *Dakota.* Towering like a vast yellow castle in a neighborhood of brown-faced town homes, the structure had been given its title not because it reminded anyone of the territory that once was home to Theodore Roosevelt, but because it was situated so far from any other buildings of similar cast that New Yorkers felt, as one wag put it, "it might as well be out in Dakota."

What the cowboys of Dickinson or Medora would say of such a building growing tumorlike out of the rough rocks of their range was probably something not to repeat in mixed company, the Commissioner suspected as he stepped from the hansom which had brought him up from the ferry at Forty-second Street. If the doorman would be so kind as to announce him to the DeLacys?

One of the features the Dakota offered its tenants was an inside telephone service: no one could pass through the gate without authorization from above. No tenement this.

"Sure thing, Mr. R." The switchboard was just inside the little guard house to the left of the entrance: the doorman uncradled its earpiece and inserted a metal plug into the appropriate hole. Teddy could hear the ringing through the horn, and the squawk of a voice re-created by a piece of foil. "Mr. DeLacy? You have a visitor, sir."

More squawks.

"It's not the moving men yet, it's Commissioner Roosevelt. From the police department; that's right."

"Official business," T.R. suggested he add, and he did.

"Yes, sir, I'll send him up." The plug was removed from its socket, the doorman gesturing Roosevelt through to the elevator in the hall. "They're on five. Apartment B."

"B, thank you." What about that reference to "moving men"?

The DeLacys were vacating the premises, it seemed. "Hard times. Someone in my position can always tell when it's coming, you know: the kind of good food they stop buying, the mail they don't get anymore. The clothes."

Some time had passed since the doorman had seen Bill DeLacy in a new anything.

▪ Edison's shoes were scuffed because Edison didn't think much about shoes. William DeLacy's were scuffed because William DeLacy couldn't afford another pair.

"Fortunes of war," he said philosophically as he ushered Teddy into the fifth-floor apartment overlooking the park, looking right now more like a warehouse than a residence. Only the largest pieces of furniture weren't crated in some carton or other and even these had been broken down into component pieces. A breakfront, for instance, separated into china cabinet and hutch.

The wings of the dining room table, stacked neatly on one of the matching chairs.

Crushed newspapers and tangles of excelsior filled the air with dust. The odor of the tomb.

"Of course," Charles's stoop-shouldered father went on to say as he returned to the dusting of the glass on the picture in his hand, "you could be here to tell us the County Assessor's office has finally discovered the long-lost deed to the property we've been claiming on Fifth Avenue."

"We" were father and second son, Charles's younger brother, Eugene, who emerged from a bedroom with a carton of unsealed linens between his arms, a stoic expression on his face. He didn't know what "property" the old man was talking about, but what the hell, if the city'd sent an official of the Commissioner's prominence to negotiate for it, better it be understood up front: "Pop and I are too sharp to accept twenty-four dollars' worth of beads."

Usually Roosevelt discouraged the pulling of his leg, but this twenty-year-old did it so guilelessly T.R. couldn't deny the grin which made a crescent moon of his mouth. "I wish I did have that kind of news for you," he said, taken by the youth. Knowing that the joke was at the expense of dashed hopes, a way to keep the bullet in the chamber and not in the brain.

"How can we help you, then?"

"By telling me where I can find your brother, Charles." Teddy would have explained the importance of it, but mention of the name itself exploded the façade DeLacy had so elaborately constructed. The picture slipped through his fingers; it crashed on the wood of the floor and the glass burst around the frame.

"Pills—" A request Eugene was already acting upon, frantically searching through the packages.

"They were right here a minute ago. Right here."

"There, see?" The vial was on the table by the door.

The Commissioner turned to find the kitchen. DeLacy would need a glass of water.

"Eugene can get it." Roosevelt wanted to know about Charles. Roosevelt was going to hear about Charles.

"If you're not up to it . . ."

"It's been two years since Thomas Alva Edison had my son murdered," the old man charged, snatching the sepia-toned portrait up from the fragments at his feet. "I'll be 'up to it' for as long as it takes to have that bastard in Menlo Park tried, convicted and hanged."

■ The *pince-nez* dropped from the bridge of T.R.'s nose as the eight by ten was thrust into his hand. "Wait a minute."

DeLacy was waving Eugene aside, pills, water and all. "Never mind those." His entire attention was focused on their guest. "You don't believe me, nobody does, but that doesn't make it any the less true."

Thomas Alva Edison, inventor of the electric light, killed this boy? This disobedient protégé? "Why?" The Estes Hanrahans resorted to murder as a tool of business and personal enmity, not the Tom Edisons, not for sass. Not even for jealousy.

"Partly for jealousy." The correction was quick and canonic. The Wizard of Menlo Park had reason to envy William DeLacy's brilliant son. "He wasn't the one who made the hydroelectric generator work, Charles was. Edison didn't personally come up with the mimeograph, that was also Charles. The magnetic ore separator."

Fluorescent light.

People had begun to talk, to mention the wrong name in the wrong place. Edison wasn't good at sharing the spotlight. "He began to bait Charles," Eugene related. "Insult him in front of everyone, whenever he could."

"Anything to get him to mouth off." If Charles talked back, Charles could be fired. "How much taunting could he take, especially when it was he who was in the right?"

Had it stopped with the firing, fine. Understandable. One shakes one's head and moves on. "But," DeLacy wanted Teddy to know, "Edison wouldn't let it lie. Charles wasn't going to compete with him for lighting contracts the way Nikola Tesla did. He wasn't going to compete at all." The technologist would make damn sure there'd be no money available for any project created by "C. DeLacy," "not in America, anyway."

"He had a project, I take it?" Spoken hushed, with perhaps a bit more anticipation than Roosevelt wanted to reveal. The genius had to have told them what the project was, or hinted at it. He just had to have.

"There was something, oh, yes." Now William could down his pill, the drama of the pause more instinctive than premeditated. "Something so incredible it was going to change the world. Change everything: how we live, how we think, everything."

"And my brother couldn't raise a dime this side of the ocean."

They didn't have to tell the Commissioner where Charles took his proposal. He knew. It fit, and the fingers crossed behind his back began to burn. The page extracted from Eleanor's doll grew heavier within the confines of his pocket. "Was there money in Europe?"

"Charles said so. The responses to his letters of inquiry were extremely positive." Fare had been raised between the three of them, Charles, Eugene and their father. The young visionary set sail for Le Havre and points beyond.

Two weeks later, no more, the pilgrimage was done. DeLacy still had the cablegram. "He'd been beaten to death. Every bone in his body broken." Spat. A piece of undigested meat stuck in the throat even now. Even now. "Not the work of one man."

Four. Five. Six, maybe, the French authorities informed them. The body had been left facedown in a muddy ravine. "A town east of Paris somewhere. Meaux."

"A long way from Menlo Park," Roosevelt was obliged to observe.

"My son could have been at the North Pole, it wouldn't have mattered. Edison would have sent those mugs anywhere. 'Make it look like an accident, make it look like he was robbed, I don't care. Just get it done.' "

They did.

"Is that what the French listed it as? Robbery?"

"They find a dead man stripped naked in a ditch, what else

could they think?" Eugene's voice was filled with challenge. "And isn't that what it was, in fact?"

"Did you tell them your suspicions about Edison?"

"Pop wrote them a letter. Two." Bitterness pervaded the recollection.

"When I got no answer to the first after four months, I wrote the second." And three months after that, in the spring of 1894, ten months after Charles had been buried, an answer arrived.

"The investigation continues. Progress is being made."

William DeLacy threw things at the wall, he broke the mirror above the hall table. He got on the ferry to Hoboken and took the train to Menlo Park.

"You saw Edison?" A buzzing began to resonate in T.R.'s ears, the inventor in conversation with the Commissioner, not more than two hours before. If you see Charles, he'd said, words to that effect, as though knowing nothing about Charles's death. As though Charles's father had never been there to confront him. To call him murderer.

Could Tom Edison forget that? Convince himself it had never occurred? Would he send the President of New York City's Police Board back to see his own accuser?

Was he that much the fool?

"I didn't see him," the old man was admitting, hating himself for his cowardice and the rationalization that gave him last-minute license to turn away. The time to face Tom down was when it could be dead to rights, good advice? "Get the evidence on the four-flusher first; then go watch him squirm."

Evidence. Proof.

DeLacy tried for a year to raise the price of another ticket to France. The hotel. The per diem. He corresponded once more with the police in Paris: could one of them investigate on private commission, and the answer came back *mais non* not one week before the last of the money was gone and the eviction notice was in the mail.

"And any day now there'll be the big announcement out of New Jersey, see if there isn't. The latest brainchild of the great thinker, Mr. Thomas Alva Edison: the world's first practical fly-

ing machine. This way to the demonstration, ladies and gentlemen, see for yourself."

Flying machine.

Practical, workable, heavier than air. *Flying machine.*

"Not a balloon," Eugene wanted to make it clear. "Not a dirigible. What my brother designed, what he invented—"

"Mankind's oldest dream, ever since he came out of the cave
and saw the birds!" The old man stood there, fevered, a figure
from the Old Testament. "No one could figure it out before my
Charlie, no one. Eastman, Edison, Westinghouse, none of them. It
took Charlie to do it. Charlie. No matter whose name ends up on
the damn thing when it finally flies."

There was merit in DeLacy's theory of conspiracy, T.R.
couldn't deny. People had been killed for less.

People had been killed for a whole lot less.

■ "I'd like to borrow this picture of Charles," Teddy said, if
Charles's father wouldn't mind.

"Will it help get Edison?" Nothing else mattered. Would giving
Roosevelt this photograph help put Edison away?

"It'll help put someone away."

Eugene went to the ringing telephone while Bill DeLacy delib-
erated. The doorman downstairs was calling to announce the arrival of the movers.

"Send them up." As he said it, the decision was made. The
picture of Charles DeLacy was thrust into the Commissioner's
hand.

"Use it well," said the old man, getting down on his knees to
collect the bits of broken glass from the oak.

10 CHARLES
DeLACY

▪ Portrait of the young inventor, once alive. Square face, thick brows, dark eyes, big, with a distant look, hair kind of scrambled. Cravat not entirely centered between the wings of the collar, not as starched as one ordinarily would see in a pose like this.

Not studio work, though. Ah. An outdoor setting: a lawn, some trees. The building in the background was faced with brick, three stories of regularly spaced casement windows keystoned. Chimneys on either end, also of brick, with clay pots topping the flues, one broken.

Familiar . . . or was it? So many houses looked like that, on both sides of the Atlantic. Something to ask either surviving De-Lacy the next time they spoke, Roosevelt mused as he stepped aside for the moving men, burly and young.

The time for questions was over today. William and son had more urgent matters to handle. And T.R. needed time of his own, to think. To wonder.

What could it look like, this flying machine? Not a balloon, Eugene had insisted. Not a dirigible . . . but balloons and dirigibles, variations thereof, were all that Teddy could imagine.

Balloons, dirigibles, adaptations of the iron-clad submersibles John P. Holland had experimented with in Paterson, New Jersey. 1878, was it? 1881? Long, pencil-shaped affairs propelled through the sky by pinwheels. Rudders.

Rotors.

Maybe it'd be more like a kite, something flat to catch the updrafts, with a tail slithering gently around the clouds, balancing things. Making them stable five hundred feet overhead.

Higher.

However the machine appeared, Charles's father was right about one thing, undoubtedly right. An invention like this would indeed change the world, how people lived, how they traveled . . . how they made war. It was the kind of device that made its creator the wealthiest man on the face of the earth, or dead.

Charles knew that. Why else would he have gone to so much trouble, separating his plans into the individual pages, secreting each sheet in God knows how many pieces of luggage, etc., aboard the *Etruria?*

Insurance, of course. Who would kill him for his airship if that airship were scattered to the winds and only Charles DeLacy himself knew with whom? What other choice would even the most violent of his would-be clients have but to bow before his ingenuity, to back off and accept the terms of his deal?

This choice: to beat it out of him. Whose luggage, in which town, sir? What street?

Come on.

People beaten severely enough usually talk: ask Lieutenant Meeghan. Unless they disappoint everybody by dying first.

"Will you want a cab, Commissioner?" The Dakota's doorman was ready to hail the one just now coming up out of Central Park.

A shake of the head. Roosevelt felt the need to walk, to pump the blood to the brain in the open air. Charles had been dead for days before the liner had sailed, miles east of Le Havre. Someone else aboard that vessel hid those plans. A confidant. Someone keeping the flame for Prometheus while he himself went out to die.

"It doesn't actually have to be someone so close," T.R. suddenly realized. "A friend would do just as well."

"Sir?" Was the doorman expected to remark on that?

" 'Here,' he says. 'Look after this package for me, an hour, two at the most. I'll be back for it as soon as I can.' By Godfrey, this was a man who considered himself absolutely safe!"

If Teddy said so.

"I do." The passion in his voice seemed to inspire the peal of laughter which came from somewhere up the street. No matter, though: Roosevelt's mind was insulated against outside stimuli now, it had room only for the picture he finally had of this friend of the inventor, left with the envelope. Waiting hours . . . days . . . learning the truth at last and splitting the seal. Seeing what Charles had wrought, inside. Realizing why Charles had died—taking the measures which eventually would bring still more death, to people as diverse as Ida Moskowitz and Elliott Roosevelt.

He had to get back to that passenger list; never mind the new, more raucous splutter of mirth over there, wherever. One of those names was going to connect up with an ex–Edison protégé, and that ex–Edison protégé's father was going to spark the minute he saw it. If not the father, the brother. "Him," one would say. "That's your man, T.R.: Charles mentioned him several times. Several times."

And, oh, as long as they were talking, what was it the Commissioner wanted to know about that building which was background in that picture of Charles . . . ?

■ It was a rather dilapidated van at the sidewalk in front of the building, the movers quick to start work, loading the larger pieces waist-high onto the bed. They were no more professional than their wagon, Teddy came to realize as he circled them on his way toward the park: William and son could no longer afford to hire even the most economical of the companies listed in the classifieds. These were friends of Eugene, probably. Students. Fellow clerks.

"Careful there." Professionals would not have piled additional bolsters across the width of the elongated sofa between them; they'd have been experienced enough to know that it took only the smallest shift in plane to topple them off. And the water trickling along the length of the curb at their feet was muddy.

Fast work with an upraised palm saved the pillows from ruin. Roosevelt accepted the youthful thanks with a modest wave, building up speed as he moved on toward the park. The quicker home the quicker to the manifest, the quicker to the eventual rubber stamp: Case Closed.

Something cracked sharply behind him. Another poorly managed piece of furniture destroyed? Before T.R. could look to see, there was a shout from up the street, urgent. "Heads up!"

Not the movers.

His head swiveled on his neck, his eyes zeroing in on the stitched missile screaming out of the sky.

"I got it," someone else was calling, a knickerbockered "outfielder" in what was an ongoing game of gutterball, cap sailing one way as he reeled the other, backward. His arm reached out, the hand encased in an oversized glove of webbed leather.

"Behind you!" This was from a cluster of spectators gathered in front of a tavern named Feeney's, across Seventy-second from the Dakota. Working men in gartered sleeves and colorful suspenders, their more moderately attired wives, their overalled children. "Steiglitz!"

Steiglitz could only veer, surprised by the outcry and Roosevelt's unanticipated presence. "Oh," he said, stumbled, the ball sailing on over his head . . . right into the Commissioner's hand.

Pure instinct shot his arm up, pure instinct closing the fingers around the circumference of the incoming sphere, snatching it out of the air. A cheer went up from one and all, players, onlookers— moving men. "Teddy!" Who else but "Teddy Roosevelt!"

Even the outfielder agreed, scrambling back up onto his feet, first to pound the hero's back, to hold the forearm up in victory. "What a catch! Did everybody see that one-handed catch?"

If Feeney didn't order a round on the house, there'd be no justice on the Upper West Side. None.

"Sure and the drinks are on the house." Feeney didn't have to be asked. It wasn't every day that his little corner inn played host to someone so celebrated, that someone swept through the door on the crest of a human wave, brought straight to the bar. "What'll it be, Mr. R.? Beer? Whiskey? Some of the good Irish?"

Dammit.

Dammit to hell.

"A man has to think, given a decision like that"; that was what was taking so long, in Steiglitz's opinion. Feeney's good Irish was rare, but sometimes the simple everyday pleasures were the best.

Dammit to hell, why did he have to allow them to pull him into this place, today of all days? Had they just waved and let him go on his way, he wouldn't have to slap the flat of his hand down on the polish of their neighborhood bar and remind them that he was an officer of the court and this place was open illegally.

"It's *Sunday.*" The Sabbath. No liquor was to be sold on the Sabbath, City Ordinance Number—the hell with it, they knew what the law was just as well as he did.

"Come on, Teddy." Steiglitz's tone was that of a reproachful uncle. "Nobody's paid that any mind for, what? Twenty years? Thirty?"

T.R. placed his back to the lip of the bar, letting his jacket fall open. His right leg bent at the knee in a casual pose, the heel hooked over the brass rail six inches above the sawdusted floor. It was as if he were in the company of cronies, genial, relaxed. Compatible.

"Look at me, boys," he said, intimate. Sharing. "Does anyone here really expect the President of New York City's Police Commission not to do his duty when it hits him in the face? Whether he personally enjoys it or not?"

Now there was disbelief on the outfielder's face, nor was the expression Steiglitz's alone. "Oh: it's going to tear your heart out to close us down, is it? The one day a week we get to socialize a little, you understand that but, sorry, the law is the law and what can a poor Police Commissioner do?"

"He can work to change the law." Which Roosevelt was doing:

he did not see the value of legislation too many would flout, no matter the lip service given.

"And in the meantime? We're locked out."

"In the meantime *everybody* is locked out. Fair is fair, gentlemen. My promise. This is the last Sunday one saloon stays open while another's shut down. I'm forming a squad and we're going to make sure this city learns what it's like, the letter of these laws."

Repeal might not be very far behind, they did it well.

"Yeah. Right." Sure. "Thank you." A shuffling of chairs, muted expressions of disappointment . . . but the customers were gathering their outerwear, polishing off whatever was left in their glasses. To Theodore Roosevelt, friend of the workingman, yeah.

Their feelings of resentment and estrangement were natural under the circumstance, Teddy knew. Even so, they were behaving like responsible citizens and he congratulated them for it. "Bully, I knew you wouldn't let me down."

Steiglitz turned in the door. "Maybe it's you who's letting us down," he murmured, reaching out for a pair of the baseball bats which were leaning against the white-painted wainscoting to his right. "What do the blue laws say about playing in the street?"

"It depends on the game," T.R. had to reply, tensing because the big man wasn't brandishing the sluggers only to test his swing and their balance before going outside.

Or was it in lieu of going outside . . . ?

"You've done your 'duty' here, Commissioner; we wouldn't want to keep you from the rest of your patrol." Not when there was a lot of other serious law being broken all over the city. "Good folks're having their throats cut in their beds, they're being jumped on in alleys, they're having their wives and daughters attacked—"

The bats made little swishing noises in the air.

"Careful, now. Careful." Roosevelt made a platter of his hand, extending it toward the bartender: he'd take the key, please. "You can get it back at Police Headquarters on Mulberry Street, anytime after eight tomorrow morning."

"Feeney," Steiglitz cautioned even as the man was digging into the pockets of his beer-soiled apron. Mr. R. was just leaving and he wouldn't really need to take that key with him, after all. He trusted them to do the right thing, "on second thought."

Swish.

"Perhaps you're right," Teddy said slowly, steeling himself. " 'On second thought.' " He started forward, the outfielder giving him just enough room to slip between his guardian body and the jamb of the door, a deliberate squeeze. The Commissioner was reminded of a similar situation in a similar saloon, eleven years before, a gunslinger in the barroom of Nolan's Mingusville Hotel, Dakota. "Four Eyes," the epithet. "You're buying the rounds."

Plural.

" 'Well,' " the bespectacled twenty-five-year-old said at the time, " 'if I've got to, I've got to.' " When he rose, though, he complied by striking out with his fists, right and left. The guns discharged harmlessly into the ceiling, whether by intention or convulsion undetermined, the bully falling. "He struck the corner of the bar with his head," the memoirs would later recall. "I took away his guns."

"Top of the evening to you," Steiglitz was bidding, doffing an imaginary cap. T.R. turned in the door.

"And you." His fist struck quick and hard, just as it had in that August of 1884, directly to the point of the jaw. The left to the rib cage came next, and a second right.

"Oof" was the sole comment the man made, even when Roosevelt wrested the bats from his hand, commandeering them, regarding everyone else.

"We were closing up, I believe?"

"That we were," said Feeney, handing him the key. "Law-abiding people that we are." Notice to his patrons: he stood with the Commissioner.

No one stood against the Commissioner, not anymore. "Has Steiglitz gotten his breath back?" someone was whispering, awed. "Talk about the old one-two!"

Corbett would have been proud of him, Teddy decided as he finally proceeded into Central Park.

▪ His feet knew the shortcut, the unpaved trail winding through a high, dark green thicket which eventually would let him out along the shore of the Lake. From there Roosevelt would head around the north side of the recently installed zoo, bidding a passing good day to the nursemaids beneath their scallop-edged parasols, gently rocking the perambulators lined up like battleships in a Navy yard. A balloon vendor in a red-and-white-striped jacket would be the next stop, T.R. purchasing one primary-colored teardrop for each of his children before exiting the park on the Fifth Avenue side.

Several bushes rustled behind him. A pair of lovers, perhaps, not expecting anyone to be using this path. Squirrels chasing each other's tails through the undergrowth, chattering. The Commissioner smiled and strode on, his mind returning to the enormity of the problem at hand. How many passengers were ticketed first-class aboard the *Etruria* on any given crossing? How many that particular voyage westward, two years ago?

Of those: which one was stand-in for Charles, altruistic in his protection of the holy grail—

—or maybe not so altruistic at all. Maybe more self-serving. What was there to stop him (her?) from betraying the inventor's memory, from selling the reunited pages to the highest bidder, American or foreign, government or private?

Another set of squirrels played acrobat in the foliage to his right, but T.R. allowed no distraction. The plan had not been put back together; it remained scattered even now, two years later, pursued piece by piece by killers. Why hadn't this acquaintance of DeLacy's reassembled everything right then and there, in those first days after docking?

Loss of interest?

Hardly.

Death: that was why. It had to be why. Death perhaps even prior to arrival. "Accidental" death.

A terrible "illness."

Reason for Teddy to check the names on the manifest again, this time to see not who was robbed but who might be dead, dead aboard or dead in New York, barely a week home from Le Havre. He increased his pace, ignoring a new shiver of the bushes, this one on his left.

Ahead.

What stepped out to block the path was much larger than a rodent and yet a rodent all the same. Tall, masked, unshaven, armed with the same kind of baseball bat which Roosevelt had faced in Feeney's, wielded with even more murderous intent. Steiglitz, unwilling to let it lie?

"Followed me, did you?" Did you?

There was no time to discern the features beneath the mask, only to dodge the descending club, ducking and twisting as it smashed with bark-bruising impact against the trunk of the tree behind the Commissioner's back. A snowfall of leaves detached from the branches overhead, green and yellow flakes which lodged in T.R.'s hair and clung to his suit at the shoulders as he hissed his defiance at the hard-breathing hood.

"One taste of the knuckles wasn't enough, all right," Teddy snarled, eyes darting around in search of a stick—a stone—anything to defend himself with. "As you wish."

Twigs littered the ground. Gnarled and skinny little branches which would splinter like kindling against the heavy ash of the bat, coming at him again. Again. Again. Roosevelt skidded around a tree large enough to act as an *ad hoc* shield and then found himself crying out in sudden pain, a second cudgel slamming into his shoulder from the side, spinning him.

The masked man had an accomplice.

Two.

Bloodlust welled in the Commissioner's head, adrenaline-enriched. The veins pulsed above his brow as he arbitrarily charged at the second of his assailants, lips feral, fangs bared. His foot kicked up at a vulnerable groin—and missed, glancing off the thigh instead. The yelp which ensued was a relief; the blow made the fellow fall, a blessing.

"Three against one, you boys don't like playing fair, do you." He was wrestling with the fallen thug for the use of the bat, seizing it only to have it swatted aside by the third of the pack.

When the business end of the bludgeon came down again, it came down against T.R.'s ear, a bright red stain gushing from the cavity.

They're out to kill me, he realized in a rush of actual panic even as his upraised forearm deflected the ferocity of the subsequent blow, this from the first to accost him. Unbalanced despite himself, Roosevelt crashed backward into a shrub covered with thorns, spines which hooked through the wool of his suit and held him. President of the Police Board, former assemblyman of the Silk Stocking District, Grover Cleveland's Civil Service Commissioner, every bone in his body was going to be broken by those whistling bats. Charles DeLacy's fate would be his own.

A smash to the back, the leg, lethal in intent. Teddy's hands and knees made a ragged path through the leaves decaying on the ground as he tried to crawl out from under while they stalked him, knowing they had him. The first of the clubs was lifted high overhead, starting its downward arc with brutal momentum.

Halfway down it was shot out of the hand that held it. The would-be assassin screamed, wrist shattered, his accomplices glancing up, startled, eyes white in the slits of their masks.

"Nobody move!" A young man's voice, backed by the authority of a patrolman's blue: Officer Lindsay Hargate—Lindsay Hargate! —firing a second time when one of the truncheons still brandished came too purposefully close to the Commissioner's head. The wood clattered against the roots underfoot, rolling aside as the bullet did its work above, piercing clothing, flesh and bone, exploding blood bursting red in the air.

Upright despite that, the wounded hood shouted a guttural "go!" to his confederates, reeling away through the denseness of the foliage, fingers clutching his mangled shoulder, unable to stem the flow of crimson. *"Go!"*

They were going, fleeing in different and opposite directions. One lone cop would never pursue, not with the Police Commissioner of Police Commissioners injured between himself and the escapees, not even on Roosevelt's insistence.

"I'm not as bad as I look," he rasped as he struggled up, the gravel in his voice thick as pebbles. "Catch one, all I need is one of them!"

Which one, though? Which shadow? Shadows were all that remained, and although Lindy was willing to obey the order, at least as far as the top of the stone bridge adjacent, the gasp of involuntary pain behind him made him turn back. "I'm sorry, sir, it's more important I get you a doctor."

Broken bones, internal bleeding: T.R. was to stay put, to move as little as possible, but T.R. grabbed at the rear of the officer's uniform and held him in place. "My insides are undamaged," he was convinced, the hell with the fire that was searing his lungs. "A doctor is not necessary." He groped as he spoke, looking for the *pince-nez* which had been lost in the struggle. "How do you, by the way, happen to be in Central Park?" Casework for Meeghan?

It took a noticeable moment for the answer to come. "I . . . guesss you could say that."

"You 'guess.' " Something was glinting over there at the entrance to a burrow: the glasses, one lens cracked into a spider's web of fragile shards, the other only chipped. Teddy retrieved them, holding them in front of his face and looking up at the patrolman.

"He did assign me. Meeghan." Lindy found himself tapping the dust off the tip of his boot.

"To what?"

"To you, sir." He wrested the boot off. Sand had gotten inside. "He—"

"—told you to bird-dog me; don't be embarrassed, Mr. Hargate. It was obviously no coincidence, your being here." How far was it from Murray Hill, four miles?

"Well, he wanted me to, you know"—dammit, Meeghan's charge had been don't let him see you, under no circumstances, don't let him see you—"he wanted me to look out for you."

"But not for the purpose of giving me a hand in an emergency," the Commissioner expected. This was Lieutenant Meeghan they were talking about, not the former Edith Carow. Lieutenant Meeghan, that long-term veteran of the department wanting to know if some of the skeletons Theodore-al-Raschid planned to rattle were those in his own well-stocked closet.

"The lieutenant didn't think he owed me his reasons," the rookie had to admit, worried now for his job. "I asked him if he could get someone else, but . . ."

Teddy could anticipate the but. "Low man on the totem pole always gets the rancid plum." Lindsay Hargate was not to concern himself with the security of his position. "I'm hardly about to dismiss the man who saved my life."

A nod. "I couldn't just let them come at you like that, not after I saw the way they were waiting for you outside Feeney's."

"Outside?" Was Lindy sure? "They weren't in there with the rest of the customers who wanted to buy me a drink?"

"No, sir." In fact, "when you came out, they ducked back into the shrubs—that's how I knew they meant business." The trio were on their victim faster than the officer had expected, "otherwise I'd have been down off the outcrop I was watching from a whole lot sooner."

"Outside," Roosevelt was repeating, adjusting the pretzeled spectacles on his nose, seeing the world as a bug does, through a kaleidoscope of views. "Everybody was supposed to think I was attacked by some of Feeney's patrons, because I closed him down, weren't they. But you just exposed the lie, Mr. Hargate. These boys weren't from the bar, they were from Meaux. They were from Monroe Street. By George, if they'd risk this kind of an attack on a Police Commissioner, that Police Commissioner has to be breathing down their neck."

The how and why were known. Next came the who.

"There'll be a commendation on your record first thing tomorrow morning, Officer," Roosevelt said in parting, eastward bound and full of pep, scratches notwithstanding.

Edith would say gouges.

■ "You're going to have to call Molly," Alice announced, ebullient as she burst in on her stepmother upstairs in Archie's nursery. Seamstress to the family out at Sagamore Hill, Molly was going to be needed because "Father really wrecked his business suit. The gray one. I don't know how many places it's torn in, wait'll you see."

It was going to be a humdinger, the melodrama Alice was instigating. Hot stuff.

Maintaining composure in the face of such news was not easy, but Edith managed, carefully turning her youngest son over to his nurse, voice modulated. Very modulated. "Father is home?"

"I told you," her stepdaughter chirped. "His face is all cut up, too. And his knee."

"Is anyone helping him in?" No point in suppressing her feelings now: Alice's description was just too alarming for pretense. "Theodore?" Her feet thundered on the stairs. "Theodore?"

They met six steps above the first floor. "Before you get all upset," he said, "know that it's nothing serious. It looks terrible, I will admit, but it's not."

She closed her hand around his wrist and led him back down to a south-facing window, the rays of the sun filtering through the moiré of the curtain. "Since when are you a doctor?"

"A little iodine, some plaster, maybe: nothing more." If he didn't need a physician in Central Park twenty minutes ago, he certainly didn't need one now.

"Have you looked at yourself in a mirror? Those gouges?" Edith's fingers fluttered in front of his face.

"Scratches," Teddy insisted as he removed his damaged jacket, a number of curl-edged leaves landing on the runner. "Can we get to the iodine?"

"Iodine won't help that eye." Was her husband aware of the swelling? The discoloration? "You aren't just going to be black and blue, you're going to be every color of the rainbow. It won't go away for a week."

His hand was in hers again, the destination the kitchen this time, a white-tiled sanctuary reached through the nondescript door beneath the stairs.

"Why are we coming in here?" The iodine was still in the medicine chest upstairs in their bathroom, was it not?

Edith had released him to rummage in the icebox. "We were going to have this steak tonight," she wanted him to know, a piece

of raw red tenderloin extracted from its keep. "It'll do more good
on your face."

"I will not walk around holding meat up in front of my eye," he
objected. "It's demeaning."

"What it is is either that or the doctor." She swept out of the
room, forcing him to follow. He did, his sense of fair play ag-
grieved.

"You'd think I went out looking for this fight, the way you're
treating me." They went single file through the oak-paneled vestibule and back up the stairs, knowing that an audience of little
Roosevelts had assembled along the railing on the second-floor
landing: Ted, Kermit, Ethel and Alice. "I was jumped!"

"How many by?" Kermit asked breathless.

"Three."

"Three: smashing!" The sentiment was echoed by his siblings as
they tagged along, following their father into the master bath.

" 'Smashing' is the word, all right." Their mother immersed a
swab into the bottle of iodine as she spoke, the tincture turning
the cotton a shade of rust. "Did they say why they were so mad at
you?"

"They weren't mad at me, ssss!" The sting of the antiseptic
seemed to do more damage than all the bats combined.

"Boy," said Ethel. "I'm glad I don't need any iodine."

"Me, too," Ted agreed.

"If they weren't mad at you why would they want to attack
you?" Random violence made no sense to Edith; it was hard for
her even to conceive.

"They think I might be on to who they are, and they just might
be right." Pride filled his voice. "Of course they'd come at me
with baseball bats, aaahhh!" Enough iodine!

"Baseball bats?" She'd been shocked enough to jab the blunt
end of the probe into the gash at the ear.

"Daddy sent them packing, anyway, right? Right?" None of the
children needed any corroooration. Their father, Police Commissioner Roosevelt, former sheriff's deputy in the Wild West town of
Medora, Dakota, could not have done otherwise. "Right?"

Right. "With a little help from one of New York's finest," he was happy to add. "One of the bravest young officers I've ever met: three cheers for Lindsay Hargate."

Three cheers it was, and three more, these for the routing of the thugs with the baseball bats.

"Put your foot up on the stool," Edith said, not one hip, hip or hooray escaping her own particular throat. She could read between the words, and she knew that "a little help" was understatement galore. What would Theodore have done had Officer Hargate not been there for the rescue?

"Done?" Come through alone, what else? "By Godfrey, I thought I said 'enough'!" The iodine was just as caustic on the knee as on the face, damn it. A lesson for his children, though: "You have to expect scratches every now and then, going through life, unless you turn out to be a person who doesn't stand up for what he believes."

"They get their scratches, too, Commissioner: the kind that don't go away as fast as yours." Jacob Riis was leaning nonchalantly against the frame of the bedroom door, looking dapper in a powder-blue summer suit, skimmer in hand. "It might be fun to ask Andrew Parker about that twenty years from now. Mark the calendar."

"Who let *him* in?" The gruffness of the inquiry to his offspring was offset by the welcoming grin quick to play with the corners of Roosevelt's mouth. If the grin was more limited than normal, it was only because it hurt to grin right now. "Are you bribing our housekeeper again?"

"Tell someone you'll get them in the Sunday rotogravure and they're yours for life," the reporter replied, cheerfully insolent as he stepped forward onto the hexagonal tiles, leaning a little to examine the extent of the damage. "Your poor suit. Really, Theodore, if you were going to pick an alehouse to close up, wouldn't you have been better off going with one in your own political district?"

"Police commissioners don't have 'districts.' " And how did Riis know that T.R. had closed a gin mill not more than an hour before?

"Everybody's known about you and Feeney's for three quarters of that time." A story so dramatic would three-alarm its way across Manhattan, fueled by desperate phone calls: Feeney to his suppliers, his suppliers to their friends in high places. "It's a three-star headline, with editorials by Hearst and commentary by Andrew D. Parker, to wit. . . .

" 'While it is commendable that the President of this Board wants to enforce the letter of the law, I really must question his methods. What sort of Police Commissioner personally goes into a saloon and picks a fight with its patrons? Can a city of New York's stature long afford leadership of this kind?' "

Uncanny as ever, Jake's imitation of the flint in Andrew's voice. He could hardly wait to hear what else the rival commissioner might have to say, once he learned about the resumption of the altercation later, in the park.

" 'Isn't it interesting, how trouble just seems to follow our Theodore, no matter where he goes?' "

"Trouble was following me, all right, but not from Feeney's. From earlier." Roosevelt ran it down for the newspaperman as he extracted a new suit from the closet: who he thought the bushwhackers were, and why. Whether it had something to do with the banning of beer on a Sunday, or the plans for an honest-to-God flying machine.

Riis's eyes went out of focus. "An airship?" Was that what it was about? "Is such a thing really possible?"

"These people think so," Teddy could only reply, slipping into new trousers. "Look what they've done to get their hands on those drawings. Jake, you can be a big help to me on this." He pulled the wrinkled photograph of the inventor out of the discarded suit. "Charles DeLacy."

Astonishment refocused Riis's eyes. "How old was he, twelve?"

"Twenty-one." What T.R. needed was Jake in contact with the *Sun*'s bureau in Paris. "Get me the details of the killing. Police reports, newspaper items. Eyewitnesses, if any exist."

"I can have the cable out within the hour." As soon as the reporter went down to the phone in the Roosevelt vestibule, in fact: whoever was manning the rewrite desk on Park Row would take care of it.

"One thing more, more important." The Commissioner stopped Riis at the top of the stairs, fumbling with the elastic of his suspenders. "I have to know who DeLacy saw while he was over there. Who he went to for funding, fellow scientists—even the ladies."

"The ladies." A young man Charles's age, of course there'd be ladies. "You think that's how he was lured to his death?"

"Anything's possible." But finding a Siren was less important than finding the person Charles trusted his papers to. Were there someone in Paris who later returned to America aboard the *Etruria,* "Eureka: we'd know who to go to next, wouldn't we."

"Tall order, Theodore." Perhaps too tall, even for a bureau chief in France.

"But the only thing I can think of at the moment." Had Jake any idea what a live shell could do to a house like this, dropped from one of DeLacy's airships? "What it might do to a structure three times the size and twice as thick—the building in this picture, say?"

Riis glanced at the photo again. "Where is that, Europe?"

"I wish I knew."

"Theodore." Honestly, his wife's tone said as she came by with the tattered suit draped over her arm. "Sometimes that mind of yours is like a sieve."

If Edith knew the place, he knew the place. They had been there together, after all, three years ago. Standing right where that picture was taken, in fact. He, Edith, Elliott—

Suresnes.

The sanitarium at Suresnes, where Elliott had gone for the cure. Where Elliott was staying when he met Mrs. Evans. France, 1893.

What the hell had Charles DeLacy been doing there?

▪ Thunder vibrated in the upstairs hall, Theodore Roosevelt acting like a madman, grabbing his jacket and using the stairs as though it were a firehouse pole.

"Where are you going?" Edith cried, spun by the cyclone.

"To see Mrs. Evans!"

"Can't it wait till tomorrow?" She was talking to his back,

watching from the top of the stoop as her scurrying spouse hailed a cab in the middle of the street, jacket flapping as he climbed aboard even before the horses could be brought to a stop. "You need at least a day to heal!"

"Three thirteen West 102nd," he said to the driver, and "I love you" to Edith. "You might have just told me who DeLacy gave his designs to!"

▪ Mrs. Evans wasn't at home. The Commissioner had rapped on the door more than once, each rap louder than the one before, and still no response from within.

Nobody home.

Impossible. He hadn't rushed across town for nothing: she *had* to be there. "Mrs. Evans!"

"Kicking the lock off won't do you any good, Mr. Roosevelt." It was a small woman in a frayed housecoat and furry slippers, speaking through the summer screen on the door of her own apartment across the hall. "She's out with the boy getting some sun."

"Where?"

"Down by the tracks that go along the river, usually: her son likes the freight trains."

T.R. nodded. "Thank you," he said, remembering an open gate he'd seen on Riverside Drive. If they were going for a walk along the right-of-way, that's how they'd do it, through there. Through that gate.

First glance made his heart sink, however: no sign of a woman and a little boy. Only an engine, a tender, several boxcars, one caboose. A stripe-hatted engineer, his stoker, a brakeman.

"Damn."

Better to wait back at 313. How long could they be, an hour? Two?

"Not too close there, sonny." The engineer momentarily interrupted the trackside conference: a child of four was suddenly poking at one of the switches up the line. A spur into a siding, where the hoppers were stored. Teddy's ears felt as though they were tugging at the rest of his head, turning him back for one last look.

"You heard the man, now, come on." Mrs. Evans was coming out from behind the brick-colored caboose, hand extended. The boy ran to her, shaken. He hadn't expected the rebuke.

"Mommy." Even as he said it his expression brightened. "Look," he gestured. "Uncle Theodore."

Her expression underwent similar metamorphosis. "Mr. Roosevelt. You've been injured."

"Not really," the Commissioner was moved to assure her, finding himself touched by her concern and his own desire to ease her mind. "And you, my boy? Isn't that a tre*men*dous train?"

"Thirty-seven cars." The little head bobbed up and down, with singular enthusiasm. "Mommy helped me count."

"Mommy thinks she might be raising the next captain of the *City of Altoona,*" Mrs. Evans allowed.

"Well, now. Maybe it's time to give the lad some experience with the real thing in that case, to see if driving a locomotive is what he really wants to do once he's all grown up."

"Little kids aren't allowed in big locomotives, though." Or so his mother had said.

"And she was one hundred percent correct," Teddy declared. "Except when exemption is made for a special friend of New York City's Police Department."

"Have you the authority, really?" Mrs. Evans was fascinated. "Isn't the right-of-way private property?"

"Since when does the long arm of the law stop at private property?" Cheerfully said as Roosevelt took a step or two in the direction of the crew. "Gentlemen, a word?"

"Commissioner?"

"Perhaps you could do me a small favor." Assuming they weren't about to start a run in the next few minutes or so?

"Got a real sweet repair job going here," the engineer informed him. "We'll be lucky to roll before ten tonight—four hours behind schedule." The eyes darted downward at the child, crinkling back to the horizontal. "That the 'small favor'?"

A nod. "Do you know anyone that age who doesn't want to work on the railroad?"

"Put the throttle in his hands, you mean."

"If it wouldn't be too much trouble."

"Hey," came the reply. "He's a special friend of Teddy Roosevelt."

"He's my nephew," Teddy Roosevelt said, loud. Clear. "Can't get more special than that."

"No, sir," the engineer agreed, taking the boy by the hand as Mrs. Evans gripped the Commissioner's arm. "Ready, fella?"

"Ready!" The four-year-old knew his engines, where to mount them, how to reach the cab and hold the control. "Wooo! Wooo!" he shrilled, as accurate a whistle as ever heard on the Albany run. Stylish, even.

"The old eight-oh-seven out of Saranac Lake used to sound like that," his mother was advised. "I think you might actually have yourself a real-live railroad man here, missus. Fair warning."

"Fair warning," Mrs. Evans was willing to agree, leaving her little real-live railroad man in heaven with the engineer. She and Roosevelt walked off into the small grassy field between the tracks and the moss-covered rocks of the riverbank, Elliott's widow finding a handkerchief and taking a moment to blot her eyes. "You don't know how much it meant to me, hearing you call him your nephew."

"It seemed appropriate, given the circumstance." T.R. kicked a pebble up with the tip of his shoe, looking back at the face of his brother in miniature, joyous at the window of the engineer's cab.

"Woo! Woo!" Not the imitation of a child. The whistle itself, an honor accorded no four-year-old any of them knew, except perhaps the engineer's son, once, and a friend of the Vanderbilt young.

"Conceived in France, wasn't he? My nephew?"

"Born in *America.*" There was to be no misunderstanding about that, or about any of the agreements they'd made. If Teddy'd come to renege.

"No." He was there because the time had come to ask her about France, at last, to hear about Elliott and herself. "How you met, when. Where."

How they'd met. Mrs. Evans found herself more touched than she knew how to say, no more having expected the inquiry from

Theodore Roosevelt than the "nephew" just granted her son. "At a café on the *Quai d'Orsay,*" she finally began. *"La Belle Hélène."*

La Belle Hélène.

"You know it?"

"She is better for me than all your doctors, my dear old beloved brother"—Elliott had said it to him there, in that very place, the shadow of the tower dappling the sidewalk table, umbrella and all. *La Belle Hélène,* when Elliott resided at Suresnes.

In the sanitarium at Suresnes.

"No longer necessary," Elliott had insisted in spite of the crème de menthe he sipped. "You see how my consumption is down. Moderation, Teedie. That's what being with Mrs. Evans has taught me. Moderation."

Nothing could drag him back to the inferno, and yet Elliott did go back to Suresnes; he did finish the "course."

"Your doing," the Commissioner presumed, watching the lady tug at a blade of wild grass growing knee-high by the water, freeing it from the hardened soil only after wrapping it around her fist.

"He saved me when I was in the depths. No husband anymore, no life: I owed that man."

She *loved* that man. If Suresnes could make him whole again, she wanted him back there, even if it eventually meant a return not to herself, but to Anna, his wife.

"Either way I was going to lose him, wasn't I." Mrs. Evans let the stalk flutter from her hand, watching it drift out toward the center of the Hudson. "Better he go healthy than dead."

Because he loved her—because she went with him—Elliott took the cure. He abided by the rules, he cooperated with the doctors, he came around. His was the example the other patients could look up to: it was possible to sober up, to return to the responsible life. It was.

They threw him a party when the time came to say *au revoir,* out on the lawn, lanterns glowing on tables draped with blue-checked cloths and Jean, the orderly, playing a bittersweet accordion. Everyone was there, all the doctors and their wives, most of the shut-ins; even Mme. D'Orsin, in whose rooming house Mrs.

Evans found shelter. There was Philippe Crais, who'd supplied her with the freshly baked croissant she brought up the hill with her Tuesday and Saturday mornings, and Henri Jouvette, whose talented needle rejuvenated some of the clothing Elliott originally believed as irredeemable as himself.

"You see how wrong you were about both," the tailor had joked, toasting the guest of honor with a tulipful of Graves while the mineral water and lime in Elliott's glass sparkled like the driest Bollinger. The laughter and the music went on well past midnight.

"Was this man there?" The picture of Charles DeLacy appeared in Roosevelt's hand.

"My Lord." Recognition transformed her: how would Teddy have gotten hold of a picture of her cousin? This picture especially? "Did Elliott have it with his papers?"

The Commissioner shook his head. How he'd come by the photograph was of less moment than the word she'd just used: cousin. How was Mrs. Evans related to Charles?

"His father was my uncle." Her mother's brother. "We were children together in Connecticut." Cos Cob. The friendship maintained itself on into adulthood, if not in person then through the mail. It was good to have someone to confide in when things went sour . . . during DeLacy's problems with Edison, for instance; during the Evanses' divorce. "I wouldn't have even been alive to meet Elliott if it weren't for Charles. He was the one who suggested Europe."

Refuge. Sanctuary. The breakup wasn't her fault but the families didn't want to hear that. Could such a scandal be blamed on anyone other than the wife?

The inventor was hoping to be on the Continent himself, "although it turned out to be months before he could collect enough money." She was already with Elliott at Suresnes by the time Charles arrived.

"Did they get along?"

"So well I might have been jealous"—Mrs. Evans smiled—"if I didn't know your brother better." Elliott had been especially fascinated by Charles's tenure at Menlo Park, short-lived though it had been. "He wanted to hear about everything we could be looking forward to in the twentieth century."

Their discussions went on for hours, sometimes, Elliott very seriously offering to help the younger man raise money for whatever he might be working on.

"Which was?" T.R. did not bother to conceal his interest, or his disappointment when Mrs. Evans had to tell him she never knew.

"Not that he didn't want to let Elliott and me in on it," she was quick to add. "He just thought the financing might be there already and it wouldn't be fair to those investors if he talked without their okay."

There was supposed to be a meeting that night, come to think of it. The night of the party, Elliott's farewell to Suresnes. Charles was going to see the investors at 11 P.M., he'd said.

"What kind of 'investors' do you meet with in the middle of the night?" Teddy couldn't help but be curious to know, a coldness at the base of his spine.

"We thought it pretty strange ourselves." Stranger still was the request her cousin had made of Elliott, pulling him off into a quiet corner while everyone else was watching the impromptu cancan Mme. Jouvette had begun with the even more exuberant Mme. D'Orsin.

"Would you mind keeping this for me?" Charles had asked, indicating a small leather-bound portfolio he'd been carrying, a padlock of appropriate size securing the handles. "It's only going to be in the way tonight."

He could pick it up at breakfast or, if that would be cutting it too close, perhaps at the station before Elliott boarded the boat train to Le Havre?

"I'll guard it with my life," a phrase which made the President of New York City's Police Board squeeze his eyes shut when Mrs. Evans repeated it. I'll guard it with my life.

At least as far as his cabin on the A Deck of the Cunard he'd guard it, France long since gone over the stern. When there was no possible last minute in which to expect that Charles would show up with the claim check.

"Why would Charles go to the *Etruria,* what sense does that make?" Hadn't T.R. heard what she'd said? "Elliott gave him his case back at the train."

"You saw that?"

"No." There'd been a mix-up with the luggage and Teddy's brother'd gone to straighten it out. "That's where he ran into Charles." Her cousin had sent his apologies back with Elliott: "his all-night meeting hadn't really adjourned, it was only in recess and he had to return to it right away; I don't see why you're having so much trouble with that."

Charles certainly wouldn't have wanted his property returned to New York, would he?

"Of course not," the Commissioner said, distracted. She didn't know. Even now, after how many years? Elliott had lied to her, deliberately lied to her, and she didn't know.

To protect her on general principles? To protect her because he was going to deal with the same people who butchered DeLacy, or others equally perfidious? Elliott, damn it, you had the word even then, hadn't you: her cousin was dead.

"Mr. Roosevelt, please. If you have a reason to think Charles wasn't there to pick up his case, isn't it time to say?"

Gently, he told himself. Gently. This was someone he'd taken a lifetime to come to terms with, a woman who'd been hurt too much, all down the line.

"You never heard from him again, did you."

Her fingers fought with the wind from Poughkeepsie: a wayward strand of her auburn hair semaphored in front of her face. "The relatives got to him," Mrs. Evans had presumed, no other alternative acceptable. Not when Charles himself was the one who'd given her the news, how badly both sides of the family had taken the divorce. The shame of it all. The reflection on them.

How deplorable that he still intended to look her up when he got to France, especially when some of his potential funding could have been contingent on the high moral character of his associations.

"Keep your distance," that would have been her own advice, but Charles wouldn't do that. "He went to France, he came to

Suresnes; I'm sure he's over there right now building whatever it is they gave him the money for."

"He's dead, Mrs. Evans."

No, her look replied. Impossible. Whoever told him that was a liar.

"The French police."

"The French police." She might have been saying Jack the Ripper.

"I wish it weren't true," Roosevelt blurted. "I wouldn't have had to come to you about any of this, I could have talked to him." How quickly they fogged, the lenses in this back-up pair of *pincenez.* "What either of us want doesn't change the facts; I'm sorry." Sorrier, perhaps, than Mrs. Evans might ever know.

A single breath, the kind you blow candles out with. "When?"

"That night." The party night. "Sometime before dawn," in the Commissioner's estimation.

"Two years ago now." Two years of being shut out. Shunned. Two years of believing Charles finally got smart and started listening to the family.

Self-deception was easy at first, all she had to do was disregard the Charles she used to know, the one who'd laugh when someone tried to dictate his behavior. A snap, until Elliott died. Until Elliott died, and a letter to France seemed the only way to expiate the grief. But the handwritten envelope reappeared in her mailbox, the purple stamp of the Parisian postmaster affixed. *Destinataire inconnu,* it said. Addressee unknown. Return to sender.

"So what?" she attempted to tell herself. "The French mails can't find people who've been living in the same place for a hundred years. They're notorious."

"Notorious," T.R. had to agree. A letter from Alice to Auntie Bye in Neuilly, properly addressed, had boomeranged back to Sagamore Hill not once but three times.

"How did he die?" It was down to that now, wasn't it. "An accident? Illness?"

"Murder." Roosevelt touched the back of her hand, watching what shock could do to the prettiest face.

"Who?" Who would want to do that to someone as decent as Charles?

"Robbers, the French think."

"You don't?"

The Commissioner let a pair of battling gulls distract his eyes upward for a moment. "His 'investors' killed him," he wanted her to know, and he wanted her to know that they then came to America, to get the plans they'd tortured him for. "I think you might have seen two of them."

Her memory needed no jog, the image immediate in her mind. "Those two well-dressed young gentlemen the day Elliott died . . . ?" The pair coming out of 313 West just as Mrs. Evans and Elliott's son were coming home?

Gentlemen. Never before had Theodore heard the word turned over like that, as though it were the rock on top of a colony of worms.

"We're beginning to close in on them now," and this talk was going to speed the inevitable arrests. It was. "They aren't going to get away with any of this."

She was in tears now, unashamed, leaning on Teddy's shoulder and crying.

"Uncle Theodore?" The child, returned from his stationary ride in the engine. "Why does Mommy always cry whenever you come to visit her?"

"Oh, no, my darling," Mrs. Evans insisted as she swept the Commissioner's nephew up into her arms. "You mustn't think badly of your uncle. We're all very good friends now." Her glistening eyes sought Roosevelt's. "Aren't we?"

"Indeed we are, madam," he was pleased to say. "Indeed we are."

11 THACKERY

▪ "I'm stymied, Jake. Stumped."

The realization struck home ninety minutes after T.R. left Mrs. Evans and ninety minutes before he finally managed to reach the reporter at home, when the Commissioner was shirt-sleeved in the basement storeroom of the Hall house at 11 West Thirty-seventh Street. When he was going through the contents of his brother's old steamer trunk for yet one more time. When all that was left was the detritus. Somewhere among these timetables and matchbooks, these programs and napkins and menus, Teddy would locate a name, react to a reference . . . know where to go.

So neat. So logical. The only place the evidence could be, he'd told himself as he traveled downtown. Was Elliott not the middleman he'd been looking for, the intermediary between Charles and the gang? Had he not established direct contact with them just prior to his death, when he was so eagerly anticipating that move up to Easy Street?

Give Roosevelt even the most cryptic of notes, let him find a diary, an appointment book—a picture—and that would be that, by Godfrey. The roundup could begin.

Eleanor's joy at the sight of him was an omen. "Look, Uncle Theodore," she'd said, tagging behind as her grandmother unlocked the door at the top of the cellar stairs. "Baby Joss is out of the hospital, see? He came through with flying colors." Her fingers unwrapped the ribbon which served as bandage from around the little rag neck, her eyes in search of sanction. Teddy agreed, didn't he? The doll was as good as new . . . ?

"Absolutely," Roosevelt assured her, not liking what the desperation in her eyes was doing to his omen, not needing the cautionary glance from Mary. "You don't see needlework like this every day, not even at Abercrombie and Fitch. If I don't know better, Nell, I'd have thought this was how Mr. Joss came in the first place."

"Grandma sews better than anybody," the girl beamed, relieved to have the endorsement. And yet there still was something unsettling about it all, wasn't there, the sense of something more changed than not. Life had seeped through those beautiful stitches, and deny it though Eleanor might, Baby Joss was going to spend more time alone on top of the dresser from here on in, alone on the floor of the closet. He'd be left behind when she sailed off to Allenswood boarding school in England.

Perhaps she'd pull him from the darkness upon her return, to hug him, perhaps, or to laugh at this relic of childhood before she threw it away. There were several steamer trunks in the basement. Eleanor's was one. Elliott's, another.

Timetables, matchbooks, theater bills and menus: none of them were annotated. No diary turned up. No appointment book.

No photograph.

"Jake," he complained when the newspaperman got on the line well after eleven that night. "I'm stymied. Stumped. I could have sworn Elliott would have kept some kind of record, something this important."

"Did you look in the lining?" Riis's question made the Commissioner laugh. He'd looked under the seam of every lining he could find, beginning with the trunk itself.

"And what good did it do me?" Was it too soon to ask if Paris had been heard from?

"You've got to give it at least two days, Theodore."

"Theodore's impatient, not being able to think of any other way to turn." An uncharacteristic cynicism edged his voice. Here he'd

had such great expectations. The pot of gold at the end of this
long hard rainbow would be in the form of a name. A bunch of
names. A final gift from a brother who had to know how important the legacy was.

Even in this, failure.

"I know Elliott, Jake. I know everything that happened on that
boat. I know everything except who."

■ *Charles is dead. He is lying with no face in the mud at the
bottom of a ditch, because of what's in this portfolio.*

Should he open it? See what it is that makes people kill?

*Or should he just throw the damn thing overboard and be free of
it before it turns on him, too?*

*They are a day at sea, with five days left before Pier 56 at the foot
of good old Thirteenth Street. Curiosity can be gratified here because, once it is, he can still send the sword of Damocles to Davy
Jones. Do with it what you will.*

An hour of staring at the case. Two.

Perhaps a crème de menthe?

The fingers tremble and go to it; the lock is picked. Not hard.

*Scientific drawings. Twenty . . . thirty . . . designs for a fly-
ing machine. An airship. For this, death by the club? The fist? For
yet one more post–da Vinci flight of fancy?*

So far, not one has actually flown, not one.

*Yet Charles is lying with no face in the mud at the bottom of a
ditch in Meaux and these renderings are the cause. Could it be that
this one would work? That this one would go up?*

*Oh, yes, this is for Davy. This is to go over the side in the middle
of the night; no one is to know it ever was.*

*Another crème de menthe. Thank you. Thank you very much, I
think I'll sip it out on deck.*

*The stars swarm over his head and reflect in the water, stretched
and spiraled and deep. Elliott raises the leather briefcase high over
his head. Perhaps he even commences the downward swing.*

*But he catches himself. It's too quick, this way, all the ramifica-
tions not really considered. They have to be considered, how they
apply to what Teedie would call the march of mankind.*

How they apply to the future of Elliott Roosevelt.

A glance over his shoulder. Who's there? Is someone there? Hello?

Hello?

No one. Only the water and the stars.

Waltz music from the salon. Distant laughter. It's too dangerous, keeping it with him in his cabin. Anyone on board, first class or belowdecks—any member of the ship's company, in fact—could be one of the men who left Charles dead.

Eliminate the purser's safe.

Eliminate any place on board in which all thirty-plus pages of diagram could be stored, ensemble.

Separately, though? Page by page?

Remember your natural history, Teedie? Remember in whose nest the cuckoo plants its egg?

Elliott descends into the hold of the Etruria, *fortified with brandy. One more crème de menthe. Is anybody on guard? Is anybody there?*

Apparently not.

So many trunks. Valises. Carpetbags. And so few protected by locks. What need? The incidence of theft in the first-class locker at sea is nil. No one even thinks about it.

Besides. Elliott isn't opening these pieces to take anything out. He's opening them up to put something in. Carefully prying up the tacks and clips that hold the linings in place. Smoothing out the fabric with each cuckoo egg beneath, flat. Imperceptible.

Of course he notes the names on the trunks, on the jewelry boxes, on the saddle. How can he not, if only for his own protection?

A crumpled piece of scratch paper, shoved into the back pocket of his pants afterward.

Steward: a bottle of your finest to stateroom 34, please; there'll be a little something extra in it for you if you make it especially quick, yes? I have the thirst again.

Damn you, Charlie. I was cured, did you hear that before you asked me your favor and left for your meeting? The doctors said I was cured.

■ He'd sent the telegram when they put in at Halifax. "My dear old beloved brother," it began. "I will be returning to New York aboard S.S. *Etruria,* docking Thursday, one p.m. Please meet me; it is of the utmost importance we speak, a matter of considerable urgency."

And then he went back to his cabin on A Deck and drank the rest of the bottle there, ordering more, until he reached insensibility. Teedie wouldn't meet the boat in Manhattan on Thursday, Teedie'd be afraid that Mrs. Evans would be there and Teedie didn't want to have to look Mrs. Evans in the face and say, "How d'you do."

Hell. Why didn't he put that in the telegram? "Am traveling alone, rest assured." Words to that effect.

Too much crème de menthe, Ellie. Too much cognac. Shame on you.

A laugh, a snore: they carried Elliott Roosevelt off the liner on a stretcher, Anna Hall Roosevelt burying her wasted face in the bosom of her mother, unable to look. Unable to breathe. Wanting to die.

They sent him to Illinois. Dr. Keeley in Dwight could cure the alcoholic with his patented Bi-Chloride of Gold Cure and after that the alcoholic could go to Virginia. There was an estate in need of management there.

The scrap of paper in the back pocket of the trousers he had on when they evacuated him from the *Etruria* had long since been burned by then, incinerated with the rest of the vomit-stained wool.

■ There were two scientific sketches on his desk when the President of the Police Board sat down to work at eight the following morning, two sketches in a familiar style, signed by a familiar name. And there was Minnie Gertrude Kelly, lingering in the open doorway between the outer office and the inner sanctum, trying not to preen *too* much.

"By Jove." Roosevelt held them up to the light, swelling a little himself. "Where did these come from?"

She handed him her copy of the ship's manifest, two names

checked off. Mr. and Mrs. Milton Shaw of Nyack, New York. The Reverend and Mrs. Timothy Singleton, the First Methodist Church of Astoria.

"You went to see these people? When?" As far as Teddy knew, his secretary had been at her desk before eight each morning, not going home until well after seven in the evening.

"Sometimes I didn't go straight home." Nyack wasn't that much of a journey by railroad: thirty-five minutes from the Grand Central Terminal at Forty-second and Park: "I could be there by eight and home by ten-thirty." Astoria was even more convenient; Minnie'd arrived at her parents' house in Brooklyn Heights only a few minutes past nine.

"What did they say when you told them who you were and what you were looking for, the Shaws and the Singletons?" T.R. could imagine the reactions greeting the girl: was it really proper for a young lady of breeding to be out on her own like this after dark?

"They recognized me, actually." Mr. Roosevelt's new girl secretary, they remembered her picture in the paper. Come in! Come in!

Her cheeks tingled even now as she relived it in her mind, how immediate it had been: the recognition.

"Makes you feel like a million, doesn't it." The Commissioner knew, and his hands beat a commemorative tattoo on the edge of the desk. Publishing Minnie's portrait under all those banner headlines didn't only keep that initial break-in at Frick's house off page one, it gave them two more Charles DeLacy originals as well. Not that either would provide them with more information than they already had, but so what? "It's two less drawings for whoever it is we're up against out there."

Had Richard checked in?

"He called me at home, last night." Atypically demure, not the Minnie Kelly who took herself to Astoria and Nyack, leading her employer to presume that the call was more personal than professional . . . ?

If so, "his intentions had damn well better be honorable," that was all Theodore Roosevelt could say.

"I'll let you know after lunch this afternoon," she replied, feeling familiar enough to let her anticipation show. "He's taking me to Tony Pastor's Restaurant."

A whistle. Who wouldn't be impressed? The hint of occasion was in the air. "You tell him for me I'll whale him within an inch of his life, he doesn't come through with a proposal. The whaling'll be for real this time."

"How to put a man in a romantic mood." Minnie couldn't help grinning as she went to answer the ringing telephone.

"Just don't be so romantic you forget to bring back any of the drawings *he* might have come up with, *A* to *H*."

The expression darkened on her face. It had been the one sour note in their conversation, Richard in frustration forced to admit no luck even half as good as hers. Not one of the people listed on his part of the *Etruria* manifest had any papers secreted behind the lining of any traveling case.

"Commissioner Roosevelt's office, may I help you?"

His mind went racing while she listened to the caller. No pages in anyone's luggage, *A* to *H*? Chance? Could the luggage in the ship's hold have been arranged in such a way that Elliott never got to even approach those particular pieces?

Possible, depending on whether Cunard's system was alphabetical or by stateroom number: Witherspoon could tell him that, although Teddy could think of another explanation a whole lot more possible, a whole lot more simple.

They had been beaten to the punch. The enemy had long since dropped in on the *A*'s through the *H*'s, looked under those linings and taken the prizes. Every last one.

Minnie was extending the phone, befuddled. Making no bones about it. " 'The Great Felice' is returning your call?"

Who?

Oh. Yes. Right. "Felice!" T.R. boomed, confiscating the instrument. *"Come state?"*

"Bene," came the response, adding to Roosevelt's delight.

"You're doing well in New York? You don't miss *Le Grand Guignol?"*

"Teodoro. How many cut throats can someone make up before

he gets bored from his mind? How many broken heads?" Dressing
the ladies of the chorus was so much more rewarding. Paris had
been gay, amusing, lucrative, yes, "but New York? So exciting
these days. So new."

"Don't tell me you've forgotten how to do bruises, though."
Mock alarm filled the Commissioner's voice. When it came to
gore, no one was better than the Great Felice. No one.

"I forget *niente.* There is a job?" The New York City Police
were in need of some greasepaint, expertly applied?

"About three days' worth of rubber hose. Can do?"

"Can do?" Was there ever a doubt? *"Teodoro,* I will make it so
people will have trouble with their lunch, looking at you."

People might have trouble with their lunch looking at him as it
was, Teddy had to think, catching a glimpse of his reflection in the
glass of the window behind the stuffed bear. What did Edith say
about that shiner? Every color of the rainbow, with an emphasis
on the black—purple and black.

"It's not for me, Felice." He told the makeup man about Richard, how the patrolman had to look when he went back undercover with Hanrahan and the boys.

"They will pin the medal on his chest when I am finished, these
scum," Felice swore. "To work on so brave a man as your Officer
Kerner, this is an honor."

At five the following afternoon Richard would limp away from
the Forty-first Precinct, face and forearms brutally discolored, his
back a mass of welts. But his head would be high: he'd have
withstood the worst that bastard Meeghan could dish out and
Estes Hanrahan wouldn't think twice about where the prodigal
was.

Or what he'd been doing.

▪ Parker's call came next.

"Theodore," he said in sandpapered tones, "what's this 'order'
you issued for next Sunday. 'Number 187-A, All Leaves and Va-
cations Rescinded'?" Since when did a single commissioner have
the right to deploy a full contingent of men on the day of rest?

"Is there a problem with that, Andrew?" For the life of him, the President of the Police Board just couldn't imagine what. "Can you think of another way to make sure we play no favorites, enforcing the Sunday Closing Act?"

"Have you any idea what that's going to cost?"

Cost? "A price tag on the equal administration of justice? Andrew." Tsk. Surely Mulberry Street's most outspoken law-and-order man wasn't calling because across-the-borough observance might mean cocktails and dinner at home rather than in the elegant Gotham Club?

"The Gotham Club," Parker wanted him to know, "is a private establishment."

"So is Feeney's Tavern on West Seventy-second Street." A shadow fell over Roosevelt's face as he spoke: Jacob Riis standing in the open door, a large cablegram held up in his hand. Have I got news for you, his expression was saying. Have I got news.

"*Gentlemen* patronize the 'elegant' Gotham Club," for Theodore's information. "And furthermore—"

"I'm sorry, Andrew, my nine o'clock appointment just walked in. Can we pick this up later?"

"My watch says eight twenty-five."

"Overwinding will do that: you might want to have a jeweler take a look at that mainspring." Parting advice, spoken into a still-squawking receiver even as T.R. was lowering it onto the cradle, turning his attention to the newcomer. "You've heard from France?"

A nod, but with a *caveat.* "Don't get carried away too fast: I'm not sure any of this is going to help get us out of the dead end."

"It can't lock us in any more than we already are." Roosevelt gestured at the loops of paper hot off the transoceanic wire. "What've you got?"

"This, to begin at the beginning." Part of a social column published in Paris, an English-language weekly.

"Inventor Arrives," according to the squib. "Mr. Charles DeLacy, recently associated with the New Jersey laboratories of Thomas A. Edison, has arrived on the Continent for a brief stay. 'Primarily a busman's holiday,' he is quoted as saying, 'the intention being to acquaint myself with the latest developments on the

European scientific scene, and to meet with as many of the people involved in it as I can.' "

"Not nearly as blunt as he was when he was the sorcerer's apprentice," Teddy observed. "Is there a date on that?"

Riis showed it to him. "Seven days before he was killed. One week." The postmortem followed, copied out by the operator at the bureau on the Rue d'Orléans. "What you want to look at is on the bottom. 'Conclusions.' "

"That DeLacy was tortured for several hours before he died, by as many as three or four men?" T.R. could draw his own conclusions all too well. "Injuries like these are damned specific, wouldn't you say?" Did the Great Felice think he could turn a man's stomach? Compared to this, the Great Felice was a rank amateur.

"But it proves the theory, I think. This was no ordinary highway robbery," not as far as Roosevelt could see. "Highway robbers don't linger over their victims like that." An interrogation: that's what went on in that ravine. "Charles's 'investors,' or should I say inquisitors? 'Where're the plans? Where'd you hide the plans?' "

He was stronger than they'd thought, wasn't he.

"You'd have a case if he were the only one." The reporter directed the Commissioner's attention to another set of paragraphs translated from the Morse.

Dismay. "There were others?"

"Two before, three after."

"Marauders at large in the countryside," this excerpt screamed. "Six victims named." Now did Theodore see why the French police couldn't regard Charles's death with anything like the special attention William DeLacy demanded? This killing was one in a series, and the fact that Charles was an inventor didn't really lead the *gendarmes* anywhere. So some "designs" were missing, according to the list of possessions supplied by the father, William? So what? Were the shoes not missing as well? The watch?

Loot was loot, T.R. could hear them say. It's disintegrating in the mud at the bottom of the Seine if it can't be fenced like everything else. No doubt.

Everything else . . . could there be something to save all the good hard logic among the rest of the valuables stripped from the corpse? Was William's list somewhere in that elongated cable?

"Page two, bottom," Riis replied, snapping at the corner with the back of his finger. "Signet ring . . ."

Signet ring. Beaver-skin coat. The pair of brown leather boots. Pocket watch and chain.

"Diamond stickpin," Teddy noted. "Matching tie clip." Had any of these items turned up on the black market?

"Unmentioned." Jake could send a new cable.

"Why not?" The Commissioner walked, he turned, he kicked the wastebasket across the room, letting it clatter against the wall.

"What was that?" Minnie asked, starting up from her desk.

"Me being even more frustrated than Richard," her boss rasped. Dammit, Roosevelt didn't care who else they found out there, "Charles DeLacy is a separate case!" His putative investors had to have either taken advantage of the ongoing crime spree, "or they went out and hired some bastards to do the same kind of knife work, nothing else adds up."

"How sad," the secretary felt compelled to observe. "Of all the people the man could have gone to for money, he picks these."

"Yes, but not out of thin air," T.R. was certain. "Not eeny-meeny-miney-mo." There had to have been a recommendation. "A Judas goat." And what he'd give to get a line on whoever that was.

"Some people accept eyeteeth. Me," Riis reminded him, "I'll go for the meager little exclusive, as usual."

"Jake?" What else was lurking in those typewritten sheets?

"See for yourself." The journalist hadn't quite known what to make of it before, if anything—the back page he was now handing over.

"Connoisseurs Gather in Paris," according to the modest headline. "Harbinger Named Spokesman."

"*Maurice* Harbinger?"

"Maurice Harbinger," Riis confirmed, "discussing an auction of fine art held a few days before, in the Hague." Including such just-sold masterpieces as *Sir William Pensionner and Family*.

"By Godfrey, look what else this says!" T.R. read it aloud, for Minnie's benefit, and his own. " 'The proprietor of New York's well-known *Galerie des Artistes* was interviewed while dining at Maxim's with former Edison associate . . .' "

" '. . . Charles DeLacy,' " his secretary didn't need to be told.

"When," that was what Teddy wanted to know next. "How long before Meaux? This is something else I need a date on, Jake." There was a date.

"Do you know what this means? Do you?" The Commissioner's whisper filled the chamber. "Not only does my friend Mr. Harbinger collect art and antiques, he invents things, just as Charles does. He is up on all the latest scientific advances, a member of the Society for Individual Accomplishment. Motion Pictures. Fingerprints. And there he is in Paris, approached by this acquaintance from Menlo Park—someone, incidentally, he now claims to not even remember—someone who comes to him for a line on capital.

" 'For what?' Maurice inquires.

" 'For a flying machine,' Maurice is told. Can he help?

"Can he help? Damn right he can 'help,' he can help turn the DeLacy airship into the Harbinger, that's how he can help."

"You wouldn't think it to look at him, would you," said Riis, taking notes. "The last guy you'd expect to kill for something that wasn't his."

"Not really," the way Roosevelt saw it. "The man knows almost every industrialist and financier in town, he's been furnishing their houses for years. Guggenheim, Belmont, Huntington, there might be twenty of them who'd jump at the chance to back a project like this. Daniel Thackery, even. Show any one of them enough of the drawings and he's on his way. He's—"

"Theodore?"

Edith was right. A sieve, his memory. Full of stupid holes. "I could kick myself!"

Blank stares. Kick himself about what?

"Daniel Thackery, didn't you just hear me say the name?" The walls began to reverberate as the backwash of Teddy's exit slammed into them broadside. Jake had to hold his hat, Minnie the desk.

"Thackery's in on it with Harbinger, is that the story?" One last question, yelled down the stairs from the landing on the second floor.

"All I know is what I got straight from the horse's mouth," T.R. called back, the front doors of the building yielding before the one-man flood. "Maurice took some kind of invention to Thackery for financing. I want to know whether it was a flying machine or not, don't you?"

▪ Daniel Thackery was not in to visitors at this time of the day. "He is in his rejuvenation chamber," whatever that was, "and will see no one." The explanation came courtesy of a supercilious factotum in a gray-striped morning coat, obese, with crumbs on his vest.

"Correction," Roosevelt emphasized. "He'll see me. *Now.*" Or the gelatinous gentleman would be seeing the inside of the tank at Mulberry Street, having interfered with a police official in the performance of duty. "Clear?"

"Since you put it that way, sir." If the Commissioner would follow him to the dressing room?

*"De*lighted," even if the Commissioner had no intention of dressing, either up or down.

"As you wish, of course," said the steward, a trace of his initial smirk returned to his face as he led Teddy into the windowless cubicle at the end of the corridor, pulling a drape aside to reveal a rack and several satin-padded hangers. "You can put your clothing in here, if you want. Otherwise, it's directly through that door." The one the stench was coming from.

"My recommendation is that you do strip down: the odor tends to permeate wool for weeks. Some say it never leaves."

T.R. could imagine. "Are you telling me Daniel Thackery, one of the richest, most powerful men in the world, is sitting in some sort of indoor outhouse?"

"Rejuvenation chamber."

Sparring with this man would be a waste of time. Teddy scowled and went inside, shoulders squared.

■ "Good for you," said the aging, wispy-haired old head sticking up out of the trapezoidal box in the center of the inner sanctum. "That's the Theodore Roosevelt I read about in the papers all the time, ducking neither bullets nor shit."

"Compost doesn't faze me, no," Theodore Roosevelt assured him.

" 'Compost' suggests the vegetable. This, I assure you, sir, is one hundred percent fauna."

"Why bother with halfway measures."

"Exactly." Thackery cackled. "You think I'm off my rocker?"

"Most people don't sit neck-deep in a vat of feces."

"Most people should. Oh, yes," the tycoon proselytized. "It's been scientifically proven. People live twenty years longer doing this on a twice-a-week basis. The combination of tactile contact with organic material and the breathing of the fumes: that's what does it."

Lesson learned from no less than Friedrich Krupp of Germany. Did the Commissioner know the name?

"Munitions manufacturer in Essen, I think."

"Bully," followed by a series of quacks and a sharp snapping sound, the millionaire releasing the catch on the slanted doors of the cabinet, rising like some prehistoric creature out of the slime. "I love an educated man, even if he didn't come here to talk about the way to perfect health."

"I'm more concerned with an art dealer named Harbinger today," Teddy had to acknowledge as Thackery in all his wizened nakedness sat himself down in a Victorian bathtub brimming with gallons of ice water. "Part-time inventor; he might have submitted something to you."

"And so he did," if memory served. "A rather ingenious 'safety' razor. 'Within two years we can eliminate the straight edge and the strop,' he told me. You can imagine how disappointed he was to learn he was already two years too late."

"Someone else has, what'd you call it? A 'safety' razor?"

"King Gillette. We've been working on it for two years now, whether Mr. Harbinger believes it or not." Thackery shifted in the tub, reaching for the cigar on the platform alongside. "Needless to say, all the papers from the patent office are appropriately dated."

Puff.

Puff.

"Is that it, Commissioner? Harbinger's claims to the safety razor?"

"No. His claims to the flying machine."

The entrepreneur swallowed his smoke down the wrong pipe, his cigar dropping into the icy water and going out with a witch's hiss. "How did you know about that?"

"Confirm it for me first: Maurice Harbinger did present you with plans for an airship." T.R. leaned forward, retrieving the soggy cigar, replacing it on the platform. Anything to keep from flying out of the room right then and there without the benefit of machinery.

"I wish," Thackery was responding. Money would have been forthcoming in two seconds flat, had there been plans, a prospectus. "All I got was a lot of talk."

Anybody could talk.

"When?" It was very important that Roosevelt know when.

"Two years ago . . . a little less." The owner of *La Galerie des Artistes* had promised to return with all the prerequisites. "I'm still waiting."

"You may wait forever if I get to him first." Now the Commissioner could leave. Now he could call Richard and Jake, and Minnie, and take a final trip to Twenty-third Street.

"Looking for something to invest in, are you?" Daniel Thackery flicked a stray piece of brownish material off his upper arm and reached for a scrub brush. Teddy handed it to him.

"Not something to invest in, sir," he crowed. "Something to hang."

12 HARBINGER

■ The maître d' would have seated them at an open table near the kitchen, but Tony Pastor was there that afternoon and Tony Pastor wouldn't hear of it. "What's the matter with you today, don't you have eyes?" The young man in the natty bow tie and striped summer jacket had brought the young lady here to propose marriage; if that wasn't obvious, nothing was. "Where is your sense of romance?"

Richard Kerner and Minnie Kelly were seated in one of the curtained booths and presented with a complimentary bottle of the establishment's finest, the Moët, 1880.

"I pop the cork," the restaurateur crooned, "you pop whatever, like the question." He withdrew before the officer could do more than blush.

"Well," he finally found himself grinning, "how could I disappoint Tony Pastor?"

She was very fond of that grin; she had been from the first. "If I'd known you could be bought for a bottle of champagne, I might have done it months ago."

His hand reached out across the table, cupping hers. "You wouldn't have needed to." The truth was that he'd been bowled over by the sight of her and what a surprise. What a surprise. "I really thought I was immune."

He preferred it, being immune. A person in law enforcement was better off not involving himself—or anyone else—in a traditional relationship, it wasn't fair. He'd be out on the street where the felons were, a lightning rod drawing knives and guns and God knows what else, and she'd be lying awake in their bed at home, wondering, worrying, waiting—

True—images of it were lambent in Minnie's restless mind almost every night, ever since she realized she wanted him: could she stand up to the strain? The potential knock on the door at two in the morning, the unexpected telephone call from the precinct captain, or even the Commissioner of Police?

"Minnie . . . there's been an accident . . ."

"Minnie . . . something's happened to Richard . . ."

"Minnie . . ."

But less than two percent of the officer corps were ever injured while on duty. Less than that ever gave their lives to protect the citizens of the city from harm. Most never even had to draw their guns, not once in their entire careers. Not once.

Not bad, those odds. And something else, more important: "I love you."

"I love you." God was his witness. "That's why I wasn't sure if it was right for me to ask you to marry me, to put up with this life."

This life which could come to a sudden end, anyday. *To*day.

"One day, one year, one hundred years, whatever we have together I'll take." It was better than nothing at all.

"Yes," he whispered, putting his arm behind the slimness of her waist, pulling her into an embrace on the red velvet banquette. "Will you marry me, Minnie Kelly?"

"Just try and stop me," she suggested, kissing him right on the lips. It was shocking and brazen. But called for.

When he caught his breath he said, "Maybe we ought to keep a symbol of our intentions in plain sight, just in case some coldhearted official from the police department happens to peek through that crack in the curtain."

"Let him."

"Why cause a scandal when I have the perfect solution to the problem right here?" The ring which had graced the pinky of Richard's right hand now found itself fitted over the third finger of Minnie's left. "It's not the diamond you're going to come with me to pick out, but this isn't the first time I've had to come up with something on the spur of the moment."

"You know what?" she confided, marveling at how much a part of her the little circle of engraved silver could become, so quickly. "This is all I need."

All she could ever want.

"Fine," her fiancé acceded. "But I happen to be a little more traditional. Which means an engagement ring with a diamond, the blessings of your father; I'm talking about doing it right. Everything from engraved announcements to a bridal shower, church wedding, sit-down reception; I want a honeymoon that starts off with a shower of rice and you throwing the bouquet."

"You're the boss."

"Not until the rice and the bouquet," said Theodore Roosevelt, stepping through that crack in the curtain, beaming. "Till then *I'm* the boss." He gave Minnie the eye, holding the *pince-nez* up by hand, remembering how much more formidable it made the eye. "That was the tag end of a marriage proposal I overheard, I hope. You did tell this fellow what I'd do if it wasn't?"

She displayed the ring, delighted to inform him that a thrashing wasn't even remotely apropos.

"*Congrat*ulations. *Congrat*ulations." Teddy pumped the officer's hand as though they were out on the hustings, candidate and voter. "Now I don't have to feel so guilty about taking you away before you've had the chance to eat your engagement dinner."

"Take him away? Now?" Rebellion. Minnie's demanding employer had asked a lot of her these past months, and she had given him a lot. But this was too much.

"What'd I say about some coldhearted official from the police department?" An aside, wry and playful, but intentional: Richard's aside to help her suppress whatever it was she'd otherwise blurt, and later regret.

Was something up with Hanrahan?

T.R. shook his head. "Harbinger." Minnie hadn't filled the officer in yet, understandable considering the circumstances. First things first.

"The art dealer? What about him?"

It was Minnie who furnished the explanation, feeling obliged, bringing Richard up to Daniel Thackery's part in the story as far as she knew it, giving Roosevelt a glance as she finished. "Thackery confirmed your guess, didn't he? The invention Harbinger brought him was the flying machine?"

"Excuse me," Officer Kerner interrupted. "Harbinger's invention was a what?"

"I'll give you the details on our way to the gallery," the Commissioner promised, sweeping the curtain aside for their departure from the booth.

"You're *leaving?*" Tony Pastor bustled over, mortified. "The complimentary champagne wasn't flat, was it?"

"Of course not," the bride-to-be started to assure him, but their host wanted to hear it from Teddy, this debacle was all his doing, and how could he? How?

"Here I thought you of all people would know when to put in an appearance." And when to not. "I am very disappointed in you. Very."

"Shall I tell you what *I'm* disappointed in, Mr. Pastor?" The voice was T.R.'s most public. "I'm disappointed that there are people in this world who take things that don't belong to them and use force to do it, or coercion. I'm disappointed that it doesn't stop at coercion sometimes, that murder is even a word in the dictionary. I'm disappointed that there are occasions I have to send a fine young specimen of American manhood like this into what might as well be called combat, often on no notice. A baseball game, a bath, a proposal of marriage, whatever it is doesn't matter: he goes, and do you know why, Mr. Pastor? Because it's his job. And his brand-new fiancée stands by him because that's *her* job. New York is damned lucky to have people like this looking after us, believe you me."

A wall of applause exploded up from the palms of every last diner present. "That's telling him, Teddy!" came the cry, accompanied by shrill whistles and the stamping of feet, the clanging of silverware against the gilded rims of leaded crystal and fine bone china. "Go get the bastards!"

"Our exact intention," the Commissioner was glad to let them know as, waving, displaying those ferocious teeth, he ushered his staff away. "Thank you!"

"Amazing," Mark Hanna of Ohio said to Thomas C. Platt, Republican boss of New York State, relieved to be at a table in an out-of-sight corner.

"Frightening," Thomas C. Platt replied, his lobster suddenly tasting like cardboard.

■ "My dear Philippe," Maurice was writing, his penmanship neat and precise, almost fussy, the white of the rag bond letterhead tinted yellow by the steady glow of the Edison lamp on the antique oak desk in his cluttered and dusty office. "It has come to my attention that you now represent the Aachenberg collection. As we discussed two years ago in the Hague, I am extremely interested in the possibility of introducing several of these pieces, particularly the inlaid tables and matching chairs—"

The delivery bell rattled on the far side of the warehouse, a block-wide building attached to the showrooms halfway between Twenty-third and Twenty-second streets. Harbinger lowered his pen and glanced up at the schoolhouse clock on the wall. Seven twenty-three. Twenty-three minutes past closing. Had his warehouse foreman forgotten an expected shipment, gone on home in the mistaken belief that nothing more needed to be done that couldn't be done in the morning?

"—to a selected group of my New York clientele. These are socially prominent persons who—"

A second ring, more persistent.

Leaving the letter unfinished, sighing an inconvenienced sigh, the dealer wound his way around the cabinets and commodes and reached the receiving bay as the bell sounded once more. "We're closed," he said through the small diamond-shaped window decorating the door.

"Please: it's very important I see Mr. Harbinger." Spoken

deferentially, hat in hand. Maurice found himself impressed by
the suit the caller had on, the piping which edged the lapel, the
bow tie.

"Yes?"

There was no delivery wagon in view behind him out on
Twenty-second Street.

"My name is Hastings, Mr. Harbinger. George Hastings. I'm
sorry I couldn't drop by till after hours, but I think I have a piece
of antique furniture you might be very interested in." Could he
come in?

"Anytime between nine-thirty and seven tomorrow: certainly."

"By then it might be gone and I wanted to give you first crack."
The voice was tinged with regret.

"Gone overnight." What kind of antique would be in that kind
of demand? "*Louis Quatorze?*"

"The period isn't the reason you'd be upset if you let it get away
from you, sir."

"Oh?"

"We're talking about something that was brought over from
Europe," Hastings wanted to emphasize. "On the *Etruria*, two
years ago August." If the collector wanted to check the manifest,
"Hastings comes after Frick and before Moskowitz."

Hastings, George. One antique dressing table, crated, among
other things.

"Sir?"

Harbinger was thinking. Looking away and thinking. When he
turned back to speak again through the diamond shape of the
window, it was in a liquid whisper. "You're not really offering me
a Louis Quatorze dressing table, are you."

"All kinds of things make an antique more valuable," came the
response, the eyes suddenly luminous blue, blinking like a Siamese
cat's.

Another pause. A stipulation. "I would have to be shown something concrete, you do understand that, I presume."

"Perfectly." Hastings would be very happy to show him a small
sample taken from the larger whole. "Which can be delivered to
you as soon as we agree on terms."

"Then this 'larger whole' is . . . in stock?" Too much saliva on the tongue made it difficult for Harbinger to speak.

"Thirty some-odd sheets." The caller's face disappeared behind one of them, held up in front of the wire-reinforced glass. "If you open the door, you can hold it for yourself."

"Come in." Of course the latch would be pulled; of course Mr. Hastings was welcome inside. The signature beneath the drawing at the bottom of the page was Charles DeLacy's, and the gallery owner couldn't wait to trace it with his fingertips, to feel the texture of the paper and smell the little bit of vinegar left in the ink.

Science and art, all in one. Harbinger knew its worth, but Hastings? Could this callow youth really understand what it was he had here?

"Really, sir. Do you actually have to hear me say 'flying machine'?"

Maurice inhaled audibly. "Yes," he conceded. "That's exactly what I had to hear." The eyes darted up from the specimen. "How did you come by this material?"

The Mona Lisa look suited Hastings well. "That doesn't make any difference, does it." His hand retrieved the paper, carefully returning it to the inner pocket of his jacket. "Before the night gets too old, Mr. Harbinger: quote me a price."

"Price." A slight smile drifted around the edges of the dealer's mouth. It was a game he was very practiced at, price. "Why don't you give me an idea of what you have in mind; then I can tell you whether I think your expectations are viable or not."

"Fifty thousand dollars is about as 'viable' as I'm ever going to get," Hastings suggested, his certitude eliciting a cynical laugh.

"Ten wouldn't be jumped at?"

"I don't think so." There was no give on the face, not yet.

"Twenty-five, then." Harbinger's face could freeze as solidly as anyone else's.

"Thirty."

"Good night, Mr. Hastings." Maurice's hand reached out for the knob on the door.

"Twenty-five thousand, all right. *Cash.*"

"Cash." Done.

"Indeed you are." The voice was neither Hastings's nor Harbinger's, and it was filled with the kind of clinical revulsion usually reserved for the sight of the pus in a festering sore, intentionally impersonal.

". . . Theodore?" What was the Police Commissioner doing there?

"Placing you under arrest," the Police Commissioner replied, ordering the arrestee to put his hands together for the cuffing. "Officer Kerner?"

Officer Kerner . . . ?

Oh, God. T.R. knew. He knew about the relationship with Charles and everything else, a lot of everything else. He knew how the proprietor of *La Galerie des Artistes* had lied when he said he'd never heard of any "C. DeLacy," how he'd gone after those airship plans for his own profit and immortality; maybe even how he'd met with Edison's repudiated protégé in Paris—"but you've got to let me explain. You've got to give me a chance to talk to you."

Handcuffs weren't necessary—!

"Have you any idea how happy it would make me to have to use force? Do you?" Roosevelt's voice was metallic.

"I didn't do anything wrong!"

Didn't he? "Your interest was solely in Mr. Hastings's antique dresser? The fact that it came over on the *Etruria* never entered your thinking at all and the only reason you let yourself be shown that sketch was simple curiosity?"

"There is no way you can arrest me for wanting to buy those plans, I'm sorry," Maurice said, sidestepping the open manacles out in Richard's hands. "Charles was dead: *he* couldn't do anything about them."

"Is that the Charles whom you might never even have heard of if it wasn't for—who was it at the Lumière meeting that night, Professor Lake?"

"People panic, what can I tell you? The most important cop in New York comes to me with part of a plan I thought lost forever, he asks me questions about the inventor I was trying to do busi-

ness with—murdered probably because of that plan—Theodore, I
couldn't think of anything else to do but lie. No one could connect
me to DeLacy here in America, hardly anyone, anyway. Maybe
you'd never find out. Why open the can of worms?"

"Especially when," Teddy imagined, "Daniel Thackery might
be willing to fund the Harbinger Airship Company. Another
name would have been so confusing."

"That was more than a year ago," Harbinger exclaimed. "He
turned me down on the safety razor, I didn't want to walk out of
that godforsaken 'rejuvenation chamber' of his with nothing."

"Even if you didn't have one single sketch to show." The collector's explanations had the air of improvisation about them. The
whole desperate cloth.

"Charles showed me the portfolio in Paris, all thirty-three
pages." If his memory was good enough, Harbinger could repro-
duce some of those pages and, as an inventor in his own right,
figure enough of the rest to make another meeting with Thackery
feasible. "I could give the world the flying machine, after all."

"Altruistic you." Touching, a story like that, especially since it
could only conclude with an admission from this inventor in his
own right that his memory wasn't "good enough." That the De-
Lacy originals couldn't be duplicated.

If only it happened like that.

"That is exactly the way it did happen!" A shout.

"*This* is the way it happened," the Commissioner declared.
"Charles said no to the deal you offered him over the Montrachet
in Maxim's and you steamed. You boiled. You burned. That lousy
little so-and-so has the invention of the century under his arm and
he won't let his friend Maurice have any part of it, not even one
tiny percent."

Could someone as proud as Maurice Harbinger just sit there
and let a fortune slip through his fingers?

Hardly. "And DeLacy'd already done his part of the job. If you
got your hands on those drawings, he'd be Mr. Expendable." The
voice went low, low and dangerous. "That's when you decided to
dangle investment money in front of his nose and invite him out
to Meaux."

Gray was now the predominant color on the face of the accused. "Theodore, you can't be serious," he breathed, sad and
scared, spittle glistening on his goatee. The resemblance to Baby
Joss was uncanny.

"I have never been more serious in my life," Maurice was assured. "You thought you'd get that boy out there, take his portfolio and kill him off. Only the papers weren't on him, so you
couldn't do that outright, could you. You had to keep him alive
and in agony, long enough to tell you the hiding place."

"Not so, I swear. I have never been in Meaux." T.R. was right
about the exchange in Maxim's, yes, "but the only reason Charles
wouldn't accept my proposal was that I came to him too late.
Other investors had already promised him more than he needed."

" 'Other investors' he somehow just didn't name for you, I'll
bet." Richard could no longer just stand by, silent. Who did this
man think he was kidding?

"He didn't volunteer, that is correct, and it was not my place to
ask." Harbinger looked back to Roosevelt. "Even in this business
there are ethics; you know that."

"Don't you lecture me on ethics," Teddy snapped, one side of
Officer Kerner's handcuffs snapping simultaneously.

"Come on, sir. We can finish this downtown."

"No!" the inventor wept, left forearm snared. "Theodore, my
God, listen to me: you're making a mistake, I can prove it. I have
witnesses."

"Do you." The Commissioner tapped Richard's shoulder: hold.
"You had nothing to do with DeLacy's death, nothing to do with
what happened at Frick's house, you've never been down on
Monroe Street or at Buffalo Bill's Wild West Show: bully. I want
to believe you."

And maybe he might just have thought of a way he could do
that, even before Harbinger would have to bring on his "witnesses."

"Just come up to 102nd Street with me. Three-thirteen West."

"Now?" The head seemed to shrink backward on the neck, the
glottis elevating in the throat.

"Right now," said Roosevelt, watching him.

"Why?" Harbinger asked, hushed. "What's on 102nd Street?"

"Don't you know?" The name Evans meant nothing to him? *Evans.* "Should it?"

"My brother's mistress." The collector might have read about her in the papers just after the birth of the child, it was all over the front page. Elliott admitting paternity, Elliott declaring himself insolvent, incompetent to handle his own affairs—Elliott agreeing to enter an institution.

"How would this Evans woman be able to clear me? I don't remember ever having met her."

"Then you wouldn't be one of the men she saw coming out of her building just before she went upstairs and found my brother dying on the floor." Harbinger wouldn't have anything to worry about once she said that, would he.

"Mrs. Evans saw people leaving the apartment house?" Richard was fascinated. "Enough to identify them?"

"So she says," Teddy affirmed, studying Maurice. "What do you want to do, go uptown or down?"

"Uptown, naturally. What are we waiting for?" He lurched forward with surprising speed, heading in the direction of the door with the diamond, Officer Kerner's cuff secured to only one of his wrists.

"Not so fast, you." The Commissioner's aide lunged to grab at the other half of the device, dangling loose. He missed the flapping steel by less than an inch as Maurice went suddenly crazy, crashing through the narrow crevasse between two high stacks of crates. Each went tumbling, backward, forward, to either side.

"Harbinger!"

Roosevelt flung himself at the fugitive, only to be met with the sharp edge of a container reinforced with a jaggedly mitered length of unfinished pine. Maurice slammed it into him, hard, feinting as he did so. Scurrying free.

"I'll get him, sir!" Richard yelled, burning with guilt. Damn it, had those cuffs been properly locked none of this would be happening now, and it was this thought which propelled him up onto another stack of crated merchandise. He'd jump the suspect from above. Come down on his head before the man knew what was what.

As Teddy Roosevelt would say, "Hi yi—"

His shadow betrayed him at the last moment, Harbinger having just enough time to impulsively snatch up a hefty piece of sculpture, a small brass lamp. He hurled them one after the other with unexpected velocity and aim, both the antiques crashing with jarring impact against the patrolman's shoulder and thigh. They broke, they bounced, they stung, forcing him to dodge and duck.

Good: T.R. could make use of the diversion, placing himself between the suspect and the door. If Maurice wanted out, he'd have to go through him. Come on, mister. Try it, come on.

Redhead Finnegan hadn't aroused the wolf in Roosevelt's heart, not this way. Not this much. Redhead Finnegan wasn't Elliott's killer. "What're you waiting for, Harbinger?"

The answer came in a shriek, the escapee plowing forward with rabid eyes and flailing forearms, scratching, biting, kicking, using the free handcuff as a weapon. It swung at the end of its chain, glancing sharply off the side of the Commissioner's face, toppling him. Unbalanced, Harbinger toppled, too.

Both men slammed hard into the wood of the floor, the joints groaning and cursing beneath the boards as the struggle intensified. Maurice's breath was pyorrheal, and Teddy tried to roll him over, to get on top, away from the fumes. If he could wrestle him flat, punch his mouth—

Surges of adrenaline kept his adversary going, feeding the muscles, strengthening the body beyond all expectation. It provided him with cunning as well, turning the fingernails into claws, the fists into hammers. The arms locked around Roosevelt's neck, twisting his tie, yanking it tight until the eyes bulged and the complexion went purple. Red.

Black.

The elbows. Jab. Harder. Jab. Hurt him. More.

And still the tie was not released. Liquid gurgles began to bubble up from inside the throat.

"Commissioner—!" Richard was up, staggered but up, behind

them. Approaching. Harbinger saw him and his concentration was broken, the grip momentarily relaxed.

Now.

T.R. bucked forward, catching the dealer's newly exposed abdomen with the points of his shoes, lifting. Maurice flipped upward in an inverse arc, heels over head, coming down against an antique harpsichord trimmed in gilded filigree. It disintegrated in a cluster of discordant twangs, the overtones reverberating off the walls, the crates, the stacks.

Harbinger reacted with all the horror of a father forced to witness the bloody demise of an only child, crawling through the debris on all fours, blubbering as he gathered some of the disattached keys to his bosom. A piece of a pedal. "Look what you've done, look. Look what you've made me do."

Something metal glinted in his hand and he came back hard at his enemy, the last of his words exploding into shocking oblivion as Richard's bullet tore a deadly furrow through his lower left lung and detonated. Like a mastiff on a chain, Maurice was brought up short, limbs akimbo, amazement on his face even as he sprawled backward on the floor.

"Are you all right, sir?" Officer Kerner reached out to help Teddy up. "He had a knife, there."

It was not far from the twitching hand outstretched, small and wicked-looking. The blade was notched, the curve designed for the quick strike. Had the gallery owner managed a thrust, it damn well would have been the President of the Police Board breathing his last, not the other way around.

"I won't forget," he promised as he crouched down alongside his brother's executioner: there were things to be said, even now. Especially now. "Mrs. Evans would have identified you, that's why you bolted, isn't it. You were one of the men she saw . . . ?"

What was on the waxen face beneath his own was dread. Blind, unreasoning, all-encompassing dread. Maurice's lips tried desperately to help his tongue form words. "Baaaahh . . ."

Blood stained the enamel of the teeth.

"There's no time left for more than a yes or no: were you there at the apartment with Elliott? . . . Maurice?"

Death's rattle replied, tapering off after the longest of moments into numbed silence. Gone. Maurice, *Pensionner, La Galerie.*

The last words.

"One minute more," Roosevelt muttered. "Thirty seconds."

Richard understood the feeling. A dying confession would have been good not only for Harbinger's soul, but for their own. They'd go home satisfied, justice done.

"Except I think we did get his confession, though," the officer had to point out. "The way he took off when you asked him to go up to 102nd Street? That was a guilty man, Commissioner."

All they had to do was go through the warehouse they were standing in if they wanted the final proof. How much did his superior want to bet that the paintings still missing from the Frick collection would turn up right here in this building? Dvořák's music case?

Dvořák's music case, yes, Teddy nodded, distracted, taking a few absent steps off into the darkness behind the shattered harpsichord. The canvas satchel that cost Ida Moskowitz her life, that was probably here, too.

"Then why are you looking like that, sir?" Why wasn't he smiling? "You solved a major case. Multiple murder. No one else could have come close to putting it together so fast; I don't think they'd have done it at all." If Kerner were Roosevelt, the old Sioux war cry would be ringing out, "loud enough for people on the Bowery to hear."

"Funny, isn't it," T.R. replied. "That's what I thought."

BOOK TWO

"The Strenuous Life"

1 BISHOP DOANE

■ Meeghan was there, the county coroner was there, Jacob Riis was there, and a photographer along from the *Sun:* Roosevelt wanted a record of it all, "something to examine in the cold light of morning when my shoulders aren't sagging so much."

They were looking for three things. One: the drawings. DeLacy's sketches. Two: the last of the Old Masters still missing, Frans Hals's *Madwoman of Leyden.* Even without the diagrams, the last lingering questions about Harbinger's guilt would be laid to rest once that painting was found, here, at *La Galerie.*

Three: notes, letters, a diary or an address book. "Maurice wasn't a one-man gang. This case isn't really closed," the Commissioner wanted it understood. "Not until every last accomplice is brought in."

Until every last page of DeLacy's collection was retrieved, given to the heirs, with the government in Washington advised.

"Just coming up with those pictures could take weeks," Richard had to observe, looking around at the multistoried warren they would have to ransack. Bins filled with oil paintings abounded, in no apparent order, shelves of canvases amid bundles of draperies, clusters of chairs, rolls of carpet—endless. Their eyes were already crossed and how long had they been at it? Two hours? Three?

Hardly a drop in the bucket. "Maybe it'd be better if we went home and came back fresh in the morning," the Commissioner's aide suggested, weary as his boss. "I don't know what anything really looks like anymore, do you?"

"Not in this light," T.R. had to admit, very much aware of his aching vertebrae. "We could have gone right past both of those paintings twenty times over by now."

Whereas in the morning they could have Henry Clay Frick himself on the premises, going through these cribs, racks, chests and lockers. His was the eye most unlikely to skip over that Hals: it was his own. His precious.

"All right. Meeghan?"

"Sir?"

"We're finished here for the night, I think." He could release the body to the morgue "and hold everything else exactly where it is for tomorrow. At least four men on guard. Six. No one in or out, except yourself, myself, Officer Kerner."

Was Mr. Riis on the list, too?

"He'll be coming back with me," Teddy decided, patting the newspaperman on the back as they went out onto the street. "I expect you're going to be busy at your typewriter the rest of the night as it is."

"At least till three in the morning," Jake had to agree. "Mr. Dana'll want it in the two-star; that'll give him the great pleasure of waking Mr. Hearst up by four-thirty. 'Sorry to call so early, Bill, I just thought you might want to take a look at the special I just put out: "T.R. Solves Baffling Murder Mystery Helped by *Sun* Reporter Riis. Culprit Killed Resisting Arrest." ' "

"Then I guess I can look forward to hearing from Mr. Hearst by five," Roosevelt said and laughed, climbing into his carriage as Officer Kerner peeled away through the darkest of alleys. Even here, even now, Estes Hanrahan might have spies.

▪ It was actually five-eighteen when the phone rang.

"Theodore." Petulance. Reproach. Sadness. "I thought we were friends."

"We are, Bill."

"Friends call each other when they've got news, or when they need help with something." Hearst was referring to the information the Commissioner got from the *Sun*'s bureau in Paris, whom DeLacy had dinner with and the like. "Their bureau over there isn't half as big as ours. We could have had twice as much for you in hours instead of days."

"Bill. Jake was right there next to me when the questions came up in the first place. I couldn't exactly not give him the shot, including the exclusive if he came through." The publisher of the *Journal* would have asked for no less, "don't say no."

"All right," Hearst grumbled. "But if I were the good politician everybody says I was, I'd make damn sure I had a few *hors d'oeuvres* left for the other boys on the block, just so they wouldn't go away mad." He deliberately anglicized the French. Whores dorvers, it came out.

Whores dorvers.

"Something like a first-person article on the subject by the President of the Police Board," was that what Hearst had in mind? "Delivered in time for Sunday's rotogravure?"

"Could you have a piece like that ready for then?" The deadline would be Thursday, 11 A.M.

"Would Theodore Roosevelt disappoint the readers of *The Sunday Journal?*"

"Listen. Theodore." The edge was gone from the publisher's voice now, replaced by the expansive tones of a mollified friend. "We can hold the press run right up to seven o'clock that night if you need a little more time."

"Appreciated, but not really necessary," Teddy assured him. "I love a deadline."

He did, too, he had to admit, as Hearst put him down on his calendar for eleven, Thursday morning, and severed the connection.

■ "Mr. Barnum would have wanted you for his circus, you know that?" Edith said it as they disengaged from the good-morning kiss which followed the call from the owner of the *Journal.*

"And why would you think I'd be of interest to the late Phineas T.?" T.R.'s nose rubbed gently against his wife's. Eskimos, Alice would have said, had she been awake to see.

" 'Hurry, hurry, hurry, ladies and gentlemen, step right up, step right up and see the amazing Roosevelt twirl Hearst and Dana and twenty-five other New York dailies high over his head, never once letting any of them crash to the ground: hurry, hurry, hurry!' "

"I'll take the job." He laughed, waltzing her around and kissing her again. "Barnum's circus has to be child's play compared to the one I've been performing in since May." Edith would have to go along as barker, though, "or no deal. Never have I heard anyone do it better."

"A female barker." Edith tried to imagine it. "That'd be new."

"If I can do it when it comes to my secretary, I can do it when it comes to my barker: another step forward for the disenfranchised half of the American population." The telephone was ringing again. "Roosevelt."

Not another daily wanting in on the story, he hoped. How many angles could one poor Commissioner of Police be expected to have on any one given piece of news?

"It's Richard Kerner, sir," an excited voice said in his ear. "I'm back at Harbinger's warehouse: couldn't sleep. We found the Hals —*Madwoman of Leyden.* It was in a carton behind the office and get this, sir, it was next to Mrs. Moskowitz's satchel. At least, I think it's her satchel. A carpetbag with a wooden handle?"

The excitement was contagious. "Expect me in twenty minutes," Teddy boomed, hanging up and whirling. "By Godfrey, Harbinger *was* our man. I thought so!"

"What'd Daddy think?" Alice inquired, she and her brothers halfway down the stairs, still in their pajamas. The question was addressed to their mother because their father had already rushed past them on his way to the bedroom closet.

"How things come together once you reason them through,"

Edith told the children, unruffled. "Have we all brushed our teeth this morning?"

T.R.'s voice pursued them back up to their own bathroom. *"East Side, West Side, all around the town, the tots sang 'Ring-a-rosie,' 'London Bridge is falling down . . .'"*

So off-key and yet so sure of himself. Dvořák would cringe, no doubt.

Mrs. Theodore Roosevelt was kinda taken with the sound.

■ *Madwoman of Leyden,* signed. Dated. "It hit me while I was lying in bed," the officer said, brimming with accomplishment. "If I were an art lover like Mr. Harbinger, I don't think I'd want to lose a picture like that in the middle of an oversized warehouse. I'd want it where I could look at it. A lot."

Insight like that couldn't wait for morning. Richard was back at *La Galerie* in less than fifteen minutes, and the painting was in his hands not five minutes after that.

"Then, when I saw that the carpetbag was here, too, well," he couldn't help but add, "you should've seen the leap I made for the phone."

"I can picture it," Teddy assured him even as he began to poke around the desk in Harbinger's office, going through the letters, the invoices, the calendar. "All we need now is a line on the accomplices and we're home."

"It's not in the desk there, I checked." The letters on the blotter were to people in the arts and antique businesses, legitimate inquiries about the availability of collections like the Aachenberg. "No address book in any of the drawers."

No diary.

"What about those filing cabinets?" Sixteen of them all told, eight on either wall.

"Bills of lading, check stubs, at least in the ones on this side." The Commissioner's aide hadn't gotten to the ones on the other, and Roosevelt made a beeline.

"You start at that end, I'll take it from this." They'd meet in the middle.

More bills of lading, check stubs. More letters of inquiry.

"Damn."

"Is it really all that important, sir?" Richard asked, last night's exhaustion returned. "I mean, we have all the proof anybody could ask for."

"Yes. But we don't have the plans. They do." Enough, perhaps, to build the prototype. "Something to show the high bidders—who don't necessarily have to be friends of the United States."

The Spanish might be a good example. Would the generals in Madrid be too civilized to consider the flying machine as a weapon to use against the *insurrectos* in Cuba? Would they refuse to attend a demonstration if they were invited to one?

"Oh, no, Officer Kerner," T.R. predicted. "They'd come, they'd buy—they'd use. Not just in Cuba: if they thought an airship would keep America out of their little fiefdom down there they wouldn't hesitate."

Getting the ringleader didn't mean the race was over. Far from it.

"Because they're a lot closer to the finish line than we are, even now. Whoever they are." Damn. Some kind of address book had to be somewhere in this place!

"Some kind of address book like this?" Lieutenant Meeghan was standing in the open office door, smiling. Tapping a small volume against the heel of his palm.

"Where'd you get that?" Roosevelt came over to claim it.

"From the table by the front door." It had been out in the showroom all the time, displayed on a desk much more expensive than Harbinger's own, one more prop in the setting. The letter opener, the rubber stamp, the inkwell, the address book. "Wouldn't you know."

The back of Richard's neck reacted as though that were a slur, and perhaps it was. He would have retaliated with something choice but Teddy issued a cease and desist with a quickly furrowed brow: his concentration had to be solely on this tablet. The names on this tablet.

"Archer, Thomas P. . . . Bennett, Mr. and Mrs. Leslie K. . . . Choate, Joseph . . ." Customers. Clients. Persons of substance and fashion whose homes were decorated by *La Galerie des Artistes*. Not a ringer in the carload, not so far.

Could Maurice have been cunning enough to slip the significant names in among all these others?

Of course.

Another possibility, from Meeghan. "What if some of these highfalutin society people themselves're a part of this little conspiracy we're talking about? I wouldn't put it past the few I've met."

Bored, rich, the sense of values warped—anything to get the blood up.

Literally.

"Get a team together," the Commissioner ordered. "I want to know everything about everyone in this book." The money, especially. "How they get it, where, from what investments. I want to know who their friends are, what clubs they belong to, how many people are in the home and what they do."

"That's going to take a little bit of time, sir." Two weeks, minimum, Meeghan anticipated.

"You have three days." A team by Roosevelt's definition was not limited to five or six men. Not when they might be under a new kind of gun, more deadly than the Gatling. "Oh. Meeghan."

The detective pivoted just outside the office. "Sir?"

"Officer Kerner wasn't here last night and this morning: I presume you understand that."

"How could he be here when he's downstairs at the Forty-first getting his head bashed?" Altar-boy innocence leavened the putty face. Meeghan had been an altar boy once, in fact, between the ages of ten and twelve, when the voice was soprano and his Aunt Bridget hadn't yet shown him the joys of the flesh.

"Good," Teddy approved. "Because if Estes Hanrahan does find out that's not where Richard is, there're only four men I'd have to call in: the three uniforms out there, and you."

"Five, sir," the lieutenant said, unintimidated. "We wouldn't want to be leaving Mr. Riis out, now, would we, if something bad happened to our friend Dick here, undercover?"

"Dismissed, Meeghan."

When he was gone, the younger cop succumbed to his curiosity. "Do you really think Meeghan's one of Hanrahan's inside boys?" The concern was all too personal.

"Let's just say it's sometimes advisable to put people on notice: it keeps the eyes wide open." T.R. was jiggling the hook on Maurice's telephone. "I think I will have a talk with Jake Riis, now that his name has come up. Central?"

The *Sun*'s number was in the low two thousands and luck was with him: Riis was at his desk. "More news, Commissioner?"

"In exchange for a favor."

"Mr. Dana would have it no other way. Shoot."

Roosevelt told him about the painting and the satchel, making Jake whistle. "Two extras in one day: Charlie might give you the shirt off his back."

"Make that an ad in the personal column and we're even. Several duplicates, maybe—scatter them all around the classifieds. One or two might even be placed at the bottom of the news columns as well," Teddy thought to add. "The more we have in print, the more chance they get noticed."

"By whom?"

"By the rest of Harbinger's gang."

Frowns formed on the faces of Officer Kerner and Jacob Riis, two miles apart. "Why would they want to answer an ad put in the paper by the President of the Police Board?"

"It wouldn't be put in the paper by the President of the Police Board," T.R. explained. "This would be from some anonymous someone who happens to have a few scientific sketches for sale to the highest bidder."

"Drawings from the steamship *Etruria*," the reporter presumed.

"Exactly. 'Technical Diagrams Available from Inventor's Personal Set, Pages 16, 23 and 31. Indispensable for Completion of Project.' How does that sound?"

"I don't know, Theodore." The Commissioner could almost see Riis hesitate on the other end of the line. "I've heard of long shots before, but this one might just be all the way up to the moon." Even if Roosevelt received a response, there was no guarantee it would be from Maurice's accomplices. "There're a lot of people who collect scientific drawings as a hobby."

"Those people aren't trying to build a flying machine with only two thirds of the plans on the workbench." What other alternative was available, anyway? "I was sure the names we were looking for would be sitting right here on Harbinger's desk, and I was wrong. What can I say?"

"Where they can write to get in touch with Mr. Anonymous," so Riis could include it in the ad. "A post office box number."

A post office box number, yes. "We'll have to get one of those, won't we."

No. Better. Why wait for the mail when it's so much more convenient just to pick up the phone?

"At Mulberry Street?" Where the switchboard said "Police Department" before anything else? "They won't ask to talk to the man with the plans after they hear that," Jake was willing to bet.

"I'm talking about a phone at the house, a new line we'll put in just for this." Not the house he was renting from Bamie on Madison Avenue: Teddy was referring to Sagamore Hill. The commissionership had kept the family city-bound more than anyone liked these yellow-aired days in the middle of August, but a full week was scheduled to commence this very Friday and what better place to combine business with pleasure? "They can run the wire right through the gun room window, two hours' work at the most."

T.R.'s third-floor aerie when they were in residence at Oyster Bay, the gun room. Just under the gables, with a view of the cove and, beyond it, the Sound. Gulls, sailboats, kids belly-whopping at the end of the pier. He could watch them play while he took the calls. Is this 952, Sagamore Hill? The person with scientific patterns for sale?

Riis was much too quiet, Roosevelt began to realize. "You see a problem, Jake?"

"With a Sagamore Hill telephone number? I'll say." Everybody from Cape Hatteras to Kennebunkport knew who lived on Sagamore Hill. "Including the unpleasant people you're trying to reach with that ad."

"Oyster Bay, then," the Commissioner extemporized, shaking his head even as he did. Still too close. "What about Cove Neck? Only the people who know Long Island well know that Sagamore Hill is situated in that township. 'For additional information contact 952, Cove Neck': how does that sound?"

"Improved," the reporter had to concede.

The President of New York City's Police Board thought it was a lot better than just improved. He thought it was Jim Dandy, that's what he thought. "Those boys're going to see a Cove Neck telephone exchange in that advertisement and the name of Theodore Roosevelt isn't even going to come close to entering their minds!"

▪ Late summer on Cove Neck was green and blue, the greens dark on the firs and the cedars, light on the lawns, the blues shading similarly from the near-black of the Sound to the near-white of the sky along the Connecticut horizon, ten miles north. Clouds puffed or trailed, the gulls like kites beneath them, their petulant outcries challenging, or boasting or demanding. When Teddy and Edith were children together, they spent much of their time down by the rocks on the shore, translating the arguments and dialogues for their brothers and sisters, none of whom knew how to speak gull, not even the basic, "Give me that fish, I saw it first," or the traditional reply, "That's not your fish, it's mine."

Gull altercations tended to revolve around fish possession, the couple agreed, although occasionally the birds would pontificate on the direction of the wind and the imminence of a squall. Of course, there was always the behavior of the human beings below to comment on, but that was merely in passing. Human beings were crazy by definition; therefore it wasn't wise to expect too much of them.

The single file coming down the hill from the house even now: what better illustration? Slow . . . steady . . . the steps were measured by the solemn rattle of the snare drum suspended from the strap around the neck of the little boy in front. Kermit, they called him.

Behind the drummer boy came the one named Ted, bearing a

cigar box on a velvet pillow. Next, a girl: Alice, playing a low three-note melody on a kazoo and, following her, another. The somber-faced Ethel, holding the hand of the baby, letting him toddle along.

Completing the cortege, the parents. Theodore and Edith Roosevelt, maintaining the slow, formal pace. "Who," they wanted to know as they approached a tiny burial ground enclosed by a tinier fence, "gives the eulogy?"

"Me," said Ted, nudging his sibling. Kermit had not yet stopped the muffled drumming.

"Don't I play under the speech?"

Alice confiscated the sticks.

"All right," Kermit hissed. "But you don't play the kazoo now, either."

"Children." Edith's voice was cautionary as her eldest son unfolded a piece of paper and inhaled.

"What is a guinea pig," he read. "Small, fra—frag—"

"*Fragile.*" The word had been Alice's contribution to the writing of the speech.

"—fragile, furry and cuddly, happy with a little bit of bark and some guinea pig food, she trusts you to be gentle when you take her out of her cage to give her a bath, or to scratch behind her ears, asking nothing in return but to live out her years quietly and in peace, and to die of old age."

"That is very touching," his father felt compelled to remark, proud.

"There's more," Alice advised sternly, giving her brother the nod. Go on. Go on.

"Today we are saying good-bye to a guinea pig who really did live to a ripe old age. She was more than five and she was very fat, and we want to thank the Dear Lord for not making her suffer because we all loved her very much. Her name was Bishop Doane because at first we thought she was a he, but we found out we were wrong when she started having all those little guinea pigs. Anyway, we're going to miss her: they're not as much fun— Mom?"

A snort had breached Edith's nose, unbidden. A sob, to be sure.

"Your mother is as touched as I am," the Commissioner hastened to explain, handing his wife his handkerchief. "More."

"Can we put him in the hole now?" Ethel was perhaps more impatient than her brothers and sister because she and their father had prepared the ground for the ceremony some hours previous, digging a rectangle three feet deep.

"Six feet for people," Teddy had explained when his younger daughter had asked, "three feet for guinea pigs."

"Drums again," Alice directed, returning the sticks. Kermit resumed the tattoo, and she lifted her own instrument to her lips. Dvořák would have been enchanted, T.R. thought, enchanted himself.

With great solemnity, Ted and Ethel lifted the cigar box from the pillow, lowering it between them until it came to rest at the bottom of the furrow. "Taps" even on the kazoo could be extremely affecting, especially when the company braced, and Officer Richard Kerner stepped out from the adjacent stand of maples to present the polished shovel, Minnie Gertrude Kelly observing from a bench a few feet removed.

Accepting for his children, Roosevelt thrust the blade forward into the waiting pyramid of loosened earth, transferring the soil to a level above the Bishop's final resting place and spilling it onto the little Cuban-made coffin. Five times he repeated the procedure, until the grave was completely filled in, the surface horizontal once more.

Someone had made a headstone for the departed, had they not?

"I've got it," Ted confirmed, pulling a piece of wood out of a pocket. Wood was easier to write on than stone.

"Here lies Bishop Doane," the engraving read, the letters more or less centered. "Guinea pig and friend, died August 21st, 1895. R.I.P."

"There's no birth date." Officer Kerner was curious as to why.

"Nobody knows when she was born, exactly." The Bishop had been purchased while still in her infancy and the children had all concurred: "Purchased September 30th, 1890" wouldn't look good on a memorial.

"Can we play hide-and-go-seek now?" The service was beginning to feel overlong to Ethel, who was ready to move on to something else.

As was her father. "That," he declared, "is an *excellent* idea." Bishop Doane would certainly not want them to spend a whole day downcast in her memory, especially now that she was happily ensconced in guinea pig heaven, having a very good time. "Why don't I be 'it'?"

"Remember: no peeking!" Hide-and-go-seek was fun only when Teddy was 'it,' because he was the only one of them who counted up to one hundred every time.

Slowly.

And then he'd come after them huffing like a grizzly, sniffing and snorting his way up the stairs, peering into closets and under the beds, talking to himself all the while. "Where *are* those children?" he would ask. "Where would I hide if I were one of them?" Behind the curtain?

In the sewing room, behind the ironing board?

The downstairs clothes closet?

No.

Growl.

"I'll find them." If only by the give-away sound of their secret little giggles, oh, yes. "I'll find them."

Gotcha!

A shriek, a hug; how they loved it when he would swing them around up off the floor and kiss their faces. No better "it" than Father, ever.

"One," he said, turning to fill his vision with the bark of the maple alongside Minnie Kelly's bench, smiling at the sound of scrambling feet.

"He's counting," Kermit was shouting. "Let's get outta here!"

"Two."

"Wait for me," Ethel yelled, her legs the shortest, not counting Archie's. The toddler would not be participating in the event: his mother had decreed that it was time for the housekeeper to see to his nap.

"Now?" What an injustice! How could they do this to him? He wasn't sleepy, not in the slightest. He didn't want to be taken

upstairs to the nursery, not when his brothers and sisters would be having fun playing a game.

"Nap time, young man." Edith wasn't about to have herself contradicted by someone just sixteen months old. Her son was hoist in spite of his flailings and kickings, his howls of outrage only momentarily diminished because Minnie was coming along upstairs and Archie liked Minnie. Their progress could be tracked by the noise, even after they were well into the house.

And then silence, Archie bowing to the inevitable. Sleep claimed him even before T.R.'s count reached seventy.

Seventy-one. Seventy-two. Seventy-three. Had Richard given any thought to where he and Minnie would want to exchange their vows?

Seventy-four.

Several appropriate Catholic churches had been discussed, between themselves and later with Mr. and Mrs. Kelly. "Why do you ask, sir?"

Seventy-five. Seventy-six.

"I don't know, maybe because I always thought this lawn here would be perfect for a wedding one of these days." Flowers, folding chairs, a vine-covered trellis set up around an altar in white: could anything be more beautiful?

Seventy-seven.

"You're asking if we want to get married here?" It had never occurred to Richard, and he was stunned by the generosity of the offer. "What can I say?"

" 'Yes' will do just fine," Roosevelt assured him. Seventy-eight. Seventy-nine.

"We couldn't put you out like that."

"Our wedding present, Edith's and mine." Eighty. Eighty-one. "It was her suggestion, and I immediately jumped."

Eighty-two. Eighty-three.

"Well?" The count continued as the officer debated.

"If Minnie agrees to it—I mean, she'd be delighted, you know that, but there might be other considerations, and—"

Teddy slapped the trunk of the tree and chortled. "Exactly what Minnie said *you* would say!" His bride-to-be had already

been consulted, it seemed, "yesterday, at the office. 'If Richard
has no objection; I mean, he'd be delighted, of course, but.' "

His laughter could be heard on the third floor of the house,
where the men personally dispatched by Alexander Graham Bell
were installing a new telephone.

"Say yes already and let me go after my kids."

"Yes."

"Bully." And then, louder, for the benefit of small unseen ears,
"One hundred! Ready or not, here I come!" Up the slope toward
the veranda, his gait ostrichlike in awkwardness and speed.

Giggles. But from where?

"Where would I hide if I were one of them?" Inside, absolutely.
The pantry? The hall closet?

The study, ah. Ted would go there. T.R.'s eldest son loved to
conceal himself in his father's downstairs domain, behind the suit
of armor nine times out of ten. The Commissioner peered around
the jamb of the door, smile broadening. Someone was there, albeit
in the armchair, the one turned to face the window.

It wasn't supposed to be turned to face the window.

"Damn it," Roosevelt said as he reached around the wings and
over the armrest to pull the boy up onto his feet. "Crouching
behind the suit of armor is one thing, turning my chair around
without permission is something we're going to have to talk
about."

"My apologies, Theodore," said Andrew Parker, unruffled. "I
didn't think you'd mind, and the view from this window is amazing. Utterly amazing."

2 PARKER

- The housekeeper was a middle-aged Irish woman named Annie O'Rourke, Meeghan-faced and practical; it was she who let Parker in, going promptly in search of "the master." Since the master had his own go-seek taking place at the same time, they missed each other until after the commissioners met . . . until, in fact, Teddy took the time to call the children together at the bottom of the stairs.

"I have an unexpected visitor," he had to tell them, regretful. "The game, I'm afraid, is postponed. But not canceled."

"Just when we found the best hiding places ever," Kermit griped, later never being anywhere near as good as right now.

"Business before pleasure," as they all very well knew, and a nod to the housekeeper as she hurried up from inside the dining room. "It's all right, Annie: Andrew Parker is a man who doesn't really need an introduction."

Roosevelt returned to the study and slid the doors closed behind him, all ears and wary. Andrew Parker was also a man who did not like to travel, not when he could simply pick up a phone. Whatever he had on his mind was obviously private, urgent and confidential.

"For your own benefit," the elder commissioner wanted his

colleague to apprehend. "A little advice from someone who might not be as much of a rival as you think."

"Someone who only has my own best interests at heart, of course."

"Theodore, I could have stayed in Manhattan and hummed some John Philip Sousa while you walked out onto the ice, never mind how thin it might be."

It wasn't about the Sunday Closing Act this time, T.R. could be sure, on guard as he seated himself at the desk which dominated the room. Andrew wouldn't have come so far for that kind of review, nor to discuss any of the officers suspended by Haroun-al-Roosevelt. Which left only the news of Maurice Harbinger and the proof of his involvement in at least two robbery-murders. "Is that your 'thin ice,' Commissioner? This Harbinger case?"

"Indeed." Even though the consensus was that everything added up, that poor Maurice got what he deserved. "Two-man judge, two-man jury, what difference? Henry's stolen painting right there in *La Galerie des Artistes:* if that wasn't red-handed, what was?"

"Having Mrs. Moskowitz's carpetbag there, too"; that was what, two pieces of solid evidence on top of Harbinger's admitted interest in things scientific. His visit to Thackery about one specific such thing. His denial of its original creator. His dinner with that very same genius in Paris, the very night the genius was killed. "Add to that the way he ran rather than be seen by Elliott's mistress? I'd say that was as red-handed as they come."

"Good strong evidence, no question." Conclusive, even . . . as long as there were no other little bits and pieces which the Commissioner and his men might have overlooked. "Not deliberately, mind you," Parker was making no accusation along those lines. "But once you think you have a killer dead to rights, well, it's only human to call it a day."

Teddy's fingers curled around the arm of the chair. "You've brought me some of these 'other little bits and pieces,' have you?" The voice smoked. "Show me."

"Really, Theodore. There are no bullets or buttons or significant strands of thread in my pocket. What I'm talking about is eyewitness testimony."

"*I have witnesses,*" Maurice had said. And Teddy Roosevelt looked straight at Andrew Parker, making an effort not to flinch. If the commissioner knew someone willing to get up in court and declare the art dealer guiltless, well. The President of the city's Police Board would be more than willing to listen.

"Why find someone when I've got myself?"

"Of all people." Dry wit. Dry mouth. What could Parker have to say for Harbinger?

"That we were friends, to begin with," a revelation Roosevelt's guest was happy to make if only because of the discomfort it engendered across the roses in the carpet.

"Your name isn't on the address book we turned up at Harbinger's warehouse."

"A friend, I said. Not a client."

The fingertips drummed once against the blotter on the desk. "All right. What are you going to tell me, that you were up on 102nd Street the day my brother was killed and, as far as you could see, Maurice was nowhere in sight?"

"As a matter of fact," his colleague informed him, "I was up fishing on Lake Placid the day your brother was killed and, please, listen to this very carefully, Theodore, so was Maurice Harbinger."

"Poppycock." T.R. stood up, fists thrust in his pockets.

Andrew Parker smiled. And smiled. "Accuse me of being a lot of things," he said evenly. "But not a liar."

"Harbinger had to have been at Mrs. Evans's apartment August fourteenth last year," Teddy snapped. "There was no reason for him to have fled like that otherwise!" If he was shouting, so be it. So be it.

"Of course there was a reason." Even though the collector hadn't been to 313 West 102nd Street that particular afternoon, he had been there before.

"He told you that?"

"When you're someone's friend, you get confided in." The late Maurice Harbinger had indeed been to see Elliott the prior April, "and I can even tell you what he went there to talk about, which was that 'mysterious scientific device' you and Jake Riis have been alluding to all week, in the *Sun* and out." The very same invention which had been the crux of the conversation at Maxim's of Paris. "Some kind of airship, I believe . . . ?"

More reason for Maurice to be scared of a command performance for Theodore Roosevelt at the site of his brother's death.

T.R. bristled. "All he had to do was let the woman take that look at him," he retorted. " 'I remember him from April, not August,' she'd have said, and two seconds later he'd have been a free man."

"Maybe." Or maybe Mrs. Evans would have gone on to say something about the flying machine she heard them discuss, "and then how fast would Theodore Roosevelt have been to let him go?"

Not very fast at all, Parker thought, picturing his overzealous colleague at the confrontation, ordering the lady to look again. Was she *absolutely* certain that this couldn't be one of the two men who came out of the house that day? " 'Take your time, make no mistake: don't let a killer go free just because the passage of time plays tricks with the memory.' "

"You do me an injustice, Andrew." The protest wasn't as strong as Teddy would have liked: the charge wasn't entirely without merit.

"An injustice, is it?" Commissioner Parker presented his antagonist with the telephone, more for the symbolism of it than anything else. "Shall we call over to the West 102nd and do the homework which should have been done before you went to set your deadly little trap?"

Or would Theodore first want to discuss the sand beneath the second of the pillars supporting the case against Harbinger?

"Something else I might have overlooked?"

"The third party at that aforementioned dinner at Maxim's, that's right."

"What 'third party'?" T.R. demanded. "The news report we got from France didn't say anyone else was present."

"So much for the accuracy of the press." Parker's enjoyment

made his face click, like a marionette's, and Roosevelt knew who
the third party was. *I have witnesses.* . . .

"Okay, Commissioner. Tell me about the dinner at Maxim's,
s'il vous plaît." It came out "see voo play," deliberately. Pointedly.
"Begin with how you happened to be there in the first place, why
don't you."

"Legal business." Andrew had been senior partner in a prominent law firm prior to his appointment to the Police Board.
"There were clients on the Continent and contracts to be signed: I
drew the lucky straw."

Two and a half weeks later the mission was accomplished and
the attorney was in Paris, as was his old friend Maurice—who felt
it might be "expedient" to have a lawyer present when he talked
business with a young inventor that night at Maxim's.

"Partnership business," Teddy presumed.

"Ah." Then Harbinger had managed to get that much out before the bullet. "Did he get as far as Charles's response?"

"About how Charles was going to leave it up in the air until
after he met with the 'investors' in Meaux? Sure." But was that
much of a defense, Roosevelt had to wonder. "Do you think anything short of an unequivocal yes would have called off the dogs?"

How much was Parker willing to put up against the hypothesis:
that when Harbinger bid them good night outside Maxim's he
didn't go back to his hotel? That, instead, he followed Charles
DeLacy to Meaux?

"Well," said Andrew, curiously benign, "you are right about
the first half of that. Maurice did not go back to his hotel."

"If you're going to tell me you know where he was after he left
you—"

"Exactly the point, Theodore: he *didn't* leave me."

The other shoe, dropped. The impact of the soft-spoken explo-
sion left T.R. numbed. "I don't understand."

"We left together, we went to the *George V* together, we spent
the rest of the night in Suite 304. Together."

"Did you."

"*Honi soit qui mal y pense,*" his opposite advised, reveling in the
corrugation of the Roosevelt face. It didn't happen often and

when it did it was a sight to be treasured. "You wouldn't want to cast aspersions at the Minister of Commerce for the Third Republic, who happens to live there." Charming man, Monsieur DuPris. "Smitten with that wonderful old American game of chance, Seven-Card Stud."

As was his deputy, one François Arnault.

"Seven-Card Stud," was it? "Or Three-Man Alibi?"

"Theodore, accept the truth. Maurice Harbinger did not go to Meaux any more than he went to 102nd Street, not while people were being killed."

"He did not have to go to Meaux!" Teddy insisted, looking every bit as overzealous and emotional as Parker had charged. "His thugs were there; they could take very good care of the young man all by themselves, and Maurice?" Why, he was in the clear—"just ask his attorney and the French Minister of Commerce!"

"Absolutely," the older commissioner suddenly railed, the supercilious façade dropped, the air stabbed with his finger, Roosevelt-style. "And the hell with the principle of reasonable doubt and the doctrine of innocent until proven guilty: you're the President of the Police Board and you have the authority to try, to sentence, to execute—and to refuse to consider anything which might show you destroyed an innocent man!"

"That 'innocent man' was coming at me with a knife!" T.R. slammed the side of his fist against the wall. "My life was saved by a piece of good, honest, legitimate shooting, and I will not condemn any police officer for doing that kind of duty under that kind of condition!"

A vein pulsed blue beneath the reddened skin stretched taut above Andrew's brow. "What you did, sir, was push a good, honest, legitimate citizen up against the wall. You stampeded him to the point where he could hardly be expected to do anything else but try to get away, and I think you might even have done it on purpose: any excuse to kill the man who murdered your brother. Except, as I just demonstrated, Maurice Harbinger killed no one, least of all your drunken lout of a brother, Elliott."

"Get out of my house." Roosevelt sent the door sliding back

into the recess prepared in the wall, gesturing Parker into the vestibule adjacent.

"If I walk out of here now," the old man hissed, his legs planted solidly on the carpet, "I go straight to the reporters. No detours." How adoring did Theodore think his adoring public would remain once they learned that the trumpets and drums were a bit premature, that the big crime wave had not been solved quite so categorically as they'd been told?

"Explain the *Madwoman* in the warehouse, Andrew. The carpetbag. Tell me how they got there."

"I don't know how they got there," came the reply. Parker was ready to leave now, on his own terms. "You don't think someone would plant them, do you? To say, 'See? No cause for concern. We wouldn't shoot the wrong man.' "

He stalked past his host, eyes straight ahead.

"Andrew." And again. "Andrew."

The hand was already wrapped around the brass knob on the front door. "I'm listening."

"What do you want?"

"What do I want," the senior commissioner inhaled, only then turning to stare at his crestfallen colleague. "I want the real killer found. Thirty-six hours ought to be more than enough time, or do you think you can handle it in twenty-four?"

"No one could reopen an investigation this big and expect arrests in twenty-four hours!"

"Theodore Roosevelt can," Andrew Parker was convinced. "Or his resignation is going to be on Mayor Strong's desk. 'Press of personal business'—'need more time with the family'—the usual drivel. We wouldn't want the President of the Police Board quitting under a cloud, would we."

▪ "Can we finish the game now?"

They were standing on the porch watching the rear of Commissioner Parker's carriage-for-hire descend the hill, Commissioner Roosevelt and his children.

Visions of lobster shimmered in front of his eyes. Oh, yes, there'd be lobster tonight in New York.

And crow in Cove Neck.

"You said it could be when the man left," Kermit was saying, tugging at the drape of his father's jacket.

"Yes," Teddy nodded, "that's what I'd hoped." Playing hide-and-go-seek with his progeny would have been a lot more rewarding than playing hide-and-go-seek with Andrew Parker. "But sometimes, children, a guest will surprise you with a problem you have to think about after he's gone."

"Think about a lot, knowing our dear departed friend." Richard was leaning over the balustrade on the second floor, Minnie to his right, Edith on his left. The sight of him brought a smile to his employer's face.

"I wondered where you'd go to wait it out."

"The gun room," Edith informed him as he climbed the stairs to join them. "Officer Kerner thought it might be better to watch Mr. Bell's men finish with the new phone as long as Andrew was here."

"Considering how hard we've worked to depict Officer Kerner as the crooked cop Theodore Roosevelt hated the most, I'd say that was a good idea." Especially after the discussion just concluded in the study.

"If you need help with whatever Mr. Parker came to talk about," Minnie offered, "we're here."

"By thunder, so you are!" T.R. boomed, his optimism bolstered if not entirely restored. "Don't think you won't get called on that tomorrow, when I'll want to know if the conclusions I've come up with tonight are sound or not."

"Wouldn't it be better if you told us the problem now?" Edith was sure they could be of more service to him before the decision was reached, but her husband thought not, with an appreciative shake of the head.

Some things you don't want to burden your family and friends with too soon, not if your one sleepless night would spare them many. "What *is* that noise up there?"

"Isn't it the new telephone?"

"Gangway!" The syllables geysered from his mouth, followed

immediately by the pounding of his soles against the wood of the narrow staircase leading up to the third floor.

"Boy," Alice could only comment. *"We* run up the stairs that loud, we get yelled at good."

■ The runner which padded the length of the third floor hall betrayed him: it skidded out from under his feet just as he was about to dash into the gun room. His arm saved him by sheer instinct, his balance restored with a push off the wall.

Six times the phone had rung. "Hello," the Commissioner barked even before the receiver was really secure in his hand. "Hello."

Click.

"Dammit," he complained to the state of Connecticut, calm and enduring on the far side of the window behind the old settee. "What am I supposed to do? Sit here twenty-four hours a day waiting for someone to answer that ad?"

Of course not, Connecticut advised, the answer plain as the brush on his face. Assign a surrogate. A young officer—Lindsay Hargate, maybe.

"Lindsay Hargate ex*act*ly," Roosevelt said aloud, reaching again for the phone. "Central?"

"This ain't 'Central,' pal." Not with that exaggerated gutter voice it wasn't, real or for the purpose of disguise. "You the party with the 'scientific drawings' for sale?"

The hang-up calling back? A second party?

"They're still available, yes . . . for the right price."

"I think I can make you happy." If these were the drawings he was specifically in the market for. "They got a signature?"

"All three."

"Gimme the initials."

Why not? "C, D and L," Teddy replied. "Satisfactory?"

"Yeah." Movement on the other side of the line. Slurping sounds. "You want to set something up, I can see a sample?"

"Name it."

"Tomorrow, the one o'clock ferry to Staten Island. Upper deck."

"Done."
Click.

■ Mrs. Evans confirmed it all in the morgue, everything Andrew claimed. She looked without flinching at the green-white face with the black goatee and she said, "Maurice Harbinger."

"One of the men you saw coming out of the building last August fourteenth."

"It was months before that. March." No later than April, certainly, soon after Elliott fled his failure as manager of the Robinson estate in Virginia. The Commissioner's letter of resignation, dictated to Minnie first thing in the morning, became lead in his pocket.

"What did they talk about, Harbinger and my brother?" Did Mrs. Evans know?

She wagged her head as the attendant lowered the sheet. "All Elliott would tell me was he wasn't going to depend on pipe dreams anymore. If it wasn't cash on the barrelhead, it wasn't going to be worth his time."

The collector was shown the door and Elliott drank himself insensible. "Because Maurice couldn't offer him anything more than promises," Roosevelt theorized twenty minutes later in the kitchen of a tenement apartment not two blocks from Murphy's Ninth Avenue Saloon. "The same kind of penniless promises he offered Charles DeLacy in Paris the year before."

"How would Harbinger even know to look up your brother, though?" Richard Kerner shifted his shoulders against the back of the chair the Great Felice had seated him in, uncomfortable under the towel and the putty knife. "If Parker is right and he didn't have an outfit to back him up? He'd have had to find out where DeLacy went before Meaux all by himself."

"Shhh, the mouth, she moves too much!" The Great Felice could not guarantee the results if the face was not absolutely still while the makeup was being applied. "The bruises will crack, the contusions will peel and, believe me, *signori,* it will look like you hired the services of a rank amateur."

After which, *zzzst!* The index finger sliced through the air between the chin and the clavicle. What had the patrolman's superior said about the job, that it might come down to life or death?

"Not 'might.' Will," T.R. was certain, gesturing his aide into quiescence. "There can't be any doubt about these 'wounds,' Richard. Not if we want Estes to buy you a drink and pat your back."

If it all went right, Hanrahan would have his new favorite lie low for a week or two more . . . and then put him to work. By which time the Harbinger affair would be settled and the Commissioner—if he was still the Commissioner—would be ready to pounce.

As for any difficulties the antiques dealer might have had backtracking DeLacy from that ditch in Meaux, that would depend on how determined Maurice was. How much money he thought he could make.

How much time and resource he had left.

"He might not have been the mastermind we thought, but he was after those plans just as much as the killers were. My guess is that he found out about DeLacy and my brother at Suresnes even before the gang did." By the time he was able to get himself back to America, however, Elliott was gone again. "To Dr. Keeley in Illinois," as Teddy recalled, "and then to the Robinson estate in Virginia. After an expensive trip to Europe, Harbinger might not have been able to afford to continue the chase."

What else could he do but stay home? Run *La Galerie?*

Time heals, or so they say.

"Except one morning he gets this irresistible urge to go up to 102nd Street; who knows, maybe Mr. Roosevelt might have come home to his lady love?" The Commissioner's aide had trouble squaring that kind of sixth sense.

"Officer Kerner, please," the Great Felice begged. "The welt is still wet. For your own well-being, *silenzio?*"

"Silenzio," Richard agreed, subsiding with a penitent wave. It had been impossible for him just to sit there and not remark on what seemed to be an open link in the chain which Roosevelt was attempting to reforge.

"There were announcements in several of the newspapers"—weren't there?

Yes, in several. "Elliott Roosevelt Returns from Virginia," they'd put it. "Plans in Abeyance." Harbinger must have seen it, and that would close the open link. Within the day, he'd have gone uptown to knock at the door.

Because of that, and because he'd also been fool enough to say "flying machine" to Daniel Thackery, Maurice had panicked in the warehouse. "What else could we think once he did?" T.R. wanted to know, suddenly wondering if the resignation might really be in order, after all. "What else could we do?"

"I have no apologies," Officer Kerner said. "Harbinger would have killed you with that knife and I wasn't about to let him do that." An "excuse me" followed, directed at the Great Felice.

"Ecco," the makeup artist deferred, magnanimous now that only the finishing touches were left. "One minute more and you can stagger out onto the street, the beaten wreck of a man." He looked to the Commissioner for approval but the Commissioner had eyes only for the events of the other night.

"No wonder we couldn't find that list of names in Maurice's office," he was muttering. "No accomplices, no names."

"Putting us back at square one," unless T.R. knew something Richard didn't—?

"Not yet." But that didn't mean he wasn't going to. "Great things could happen on the deck of the Staten Island Ferry this afternoon: you never know."

True. You never did.

"Listen to Teddy," the Great Felice counseled, seeing doubt beneath the cuts and coagulations on Officer Kerner's face. "Optimism, she is much better than pessimism, yes?"

"Decidedly 'yes,'" Roosevelt affirmed. "What a beautiful day for a boat ride!"

3 HANRAHAN

■ As a matter of fact, it was not a beautiful day to be out on a boat of any sort. The sky was overcast, rain misting in a steady drizzle which licked at Lindsay Hargate's cheeks: cat's tongues, only cold. He was standing alone at the railing at the edge of the upper deck, just above the bow, glad for the warmth of the slicker and knit cap the Commissioner had him wear.

"You're in civvies on this one," that was the order, issued when the rookie obeyed the unexpected summons which brought him first to Mulberry Street. "And this is the hot little item you're taking onto the ferry, presumably to sell."

Page 16 of the set signed C. D.L. was out in Teddy's hand.

Lindy would be on the one o'clock to St. George, "studying" the diagram until approached—by whom?

"By someone interested in purchasing a scientific sketch 'just like that one, sir. To complete a set I'm collecting, you see.'"

Once the transaction was complete, once dollars changed hands, T.R. would close in. Handcuffs would snap. "And then?" Officer Hargate asked, receiving one of his superior's finest smiles, tooth-filled and challenging.

"We pray we haven't caught some dilettante who collects material like this just for the fun of it."

Which of these few hardy souls braving the fog halfway out

from the slip at the Battery was his man, Lindsay wondered, glancing up from the drawing held conspicuously on the wood of the rail. Most of the passengers this trip were inside the salon; that narrowed the number of possibilities down to five.

That gentleman there with the lean look, the one with the peeling shoes, would he approach and open a not-so-casual conversation? Or would it be the fat figure some fifteen feet to the left, thick lenses focused on the torch-bearing statue on Bedloe's Island?

Could it be the third man there, the one on the slatted bench who brandished his New York *Times* the way Sousa brandished his tasseled baton, fingers stained with printer's ink? Or that couple behind him, the look on the face of the wall-eyed wife suggesting that she, unlike her spouse, derived no pleasure from the feel of a million tiny droplets wind-whipped off the Kill Van Kull?

Where was the Commissioner, Lindy was curious to know. Watching from somewhere in the salon? What better retreat could there be for someone to view whatever might happen on deck, his own presence hidden behind the reflections which turned the glass into mirrors . . . ?

It was the perfect place to set a trap, the fore of this ferry. Where could a suspect flee once the jaws snapped shut? Nowhere but into the swells, as far as the officer could see, his eyes glancing up at the bridge, at the helmsmen in their white brass-buttoned uniforms piloting the vessel to a harbor still twenty minutes away. Strong swimmer though he was, Lindsay Hargate would not risk a dive into these choppy gray waters. The distance, the clothing, the temperature beneath the surface even in August: exposure would get you if the bay did not.

Oh, no. Whoever came forward to buy this drawing would rather return to land in handcuffs. Anything else was madness.

Movement starboard. The fat man had finally wrenched himself away from the lure of Miss Liberty, removing his glasses to shake the rain from the lenses as he turned, lumbering up toward the waiting cop. This was it. Every muscle in the washboard of Lindy's belly tensed, the breath suspended midlarynx.

"Sir," he managed to say, with a nod.

"Fine day for ducks," came the churlish response, nothing more. Instead, the behemoth circled past the officer, working to maintain his balance against the roll of the boat as he headed into the salon.

A gust from Bayonne swallowed the slam of the door. Patrolman Hargate was left alone with the lean-faced gent and the unhappy couple; the man with the *Times*.

What if they were all in on it, all waiting for the right moment to surround him, to press his back to the rail and snatch the drawing? There'd be a gun at his ribs, at least one, and orders given. Take us to the other pages, no tricks.

Had T.R. brought backup?

Was it really needed? Dammit, man, no one was making any moves. No one was even sneaking him a look, curious, speculative or otherwise. Could the caller have backed out?

Could he have simply missed the boat?

Staten Island was beginning to assert itself now, as if God were blowing air into its outline: an expanding balloon, black, the surface pocked. Resignation began to rise in Lindy's thorax. Were he to have been approached, it would have been before this.

Long before.

And then the cabin door behind him opened, and a tall figure stepped out onto the deck, Inverness coat whipped by the wind.

■ "Nine five two Cove Neck?"

You really don't jump out of your skin in the slightest, do you. You stand there reserved and careful, watching the hands and the eyes; you say, "Yes?" noncommittally, and you feel good because you can handle it. However it plays out, you can handle it.

"I thought you'd be older." The voice was blunt, used to getting its own way.

"People say I sound older on the phone." Were they going to spend time talking about how the little foil diaphragm in Mr. Bell's earpiece distorted tone and pitch? "We're going to be on Staten Island before we get down to business, we do that."

"We're not going to do that." The pomaded head indicated the paper still out in the young man's hand. "Do I get to touch it or do you want to just hold it up in front of my nose?"

"All yours," Lindy said, surrendering the sheet. "Straight from the *Etruria.*"

Roosevelt wanted it said, loud and clear. This was one of the documents which came to America aboard that particular Cunard. Signed, *C. DeLacy.*

" 'C. D.L.,' " a quote remembered from the telephone call of the previous afternoon as the prospective buyer raised the prize to the light.

"It's real," he was assured. Was there going to be an offer?

"Five hundred, for all three diagrams."

"One thousand—for each." Officer Hargate made a point of taking the sample back.

"One thousand for the three," the final offer. "Take it or leave it."

Taken. "Only do that slowly," Lindy had to advise as the tall man slipped a practiced hand beneath the lapel of his coat.

Pity soured the smile preceding the reply. Poor you, it seemed to say. Don't you realize? "Pulling a stunt like that would hardly get pages 23 and 31 in the collection, would it."

Greenbacks of large denomination fanned out in his fist: one thousand dollars.

"Three hundred now," it was decreed. "Seven hundred more when we meet again." Which would be when and where?

"Uh . . ." The undercover cop stood there fingering the trio of C-notes tendered, at a loss. Wasn't this the moment Roosevelt was supposed to step in?

"Why don't we do it in Manhattan this time," the stranger was suggesting. "Now that we trust each other so much, there's no reason to go to hell and back, is there?"

"Manhattan is just bully!" a scathing voice interjected from above, amplified by megaphone. Both Patrolman Hargate and the suspect pivoted, shocked to see the Commissioner there on the bridge, white-jacketed, a member of the ferry's crew. "Three hundred Mulberry Street will be even bullier: you, sir, are under arrest!"

Even as he was saying it, the hand holding the megaphone was dropping, the face detonating. Teddy knew this man.

"Hanrahan, you son of a bitch, what the hell're *you* doing here?"

▪ "Hanrahan?"

Lindy knew the name, certainly: everyone in New York law enforcement knew who Estes Hanrahan was. No robbery, burglary, murder or rape took place west of Sixth Avenue without this man getting his cut. No protection racket or other form of extortion, strong-arm or by threat, flourished north of Christopher Street or south of Seventy-ninth without his approval, if not his personal participation.

Why would he come alone to a setup like this, prepared to lay a thousand down on a set of scientific diagrams, incomplete?

There was no time to ponder the question. An inhuman howl was erupting from the hoodlum's throat, so coarse and splenetic that Officer Hargate could not immediately isolate the words which were making up the sound. "You suckered me," Hanrahan was saying, it seemed. *"Roosevelt—!"*

The rage became physical, Lindsay shoved aside so that the tall man could clamber monkeylike up the side of the bulkhead connecting the salon below with the bridge above—anything so that Hanrahan could wrap his hands around the neck of his enemy, popping his Adam's apple, flinging him into the waves. The foot kicked out backward as the thug climbed, the heel of his shoe catching the rookie square on the forehead as he tried to pursue, slamming him into an air vent. Both legs buckled on impact, and Lindy found himself on all fours, dazed, everything coming at him in sets of two: two Hanrahans on two railings, reaching upward to grab on to two ladders.

Two Teddys were also in motion, scissoring four feet around two distinct hawsers, sliding with crescendoing speed down at the twins which were his opponents. "Hi yi *yi,*" the Teddys whooped, the sound abruptly cut off when the underside of their soles crashed flat into the Hanrahans' midriffs, making them hiccup.

Optic unity returned. Now only one Commissioner grappled

with one Estes Hanrahan atop the ferry's railing. The suspect in his madness had the advantage, it seemed, one hand tangling with a rope, the other punching. Each new blow knocked Roosevelt farther over the edge.

It was imperative that the patrolman regain his footing. He had to pull himself erect against the air vent and get in there; he had to yank Hanrahan away before T.R. lost what little grip he had and went into the bay. The backwash would catch him, this close to the keel. The undertow from the propeller.

"Right here, sir," Lindy cried, fingers clawing, coming down hard against the back of the criminal's coat, bunching the cape. Hanrahan wavered off-balance, arms flailing.

"You bastard," he cursed, swinging wildly as though the momentum alone would brush the fly from his back. Indeed, it did, but the momentum was too much: the main mass of Estes's body followed his arm outward, twisting, unable to stop.

"Hold him," Roosevelt shouted, lunging as Lindy was lunging, grabbing for the tail of the Inverness. "Don't let him go!"

"Got it!" Officer Hargate doubled himself over the rail, arm extended to its limit, fist trying to maintain a grip on the little bit of fabric left above the deck line.

"All right," the Commissioner exclaimed, dropping belly down onto the planking, crawling forward to reach out: "I'll pull him in—"

"Too much weight," Lindy warned, hearing the rip of a seam giving way, one stitch, two, threefourfive.

"Save me," the leader of the West Side mobs implored, face contorting. The words were lost in a shriek which rose and then died away as, despite all their efforts, Hanrahan's coat opened up, its owner plummeting. Water cascaded upward, inundating the lawmen above, smelling of clams and seaweed.

"Mine," the patrolman yelled, feeling responsible, diving into the bay even before the last of the brine rolled back off the deck. Teddy was right behind him.

■ Darkness doesn't come monochromatically at all, T.R. found himself thinking as his open eyes peered upward through the liquid night. He was several feet below the flatted keel of the ferry, and he was trying to scout a way to the surface. Sooner or later he would need a way to the surface.

There, that brightness on the diagonal. He kicked out at the water below him, propelling himself upward, closer, closer, breaking through off starboard. Air.

"Mr. Roosevelt," someone was calling. "Over here." One of the crew rushing onto the lower deck, extending a pike. Several of his mates made a semicircle behind him and, behind them, a crowd of passengers was gathering. "Mr. Roosevelt?"

"Not yet," he told them, inhaling again, expanding his chest to the limit and divesting himself of his brass-buttoned jacket. Mr. Hargate was nowhere in view. Neither was Estes Hanrahan.

The Commissioner flipped forward, descending, more prepared for the darkness, steeled now against the cold and the sound of the underwater, that hollow thudding that bubbled up against his ears.

Nothing.

Forty seconds, sixty—he returned to the surface, gasping.

"Mr. Roosevelt, sir!"

"Wait!" He'd seen bubbles. White bubbles fulminating down there.

Mr. Hargate.

Churning his feet behind him, T.R. plowed through the water, downward. It *was* Lindsay Hargate, looking up at his approach, urgency in his eyes, forearms burdened by a horizontal figure with trailing limbs: Estes Hanrahan, drowning.

Help me, the officer was gesturing. I don't know if I can hold on to him much longer.

Together, however, from opposite sides, they could hammock the body; they could bring it up to the surface. Together, hands clasping beneath the back.

Hanrahan's head, unsupported, turned its face. Cold blue flesh with a purple orifice gaping in the center. The lips suddenly twisted to brush Teddy's cheek.

Up, quick. *Up.* Before the poison from the kiss of death dragged him to the bottom.

Air, quickly!

Now the men on the lower deck could extend the pike. Now they could throw the life preservers onto the whitecaps.

"Make sure there's a line we can wrap around his feet," the Commissioner heard himself saying to Lindy through chattering teeth. "We don't want him going under again."

His hand signaled the crew on the ferry: pull. The faster they could reel the victim in, the faster they could pump the bay from his lungs.

"This man cannot be allowed to die," he informed them as he dragged his own sodden weight up over the lip of the deck. "He has to talk!"

Rest was out of the question. Officer Hargate was still in the water, shoving Hanrahan upward into the waiting arms of the boatmen, Roosevelt himself helping to flip him over onto his back.

"Give me room."

"Give him room, he said." The captain was there, pushing through, the authority in his voice backing the expanding crowd to a manageable distance while Teddy straddled the pelvis and spread his hands out just under the rib cage. He pushed forward, releasing.

Again.

"Breathe, damn you." The fingers dug in harder this time; with even more pressure the next. "Breathe."

Still inert.

"Commissioner." Lindy was kneeling alongside Hanrahan's head, flooding the deck.

"Not now." His fists were punching the belly beneath him, the spectators reacting with burgeoning horror.

"Stop him," someone was saying, aghast. "Can't someone stop him?"

"Are you an expert in the techniques of lifesaving?" T.R. made the inquiry without missing a stroke. "Will you take the responsibility if you prevent me from using my knowledge to revive this man?"

Liquid vomit suddenly gushed, Hanrahan's mouth open, spasming. He coughed and shuddered, vomiting again.

"Dear Lord." It came from a woman in the front circle of spectators, pale beneath the brim of her hat and netting, turning the face of her six-year-old away from the scene.

"Is he alive?" the girl was asking, resisting. "Did Mr. Roosevelt save the man?"

Another regurgitation. But he was breathing now. They could all hear it: the living wind that whistled through the nostrils. Teddy could withdraw his hands, allowing himself to sag back on his haunches.

"Blankets," he ordered.

"For Mr. Roosevelt, too," the captain amended as a deckhand hurried toward the supply locker. "And this man here." Lindsay Hargate's skin had gone translucent blue, his palsied lips purple. All this effort to save a man the Commissioner called criminal? "Excuse me for saying this, sir, but wouldn't the bottom of New York Bay be the perfect place for him?"

"He has information I want. When he wakes up, we're going to have a serious talk, the two of us."

"Sir." Lindy's tone was the same as it had been when he tried to interrupt the giving of the artificial respiration. "He might not wake up so soon."

"I've seen cases of near-drowning like this before," his superior assured him. "Five or ten minutes: they open their eyes."

The rookie was very gently altering the angle of Hanrahan's head, lifting it so that T.R. could see what he'd seen even in the dark waters beneath the ferry's hull: a crimson gash almost two inches long, haloed white on the hairline behind the left ear.

"The propeller?"

Of course the propeller. The edge of the blade. What else could have so neatly trepanned through the skull like that?

"There's a hospital not far from the slip, up the hill from St. George," the captain volunteered, compassion hushing his voice. "It's not Bellevue, you understand, but—"

"It doesn't have to be." If the surgeons required weren't on this side of the bay, they could be telephoned. "Twenty minutes by carriage from Bellevue to the Battery, thirty minutes on the boat —five more up the hill—that's less than an hour, isn't it."

All right.

"Our job is to get this patient to the hospital alive, and to make sure he stays that way," the Commissioner declared, rising. "These doctors won't be making the trip for nothing, by Godfrey!"

Where the hell were those blankets?

■ "I'm not going to lie to you, Commissioner: that man might never wake up."

They were standing in the dusty corridor of Mount St. George, the hospital up the hill from the slip—T.R. and a man in the khaki uniform of the Army of the United States, a wool-headed major of imposing height named Reed. Head but one of the Medical Corps, Eastern Sector, he had been in conference at Bellevue when the call came through from Staten Island.

Opportunity to observe Dr. Edward S. Crichton operate under what would have to be considered field conditions, this was providence, and Walter Reed wasn't about to let it pass.

"Dr. Crichton isn't about to let you let it pass," Dr. Crichton replied; if there was anyone more qualified to assist in conditions like these, he would like to know who. "You're on."

This meant an hour's journey by carriage and ferry and foot, followed by three and a half hours in the amphitheater, under the watchful eye of Police Board President Theodore Roosevelt.

"Don't expect me to pace out in the corridor like an expectant father," Teddy warned them before it began. "I have seen wounds in my time and cutting, too: precede me, gentlemen?"

He watched, he questioned, he left his seat on occasion and looked over their shoulders, fascinated with the scalpel and the drill. The forceps.

The brain, exposed. How similar to those he had scraped out of the skulls of deer, in appearance if not in size.

Why the glances exchanged across the man anesthetized on the table? Was it not going well?

"It rarely does when the injury is that deep," Dr. Reed advised him, directing him with a pat on the shoulder to their conversation outside. "Edema sets in—swelling of the brain." Because of which the Commissioner could not expect to have a lucid exchange with Hanrahan, "not at any time in the near future."

What was the near future, exactly? "A week? Two?"

"Or longer."

"Or longer," Roosevelt repeated, his eyes on the comatose patient being wheeled away, the head turbaned in gauze. Would it help to shake him, to slap him, to splash a bucket of water in his face?

More than a bucket had already been splashed all over him, hadn't it.

Crichton, who had interned at Shiloh and Gettysburg, who had treated hundreds of cranial wounds on the march with Sherman from Atlanta to the sea, had often claimed that he could have saved Lincoln had he been in Washington the night of April 14, 1865. "What I didn't claim," he emphasized as he joined the pair in the hall, "was that I could restore his ability to think, to read, to speak—to do anything other than breathe." It would be wise to expect the worst. "The cases are very similar."

"And all I have is two hours." Teddy glared down at the watch in his palm, as if the glare would slow the sweep of the second hand. "Three at the most."

"There'll be no change in that time," the surgeon said, echoing Reed. "You might as well go back to Manhattan."

Resignation in hand.

■ "I wish there were something I could say." Empathy filled Lindsay Hargate's youthful face, he and the Commissioner alone on the terrace outside looking north to the island of Manhattan, white against a sky suddenly blue. The front had moved out into the Atlantic, and the last of the fog scurried to keep up. "Isn't there someone else who'd know what Hanrahan was up to out there?"

"Maybe." But the man's demeanor on the vessel had all the earmarks of close to the vest. No confidants came to mind, certainly none of the West Side boys.

"What about Dannemeyer? The lawyer?"

"Dannemeyer." Who would plead his privilege, even should the client die. Meeghan might sweat the confidentiality out of him in the basement of the Forty-first . . . but it would take more time than Roosevelt had available, with no guarantee of success. "A good suggestion nonetheless, Mr. Hargate, and I wish it were the way out, I really do."

There might not be a way out, not this time.

What would Theodore Roosevelt do with the private life staring him in the face? Return to Harvard for the long-abandoned Ll.D.? At thirty-six?

"Somebody's got to know why a gangster like Hanrahan would be interested in something scientific like that," Lindy said with sudden fervor. "Could they have known each other, you think?"

"Who?" T.R.'s mind was not quite returned from Cambridge.

"Hanrahan and DeLacy." The "naah" which would have automatically followed was cut off by the shock which seemed to snap the Commissioner erect.

"Great jumping Jehoshaphat."

"Sir?"

"Sir" was already on the move. There was somewhere to go. Someone to go to. Two someones. "Officer Hargate, you are promoted," Teddy boomed, scrambling for the portico and a cab. A carriage. A bicycle. Anything to get him down the hill to the ferry. "Stay with our friend Estes upstairs till you hear from me— if we're in luck, all we're going to need from him is a nod; maybe not even that much!"

■ "Rough neighborhood here, Commish," the cabbie said as he pulled the one-horse hack up in front of a fleabag across from the Vesey Street docks. "The Strand," it was called, rooms by the day and week, and sometimes the hour.

The slit-skirted young lady leaning against the lamppost adjacent might have the key to one of those rooms, and the narrow-eyed pug keeping his eye on her from the stoop might have a knife waiting for anyone foolish enough to accompany her.

"You sure you don't want me to wait?"

Roosevelt was sure. "This might take some time," he said, more concerned for the cabbie's welfare than his own. "I'll be all right."

Doubt and a desire to believe mingled on the driver's face as he finally flicked the reins against the flanks of his animal and rumbled away, T.R. hurrying up the stairs into the narrow vestibule of the rooming house: this was a hotel without a lobby, a half-open Dutch door to the right of the entry serving as desk. "Checkout Time 11 A.M.," according to a sheet of hand-lettered foolscap, propped up by a flat-headed bell which Teddy didn't have to ring.

"Yeah?" The woman behind the makeshift counter was leathery and sparse-haired, wearing a robe patched with quilted calico in some places and with nothing in others.

"William and Eugene DeLacy: they live here now, I believe?"

"Who wants to know?" She knew who, and the calculated indifference on her face infuriated him.

"Give me the room number, madam. This is police business and it is urgent."

"Just so you know I run a respectable establishment here. Pinch them all you want, you leave me out of it." She made a show of the disintegrating composition book which served as register. "Fourteen; it's at the head of the stairs."

"Thank you." Brief. Grudging. The wife of Rabbi Baline was poor, also, but she kept herself clean. Her clothes knew the washboard.

"Mr. Roosevelt?" Eugene DeLacy was on the stairs, stopped halfway down the flight from the second floor, his father behind him. Distress was mounting on their faces, that the Commissioner would find them in circumstances such as these.

"Exactly who I was coming to see: *ex*cellent." Ebullience was better than commiseration, Teddy's instinct told him, their embarrassment needing no explanation. The fall from the heights of the Dakota was a lot farther than a mere ninety blocks.

"Coming to see us about what?" Not about Charles's death, certainly: "the papers said you solved that days ago."

"We never gave Maurice Harbinger even the slightest consideration," the father revealed. "Charles hardly mentioned him."

"Some questions have arisen." They made their way back down the stairs, the DeLacys tacitly on their way to some kind of appointment.

" 'Questions'?" No mistake had been made, Eugene hoped. "Pop and I were just making our peace with how you put it all together. The sequence of events."

Leaving Edison out of it.

"Is that what's troubling you, Commissioner?" William De-Lacy paused on Vesey Street to probe the eyes behind him. "The fact that you can't leave Edison out?"

"It isn't Edison I've got the questions about," to put the obsession aside.

"Who then?" Asked by Eugene.

"Estes Hanrahan."

"Who?" Not a flicker of recognition appeared on either face.

"Charles never mentioned anyone by that name? Think, please," T.R. urged them. "I can't emphasize the importance of this too much."

"Hanrahan," William repeated, regarding his son. "Does it mean anything to you?"

"This's the first I've heard of it." There was no doubt of his truthfulness: Charles's brother was at a total loss.

"He *has* to have said something!" The walls were closing in again, the cell door slamming—the way out was turning into a dead end.

"I'm sorry."

"In passing, perhaps." Roosevelt could only persist. "A reference which might not have meant anything to you at the time, before he sailed to Europe."

"A possible investor, you mean." Eugene was searching the nooks of his mind as they cut through Washington Street to Barclay, the effort wizening his face.

"If not an investor, a go-between. Some kind of broker." Had Charles kept a list of the people he'd been in contact with on this side of the Atlantic?

"Why would he have bothered?" As DeLacy had mentioned before, every last one of those potential subscribers had withdrawn their support in deference to the wishes of Thomas Alva Edison. "My son preferred to look forward, not back."

And there it went, the last little hope. With Hanrahan unconscious, with the DeLacys unfamiliar with the name—with the time running out—what else was there but the office of the Honorable William L. Strong, Mayor, the City of New York?

> *Dear Bill, personal reasons which must remain private compel me to resign my position as Commissioner of Police and President of the Police Board, effective this date. While the job has been challenging and exciting, it would seem that my true interest lies more on the national rather than the local scene. . . .*

Thanks for William DeLacy and his son formed on his lips as they turned into the Greenwich Street establishment that had been their destination: a downtown equivalent of Clinton's Ninth Avenue Pawnshop. He was grateful for their help, their honesty.

"We're as disappointed as you are," DeLacy said, shaking Teddy's hand in parting under a valance of overcoats and clarinets suspended from the cast-metal ceiling. "To have come so far for nothing. A shame."

"What is? What's 'a shame'?" The inquiry came from the moonfaced man emerging from the cage, Lyman Galloway of Galloway Loans, flat-nosed and liver-lipped. "Don't tell me another venture fell through, Bill, please. When does it end? When does a good man get a break?"

"When God says," the old man shrugged. "In the meantime, my son thought it might be time to give you a closer look at that ring you were interested in."

"The signet ring, yes." Lyman Galloway did not have to have the finger raised in front of his eyes; he remembered it very well. "But you must be heartsick, an heirloom like this."

"You can't eat heirlooms." Eugene was twisting the band off the middle finger of his right hand, stoic.

The hell he was, T.R. thought, lingering, wondering what it was that was catching his eye, making him stay. Eugene, dying inside, was that it? Galloway's condorlike patience? The shame he felt in his own gut, thinking Theodore Roosevelt was at the end of the rope when Theodore Roosevelt wasn't anywhere near as gone as this?

"Beautiful," the pawnbroker was saying, holding the offering up to the shaft of dusty sunshine filtered through the opaline skylight overhead. "You don't see craftsmanship like this anymore. Worth at least . . . twenty dollars, would you say?"

"Twenty dollars?" The elder DeLacy flushed. "Sixty would be more like it, and that would be a steal!"

Which Lyman knew damn well.

"Pop." The sudden reddening of the skin on his father's forehead was a warning, and Eugene was not about to let it go unspoken. Had they remembered to take the pills when they left the room?

"Why are you talking about my pills?" DeLacy's fingers were making little curlicues in the air in front of the entrepreneur. "Why aren't you telling this man what a fair price would be for a ring like that?" A snort. " 'Twenty dollars.' "

"I might be able to go up to thirty," Galloway proposed, speaking from the goodness of his heart, of course. "Thirty-five if I stretched it."

Because the DeLacys were such good customers.

"My competition won't be so generous, believe me." He rolled the little metal hoop between his thumb and forefinger, checking its heft. Its finish.

Theodore Roosevelt suddenly recognized it. He suddenly remembered where he'd seen it before.

This very ring.

"How could that be possible?" he couldn't help but ask, out loud. "She had it on."

They looked up at the outburst, confused. Who? Who had it on?

"Are you saying you know someone with a ring just like this, sir?" Eugene had retrieved the circle of silver and was extending it toward the Commissioner.

Snatched. "That is precisely what I'm saying." No magnifying glass was necessary. This was the ring, the identical ring, or the identical twin. "Mr. Galloway."

"Sir." At his service.

"Could I go over to Wanamaker's and buy a duplicate of this? An exact duplicate?"

"To match the detail of this engraving? The hand tooling?" The pawnbroker expected not: this was custom work. He was surprised, in fact, to hear Teddy's claim of reproduction. "Things like this are usually one of a kind."

"Unless they're a matched set," wouldn't Eugene agree? "Mr. DeLacy?"

"Charles had one just like Eugene's," the old man confirmed, whispering. "It was their Christmas present, 1890." Made to order by a silversmith named Donaldson, when the DeLacys were well-to-do. "The shop is still on Astor Place, if you want to verify it."

"Only that he didn't go on to make a few more." He didn't: T.R. knew it in his bones. There was only the one here at Galloway's and the one on the list that came with the rest of the information Riis received from the bureau in Paris, the valuables stripped from the body in the ditch. The pocket watch. The beaver-skin coat.

The signet ring.

An awful sound was emerging from Roosevelt's throat, half a sob, half a ragged scream, filled with anger and betrayal, and the others present blanched in the face of so much emotion, wondering what to do.

"Sir—"

Three steps one way, three the other, head low on his neck now, eyes like irons. Control. Control. "Maurice Harbinger did not kill your son, Mr. DeLacy."

"But you said . . . I mean, in the papers . . ."

"As good a *prima facie* case as any prosecutor could want: the interest in science, the access to Charles in France—the plans—the visit to Thackery and, on top of all that, his reaction in the warehouse when we confronted him? The knife on the floor?"

"So it has to be him," Eugene protested. "No one comes at you with a knife if they're innocent."

"Eugene," the Commissioner said. "Maurice Harbinger didn't come at me with that knife, no more than he followed Charles to

Meaux. He wasn't on 102nd Street the day Elliott Roosevelt died, and you want to know something else? Elliott's brother Theodore's been a blind, pigheaded, self-satisfied ass too damn happy to take his bow one act before the end of the play."

Ring in hand, he headed out to the street.

"Wait," Galloway yelped, following. "Where're you going with that?"

"Evidence!"

"Commissioner," DeLacy called, hurrying to keep up, his son on his heels. "This woman who might have Charles's ring: don't you think we're owed a name?"

"Yes. You are." Teddy paused on the sidewalk. "But I'm not going to give it to you now."

Why not?

"Because I've learned my lesson, gentlemen. Knowing who isn't good enough if I don't also know why. How. When. Where. All the odds and ends, which are going to fit this time," he swore. "They are going to fit like the hide on a taxidermist's mold."

The letter of resignation was no longer in his pocket. It was out in his hands, being torn in half, in quarters, in eighths. Confettied. Up into the air they went, all the little shreds, snowing down on the group while the President of New York City's Police Board stood there smiling till the last of the flakes fluttered onto the ground between their feet.

"You have no idea how bully a sight this really is," he declared, a spring in his step as he turned to resume his walk to the el station over Barclay—stopping two storefronts later when he realized that the cab pacing him was the cab which brought him to Vesey Street in the first place.

"Like I said, Commish: rough neighborhood." The driver grinned as he reined in and craned his head. "You want out?"

"I want Police Headquarters on Mulberry Street," T.R. replied, hopping in and gesturing east. "On the double!"

His appointment wasn't going to be with Mayor Strong, after all. It was going to be with Minnie Gertrude Kelly.

4 LINDY

"Thank goodness you're here," she said, agitated as he walked through the door. "I've been calling all over town."

He took her by the hand, not only to calm her down: Minnie did not have to know that his interest was focused almost exclusively on the third finger of her left hand. "Because?"

"Andrew Parker telephoned—three hours ago now." He'd been curious to know what progress Theodore had been making following their conversation out at Sagamore Hill, and he was dreadfully disappointed that the secretary couldn't provide him with any specific information. " 'I was so hoping he'd have found the rabbit for his hat by now.' "

"After only twenty-three of my thirty-six hours?" Roosevelt's thumb traced the stipplework on the side of the ring, line for line the pattern engraved on the mate tucked in his pocket. "The man does like to put the pressure on, doesn't he."

"The man likes to change the rules of the game after it's started," Minnie advised, chafing at the unfairness. The blatant unfairness. " 'Tell him I've thought it over and I've decided that it'd be just plain wrong to withhold the news of Maurice's innocence any later than five o'clock this afternoon'—he's calling a press conference, Commissioner."

"Which is getting under way right now," said Jacob Riis, looming behind them in the double doors open to the hall. "By six-thirty it's all over the newsstands, just in time for John Q. Public to read on the el going home."

"That two-timing snake in the grass." Minnie's hand was dropped even as Teddy pivoted on his heel. "The board room, is it?"

"What better place for a palace coup when you don't have a palace?" The reporter stood aside to clear the path, T.R. storming past him—

—but then there was a last-minute instruction for Minnie, not to be forgotten in Teddy's haste: she was to close the office.

"At two minutes past five?"

"Right now, yes." He wanted her to answer no more telephone calls, to leave any filing on her desk. "Just get your wrap and go tell one of the officers on the desk that Commissioner Roosevelt wants you driven to his residence on Madison Avenue. I'll meet you there as soon as I can."

"What about Richard, though?" Officer Kerner was scheduled to call in by five-thirty, and his fiancée was certain he'd worry that no one was present to pick up the phone.

"He'll be contacted," her employer promised, gone even before the last word could register in her ear.

As was Jake.

■ "Gentlemen. Thank you for coming. I have a brief statement and after that I will be available to answer your questions for about ten minutes."

Andrew D. Parker sat very comfortably in the Board Presi-dent's chair, relaxed and uncharacteristically smiling, toying with the typed sheet of paper in his hand as he surveyed the turnout of reporters. Not as many as his rival might attract, perhaps, but a goodly crowd. There was Lincoln Steffens of the *Post,* Stephen Crane of the *Herald,* and Riis? Was Riis there?

Not yet.

Damn him, that Roosevelt sycophant, the new administration here at Mulberry Street would see that he regretted the allegiance. So shortsighted. So circumscribed. In less than two hours the *Sun* would no longer have its "in" upstairs and, were the gods in their heaven, Charles Dana would be shipping his overrated *wunderkind* off to assignments in the Bronx.

"As everybody knows," Parker began, "the President of this Police Board has recently announced a solution to the baffling series of burglaries and homicides plaguing our city, pointing a sensationalized finger of guilt at an art dealer named Maurice Harbinger . . . a man with a reputation heretofore unblemished, a man shot purportedly 'while trying to escape.' Mr. Roosevelt claims to have built his case against this silenced citizen carefully and thoroughly and not for a moment do I intend to impugn his motives. Nevertheless, I feel it is my civic obligation to point out certain facts which might very well affect the validity of the conclusions he has drawn." The voice rose. "If an innocent man has been unjustly accused, if an innocent life has been forfeit because of haste and poor judgment, then the responsibility must be placed squarely where it belongs."

"On the shoulders of Police Commissioner Theodore Roosevelt," Teddy concurred, stepping out of the shadows obscuring the door at the side of the room, confident. Bright. "If it turns out that I was responsible for the death of an innocent man, I am here to promise the people of this city that I will not only resign my office, I will present myself for trial on criminal charges." The *pince-nez* were once more the magnifying glasses in front of his eyes, shifting the attention of the room back to the commissioner on the dais. "As it happens, though, I've just come onto some new evidence which I'm sure my colleague will want to look at before going on with this public forum, particularly if, as he claims, the object is to avoid the hasty judgment and the protracted sackcloth."

" 'New evidence.' " The eyebrow arched. How timely, it seemed to say. How convenient.

"See for yourself in the file room downstairs," T.R. suggested. "Five minutes, perhaps?" A wave to the newspapermen gathered even before Andrew could give him the yes or no: Teddy was swallowed by the darkness beneath the arch that framed the recessed door.

Questions flew after him rapid-fire, overlapping like the arrows unleashed by the Indians in Buffalo Bill's Wild West Show. What evidence was Roosevelt talking about? Could he give them an idea of the area, at least? The kind of material it was? Would it confirm Harbinger's guilt, or exonerate him in death?

When could they expect to see it for themselves? "Commissioner?"

They clustered under the arch, opening the door and peering through to the corridor beyond. The President of the Police Board was nowhere in sight.

And behind them Commissioner Parker was slamming the flat of his hand down against the table, pushing himself erect and gathering his dignity. "Gentlemen," he said in parting, the gentlemen rushing back before he, too, would be gone. Did Parker intend to take Teddy up on the invitation and meet him in the file room?

Would he give Teddy the satisfaction?

"It's not what I give Teddy," Andrew wanted them to know. "It's what he gives me."

■ For a moment Lindy held his breath. Hanrahan's eyelids had fluttered. The eyes had moved underneath. No mistake, it was happening again, look.

Perhaps the surgeons had been needlessly pessimistic. Perhaps the man was waking up even now, barely an hour out of the operating theater.

"Nurse?" Officer Hargate held on to the frame of the door, leaning out into the corridor to call. Was Dr. Crichton still in the hospital? Or Dr. Reed?

"Something wrong in there?" The nurse was a grizzled one-armed veteran of the Indian Wars, Luther Boyd by name, ex of General Winfield Scott Hancock's Seventh Cavalry. He'd gotten a glimpse of the patient's wound when Hanrahan had first been carried in and if they'd asked him he'd have given it to them straight. All the medical expertise in the world wasn't going to save this poor bastard, take it from someone who'd seen too many

axes and hatchets leave too many soldiers scalpless, either entirely
or in part.

Better instantaneous death than, what, "convulsions? Choking?
Delirium?"

"Just the opposite, I think," the patrolman said, more apple-
cheeked than ever in his youthful zeal, bundling the old-timer into
the room. "He's trying to talk." Wasn't that a good sign, "a man
in a coma trying to say something?"

"Instead of lying there quiet, you mean." Luther saw what
Officer Hargate saw, the arrhythmic eyelids, the movement beneath. He heard the noises in Hanrahan's throat, the low rumbles
which might have been words . . . or the beast within struggling
to get out.

The beast knew when it was time. It always did.

"Seen many people die, sonny?"

"A few." The name wasn't "sonny."

"A few *old* ones drifting off peaceable, maybe." Luther displayed the gap between what teeth were left in the front of his
mouth. He wiggled the stump of the arm amputated on the back
of a buckboard outside Wounded Knee. "We ain't discussing your
dear old grandpa on his clean white deathbed, this's someone
whose guts're coming out over his tongue."

"I don't see any 'guts,'" the patrolman retorted, holding himself in check.

"Stick around." The words Lindy thought Harbinger might
have been saying? "That's someone choking on his own spit, boy.
The man ain't swallowing right. Soon he ain't gonna be swallowing at all."

Unless he held the tongue down with his own fingers while
Luther ran for an M.D.

"Go." The bandaged head was in the cop's hands even before
Boyd left the room, the mouth pried open, the fingers between the
teeth.

"Ahh," the patient exhaled, a pool of saliva at the back of his
throat. Boyd had been right. This wasn't the way it was when
Lindy's grandfather lay on the mahogany bed upstairs in his Aunt

Rachel's house, the sunlight dappled by the lace of the curtain and the Reverend Mr. McCann reading from the Psalms.

Hanrahan's tongue fought him, whipping like a snake. The body spasmed, and Officer Hargate found himself using both hands, the left at the grimacing face, the right at the chest. "Shh," he whispered, sweat breaking out on his brow. "It's all right."

Heavy footsteps crescendoed behind him, Dr. Crichton preceding Luther Boyd through the door. "We'll need straps," he said after a one-glance assessment of the patient's condition.

"Attached," the nurse informed him. "Underneath." Luther dropped to his knees, probing with his remaining arm for the lengths of leather looped around the springs, pulling them free.

"Here's the buckle." Lindy was on the far side of the bed to receive the toss, to fasten the ends while the physician struggled to keep Hanrahan from curling up into a fetal ball. With the first of the straps tightened across the chest Crichton could breathe a little easier, enough to tell the cop that he'd actually been on his way up to see him.

"There's a call for you in the office." Commissioner Roosevelt was waiting on the line. "He said it was urgent: go." Estes Hanrahan was in three good hands. "Go."

"Yes, sir. Thank you, sir."

"And tell Theodore we haven't lost this one yet."

A nod as Lindy left the room, hurrying down the hall to the office, his hand clamping down around the earpiece of the phone even before his legs came to a complete halt. "Commissioner?"

"Mr. Hargate."

"I'm sorry it took so long: we had a crisis with Hanrahan. Convulsions. Dr. Crichton says we aren't giving up on him but I don't know, sir; I hope he's not just trying to put a good face on a bad situation."

"That's not Crichton's style," Roosevelt was certain. The fact that the surgeon was still on the scene was indicative—a good many of his fellow practitioners would have been long gone. "How fast can you get up to Hell's Kitchen for me?"

"About an hour, I guess." Less if luck were with him and he managed to catch a ferry just about to leave the slip at St. George.

"But don't you want me here if Hanrahan does wake up and say something?"

"From what you've just told me that isn't going to happen anytime soon. And I want someone I trust doing this job for me." Lindsay was to drop in at Murphy's Saloon on Ninth Avenue— "you're looking for another undercover cop. The name is Kerner. Richard Kerner."

Wasn't that the officer T.R. had the fight with? "In front of headquarters?"

Everybody knew: the news had been like a brushfire, precinct to precinct to precinct. A bad apple, the word was—just as Roosevelt and Kerner intended.

"But maybe not so far off the mark, after all," the Commissioner couldn't help but add, acerbic. "Act accordingly, especially when you're with his 'friends' in Murphy's."

"How do I act when I get him alone?"

"Tell him I want the both of you at my house tonight, eight o'clock. We're going to talk about what happens now that Estes Hanrahan is out of the picture, say. And then, Lindy?"

Teddy hadn't called him that before. "Sir?"

"Do not let him out of your sight. Drink with him, joke with him, take a walk with him—even if he wants to make a private phone call. No. *Particularly* if he wants to make a private phone call: I cannot stress the importance of that too much."

"You want to know who he calls."

"What number he dials, at least," T.R. said, confident that the young man would do the job with alacrity and ingenuity. Better, perhaps, than Richard himself might do, in fact, and damn the sudden catch in his unreliable voice.

"Sir? Are you okay?" Had Lindy heard something other than the meaning of the words? Would a proud man like Theodore Roosevelt allow emotion like that to show?

"Dammit, Hargate," the Commissioner barked, loud. Defiant. "We're closing in on a murderer tonight and we're a lot more than just 'okay.' We're bully, mister. We're raring. We're out for blood."

Click.

It had been a sob, the rookie was convinced. He knew the sound a broken heart made: he'd heard it before, when his older brother Leonard had fallen beneath the ragman's runaway rig and his mother had come careering out of the house to cradle him while they sent for the doctor. She'd laughed for him, because if she didn't he might realize that he was done for and give up the ghost too soon.

Lenny knew, anyway. The laugh wasn't right.

There's no denying that sound, Mr. R., there really isn't. Which of your sons have you lost today?

▪ He'd brushed the blur from his eyes even as he'd barked. Dammit, he *was* bully, mister. Raring to catch a man who had played him for fool. One does not cry over bad apples; one roots them out and throws them away, clear-eyed.

Level-headed.

All the way down the metal-edged stairs to the basement, to the file room on the left; even as he pulled the drawer marked *A–K* out on its tracks and thumbed the tabs. Jenkins, Jones, Jordan, Kane, Kay, Kerner.

Kerner, Richard. An address on East Eighty-fifth Street? Four-forty, was that what it said? Four-ten?

Blinking didn't help, no more than it had helped when he was on the phone with Officer Hargate, and the *pince-nez* were just about as useless, no matter the distance from the bridge of his nose. It wasn't until Andrew Parker walked in that Roosevelt's vision cleared.

" 'Evidence,' you said," the elder commissioner recalled in the driest of voices, regretting his own damned lack of willpower. Why was he allowing Teddy to use him like this? Why couldn't he be strong enough to play it smart, to let his rival hang by the weight of his own mistakes until the stretched neck parted like the strands of an old, frayed rope?

"You really should have just handed the resignation in, Theodore. It would have been a lot easier on everyone; I'm thinking of your own family." Had Roosevelt considered their feelings, "or were you too busy cooking up this last little fireworks display?"

"The only thing I considered, Andrew, is who'd want to add your friend Maurice to the list of victims in this case." T.R. spread Richard's file out across the others that filled the extended drawer.

"Now I've heard it all." Parker would have laughed were his intelligence not so insulted. " 'My friend Maurice' *wasn't* shot by your deputy, is that the new story? The bullet came from some sniper perched in the warehouse rafters?" If Roosevelt had honest-to-goodness proof of that, he was truly a magician. "Truly."

Teddy rested his forearm across the open folder. "I wouldn't dare say my deputy didn't shoot that man, Commissioner: he did it, all right. Just as he engineered the deaths of Charles DeLacy and my brother, and those people in Frick's house. Ida Moskowitz."

G'wan, Parker's expression seemed to say, as though he were a bellhop at the Waldorf and the tip had been in Confederate. "A New York City police officer. Aide to the President of the Board, no less. *This* is your new American Moriarty, a man who leads a band of cutthroats on both sides of the Atlantic?" What a straw to grasp at. What a desperate, desperate straw.

"He's not American, Andrew," Roosevelt stated, stopping the walkout before it began. "Not native-born, anyway." The folder was turned as Parker about-faced to see the moving finger tap against the uppermost of its documents.

Kerner, Richard. 448 E. 85th Street. Born 9 January, 1871, Hilgertshausen, Bavaria.

"Germany?" Wasn't he a citizen?

From the same document, four lines below: "Citizenship conferred, 21 March, 1878."

"Then you're talking about someone who came over when he was a child?" Andrew could only wonder what the fuss was. "The man is an immigrant, therefore he's a killer? Is this information the big evidence you dragged me down here to look at, Theodore? Should we close Ellis Island?"

"This is what I 'dragged' you down here to look at." Theodore held a ring up in his hand.

"Very nice." It would have to be a lot more than very nice to hold Parker's attention.

"Eugene DeLacy owns this particular ring. His brother Charles had the other of the set." Did the Commissioner want to know where that one was, "at this very moment?"

"I'll bite."

"My secretary has it, on the third finger of her left hand. A temporary engagement ring, until her fiancé can take her to the jewelry store." T.R.'s smile was grim and ironic. "Miss Kelly wouldn't know who the original owner was, of course—it's not the kind of thing a groom likes to mention to his bride."

"The groom being this selfsame adjutant," Parker presumed, "the one who killed Maurice and everyone else. Richard . . . Kerner, is it?"

"Kerner."

"Don't I know that name?" Wasn't this the officer accused of extortion in Roosevelt's office? "He beat a pharmacist, didn't he? And didn't we suspend him pending charges?"

How could this disgrace to the department turn out to be the deputy at Teddy's right hand that night in the warehouse behind *La Galerie des Artistes?*

"What's going on here, Theodore?" The prosecutor speaking, nostrils aquiver. If the corruption he sensed was only the tip of the iceberg, what rot would there be under the surface? Good Lord, could this self-proclaimed paragon, this darling of yellow journalists from Boston to Charleston, be even more of a fraud than anyone thought?

God help the country if he weren't exposed. God help them all.

"Officer Kerner was working undercover for me," Teddy was explaining. "He was Estes Hanrahan's latest 'recruit' from the department, which is why we went to such extremes to make him look as corrupt as they'd come." Since he was already after the gang on his own, or so he claimed, "of course we'd join forces."

"Excuse me," Andrew interrupted, irritated. "Two minutes ago this aide of yours was the vilest of the vile. Now you say what he was really doing was pretending, to dupe Hanrahan. Which is it, Theodore, or don't you know?"

"The man was playing his own game for his own ends. He was Hanrahan's man when it suited him; he'd be mine if that card came up . . . both ends against the middle. And *that's* why Maurice Harbinger died in that warehouse, not because he was coming at me with a knife."

"You're admitting it, then? There was no knife?"

"Not until after the shot and the confusion there wasn't. But when your deputy yells, 'Look out, sir, he's got a knife'—firing right away to save your skin—what else can you believe?" The voice shook. "That a man as close to you as a son would kill someone in cold blood and then drop a weapon of his own to make it look like self-defense?"

Parker could understand that, dammit. Courage under fire: something a warrior like Teddy Roosevelt would value above all else. So much so he wouldn't question the reality behind the heroism. Never.

"I wouldn't have thought about it twice, Andrew," the Commissioner had to concede. "But then I saw the ring, and I remembered who gave Minnie hers."

"And there's no doubt?" It could only be the one taken from the body in that ravine outside Meaux? France?

"Only two were made."

"Which still doesn't mean Kerner personally took it off a finger four thousand miles across the ocean." Loot frequently wound up for sale in legitimate jewelry stores: "Couldn't he have just gone into one of those and bought it?"

"Why tell Minnie it was an old family heirloom if that was the case?" Richard had done so: his fiancée had mentioned it to Edith over the weekend at Sagamore Hill, and T.R. could see no advantage such a story would give to the groom. Could Parker?

"Yes, as a matter of fact." Something store-bought wouldn't have anywhere near the sentiment of an old family heirloom, "I don't care how much it cost."

"It wasn't bought in any store, believe me," Roosevelt insisted, showing his colleague the attachment clipped to the back of Richard's folder. Paperwork leading up to a leave of absence dated late summer, 1893. "Note what's down under 'Reason for Request.' "

Travel. To return with my brother Wolf to the place of our birth, Bavaria in Germany.

Approved, August 1, according to the stamp. Duty resumed 19 September, 1893, 6 A.M. Did Police Commissioner Andrew Parker want to say it still wasn't proof that Patrolman Kerner could have been in a town named Meaux at least one night during that time?

"Police Commissioner Andrew Parker is going to withhold judgment." For the moment.

"Now you're talking!" Teddy sent the open drawer sliding back into the oak of the filing cabinet with the heel of his hand. The impact rocked the unit and, in fact, the entire four-tiered row. "Meet me at my house at eight o'clock: if my hunch is right, this case could be signed, sealed and delivered, right then and there."

"As per who?" Parker was curious to know, following the dynamo out into the hall and back up the stairs. "Where are you going now?"

"The *Deutsches Journal* on Eighty-sixth Street." A German-language daily recently purchased by, of all people, William Randolph Hearst.

"Just because Kerner and his family came from Bavaria?" Wasn't Theodore being overly optimistic, expecting the editors of that publication to oh-so-conveniently have that last piece of telltale evidence—the smoking gun which would get the hangman another night's work?

"Then you didn't notice what Richard put down under 'Previous Experience' when he applied to the department, did you." Roosevelt had. "Circulation Assistant, *Deutsches Journal,*" the handwriting said, beneath shoeshine boy and—"Get this, Andrew"—clerk in the offices of the Cunard Steamship Line. "Indicative, wouldn't you say?"

They were outside on Mulberry Street, and the President of the Police Board was climbing up into the carriage he'd had on standby for the past twenty minutes. Parker watched for a moment and then swung himself up into the vehicle, joining Teddy in the rear. "I've always wanted to see what the offices of the *Deut-*

sches Journal looked like," he said, smiling as the driver got them under way. "Thank you for giving me the opportunity."

"My pleasure," Roosevelt replied, settling in and smiling back.

▪ Edwina Smith was surprised. Julius J. Dannemeyer was a Thursday night regular, and this was Monday. "Monday's Lulu's night at the charity ward," she divulged as she gestured the attorney through the door. "You remember: Judge Cockran said it'd be good for business if the girls could show a little civic-mindedness."

Who was Julie's good-looking young friend, the one in the shadows behind the garbage cans over there?

"What good-looking young friend?" Dannemeyer had come alone.

"Ain't that a shame." Here the madam had assumed the youth was Dannemeyer's son, daddy coming out on his own off-night to arrange the rite of passage with people he could trust. "But it doesn't really matter who your old man is," Edwina wanted the fledgling to know before she shut the door. "Virgins always rate a special discount, dearie—except on Saturday night."

Five minutes on the inside, she estimated as she led the lawyer to the red velvet sofa in the parlor. Twenty on the outside. The good-looking young man would get up his courage and knock.

"Drink?"

A shake of the head. "Several of the boys are here, I understand," or so they'd told him over at Murphy's. "Bova, they said. 'Tiny' McPhee. The new kid, Kerner."

Verification appeared on the painted face, and admonition. "You're not asking me to go up and bust in on them, I hope: they just got going six, seven minutes ago." Surely Dannemeyer could find something to occupy himself with in the forty more minutes or so it would take for them to trickle back down. "There's a new girl you might like—sixteen, peaches and cream. Long legs."

"Which rooms are they in?" Mrs. Smith could not keep him from the foot of the stairs.

"Mr. Hanrahan isn't going to like this."

"Mr. Hanrahan isn't going to be liking much of anything from here on in," the mouthpiece informed her. "Roosevelt got him."

Her gasp propelled him up to the second floor. "Bova, you in there? Tiny?"

Kerner?

They knew the voice, and that they had to appear, each in an individual door. Richard wore Felice's black eye and, like the reinstated sergeant, a blanket. Tiny, a man who broke scales in drugstores all over town, used both a blanket and a sheet. *Coitus interruptus* made him look like a cross between Marc Antony and Sitting Bull.

"This better be good," he grumbled.

"It's not." Dannemeyer relayed the news. If the boss wasn't dead, he was close. "Everything goes on hold until I have a look at the operation overall."

Bova regarded him with almost clinical interest. "Taking over, are you?"

"Any objections?" Julius J. Dannemeyer put his spectacles in the breast pocket of his pinstripe. The owl became the falcon, if not the eagle.

"From me?" Bova turned to the giant, feigning amazement. "Tiny, you hear that? Mr. Dannemeyer thinks we got aspirations, like Sammy the Shoe"—a bill collector noted for the metal on the tips of his brogans, heavy enough to eliminate the need for weights on his final descent to the bottom of Hell's Gate.

"Keep it that way, we'll get along famous." They'd be in touch, he added, heading back down the stairs.

"Hey," said the girl on McPhee's bed. "I'm getting bored in here."

She found a knob-headed candlestick pressed into her hand, and Tiny putting his clothes on. The door was still open and Bova watched with his arms crossed and his shoulder angled off the frame. "What d'you think? Dannemeyer got the stuff?"

"Depends on whether they find him floating in the river tomorrow morning, don't it." The big thug grabbed his coat and followed the attorney's path down the stairs.

They caught up with him on the sidewalk outside, the red of the

light in the window alongside the stoop turning Richard's black
eye purple. "Where're you going?"

"St. Francis."

"You're kidding." Tiny hadn't been in church since he'd stolen
the crucifix off the altar the day before Father O'Brien canceled
his confirmation. "What're you gonna do, light a candle?"

"Yeah," McPhee said, surprised himself. "That's exactly what
I'm gonna do." He started across the street, ignoring the youthful
figure still crouched in the alley. After a moment the sergeant
hurried after him.

"What the hell," he said over his shrugging shoulders as Richard stood there, smirking. "Two candles've got to be better than
one."

"Catholics." Officer Kerner thought they were superstitious
fools, the lot of them. How could so intelligent a girl as Minnie
Gertrude Kelly come from so crude a crowd?

"Mr. Kerner?" A hiss in the dark. Mr. Kerner whirled, hand
quick to the knife in his pocket.

"First you tell me who the hell *you* are."

Mrs. Smith's virgin stepped into the pool of light which hooped
the base of the streetlamp. "Lindsay Hargate," he responded, low.
"Commissioner Roosevelt sent me for you."

■ T.R. stood on the sidewalk, hand extended upward to help his
colleague out of the coach. Parker grasped it and stepped down,
amused. "What a picture for the front pages," he remarked. " 'Ri-
vals Declare Truce, Harmony to Reign on Mulberry Street.' "

"You're right," said Jacob Riis, strolling up to join them, casual, nonchalant. "I wish I had the foresight to bring a photographer."

"Jake." Teddy found himself filled with genuine surprise.
"What are you doing here?"

"Oh, really, Theodore." A curl of the elder commissioner's lip.
" 'What is he doing here' indeed." Was there anywhere the ambi-
tious young politician would go without notifying his friends of
the fourth estate?

"The question is," the reporter smiled, "is there anywhere Mr.

Roosevelt can go without his friends of the fourth estate right there on his tail—especially when he goes there with someone who usually says 'hot' whenever he says 'cold.' " The eyes flickered past them to the brass plaque to the left of the building entrance behind them. "The *Deutsches Journal:* I'm intrigued."

"Aren't you, though." This was going to be one event in the Board President's career uncovered: Parker would insist on it.

"Felix Wiegand might insist on exactly the opposite," in Jake's opinion.

"Felix—"

"—Wiegand, editor-in-chief here. Old pal of mine." Riis was sure the ink-stained newshawk would expect the answers to his questions to be for the record. "What the two most influential members of the new Police Commission were doing to decrease the crime rate in Yorkville, how many additional cops they plan to put on the Eighty-sixth Street beat. Whether any of them are going to be given lessons in the language. You know."

"We're not answering questions," Parker informed him. "We're asking them." If the journalist would excuse them, now?

Sure. "I just hope the information you think he'll give you isn't crucial to anything."

"He isn't going to withhold evidence." Withholding evidence from any duly appointed member of New York City's Police Commission was a jailable offense, for William Randolph Hearst as well as for a subordinate like Felix Wiegand. "Buttoning his lip would not be very smart."

Jake agreed. "Felix'll talk up a storm." And when the officials return to Mulberry Street, they'll suddenly realize that he hadn't actually said much of anything. "It's an insulated little enclave, Germantown. They're very selective about what linen they wash in public and what they don't." There'd be no way for outsiders such as Parker or Roosevelt to know if the truth they received was the whole truth or only a selected sampling.

"Unless," T.R. broke in to say, "there was an old friend present in the room to break the ice . . . ?"

The reporter played doorman, gesturing them into the lobby.

"Always a pleasure to do business with such a perceptive individual."

"Theodore," Parker complained, balking until Riis relinquished the door and went in after the more venturesome of the commissioners.

■ "Richard Kerner. Richard Kerner."

It was an accent more Swiss than Prussian, Felix Wiegand having, in fact, been born in Bern. He stood separated from his visitors by his desk and the mock-up spread out over the top, making corrections in blue as they waited for the mulling to end.

"Richard Kerner."

"A circulation assistant back in '88," if Teddy's facts were correct.

"Not quite." The circulation assistant had exaggerated somewhat when he'd later presented himself for police work: he had in truth been nothing more than a copy boy at the daily—"although I did think he might make a career in print, those first few weeks."

"Something changed your mind," apparently.

"Something changed *his.*" Young Richard had quit, cold, not two months after starting.

"Why?" Riis asked the question.

" 'Circumstances.' " At the time the editor thought he was referring to his father's physical condition, deteriorating rapidly—"Rupert had about six weeks to live."

Someone had to stay with him.

"That couldn't be the brother? Wolf?" Roosevelt paced around the chair in which Parker was seated, watching as Wiegand shook his head and excised a misplaced umlaut.

"Wolf was in Buffalo that year, I think . . . *ja.* With George Westinghouse." A machinist of some sort, if memory served. "An engineer."

An engineer. Someone familiar with scientific designs. Generators. T.R.'s fingers curled against the frame of Parker's chair.

"That would leave only Richard to take care of the old man, all right."

"Except," Jake interceded, his eyes going in the direction of the editor, "didn't you just suggest that his father's illness wasn't really the reason Officer Kerner left the job?"

"It wasn't." Richard was conscripted to be the companion of his father's last days, not at a New York City bedside but on a trip back to a deathbed in the fatherland, yes, but Felix would have held the position for him, granted him leave—"the boy wanted no part of it."

"Perhaps he'd already decided he wanted to become a policeman when he got back to America." It made perfect sense to Andrew Parker, who found the editor's bemused reaction to the remark somewhat offensive.

"You don't know much about the Kerner family, I gather."

"The reason we came to see you," Roosevelt affirmed, watching as Wiegand turned to the files behind his desk, thumbing through the folders in an upper drawer.

"This is an article we ran this past March," he said as he searched, "twenty years after what used to be known as 'the Little Munich War.'" His guests would want to hear about the Little Munich War: "It began in the courtyard of the Kerner *Maschinenwerkstatt* there."

Six dead when the smoke finally cleared. "Responsibility must be placed on the shoulders of Rupert Kerner and his son Wolf," State Prosecutor Ernst Dichter wrote in his report. "Were the crowd assembled at the foundry not addressed in so inflammatory a manner this disorder would never have occurred."

"'Disorder.'" Wiegand snorted. "Troops had to be brought in, and even then it wouldn't have ended, not without the personal intercession of Ludwig Second."

"All of which went on over what?" Teddy wanted to know. "A labor dispute?"

"At first it was over property rights and government interference." In their zeal to expand their facilities the Kerners had run roughshod over their neighbors; "the fines were the stiffest ever levied in the area."

When Rupert returned from the courthouse, he and his teen-aged son stood up in front of their employees and told them they might have to shut down as a consequence. No factory, no jobs—for which the workers and their families could thank a pair of judges named Gottlieb and Seligman.

Jews.

By nightfall knots of angry people were gathered on the street, bearing torches and weapons, joining together to march on the homes of the judges. Those grasping Hebrews, it was said. The only reason they ruled for the opponents of the tool and die was that they, too, were Jews . . . could any other explanation be possible?

No. Not even when the chief of police himself appeared, trying to tell them that Judges Gottlieb and Seligman were Lutheran. "Their grandmothers must have been Jewish," Rupert Kerner was heard to shout, and the riot was on.

Were the dead from the ghetto—the *Judenviertel*—a trial might not even have been held, or the verdict been token. But none of the six were of those narrow, twisted streets. They were German, full-blooded, and the sentence was twenty-five years at hard labor.

Or exile.

By mid-August the family was in America, assimilating as well as could be expected, the editor recalled. "Except for the time when Rupert was ejected from the Century Club for calling Jay Gould a kike—Mr. Gould refused to loan Wolf the capital he needed to start an engineering business—and when my copy boy discovered that two of his supervisors here at the *Deutsches Journal* were, in fact—how did he put it?—'*Untermenschen*'?"

As Jake had said, his father's illness wasn't really the reason Officer Kerner didn't return to the paper.

"He sent me a program from the *Festspielhaus,* Bayreuth. *Götterdämmerung.* 'We are the *Wälsungen,*' he wrote, in the margin."

"'The *Wälsungen.*'" When Richard Wagner was performed, Andrew Parker stayed away.

"The children of the gods," Wiegand explained. "A race of superior beings destined to bring order to the Western world. It's all there in the music, everything these people believe in." Wagner himself might not have been as dedicated to the ideology as his disciples—"most of whom would like to evict half the population from Alsace to Estonia; not just Jews. Slavs, Serbs, Greeks. Gypsies. Cripples."

"Madmen." It seemed a logical addition to the illogical list, Roosevelt thought.

"No doubt."

Parker moued. "You're talking about millions of people."

"So are they," his host agreed. Pamphlets to that effect were in circulation all over the Continent, and if the commissioners wanted to know the truth, " 'evict' is a euphemism."

"First they have to get into power." Was Wiegand seriously telling an old pragmatist like Andrew Parker that people in civilized Europe would support such a regime? "In numbers large enough to make a policy like that feasible?"

"You don't need a majority to make an insurrection succeed," T.R. declared. "Not if you have the guns and enough of the pencil pushers."

Not if you owned the air.

"There can't be any more pussyfooting, Andrew: we've got to shadow this scoundrel—sooner or later he's going to lead us to the rest of the band."

Where the band was the plans were. DeLacy's plans, perhaps realized. Roosevelt didn't think he'd be surprised to find the device already constructed. Brother Wolf was an engineer.

"Heidelberg."

Heidelberg. Where the students scarred their faces to prove their manhood. "Did Wolf have a scar?" Teddy's hand reached out to clutch at the editor's sleeve. He'd met Richard's brother before, hadn't he, on the railing of a bridge. On the trellis at the rear of a house on Thirty-seventh Street.

"I wouldn't know if the man had the Heidelberg scar, I was never introduced to him but," Wiegand was quick to add, "you can be sure he'd have the insignia of the *Bund* tattooed on his arm, sir. You can be damned sure."

"An eagle? Ruffled feathers, with spears in the talons?"

"Jawohl, ja." They thought of themselves as eagles, these firebrands, "and I promise you: there isn't one person in this building here they'd consider 'pure' enough not to swoop down on."

"Don't worry," the Commissioner assured him as he took the phone in his hands and jiggled the hook. "If there's one thing we're going to do now, it's make sure these birds never fly." Could Central please connect him with Lieutenant Meeghan at Police Headquarters? Plans had to be made, quickly.

Officer Kerner was nobody's fool. It would take cunning to bring him to heel. Cunning, ingenuity and wit.

"Sir?" The brogue crackled through the wires.

"What kind of man-in-the-street outfits have we got over there? Any street sweeper whites? Iceman uniforms?"

"Both." What did T.R. need them for?

T.R. explained. Could the lieutenant get a squad up to Madison Avenue and Sixty-second, appropriately dressed, in—"what do you need, an hour?"

"Forty-five minutes." There'd be the sweeper, the iceman, a postman, one or two swells in evening attire. "Natural as the little bit of wrought iron in front of your stoop; the devil himself wouldn't think twice, seeing them."

Breathing down the suspect's neck they'd be, all the way home, and then?

"The roundup, Meeghan. We move in and we take the bunch. By Godfrey," Roosevelt chortled even before he cradled the earpiece, "there really will be a hot time in the old town tonight!"

■ "Up here," Edith beckoned, Minnie with Alice and little Ethel on her heels going up the staircase to the third floor. "I was going to show it to you this weekend, but as long as Theodore had you come over now we can take advantage."

"Are you sure you want to go to all this trouble, Mrs. Roosevelt?" The present awaiting her in the sewing room was not going to be inconsequential, not if Mrs. Kelly's bright-eyed daughter was any judge of giggles and winks—how could she repay these new and ever more lavish kindnesses? Wasn't the loan of Sagamore Hill more than enough?

"Nonsense," the unoffended Edith replied. "How can you have a wedding without the wedding dress?" She threw the door open at the top of the flight, and there it was in a shaft of afternoon

sunlight pitched through the curtained glass, as though God Himself were lighting it.

"Oh, my." And again. "Oh, my."

This was not just any gown on a dressmaker's dummy. This
was lace and organdy at its most enchanting, the fabric shaped
into button-sized roses at the waist, with ribbons of eggshell silk
and ruffles at the cuffs. Pearl eyelets down the back. Even a child
of potato-poor Ireland knew that it could have been worn only
once before . . . on the occasion of the marriage of Miss Edith
Kermit Carow to Mr. Theodore Roosevelt of New York and Oyster Bay.

"Mother says she doesn't think there'll have to be too many
alterations," Ethel piped. "A little at the waist, maybe."

"*Eth*el." When Alice was her sister's age, she knew how to be
more sophisticated than that. Ask anybody.

"All right, you two, either act like young ladies or leave the
room." Edith had taken Minnie's hand in her own and together
they circled the mannequin, inspecting the embroidery, the quality of the cut. "Almost ten years now," she marveled. "Still in
style."

Did the bride-to-be like it?

Her husband's secretary approached the offering with tentative
fingertips, as though even the most innocent of touches would
bruise the delicate Valenciennes lace. "So beautiful," was all she
could whisper. "So beautiful."

"I'll get Molly with the pins. Try it on." Before Edith could
step to the door, however, she found herself hugged, and kissed,
too.

"Nobody's ever been so good to me. Nobody ever."

"You deserve it." As she'd said to Theodore at breakfast the
other day, why should Miss Kelly have to spend a fortune in a
store? This was the perfect dress and all it was doing was biding
time in a trunk.

"It's been in there since the wedding in London," Ethel confided. "Father says he never saw a prettier bride."

Alice kept her counsel. Edith Kermit Carow was not her
mother, she was her stepmother, and no one ever spoke of the

tragic Alice Lee in this house, not since the night she and Teedie's mother had died, and Alice was born.

"London to be married in." Minnie Gertrude Kelly found that exciting and romantic, and her benefactor smiled in remembrance.

"Gray morning coat and orange gloves. Iridescent orange gloves."

Why would a man have iridescent orange gloves on his hands when he went to say "I do"? Because a man on his way to the church might sometimes forget even to bring his head were it disattached, never mind a trifling little pair of velvet gloves. Going back to Brown's Hotel on Dover Street was unthinkable in the pea soup which had inconveniently if traditionally descended on Victoria's capital, and why risk being late when right over there was the most convenient of haberdashers?

"Gloves? Oh, dear, all we have, I'm afraid, are these in apricot."

Overripe apricot.

"Done," the bridegroom declared with a slap of the hand to the top of the counter. The prospect of marrying in carnelian gloves appealed to the Roosevelt sense of humor, and the sight of them brought Edith down the length of the aisle much faster than originally intended. Minnie could imagine the other reactions that afternoon in St. George's, Hanover Square, especially that of the distinguished and basically humorless Canon of York, the Reverend Charles E. Camidge.

How charmed the life had been since then. How perfect and fulfilling, in almost every way. "There's magic in this dress," Edith wanted Minnie to know, the girl standing resplendent on a chair as Molly the seamstress adjusted the hem and pinned the waist.

"If it gives me a tenth of the luck it gave you and Mr. Roosevelt, I'll be happy." Something so stunning, fitting her as though no one else had ever worn it before: could it be anything other than lucky?

"And I think I can make sure of that." Edith was suddenly rummaging through a drawer full of notions. "Look." Her hand emerged with the prize, raised torchlike over her head: a pair of iridescent orange gloves, the kind no gentleman on his way to the altar would want to go without.

■ An avalanche of boy—plural—came tumbling down the stairs, Ted and Kermit vying to open the door first. "Officer Kerner," they shouted, voices overlapping and cacophonous. "Officer Kerner's here!" They'd looked down from a second-floor window when the bell first jangled, whooping.

Officer Kerner was their favorite, ever since the weekend at Sagamore Hill.

"Hey," Richard beamed when the door was slammed open, the curtain flapping on the inside of its window. "Ted. Kermit. Look at you." They were all over him, Kermit having leaped directly into his arms and Ted only a bit more reserved at the sleeve of his jacket. Neither paid more than passing attention to the even younger plainclothesman standing beside him, automatically backstepping from the unexpected physicality of the youthful onslaught.

"Is that the fake shiner you got from the Great Felice?" Kermit wanted to touch it, to feel what texture it might have against the fingertip.

"Does it look fake?"

"It looks like somebody gave your eyeball a knuckle sandwich but good," said Ted, remembering what the side of their father's nose had looked like after Gentleman Jim Corbett got through with it that morning in the parlor. Now that the boy thought about it, the Roosevelt bruise was a piker compared to this, and it went away over the course of a week little by little.

"This one goes away like that, too," Richard assured him: his next appointment with the cosmetician was tomorrow morning, as a matter of fact. "Have you kids met Officer Hargate?"

"—You're the one who saved Daddy's life," Kermit recalled immediately. "In the park."

" 'Three cheers for Lindsay Hargate,' right." Ted regarded the rookie with new and increasing respect. "Did they really have baseball bats, the men Father was fighting?"

"They did. But I had a gun."

"And you shot one of the bats with it—right out of the killer's hands." The boys could hardly wait to hear the details, every last thrilling one.

"Well, I don't know," the younger of the cops demurred, looking to Richard for rescue. Weren't they supposed to go into an urgent meeting with the Commissioner just about now?

"So you said." Richard's eyes were focused elsewhere, on the girl at the top of the stairs. "Minnie Gertrude Kelly," he sighed happily. "You are a sight for sore eyes."

Six steps up and six steps down: they fell into each other's arms while the children jumped and yelled "surprise," the ringing telephone punctuating their excitement.

"Can someone get that?" Edith's request was made over the railing at the edge of the second-floor landing.

"Sure," Lindy volunteered, going to the phone in the vestibule beneath the staircase. "Commissioner Roosevelt's residence."

"Officer Hargate." The Commissioner himself was on the other end of the line.

"Yes, sir. We're all here." Was T.R. on his way?

"I'm 'here' already. Is Richard in hearing distance?"

A glance upward. Edith on the second floor was indicating the bathroom and Officer Kerner was thanking her with a gracious nod, disappearing from view. "Do you want to talk to him?"

"No. Just tell him I called to cancel the get-together this evening: 'Andrew Parker's keeping me late downtown' or something." Teddy couldn't help being amused by the look the spur-of-the-moment excuse engendered on the face of his competitor, standing beside him in the living room of the brownstone directly across Madison Avenue from 689 . . . a stopgap command post donated by Roosevelt's accommodating neighbors, Mr. and Mrs. Clarence Day.

While the Commissioner thought of it, incidentally: had Richard made any of those personal phone calls Lindy was to watch out for?

"Not a one," the patrolman reported, a bit surprised to hear the relief which followed.

"Splendid! You can call it a day, Mr. Hargate—as soon as you escort Miss Kelly home to Brooklyn Heights. You, not her fiancé: I want him back undercover with the West Side boys, fast as he can. Yours Truly thinks he might have come up with a connection between Estes Hanrahan and the DeLacy case and I want his ear to that ground." Lindsay was to tell him that, "that way," in spite of the horror T.R. could see mushrooming in Parker's incredulous eyes, the waving of the upraised palms. No. No.

What the hell did Theodore think he was doing? "Why would you want to let Kerner know we're on to him? Why?"

"Because if we don't give him reason to start worrying, Andrew," Teddy explained as he hung up, "he just might follow orders and lead us nowhere but back to the West Side."

■ The burr under the saddle, of course. Ingenious. Instead of the crosstown coach and the Tenderloin, Richard Kerner would rush first to his brother, to the other members of the eagle squadron gathered; he'd want to get their opinions of Roosevelt's newest insight, the "link" between themselves and the soon to be late Estes Hanrahan.

Was their timetable to be accelerated as a result? Would their hideout have to be moved?

Hardly would their deliberations commence when the doors would burst open, the glass in the windowpanes shattering. "Police! The place is surrounded! Throw down your weapons and come out with your hands in the air!"

And Officer Kerner would curse and kick himself, the *Dummkopf* who hadn't thought anything of that iceman at the curb when he left 689, or that inebriated swell who sang "Love's Old Sweet Song" as he balanced a topper on the head of his walking stick.

Cops. Like the street sweeper and the mailman, the milkman and the priest. "I do believe it's going to work," said Andrew Parker, impressed by the accuracy of Meeghan's prediction. Those officers out there did look as natural as the little bit of wrought iron in front of the Roosevelt stoop.

—Except perhaps for the handle of the sidearm the "street

sweeper" was wearing on his hip, sticking out beneath the drape of the white jacket. Exactly the kind of blunder which even a man blind to danger might find too obvious to ignore.

"Just what we need." Theodore's senior left the living room. He was on the street side of the threshold before the President of the Police Board realized where he was going.

■ After Richard washed his hands in the basin of the lavatory on the second floor of 689 Madison, he took a towel from the rack and, attracted by what sounded like a front door too hastily opened, glanced out the window.

What he saw was a man with a face familiar and yet not immediately identifiable, a man hurrying over to the street sweeper at the curb. The exchange which followed was brief—something to do with the bunching of the man's jacket at the side: it seemed to be caught around the end of a curving object, perhaps the handle of a gun?

Commissioner Parker? Was that Police Commissioner Andrew D. Parker out there straightening the fall of the fabric so that the gun—if it was a gun—could be better concealed beneath?

One final word and then the official went back into the house he'd come from, the sweeper returning to his broom and shovel, the high-wheeled cart which held the refuse can.

Not, however, before his eyes looked over to the iceman at the corner, a surreptitious little high sign, returned. These people were not unacquainted, were they, and what about the mailman over there?

Working late, unusually late, Officer Kerner thought, as he stepped out of the convenience, smiling to see Minnie with Officer Hargate, waiting for him in the hall. "What's this?" he joked: "my bride-to-be and my best friend?" A satirically melodramatic forearm covered his forehead. "Do I dare ask the *Truth?*"

"Hearts and Flowers" in the background.

"That call just now was from the Commissioner," Minnie related, amused by the improvised excerpt from *East Lynne.* "Parker's holding him downtown, something political."

No meeting, therefore.

"I see." Downtown. Parker keeping Roosevelt four miles south of Sixty-second Street, at this very moment. "Any details?"

The younger cop shook his head. "All he said was he wanted you back in Hell's Kitchen right away."

" 'Right away' means after I escort Miss Kelly home, I hope." Richard's hand closed around Minnie's, the merest touch enough to send a thrill through her skin.

"There isn't time," she had to say, reluctant. "Mr. Roosevelt thinks there's a connection between Estes Hanrahan and the De-Lacy case."

"He wants you to put your ear to the ground." Quoted exactly, as per Lindy's orders. "The quicker the better."

"Boy." An echo of Kermit and Ted, to stall. To think. What to do. How to do it. "If that's true it could be one hell of a break in the case." His grip tightened on Minnie's hand.

"You're hurting me." The words surprised them both. He released her immediately.

"Forgive me," he said, flustered. It was the news. The implications. Of course he would go directly to Hell's Kitchen; could he trust Officer Hargate to escort his fiancée across the Brooklyn Bridge? "You look like a man of integrity."

Charm. Personality. Miss Minnie Gertrude Kelly could not be more safe were her escort the Sisters of Mercy themselves.

"Now there's a disguise for an undercover cop," the elder patrolman allowed as they descended the flight to the vestibule below, Edith and the little ones assembled for the farewells. Had he seen a wimple out there on the street . . . ?

In a manner of speaking, yes. A priest, if the photographic plate in his mind wasn't already too faded.

Edith was speaking to him. "Excuse me?"

"Mother wants you to remind Daddy when you see him," Alice paraphrased, unbidden. "He's supposed to let Miss Kelly off early Saturday afternoon. The first fitting is at four o'clock."

"Are you kidding, Mrs. R.?" The bridegroom's final sally, delivered as he ushered the bride down the stoop steps to the sidewalk outside. "The Commissioner's going to have her there by noon himself. You know that."

Of course she did. If this was the same Theodore Roosevelt Edith had known since they were six, she'd hardly be surprised if he gave Minnie the whole day off, just to make sure she wouldn't be late to so important a preliminary.

The carriage which Edith had telephoned to arrange was waiting a short distance up the street at the curb, behind a pair of back-to-back surreys hitched closer to the house. "Allow me, sir," the driver petitioned, opening the sidewalk-side door for his passengers, Minnie to precede Officer Hargate within.

"Without a kiss?" A comical pout came to the face of her intended as she moved to disengage from his arm: funnier even than his *East Lynne* in the second-floor hall. Minnie laughed and kissed him, a long, loving kiss.

"Will you be there on Saturday?" The blue eyes reflected the flicker of the gas lamp adjacent.

"Do you want me to be?" The view over Minnie's shoulder was clear well beyond Madison, almost all the way up to Fifth. The brownstone across the street was dark, as though all inside had gone to sleep. No sign of Andrew Parker or any other of New York City's police commissioners.

Eight o'clock. And still the street sweeper in his white Sanitation Department jacket trudged behind his broom, tipping his cap to the souse. Not far away was the iceman's wagon.

"Do I want you to be: what a question." Whispered as her lips brushed past his ear.

"Then I guess I'll be there," he said, placing himself between Minnie and Lindy so that Roosevelt's secretary could have the rigidity of his palm to push up from as she stepped into the waiting conveyance. His younger colleague stood aside, automatically expecting that Richard would make room once Miss Kelly was seated within.

"She'll be home before nine," he wanted her fiancé to know as the bullet from the gun concealed in Officer Kerner's hand blasted into his unprotected chest, point-blank.

5 ROOSEVELT

■ No time to think. No time to know what to think. A pain so immense as to obliterate all other feeling was serrating through his chest, slamming him backward.

What was happening—?

The scream was his, ripped from the throat—or was it Minnie screaming? He could see the sudden horror on her face as it peered in shock through the open door of the carriage, hear the "someone shot Lindy" that came from her mouth. "Richard?"

Not an accusation. A cry for help, instinctive and devastated. Who? it asked. Who fired? Who fired at Officer Hargate?

In that first second of panic and confusion, she couldn't know. No one could, not even Lindy himself. Where was the weapon? Discharged by a sniper from a rooftop across the street? Behind the bushes in front of 20 East Sixty-second Street, was that where the assassin lay in ambush?

No time to think. No time to assess the blue-orange flash which had spewed in a narrow jet from the front pocket of Officer Kerner's jacket. This was not a single occurrence, complete unto itself. There was more, all at once. Horses neighing in fright, the cabbie lunging forward even as Richard swung himself up onto the footrail of the hack. Two more shots in rapid succession.

Now the gun was out, spitting, the blasts echoing off the cornices atop the brownstones. The crown of the driver's head exploded, a fountain of blood and brain showering the younger patrolman even as the third of Richard's rounds crashed into his body, spinning him.

Lindy's legs buckled, bringing him down in a tangle of arms and legs, his own and the driver's. His fingers caught inside the man's eviscerated skull, hooked beneath the open bone. "Yaaahh!" he heard the killer shout, frenzied in the driver's seat of the cab, reins in hand. "Yaaahhh!"

Snap!

Never had either horse felt so sharp a pain: their master had been good to them, had treated them with affection and kindness. This was unexpected, new, and their instinct was simultaneous. Run. Run. Get away.

They bolted forward. Minnie, aghast, speechless in her terror, felt an invisible hand shove her backward against the seat, the wheels bouncing, lurching, breaking the outstretched arm of the cabbie sprawled out across the cobblestones, coming within an eighth of an inch of Lindy's leg.

"Down!" Commissioner Roosevelt was scrambling out of the Day house, *pince-nez* flapping at the end of the ribbon attached to his vest, careening against his belly like a hanged man in a hurricane. It was an instruction yelled at his own family, his wife and children frozen on the stoop and in mortal danger. "In the house, damn it; duck! Move!"

Ethel whimpered, Edith yanking her toward the door behind them even as a new burst of bullets breached the barrel of Richard's gun, these missiles aimed wild behind him as he whipped the animals and headed east on Sixty-second. The iceman leaped sideways, seeking shelter behind the paneling of his wagon. The inebriate dropped to one knee and returned the fire, one of his charges ricocheting off the keystone above the gilded 689 framing Edith's head, peppering her with chips of stone, panicking the children.

"Daddy!" Ethel's whimper had become a scream. "I want my daddy!"

"Is she all right? Edith?" Had the ultimate catastrophe occurred? Had his daughter been harmed?

"Edith—?"

"We're all right." In one piece, she meant. They were definitely *not* "all right."

"Inside, then—*now.*" The President of the Police Board pivoted, arms up, fingers cutting the night. What was Meeghan waiting for? "Isn't anyone going after them? Meeghan?"

"*Meeghan.*" Parker was cold fire alongside the stunned official. Parker, to atone for the mess he had made of things.

"Are we just going to stand here?" Meeghan in turn, yelling at his men. "Baker? Esterbrook? —Williamson?"

"Send some of them up Madison and around Sixty-third," T.R. barked, getting down on his knees beside the fallen rookie. "See if you can head them off on Lexington—no: Third. They must be at Lexington already. And get reinforcements, Meeghan. Empty the Sixteenth Precinct if you have to; I want every last able-bodied man in on this, that's my secretary that bastard just kidnapped."

Clattering hooves, monosyllabic threats directed to neighboring equines. Meeghan's men were making up for time lost, moving fast, spurring their steeds. The lieutenant himself made for the Roosevelt home, the telephone within.

"Use the phone in Mr. Day's house," an irritated Theodore Roosevelt rasped. Didn't Meeghan know anything? "We're calling the ambulance from my phone. The doctor." A pair of small heads with tousled hair infiltrated the periphery of his vision as he spoke, filling the window adjacent to the evacuated stoop. "You hear that, children? Have Mother call a doctor for Officer Hargate. An ambulance."

"Mother," he could hear them cry, and the immediate response from his wife, farther within.

"I'm on the line now, tell him."

"Good." Roosevelt could turn to Parker and ask for a hand. They couldn't leave the wounded youth in the gutter, the flow of his blood unstaunched, mingling with the sewer water at the curb.

"Should we move him at all?" Parker fought the nausea turning his stomach.

"It's fifty feet—sixty at the most." Not a major move.

"How many steps up, though? Eight? Twelve?"

"This man is not going to bleed to death in the street, by God. Either pitch in or get that man there to take your place." His hand was already insinuating itself beneath the officer's shoulders, the other getting a grip on the thigh.

"Please, sir." The request of the fallen cop, the unfocused eyes trying to find the elder of the commissioners, to allay the fears. "It's wet out here. So cold."

Was it the trickle of water beneath him that brought the chills? Parker plunged in, helping Teddy make a seat for the officer between their gripping hands. "On three" they lifted, letting the legs dangle, the trousers soaked from cuffs to knees.

"Okay," T.R. nodded as they struggled with 180 pounds of nearly dead weight, taking the steps of the stoop sideways as they ascended. "We'll make an officer out of you yet, my friend."

Could someone inside open the door? Alice? Ted?

Kermit?

They were there, a widening wedge of light illuminating the precariously balanced trio as though its members were actors on one of Mr. Albee's stages. Lindsay Hargate groaned as the commissioners lifted him across the landing at the front of the entry.

"Shh," his immediate superior whispered, encouraging. "Almost there." He looked daggers across the slumping body. "Careful."

"It's okay, sir," the youth wanted him to know. "I'm not as bad as I look; I'll make it. I swear I will."

I'm not as bad as I look. Wasn't it Roosevelt who'd said that to Lindy once? Where was that, the park? There are balances in this world, after all, aren't there, T.R. couldn't help but think as he and Andrew brought the casualty to the couch in the parlor. Every once in a while the favors are returned.

"Edith?"

"The ambulance is on the way," the announcement preceded by a knock on the door, still open. "In here, Dr. Dietz."

"My God," Parker said, impressed.

"My office is just around the corner," the physician explained as he entered the room. He was a lean little man, barely five and a half feet in height, the beard outlining his jaw curving up around his ears to become the fringe encircling the polished skin on the top of his skull. Teddy always thought of him as a burrowing animal, the kind which tunnels just under the surface of the land, popping up bright-eyed and unexpectedly competent at precisely the destination intended.

"Is there anything we can get for you?"

"Hot water." The hands were already on the patient, spreading the lids of the eyes, checking the strength of the pulse at the side of the neck. Lindy did not seem to differentiate this newcomer from the others in the room; they were all wraiths to him, barely corporeal.

"Have Annie boil water," T.R. said to Alice. Did Dietz want them to help get the clothing off?

"Better I cut it away, all this blood coagulating here." The surprisingly slender fingers were delving into the leather bag placed at the foot of the coach, retrieving a pair of snips as a new racket arose outside. Hooves. The rattle of iron-rimmed wheels interacting with cobblestone.

"It's the ambulance, Father," Ted called from the watch he and Kermit were keeping atop the window seat. "The ambulance is here."

"Bellevue, it says." Kermit read the name off the side of the red-painted wagon, tentatively. He was still feeling his way when it came to the letters.

The Commissioner flew at the front door, swinging it wide in one fluid motion. "In here, gentlemen. The parlor; the doctor is with him."

Four white-jacketed young men carrying a stretcher came up the stone steps in tandem, the tips of their shoes resounding as though they had taps on them. Roosevelt led them to Dietz, who was kneeling beside the blue-skinned rookie, chromium instrument in his hand, pronged: a tweezer inserted beneath the surface of the wound. Blood welled as he tugged, and despite the towel the physician had thought to place on the sofa, browning splatters and droplets discolored the velvet and dripped to the carpet on the floor adjacent.

"One moment, I think I've got the slug. Yes. Here." Was there an extra cloth? A sponge?

"Coming." Edith was returning with the requested pot of boiling water and a pair of kitchen towels. The sponge.

"Capital," her husband decreed, taking the weight off her hands as, with one last yank, Dietz freed the bullet from the sundered flesh. Lindsay Hargate gurgled, inhaling.

Nothing followed.

"No!" the doctor shouted. "You are not slipping away from me now." He punched the broad, trapezoidal chest. "Breathe, dammit. Breathe!" A spray of blood slashed his face, goading him.

Another punch.

"Theodore," Edith gasped, but then Lindy hiccuped and started to breathe again, moaning.

"Better." Dietz glared at the patient as he took the sponge and used it first to wipe the blood from the wound and then to clean his own glistening countenance.

A glance in the direction of the newcomers. "Bandages. You did bring bandages, yes?"

Yes.

"Daddy." Ethel jiggled his sleeve.

"I'll be with you in a minute, sweetheart." They were bucket-brigading the bandages, and he couldn't look up.

"But Mommy is crying."

He could look up.

She wasn't in the room, his wife, his devastated wife, she was halfway up the stairs, clinging to the banister and weeping. "Edith?"

"Don't *touch* me," she said, brushing him away when he came to her, fleeing up to the bedroom, slamming the door.

■ Composure. Control. Common sense. For ten years now she had been his rock, the wall against which he could always lean. Understanding always came into her eyes when he had his problems and confusions, when he acted impetuously and regretted it.

To flee from him like this was a concept terrifying to him in itself, especially when he thought she'd bolted the door, turned the little brass lever beneath the knob and locked him out. Of course she couldn't really do that, could she, not so long as he had shoulder and shoe leather—but his ears had deceived him in his anxiety. The knob turned in his hand.

She was stripping the bed of its spread, its sheets, its blanket, piling the linen on the chair alongside. "If it's the blood, Edie, if it's what Dr. Dietz was doing with his fist—"

"Is that what you think it was? The blood?" One of the pillows was flagged by her hands; Edith swung it at the wall. The case peeled away and the resulting impact resounded like the concussion of a mortar, slamming hard against the Commissioner's ears. "You don't remember when you broke your arm on that hunt before the Meadowbrook Ball? Who pushed the bone back?"

No flinching from blood in 1885. No flinching from blood in 1895. Active people bleed, and you damn well better get used to it if you want to stay married to them. You damn well better not mind it too much when you're raising their kids.

"Then what?" he wondered. "Minnie?" Was it worry that Richard would do her harm, or worse? "That we won't get to them in time?"

They'd get to them, Teddy promised her that; hell, it was a promise he'd made to himself the minute he saw what his unfaithful aide had done. They'd be breathing down the back of that renegade's neck before the sun came up.

New bedding filled her forearms, fresh from the linen closet. The bottom sheet whipped up into the air, crackling like a sail in a windstorm. "How long have you known?" she hissed, furious. "How long has it been since you found out it was Richard?"

"Late this afternoon." At a pawnshop near the West Side piers. "I've never had to move so fast in my life."

"And the first thing that comes to your mind was to get him up *here?* To our house?" Edith circled the mattress, tucking and folding, lifting the next corner to tuck and fold once more. Her hands would either be busy with this or they'd strike out at him.

"I had to have men in position to start following him"; it was not a job that Roosevelt could undertake alone—there had to be reinforcements, "and this was unquestionably the perfect place to start them all off."

"Where our children live." Only once before had the Commissioner seen Edith's lower lip tremble the way it was trembling now; that was on a dark afternoon in 1878 when the twenty-year-old Teedie had come to Thirty-sixth Street with his heart in his mouth, come to tell his dear Miss Carow that that very heart had been snatched away from her, stolen by a beautiful stranger in the wilds of Massachusetts. A Lee of Chestnut Hill.

"Just like that," she'd said to him then. "Just like that."

It had been just like that, yes, no matter how hard it was for him to say and for her to believe . . . as hard as it was for Edith to believe him now, seventeen years later. Had he considered the safety of his children? His wife?

Had he really?

"Officer Kerner wasn't a random killer: everything he did he did for those plans. That machine." Would Richard even think of doing harm to the very people who gave him the patina of respectability? T.R. thought not. "He loves Miss Kelly, Edith. He really adores her."

A gamble worth taking, therefore. Had Andrew D. Parker not leaped before he looked, had Richard Kerner not looked . . .

"If it weren't Andrew it would have been someone else," Edith cried. "Some*thing* else." There was no way for Theodore to have controlled the perimeter of his clever little trap, "and once that man realized it was a trap, no one was going to stand in his way, I don't care how old, or what gender." The top sheet billowed out from her hands now, another sail, another wind. "Should I be grateful that we were lucky and it wasn't Kermit he shot? Ethel?" Archie or Ted?

"You cannot say anything to me I haven't already said to myself," her husband assured her, stepping between Edith and the bedspread waiting in folded silence on the dresser, opening it. "I have a good man downstairs dying, perhaps—close to it—I pushed a fine, virtuous young woman into a romance with a murderer and as a result she's now somewhere out there maybe alive, maybe dead; either way it's because I was so damned sure the brilliant intellect couldn't possibly be anything but on the money. If I did go off, it wasn't going to be by enough to change the whole outcome—Destiny's Anointed doesn't ever make *that* kind of mistake."

Aligned: the edge of the mattress with the pleat in the spread. Mr. and Mrs. Theodore Roosevelt smoothed the wrinkles on either side of the bed and regarded each other. "I thought as much of Officer Kerner as you did," Edith finally said. "Stop kicking yourself." Her feet brought her from the headboard to the window, one more of the neighbors looking out at Meeghan's men milling with apparent purpose down on the street below, more arriving with every passing minute. "Now I know what it's like, being married to a policeman."

"Not just any policeman." He stood beside her, hand lifted behind her back, ready to rest on her shoulder. Were Edith willing.

She was, even as she looked at him over her shoulder, one eyebrow elevated. That was the point, wasn't it, that this husband of hers was wearing two different hats all of a sudden, and the balance was shifting—from inside the office to out. The Commissioner's wife hadn't bargained for that, the disorder it brought to the shape of their lives.

"Andrew asked for my resignation. Are you?"

"I'd just like to know which hat I'm married to, that's all: cop or Commissioner. I can deal with either." Not both.

"Edie," he whispered, fingers kneading the ruffles covering her slender shoulders. "As soon as this is done with, I promise you there'll be no more cases. No more playing inspector." No other case could involve him so personally.

None.

Her response was delayed by a tumult outside, several vehicles arriving at once, horses lathered. Lieutenant Meeghan himself led the charge to a halt in front of 689, his hair a bird's nest, uniform rumpled. "Are they still in there?" he asked in a high-pitched voice intolerant and beset, the officers on the sidewalk flinching: the fuse was lit, and short.

"Up here, Lieutenant," Roosevelt called, thrusting the casement up. "Am I right in assuming you lost them?"

"Look at the head start he had, Commissioner." And how heartbreakingly close they came: "For a minute down on Fortieth I thought, 'We're going to get that skunk, we're going to have the cuffs on him by Thirty-sixth—Thirty-fifth if we're slow.' "

"And?" As if Teddy couldn't answer that himself.

"Pulled a switch on us, the bastard." Meeghan pawed the ground, tracing the periphery of an isolated cobblestone with the flattened tip of an unpolished shoe. "The cab was there, going like fifty, but no Kerner."

No Kerner, no Kelly. Just a runaway carriage and pair and the fugitive could be anywhere by now, with or without his hostage.

"Maybe not 'anywhere,' sir." Meeghan was proud of himself: he'd sent some of his officers up to East Eighty-fifth Street. "That's his address, y'know, 448 East Eighty-fifth Street."

"They're not going to find anything." Richard was taking Minnie to the hideout of his gang, which wouldn't be in his apartment.

"How can you be so sure?" Bristling.

"Where did you say you lost them? On Fortieth? Heading *down*town?"

"Can't they have circled back?"

"To an address we have on file? Lieutenant," T.R. said in a voice which tolerated no further argument, "get ahold of Felix Wiegand at the *Deutsches Journal;* you can use the phone downstairs this time. What I need is any address he might have not on Richard so much as on his brother. Wolf. Maybe he gets the paper by subscription, that'd be dandy; if Wiegand can't help, find Jake Riis: somebody's got to know something over at the *Sun.* " Someone on the Franchise Tax Board, perhaps. "Fingers crossed, Wolf owns property. Even if he rents we could be okay: my guess is he'd be wired for lights and that means Edison'd be billing him."

"We could do the same with Bell," Meeghan suggested in the hope that his superior would be impressed by the belated attention to detail. "Someone like that'd probably have a phone, right?"

"Right." A wave sent the man on his way, Roosevelt ducking

back into the bedroom, incongruously perky as he grinned at his wife. "You're right, too," he wanted her to know. "I *do* love being in the thick of it, out on the street. It's fun. Exciting. Shuffling papers? Edie: Parker shuffles papers. Freddie Grant. I'm better than they are."

Would she have married Andrew, or the son of the late President? Why had the mother of his children waited for him the way she did, unwilling to give herself to any Avery Andrews who'd come along, unwilling to put her "Mrs." in front of just any name?

"Because, Mrs. Edith Kermit Carow Roosevelt, I don't think you mind it anywhere near as much as you say you do, not knowing which hat I have on. Cop, Commissioner, it keeps you on your toes. It keeps me on *my* toes, by George!"

"You're not going to stop playing inspector when this is done with at all, are you."

"Being Police Commissioner means playing inspector sometimes. It means being cop and administrator, politician, scientist, all at once, or one right after the other." He'd lied to her when he'd said he'd stick to his desk once the case was closed; it was dishonesty for the sake of expedience and he regretted the weakness, which was unworthy of him. Utterly unworthy. "Of course, you didn't believe a word of it, did you."

"No." She had not. No more than she believed that he would alert her the next time (oh, yes, there would be a next time!), or consult her beforehand. Or warn her. And if Edith railed and cried and kicked, he'd come to her again with that same contrite-little-boy look on his face and eventually—sooner, perhaps—the anger would wear off. The acceptance would return. And the forgiveness.

Oh, if only he could go to the door right now and turn that little brass lever beneath that knob.

■ "Is Lindy going to die?"

Dr. Dietz was not going to get past Ethel Roosevelt, not without giving her the prognosis. He was going to have to stand there between the sliders separating the parlor from the vestibule, bloodied towel in hand, and speak. The four-year-old might not have known the wounded rookie well but she had to like him and wish him Godspeed: he'd saved her father's life once and it was only fair that now the same be done for him.

"Do you want it honest, young lady?" There was a glint in the eyes staring down at her. "Or do you want it sugar-coated?"

"Father says sometimes sugar isn't very good for you." Kermit moved up to stand tall alongside his younger sister, shoulders squared.

"Then you'll understand why I can't give you a definite answer to that question," the doctor replied. "I don't know if Officer Hargate is going to live or die. I won't be able to tell you that until at least tomorrow morning, maybe not until the morning after that." It was, indeed, touch and go. Thoracic wounds were difficult, even when the major arteries weren't involved. "He's young, though. Tough. Points in his favor."

"And he's getting the best medical care," Ted was convinced, or wanted to be convinced, the stern visage looking down at him surprised by the unsolicited testimonial, enough to crinkle.

"Well." Even so. "There comes a point when nothing more can be done, no matter how good the doctor. If it's in the patient to live, he will. If not—?"

A shrug: Hiram Dietz had done his best. Understanding illuminated their scrubbed little faces. "Like when Bishop Doane died," Ethel recalled. "We couldn't do anything after the breathing stopped."

"Bishop Doane died?" Andrew Parker emerged from the hall beneath the staircase, aghast. When last he'd heard, the good cleric had been alive. Vibrant. "This is terrible."

"I think the Bishop Doane my daughter's referring to is the guinea pig Bishop Doane," Theodore Roosevelt felt obliged to explain as he descended the stairs from above, Edith beside him. "One of the menagerie out at Sagamore Hill."

"You let your children name a rat after a man like Bishop Doane?" The impropriety was almost as shocking to Parker as the possibility that the human ecclesiast had succumbed without his knowing.

"Not a rat, Mr. Parker. A guinea pig." How a fully grown man like her father's friend on the Police Board could mistake one for the other was beyond Ethel. *She* knew the difference, and she was only four.

Archie knew the difference, and he wasn't even two.

"See here, Theodore—"

"Andrew," T.R. interrupted, the flat of his hand pressing forward against the shoulder blade, "when we have Minnie safe and Officer Kerner in jail with the rest of his bunch, then we can take the time to discuss the naming of pets. In the meantime I'd rather see if Lieutenant Meeghan's come up with an address for brother Wolf."

"Nothing yet, I'm afraid," the detective had to admit, the angle of his body in fatigue stretching the cord connecting the earpiece to the body of the phone, enough perhaps to rip the instrument off the wall. "Not at this time of night." No one was home at the Edison company, for instance, and the same went for Bell—"all that the operators could tell me was that they had nobody named Wolfgang Kerner in their directory."

"What about Wiegand?" Teddy asked. "Somebody has to be up at the *Deutsches Journal;* they put it out daily."

"And the subscription department locks up at six." Editor Wiegand was attending a function in the middle of the Hudson River, believe it or not. "By now the cruise boat he's on should be halfway up to Bear Mountain."

Not that the man would have the information they sought, not at his fingertips he wouldn't; "so what difference does it make if we get a man on board up there or not?" Parker had already told Meeghan not to waste the time.

"How practical of you," Roosevelt growled, breathing fire and brimstone onto the lenses of his *pince-nez,* scrubbing them spotless with his handkerchief. Had the lieutenant remembered to get Riis on the job, at least? "I did suggest you have him call over to his office, I believe."

"Nobody's seen him," Meeghan replied. "Not outside, not down on Fortieth Street; he wasn't at the paper, either." The detective wasn't particularly surprised: "the minute the shooting starts, these writer guys head for the nearest saloon." By the time Teddy got him out from under, Meeghan's boys would have the Kerners hog-tied and ready for the hangman.

"Then you won't be needing these addresses I went out and got while I was 'under' in the nearest saloon." The sound of the journalist's voice turned them all in the direction of the open door, Jake there looking more rumpled than ever, and a bit more winded. "I figured it might be a good idea to hurry out and do some fast research, we wanted to get a line on where Richard might've gone."

"Those addresses, sir," T.R. hissed. "Everything else can wait —Minnie's out there at gunpoint!"

"I've got three addresses under 'Kerner,' the first one right here in Manhattan. Eighty-fifth Street."

"Four forty-eight East, yes." They'd discussed it and dismissed it, Teddy's hand was quick to signal. "An airship wouldn't be built on top of a tenement."

"All right," Riis acceded, uninsulted. "Here's a Kerner in Brooklyn. Red Hook."

"Even more of a warren than East Eighty-fifth," as Jake damn well knew. "Out with it, man, come on." Roosevelt recognized the look on the newspaperman's face: the best was being saved for last.

"Captree Island." It had been on the list of registered voters kept in Mr. Dana's safe. Kerner, W. F., Captree Island, New York.

"Captree Island," a name to roll over the tongue. Somewhere off the southern coast of Long Island, wasn't it? "More sandbar than island," if the Commissioner remembered right.

What would the nearest town be? Bay Shore?

"Bay Shore," Riis nodded. "About two hours by rail. Two and a half."

"Two and a half hours by train," Parker repeated with a shake of the head. "All to look up a Kerner whose first name happens to start with a *W*—which could just as easily stand for William as Wolf. Walter."

"But it's not going to be William or Walter, Andrew, it's going to be Wolf." How right it felt, deep in the marrow of Theodore's bones. Of course it was Richard's brother out there on that flat, barren excuse for an island. "Isolated, private—just what you'd want if you were working on something secret."

Something intended to *fly*.

"These airships don't just pop up off the ground," Teddy imagined. A long, narrow strip barely twenty feet above sea level: what better place for the requisite speed?

"Maybe." Parker's impetuous colleague would have to give him more than intuition and circumstance; otherwise it would be too much like a wild-goose chase.

"Unless it turns out right."

"In which case," Andrew Parker smiled, "I will naturally have been in the vanguard from word one."

"Just so long as you aren't standing in the way." Teddy pushed past him, snatching the earpiece up from the phone on the wall. "Police Headquarters," he demanded, his voice sharp with excitement. "Mulberry Street."

Sergeant Conrad Balter was on duty at the desk. "Sir!" he exclaimed as soon as his commander identified himself.

"Commissioner Parker and I are on our way downtown. We are in need of a fully equipped patrol, Sergeant, twenty men at least—six mounted. Wagons to transport the remainder. *Fresh* horses, well rested—even if they are going to be spending the first hour or so of this assignment eating oats on a train."

Bewilderment came through the receiver in Roosevelt's fist. "Train?"

A nod. "See if we aren't too late to catch the last run to Bay Shore, Long Island. If we've missed it I want you to speak to the stationmaster at the Atlantic Avenue depot, Brooklyn: tell him Theodore Roosevelt wants him to make up a special express, police business. Make that *urgent* police business—those tracks have to be cleared."

"Do we have that kind of authority, Theodore?" Doubt made Parker's face pucker; the sight reminded T.R. of figs. Overripe figs. T.R. was allergic to figs.

"If 'hot pursuit' doesn't give us the authority I don't know what does." Richard wasn't going to be driving his kidnapped fiancée halfway across the length of Long Island in a horse-drawn carriage; Andrew could figure it out for himself. "The fastest way to get where he wants to go is by railroad. Following them by any other mode of transport wouldn't say very much for our intelligence." Was Balter still there?

"Sir."

"All right: those men you're getting us. Volunteers, Sergeant. This business tonight could be dangerous—warn them. I can't guarantee anybody's life."

"There isn't anyone in the department who wouldn't follow you into hell, Mr. Roosevelt. Myself included."

"Well." The officer's passion was unexpected: Mr. Roosevelt found himself incredibly touched, enough to necessitate a clearing of the throat. "Splendid. Because after you've gotten us the train and those twenty men are waiting for us downstairs, you've got another job to do for me, just as important." Was Conrad Balter a tactful man?

Conrad Balter hoped so. "I don't think you can sit at this desk ten hours a day, tactless." What was T.R.'s interest in his sense of discretion?

"Bay Shore," Teddy advised. "You're my personal liaison to the authorities there tonight." Telephone calls were to be made, to the mayor, the police chief, the fire chief, "the president of the Town Council—"

"Commissioner, are you aware of what time it is?"

"Why do you suppose I asked you about tact?" Sergeant Balter's job was to alert the aforementioned officials; "I don't care if you catch them in their pajamas." Police Commissioner Theodore Roosevelt of New York City was on his way to their community with an armed patrol, "hot on the heels of a gang of, I don't know, how does 'anarchists' sound?"

Balter thought it sounded fine.

"Just make damned sure those people out there don't overreact to the news, Sergeant: we've got a kidnap victim in the middle of all this and the last thing we need is a lot of bells and si*reens* going off at one in the morning. Her life would be worth about as much as the money in Jefferson Davis's vault, tell them that."

"I will," the officer promised, imbued as his superior terminated the call and plunged headlong into the hall closet.

"Edith, what'd I do with my fringed jacket? The buckskin from Abercrombie?"

"The one Father wore when he brought Redhead Finnegan in to the sheriff's office at Dickinson, Dakota," Ted interjected from the top of the stairs. Best seats in the house.

"Didn't we give it to charity last year in Washington?" Edith emerged from the parlor. A few extra logs on the fire would hardly do Officer Hargate any harm.

"When did we decide that?" There had been a request for garments to clothe the poor of the First Episcopal; Teddy vaguely remembered something along those lines, yes, but that meant old suits with shiny seats. Shirts holey in the elbow.

Not a suede hunting jacket with sentimental value!

"Really, Theodore," Parker had to observe. "It's not necessary to wear a Wild West costume just because you're taking a patrol out."

"Especially," the Commissioner's wife agreed, "when it was ripped from here to here and two sizes too small." Roosevelt had forgotten how he had tried it on, apparently. How he couldn't get any of the buttons near any of the eyes.

"Call Abercrombie first thing tomorrow morning," he said, selecting another coat from the rack and shrugging it on. "Give them the new measurements; let them duplicate the one they made for me back in '84. If they can add a scarf I can button in under the collar, so much the better." The Dakota wind had infiltrated his neck back there on the Missouri, now that he thought about it.

"How about a hood?" Cynicism from his rival, not entirely without cause. "A sewn-in set of earmuffs?"

"By George, that happens to be a capital idea!" Edith would make a note of it, he trusted, opening the door to the street and gesturing the menfolk through. "Who knows what criminals we might be after when December rolls around?"

His teeth blinded them, the pluck-filled gleam of pure white enamel defusing any potential retort other than Edith's "Be careful, Theodore," and the "Good-bye, Father" which came stratified from the mouths of his children.

Richard Kerner didn't have a prayer as far as they were concerned. The traitor was *finished*. Anyone with ears to hear the way Teddy Roosevelt said "Onward!" as he crossed the sidewalk to the carriage waiting had to know that, even Andrew D. Parker.

If he didn't, said Kermit when he and his brother Ted were upstairs under their counterpanes, he would. First light tomorrow . . . at the same time as the boys would be setting the ladder out on the stoop, climbing up with their pocket knives to dig the bullet out of the keystone over the front door. They'd make a cardboard plaque of it, for when their father came marching home.

■ Joseph Healy had been the conductor of the ten-eighteen out of the Atlantic Avenue terminus that night, a new employee of the railroad, barely nineteen. After no more than twenty-five runs to Riverhead and back passenger faces were already becoming indistinguishable to him, merely eyes and noses. Mouths which were more like curving lines, up at the ends or down. And yet when questioned by Lieutenant Meeghan the following afternoon the youngster could indeed remember Richard Kerner and Minnie Kelly as being aboard his train, as Commissioner Roosevelt had anticipated. "The couple at the front of car 145, by themselves in the corner, talking quiet."

Richard was the gentleman in the picture the lieutenant gave him to look at, yes, sir—but it wasn't anything about the male of the couple which had made such an indent on Joseph Healy's brain, it was the beleaguered expression on the face of the female. How, he'd asked himself all the way out to Bay Shore, could any girl be so pretty and so unhappy all at the same time?

"You should have seen her, sitting there all scrunched up around herself," inexplicable until the detective told him about the gun concealed in the lower right-hand pocket of the bridegroom's jacket, still warm from the recent discharge of bullets. As for the hole in the weave, perhaps Mr. Healy was lucky that it was tucked so unobtrusively into a fold of the garment, and that Minnie Gertrude Kelly had not attempted to communicate.

"I'm glad you didn't," Officer Kerner had in fact whispered to his companion after their tickets had been punched and the conductor moved on to the car ahead, spared.

"And have you shoot some other innocent bystander?"

"Do you honestly think I wanted to kill either of those men in front of the Commissioner's house?" Would he have resorted to that had there been any other less bloody means of escape? "Two years we've been putting this flying machine together."

"Two years and how many lives?" Sharp. Ironic.

"Yes," he was quite willing to agree. "Exactly. What was I supposed to do, forget all that and lead them to it?"

"Once you knew they were tailing you, you would have led them anywhere but." The voice trembled, not so much with fear as with rectitude. "You could have lost them anytime you wanted, clever policeman that you are."

Wasn't the night dark enough for him? Or was it that her beloved Richard wouldn't have regarded those men as individuals in the first place—how much easier to clear the inanimate object from the path, what difference the means?

"Killing is wrong by definition, is that what you think?" He reached out to turn her face back from the window, from her sudden fascination with the moving shapes snatched by the night. "There's never any reason for taking a life?"

"Other than self-defense?" Was that his plea? "Lindy wasn't coming at you. The cab driver wasn't coming at you. My God, you were perfectly safe."

"In the short run, yes," Officer Kerner acknowledged, "I was perfectly safe." But more than his own safety was at stake. Other people were depending on him. A race. A whole race. "We either act at the first sign of danger or we're not fit to survive. That's how the world works, Minnie; there's nothing immoral about it."

Just the opposite. This was a test of the Nordic will. God was watching, wanting to see if this generation had the guts to make its nation first on the face of the earth, the strength to keep its birthright pure.

"You can believe that and still want to marry me? How?" Richard's intended wasn't from any branch of his Northern European stock; she was Irish. "The blood is Celtic."

" 'Celtic.' " As if anyone could ever make him accept that. "My ancestors went to Ireland, Minnie Kelly; they left their traces." She was a descendant of the *Wälsungen,* it was obvious. "You can tell by the eyes, the shape of the head, the bones. Everything." Mr. Roosevelt's secretary wasn't going to be stuck for the rest of her life with typewriter ink on her fingers and a son of pompous Dutchmen for a boss. "You deserve better."

"What if I don't want better?" she asked. "What if I just want you to let me off this train here, in—"

—Lindenhurst, the sign said on the other side of the window, the train coming to rest. "Next stop, Bay Shore." Joseph Healy's baritone rang through the car from the door at the end.

"Richard, please, let me go. You don't need me anymore." The escape had been made good: could Minnie be anything other than excess baggage now?

Incomprehension stretched the patrolman's features into the semblance of a smile. She was teasing him, wasn't she, getting some sort of perverse enjoyment from it, testing him the way God was testing them all. Didn't she know how he felt about her? Hadn't he said it a hundred times over, "I love you"? The future Mrs. Kerner couldn't want to get off the train now, not after having come this far with him tonight. She just couldn't.

"I do, though. I really do." Barely audible, spoken from a crouch. Bullets would reward the bravery, Minnie waited for the blast, but so what? She did not want to be with him anymore. She did not want to see his flying machine.

No. *Charles DeLacy's* flying machine.

Had the terror not constricted her throat on Sixty-second Street, she'd have said so there. She'd have said it again once they were across the bridge, on Schermerhorn Street, and she'd have repeated it in the railroad station at Atlantic Avenue when Richard was purchasing their tickets east on the ten-eighteen.

She was saying it now, thirty-five miles later. I do not want to see that airship.

"You *have* to see it," Roosevelt's aide could only aspirate, gathering himself up like a judge on the bench. "None of this can mean anything until you look at it with your own eyes." The reality was everything, that the device had actually been built.

That it had actually been flown.

"Once you know that—I mean, really know that—you'll stay." Officer Kerner was convinced of that. His hand wagged in the jacket pocket. Sit. Be fair.

Sit.

"If not?" Minnie was still half up on her feet even though the train was lurching, starting up again. "If I still don't want to stay?"

She'd be free to go then. Of course. "But you won't want to do that, I promise you. You won't."

"Bay Shore," the conductor called. "Bay Shore next stop."

■ "Someone has to sign for this." The stationmaster stood with a letterhead on Platform 16, Atlantic Avenue, the center of a triangle made up of Commissioners Parker and Roosevelt, and Jacob Riis. Behind them nineteen men in the blue uniforms of the New York City Police Department were boarding a parlor car labeled *City of Syracuse,* a twentieth man leading six tethered mounts into the slat-sided boxcar behind.

"Theodore?" Andrew Parker certainly wasn't going to affix his name to this handwritten document: it was an admission of responsibility which sooner or later might come back to bedevil the signatory.

"My pleasure." T.R.'s Waterman was already up, unsheathed with a flourish. He trusted that Mr. Beemer, the stationmaster, had arranged to have the tracks cleared between Atlantic Avenue and Bay Shore and that "the engineer knows how to get up a full head of steam."

"Mr. Kennedy is as capable as any accredited man in our employ. And the engine he's using tonight happens to be one of our finest"—protection more perhaps for the railroad than for the

party of officers and officials boarding this four-car special, Teddy
Roosevelt's reputation alone making that imperative. This boiler
tonight was going to be pushed.

"Splendid." The President of the Police Board beamed, swat-
ting the stationmaster's shoulder as he handed him his paper,
signed. "Shall we?" It was time to follow the men onto the *City of
Syracuse* and get under way.

Puffs of thick white smoke were beginning to pucker out of the
smokestack atop the locomotive, the space between each dimin-
ishing until finally the balloons all merged together, the plume of
an upended volcano. In the cab beneath, Mr. Sean Patrick Kennedy yanked at the chain to the left of his controls and a long low
howl rang through the night.

"Doesn't that make your blood run, Jake? Isn't that the most
wonderful sound in the world?" Teddy stood on the platform
outside the door at the end of the car, peering forward along the
length of the train, impulsively leaning out to wave at the men in
the switching tower they were leaving behind. "Full steam
ahead!"

"Come inside, will you?" The romance of the rails had never
infected Commissioner Parker. The damn things were merely
conveyances, no better than carriages or rowboats, useful only in
that they could get you from one place to another faster than your
feet could, with less wear on the soles of your shoes. *Coq au vin,*
now: if there was anything to set a sophisticated heart aflutter, *coq
au vin* was it. *Ris de veau.* Whistles screeching through the night
gave Parker a headache.

"Weren't you ever a boy, Andrew? Didn't you ever dream of
laying your hands on the throttle, roaring your own train through
the country at sixty miles an hour?"

Mrs. Evans's son did.

"Some of us," Theodore was informed, "couldn't wait to grow
up." Parker left his colleague to enjoy the clacking below and the
huffing above. He and Riis could be deafened to their hearts'
content, and welcome to it.

"Odd," Roosevelt had to remark. "A man that wealthy being
so deprived as a child." The darkness swallowed up the signs

attached to the standards lining a platform ignored. Jamaica. Jamaica. Jamaica.

"Twelve minutes," Riis calculated, pocket watch in palm.
"Pretty good."

"Ten minutes would have been better." The Commissioner
swung himself onto the catwalk skirting the coal car which separated the *City of Syracuse* from the engine ahead. "At this rate it'll
be midnight before we pull into Bay Shore."

Where was he going?

"To see if I can lend a hand up there in the cab."

"Lend a hand doing what?" The reporter had to extend his
body out from the metal handhold at the corner of the coach and
shout forward in order to be heard. T.R. had already inched himself halfway down the length of the ledge, animated more than
Jake thought good for him. "You don't really think the engineer is
going to hand you his cap, do you?"

An answer came back with the wind but Riis couldn't make it
out, the train plunging headlong into a smoky tunnel, shrieking at
the top of its iron lungs. The clearance between the edge of the
tender and the jagged stone of the soot-coated walls couldn't have
been more than half an inch.

"Theodore—?" And again. "Commissioner?" God. The belt on
the rear of the coat could have snagged against one of those out-
croppings, and this tunnel was endless.

It fell away even as the image gripped his mind: the Bay Shore
special was back out under the open sky, three-quarter moon
bright enough to powder the landscape white.

"By George, that was close!" Jake didn't have to hear the Police Board President say it; he could read the lips. He could see
the exhilaration all over the shining face.

He could imagine the motorman's shock when the most celebrated of his passengers suddenly appeared in his den, beaming.
Booming.

"*Mis*ter Kennedy! Theodore Roosevelt, at your service. Is there
an extra shovel?"

6 WOLF

■ "Don't say anything till you look at it." That's all he asked of her, to just look at it, the request made as Richard escorted his bride-to-be up the slope from the skiff tied up on the reed-speckled shore of Captree Island. There was a hoarseness in his voice, the awed sound men make when they are entering the presence of their God, or when they have for the first time encountered the woman of their dreams. "Tell me it doesn't fly, then. Tell me we don't have to keep it roped down. Minnie, I swear to you: that thing wants to take off. It wants to live in the air."

"Halt—!" Not the English word. The German, underscored by a metallic click, the sound of a rifle bolt.

"Claus."

Claus, nineteen, on guard in front of the shed at the top of the hill, a snub-nosed individual with fanatic's eyes and an expression of perpetual dismay: what was so fanatic about a belief in the ascendency of the Aryan? "Richard?"

The gun was lowered slowly, the girl regarded with continued suspicion.

"We weren't expecting you till tomorrow."

"Plans change on you in this business." And Miss Kelly was to be treated with the respect due the future *Frau Kerner,* "verstehen, ja?"

"*Jawohl,*" came the chastened response, immediate. The dull clang of a hammer from within the salt-stained structure accompanied the congratulations which followed.

"What's going on in there?"

"Changes. Big changes." Claus leaned in. "Wolf says it's going to be ten times better once it's broken down and rebuilt. The machine."

"Now? Tonight?" Richard kicked the door open, infuriated. Minnie found herself dragged by the wrist into the shell, two stories high and held together with crossbeams and bailing wire, illuminated by kerosene.

There it was, filling the vastness of the place like a giant insect queen in the center of its hive, twin wings of gossamer fabric on either side of the body, angled backward. Four, five, six drones surrounded her, surgeonlike, parts of their mistress removed in pieces all over the floor.

"Wolf?"

The elder of the Kerners was perched atop a ten-rung ladder, screwdriver and oilcan occupying his hands as he labored over the bicycle chains attached to the propeller assemblies, sleeves rolled up and fastened with a pair of maroon-colored garters just above the eagle on his biceps. The scar on his cheek forked like summer lightning, phosphorescent in the flicker from the lanterns. Mr. Roosevelt hadn't half described the dread it inspired, Minnie thought; he hadn't even mentioned the quick breath that flew to her lungs, the sharp extra beat of her heart.

"What the hell are you doing, coming here twenty-four hours ahead of time?" Wolf's hand swept in front of him. "This was supposed to have been a surprise."

"It is." Particularly when the patrolman remembered how his brother himself said the flight last Sunday evening had been . . . "perfect"?

"Two hundred yards is hardly perfect." These improvements to DeLacy's original design, however, would double that distance, "and by the end of November I think we can double it again."

"We might not have anything to 'double' if we can't get this machine put back together in the next hour or so," Richard snapped. "The faster we move it out of here the better."

"Is that so." Wolf slid down the rails of the ladder as though he were eight instead of thirty-eight, gray eyes marbling. "Perhaps you'd care to explain that?" An explanation for the unauthorized presence of Miss Kelly might be forthcoming as well.

"She's here because she's my fiancée and from now on she goes where I go. Theodore Roosevelt will be here whether we like it or not: he's on to me, *meine Herren,* which means he's on to all of us. I had to shoot my way out of a trap tonight." The officer's getaway, clean as it was, didn't put his band in the clear. "That man is a highly placed official; he can pick up a phone at any hour and open any archive. The name of this island could be in his hands right now."

"Quatsch," as far as Wolf was concerned: poppycock. The odds against were so wide as to be astronomical. By the time the department heads were aroused, by the time the clerks were located and the locks unlocked, dawn would be chasing them all. By the time the connections were made and the manpower organized, the sun would be casting shadows east. "Ten hours leeway, at least. Twelve, more likely."

"You'd actually take the chance." The head shook in amazement. "Just to add a few 'improvements' we can always talk about later, when we're safe."

"Tapering those wings is not an improvement that can wait, especially if your brilliant Commissioner really is coming after us. If my figures are right," and Richard's brother had no doubt but that they were, "it reduces wind drag by a coefficient of seventeen. That's enough to get us all the way across the Great South to Bayberry Point."

"If my former boss doesn't show up with an army before you have all those parts screwed back in."

"Claus," the elder Kerner called out, the snub-nosed guard turning in the half-open door. "Are there any boats coming this way? Anything moving out there at all?"

"No, *Gruppenführer.*"

"Danke." Wolf circled his brother as he waved the boy back to

his post, directing Richard's attention to the nearest cluster of disassembled airship pieces. "Just putting it back the way it was would still take us over three full hours. And where would we be able to fly it after that?"

Across the narrow channel to Sexton Island, adjacent. No more.

"What do we gain by going to Sexton Island? A hiding place Mr. Roosevelt wouldn't think of exploring?" All the man had to do was use his eyes, Sexton being no more wooded than Captree. "Try hiding a shoe there, much less a flying machine."

"Listen to him, Richard," a *Münchner* named Ahrens advised, big and stocky in bib overalls. "If we really can get it to fly over to the mainland . . ."

Another alternative came suddenly to mind; Officer Kerner cut the argument off with an upraised palm. "How long would it take to crate?" he wanted to know. "The whole thing, in boxes we can ship back to the fatherland?"

"Even if we had the crates to begin with—"

"Verflucht!" There was enough wood and nails in the building to make a hundred crates. Two hundred crates.

"By which time we would be safe on the other side of the bay." A raised voice could be equaled, or exceeded. "Of course, if you want to stand there and argue some more, we can do that, too," Wolf snapped. "Not terribly productive, especially if you really think the bloodhound's breathing down our necks but, what the hell, Richard, I've spent a lifetime indulging you. What's an hour or two more?"

"Stop it, both of you." Ahrens came between them before the younger Kerner could throw a first punch. "Crating is out of the question, and so is putting it back together without any of the improvements." He whirled on the engineer before Wolf could presume vindication. "Five hours, I'd say: that's all we have. If you're not equipped to do it properly by then, I say burn it. Right here and now, burn it in this shed and take the plans with us back to Bavaria."

"Start from scratch," Richard mused, for clarification's sake.

"Where there are no Theodore Roosevelts." The more Ahrens

considered it, the more he preferred it. With DeLacy's sketches
virtually intact and Wolf's interpretive genius given free reign to
amend, to refine, to build—

"We are burning *nothing!*" Wolf recoiled from them, these
friends and disciples who asked the sacrifice of his only begotten
child. "I will not allow it!"

"Then, *Bruder,*" Officer Kerner suggested, the accommodation
in his smile aimed not at Wolf but at the woman shrinking beside
him, "hadn't you better get back up on that ladder and fix, fast?"

■ They lined themselves up along the length of the Bay Shore
station: Mayor Cleveland Hodges, his council and police chief, all
in soup and fish, all rehearsing their smiles of welcome as they
waited for the four-car express to come to a halt. It did, at last, a
bit farther along than anyone expected, brakes squealing against
the shining rails. The sound startled several birds awake in the
nearby elms; they fluttered up out of the branches with frightened
squawks, their alarm increased by the sudden blare of trumpet,
tuba, glockenspiel and snare, the only members of the high school
band Mayor Hodges's wife was able to gather on two hours' notice.

Down went McGinty to the bottom of the wall . . .

Behind them were half the ladies' auxiliary, surrounded by several volunteer fire fighters and the denizens of the White Star
Tavern. "Who're we meeting?" one inquired in tones lubricated
by Kentucky bourbon, his attention directed to several colored
signs, hand-held.

"Welcome, Teddy!" And, "T.R.'s Our Man," even though he
wasn't running for anything as far as anyone knew.

Down went McGinty to the bottom of the pit . . .

So far, none of the people detraining even remotely resembled
Theodore Roosevelt. Was Mrs. Hodges's husband absolutely sure
that the sergeant who telephoned said the man himself was going
to be on board?

"Absolutely," he assured her, stepping forward with a flourish
of his topper, less graceful than he would have liked. "Gentlemen.
An honor."

"Ask 'em where Teddy is, Mayor," a brash young voice called at exactly the same moment, an eleven-year-old in a crushed hand-me-down parody of Hodges's beaver, tactless on the roof of a nearby porch. "Ain't he coming like they said?"

"Riis?" Andrew Parker had, in fact, not seen hide nor hair of his fellow Commissioner since, when was it, now? St. Albans? Ridgewood?

"Halfway between." The reporter gestured at the figure jumping from the catwalk that edged the coal tender, jacket draped over the forearm, soot powdering the face. Dockstader's Minstrels came to mind.

"I think we set a record, by gum: you see what people can do when they pitch in?" T.R.'s hand shot out to clasp Hodges's, blackening the palm of the gray velvet glove encasing the pudgy fingers. "You must be the mayor; what a splendid reception."

"Thank you." There'd be more of it, to be sure: a speech of some duration. The President of the Police Board recognized the portents.

"If only we were here simply to enjoy the hospitality of this magnificent community," he declared, quickly moving to usurp the floor. "Unfortunately, as Mr. Parker and Lieutenant Meeghan here will confirm, urgent police business is the reason we've come from Manhattan tonight." Teddy would have to beg their indulgence, one and all. "It's nip and tuck, this case we're pursuing. Every minute counts, and we need to confer with your mayor in private. Your police chief, too."

"Is it really that important?" Hodges spoke in a lowering voice as he escorted the company across the square to a booth in the rear of the White Star, more and more intimidated by the jut of the Roosevelt jaw and the gleam in the magnified eyes. "I mean, we all thought the sergeant who called us had to have gotten your message backward. Theodore Roosevelt wouldn't make a point of refusing sirens and skyrockets, that isn't his style."

To discover that it *was* his style this time around, well, that was disconcerting, to say the least.

"There's a kidnap victim involved," the Commissioner explained. Mayor Hodges could imagine what her captors might do to her if they thought the law was closing in. "Let's just hope they didn't get the word all the way out there on Captree Island."

Was that where T.R. thought they were? "Captree Island?"

"One of the kidnappers owns property there, it seems."

"Really." Bay Shore's chief of police found that hard to believe. "Why would anyone spend good money for even one square foot of that breakwater? All it is is a nesting place for sea gulls."

"Could be some good fishing out there," Jake drawled, not really making small talk.

"Better fishing farther out." Local fishermen hardly gave the place a second glance on their way through the channel to the open ocean.

"So they wouldn't have noticed if anything unusual was going on?" Yes, indeed, Teddy would accept the brimming mug the bartender had come to volunteer: just what the doctor ordered.

"Hey, Wyman," Chief Broward was calling, addressing a flat-faced old-timer alone on a stool at the end of the bar. "You go by Captree recently?"

"Took the *Molly G.* past there this morning." Wyman swiveled on his stool, grizzled. "Why?"

Roosevelt answered. "We think that's where we're going to find this bloodthirsty bunch of gunmen we're out to get," he said. Had the skipper sighted anything on that sandbar, or any*one,* "we want to hear about it; I don't care how insignificant it seemed to you."

Thought, and then a little shrug. "Wish I could help you gents, but—wait a minute." There was one minor little something, now that Wyman thought about it. "I don't even know if it's worth mentioning."

"Mention it."

It had to do with the old shed on the rise which looked down on the Great South Bay. "Maybe I'm wrong but, I don't know, I think it's been fixed up a little."

"How?" In what way?

"You know, repaired. New boards. There used to be gaps between the slats." Not anymore.

" 'Not anymore.' " If that wasn't the clincher, the Commis-

sioner would eat his hat. "Boats, gentlemen. We are going to need
boats and we are going to need them now."

"Mine's right down by the slip," Wyman gestured, off his stool
and rounding up the mariners occupying the adjacent table. "You
boys know the currents around Captree like the veins in your
eyes: say yes."

Before that could happen, a low, undulating lament made them
all turn. The source was a progerial apparition in the semidark-
ness, a creature with the body of a child and the face of a ninety-
year-old man, bald, with small round eyes. No whites.

"Here we go again," said someone at the bar, throwing a handful of nuts at the simpleton. "Will you shut up?" He looked quer-
ulously at the President of New York City's Police Board. "It
couldn't have been Thatch or Cedar, it had to be Captree?"

"That's why he's doing that, because you said 'Captree Island'?" Teddy was fascinated, attempting to approach the halfwit,
who backed away from him, timorous.

"Go on, Jeremy," the nut thrower urged. "Tell him. Tell the
nice man about the bird."

" 'The bird.' " Had Jeremy seen it out by that reef, this thing?
The men at the bar didn't believe him, did they, his description of
it was too fantastic for them—but T.R. wanted to hear it for
himself, he really did. "How big it was, for instance?" Could
Jeremy tell him how big it was?

With a gesture: the spread of his arms.

"Color?" White? Brown? "Silver?"

A shake of the strange little head. "Dark." The voice was stran-
gled. Metallic, as though prerecorded on one of Mr. Edison's cylinders. "Night."

"That's the only time it flies, he means," this according to one
of Wyman's seafaring friends at the free-standing table. "Night."
When only idiots could see it.

"When you don't want to attract attention, more likely." Roosevelt whirled, exploding. Dancing. "Substantiation, Andrew?
Proof? They've done it, those bastards out there—not only have
they built the damn machine, they've taken it up!"

"Assuming we can take the word of the village imbecile."

Teddy could take the word even if Parker couldn't. "How many nights?" he wanted the fool to tell him. "Jeremy, think very hard, it's very important. Did you see it only one time, or did it happen more?"

". . . Two times."

"Two times." There'd be no waiting for dawn to come up before they got into those boats, not as far as Commissioner Roosevelt was concerned. "That bird could be flying the coop right now, for all we know. Gentlemen?"

They didn't have to say anything, so long as they followed him out the door.

■ He stood in the prow of Wyman's trawler, inhaling the salt and the smell of fish both living and dead, one foot up on the gunwale. "All you need is me carrying the flag and some ice floes for Andrew to pole out of the way," Riis said, grinning.

"Let's get Minnie back safe and Richard behind bars." Then they could joke about commemorative paintings.

Fifteen more minutes to Captree, Wyman had estimated, two minutes before. Another fifteen would be needed for the other boats to position themselves on the far shore of the island and then the flare.

It was the basic pincer, two boatloads of men attacking from the north side of the island, two on the south, out of the Atlantic. The twenty officers divided five apiece to each of the vessels would charge forward, converging on the shed at the apex of the hill. If all went well, they'd batter through the door in less than three minutes' time, very much in the manner used at Trenton, December 1776.

"Another surprise for another pack of Hessians." Jake thought the symmetry of it splendid, but T.R.'s head was cocked past him.

"What's that?"

"One of the horses?" Two of the six were aboard the *Molly G.*, three on the larger *Noontide Dancer* off the bow, a trawler with a wider stern. The last of the horses had to be left behind in Bay Shore: Roosevelt would not risk bringing it in by sea.

"Out there, ahead." What would Riis call that, "a sawing sound? A rasp?"

"An engine." The flying machine?

"Would anything else have a motor on Captree Island?" Teddy scrambled past Jake in a head-on fever, rushing toward the base of Wyman's pilothouse to address the quintet of patrolmen positioned there. "We'd better talk about what to do if that bird goes up before we get to it: I seem to have overlooked that detail."

"We shoot it out of the sky, right?" Simplicity itself as far as the officer speaking was concerned. As far as they all were concerned.

"God love you," T.R. said, voice thick with appreciation. Sergeant Balter had chosen well. "Wyman!"

"Sir?" The captain glanced up through the uppermost handles on his wheel as the Commissioner ricocheted onto the bridge.

"When were we supposed to shut down and coast?"

"Right along in here." He had, in fact, just been reaching for the throttle as per Chief Broward's pocket watch.

"Forget it, we just ran out of time." Coasting to shore from this far out wouldn't get them there in time to save anything. "Or anyone."

Go all the way using the engine, was that the suggestion? "They'll hear us."

"Over the sound of their own motor?" Roosevelt didn't think so. "Not with the wind south-southeast." Most of the noise they'd make as they approached the shore would be blown north, away from the men at the top of the hill . . . "who have to be busy as hell if I'm right and they're taking to the air."

It was worth the risk, going in full steam ahead, cutting the engine off only when they were within two hundred feet of the reeds. Those few minutes might make all the difference when it came to saving the life of Minnie Gertrude Kelly.

"*Four* hundred feet," Wyman was willing to grant. "Two hundred is crazy."

Perhaps. "All I know is if that machine gets off the ground, we've lost the whole damn shooting match." Good as the men on deck were with their arms, "there's no guarantee they'll be able to blast it into the water," orders or no orders.

"Mr. Roosevelt." Chief Broward uncurled his considerable frame from the hammock he'd made of it, feet on the compass, shoulder blades against a bracket. "If we do what you suggest, we'll be putting ashore six or eight minutes before the boats due in from the ocean. It's not much of a trap if it only bites with one jaw."

"We fan out right, we'll bite." T.R. swore it. They had a dozen men—more, counting Wyman, Jake, Parker and himself. The chief.

Who persisted. Just how far did Teddy think that contraption up there could actually fly? "What're we talking about, miles? Yards? Feet?"

"Figure the worst."

"Then let me tell you something else your friend Jeremy had to say." Which was that his fabled night bird had in fact flown no more than several hundred yards at the most. "All it did was circle around and come straight back; the damn thing didn't even get a quarter of the way across the channel to Sexton Island."

Not much of a machine to make the great escape in, was it.

"*Last* week. Who knows how far it can travel now?" The Commissioner wheeled, addressing Wyman. "What's it to be, Captain? Do you open it up or do I?"

The master of the *Molly G.* opened it up, and Bay Shore's chief of police shrugged, going back to the unsupported horizontal he'd been occupying two and a half feet above the floor. Not his show, this landing. Not his show.

▪ "Turn the motor off."

"In a minute," Wolf replied, limbs pretzeled around one of the struts uniting the upper and lower wings on the left side of the airship, his elongated screwdriver probing something delicate within the depths of the engine, making it rasp.

"Now, damn it." Richard swung himself up onto the wing, reaching over his brother's shoulder to shut the machine down. It lurched and hacked, as though it were in the throes of a tubercular seizure.

"What is the matter with you?" The screwdriver was gone from the elder Kerner's hand now: he held a wrench instead, gripped not as a tool. "If the timing isn't one hundred percent with that cylinder, this thing could do this, midair." The wrench, released, clanged against the ground below with a harsh, metallic ring.

"You can't let it get quiet for one little second?" Was that too much to ask, "one second of silence?"

"Why?"

"I thought I heard another motor just now, out on the bay." Motor, as in boat.

A straining of ears. Nothing. No. Not nothing. The sound of something scraping—the legs of a heavy piece of furniture being pushed across a floor not entirely level, repeated, coming from within the shed itself, from the door in the rear which separated a set of smaller structures from the larger: quarters for the group. Storage.

"Apparently you're confusing the sound of a boat with the sound of a lonely fiancée." The engineer dropped to the ground, in need of his wrench. "Why don't you go hold her hand while we finish up here?" He turned back to the ladder before Richard could respond, suddenly stopping two rungs up to angle forward, examining a juncture of joists wrapped with bailing wire. "Who made this tie?" he demanded to know, glancing around with flaring eyes. "Fritz? Hermann?"

"Hermann," one of the men confirmed, nervous, embarrassed to be singled out.

"Where is he?" How many times had Wolf told them, one and all: "The wire at the joint has to be wrapped back on itself not two times but three. Any little vibration could make this come loose."

Had they any idea how deadly a snake metal this solid could be, whipped suddenly from its mooring midflight? Had they?

"I wouldn't want to be in that seat," he snapped. "Get out here, Hermann. Now."

"Wasn't he taking some chocolates to Miss Kelly?" Claus, speaking from his position at the door, the cock of his head indicating the house within the house even as there was a metallic crash behind the wood of the door. A metallic crash and a shriek, cut off. Minnie's voice.

"Hermann, you swine—!" Richard knocked things over, shoved people aside, kicked the door in. The vertical vein pulsed blue in his temple. "No one was to come in here, I said, didn't I? Didn't I say no one?"

His fingers clamped down on the collar, using the fabric as fulcrum, throwing the man in an arc. Hermann collided with a workbench and went spilling along with a set of tools and a box of double-duty nails. "All I did was bring her chocolate," he tried to explain, but the fanatic was kicking at him and it was hard to make words.

"Richard, no—stop—" Minnie tugged at the shirt on the officer's back, trying to pull him off. "It wasn't what you think: the tray dropped, that's all."

"The orders were, 'Stay on this side of that door, no exceptions, no excuses,' I don't care what innocent little errand he had in mind." Another kick, another cry of pain, the brute injustice of the attack adding insult to injury.

"I'm sorry, please," Hermann begged, but Patrolman Kerner was not yet assuaged. The face had to be pulp, the arms cracked, perhaps, or honor would want.

Wolf stepped in, blazing. *"Genug!"* Enough. "I need this man with hands that work and eyes open to see . . . if my anxious little brother wants to get the baby off the ground before his precious Commissioner does happen to show up."

Heavy breathing. "We have a sacred trust here, all of us. This man broke the oath." The *Gibichung* oath.

"This man was doing nothing but wasting time he could've been putting to good use because you," Wolf shot back, "decided to think with everything but your brain. We are scientists first, Richard; that's how we get to be *Übermenschen*. And let me tell you something: we wouldn't be under any gun tonight if you'd been smart enough not to have come here at all. Now? Now we've got this 'fiancée' of yours underfoot, making everyone crazy just by her presence—and you start hearing things in the bay instead of leaving me alone to do my work!"

Richard's eyes narrowed. "You don't give a damn about Poppa's dream, do you. The airship: that's all you care about, the hell with who pays for it, the hell with your Aryan brothers—if we were all Jews you'd say, *'Schön. Wunderbar. Ich liebe dich.'* "

"I killed to get us these plans!" The engineer sprang to the table adjacent, yanking DeLacy's sketches out of the old briefcase spread open across the surface. "I tortured a boy in a ditch, I stuffed an old woman in a closet with her throat cut, I stabbed a guard in a garden, and you're going to stand there and question my commitment to your God-damned Master Race? How dare you!" A slam. The pages were back in the case, shut, Minnie alongside recoiling from the onrush of sound.

"You didn't do it for the *Wälsungen,*" the patrolman countered. "You did it for yourself. Wolfgang Freidrich Kerner, inventor of the flying machine, the new Edison. Next year's Graham Bell. Well, you listen to me, *Herr* Bell, inventing the Ultimate Weapon doesn't mean a thing if the first thing you do is to let it fall into the hands of your enemy. Which is why we are flying this thing out right now, no more last-minute 'adjustments,' no more time for 'a hundred percent.' "

"There are bolts that still have to be tightened," Wolf protested, shocked despite their previous exchange. "I still have to check the chain, the rudder mechanism—"

"That's all right, Wolf: I can fly it if you've got misgivings." A snap of the fingers, at Ahrens, at Claus, at the others Richard had been talking to back in the shadows. "Roll it out."

"No!" But they were at the double doors, swinging them wide until the master builder rapped the side of his wrench against the table: Donner's hammer reverberating throughout the edifice. "This is my life's work, this machine! *I* am the one who says when it can be moved and when it cannot."

"Then say it."

"If I don't?"

The hinges on the barn doors cried out under duress: the wail of the heretic stretched out on an inquisitor's rack. His kinsmen were siding with Richard, making off with the brainchild, afraid that all of Wolf's zealous attention to detail would snatch the victory out of their grasp.

Of course they'd push the airship out into the open before it was too late, whether that noise from the bay was Theodore Roosevelt or not. They'd see the machine take off, and then follow it away in the boats. The Commissioner might arrive in time to find their campfires still glowing but what could he do? How could he know which way they'd have gone?

"Okay," he blurted as the craft was rotated into position at the top of the long, shallow incline which led a hundred yards to the edge of the estuary separating Captree from Sexton Island. "You're right. I'll fly it." No one else could—none had his experience with downdrafts and crosswinds, the balance and weight of the airship itself.

Officer Kerner looked at him over his shoulder, as though surprised to find his brother still there. "I think it's a little late for that," he said coldly. "You're in default."

"Am I." Wolf started across the open space between himself and the biplane, stopping when Ahrens and the snub-nosed boy, Claus, stepped in the way. A glance had dispatched them, no more.

"Don't, *mein Herr*," the man in the overalls found himself begging, sorrow in his eyes. "I would only have to harm you and I don't want to do that."

"This is madness!" The engineer spoke to them all, wheeling slowly in his desperation like the stars in the arms of the galaxy. "Have you any idea of the odds, a man with no instinct at the helm? What happens to all our plans if he gets into trouble? I'm talking about up in the air. Over the water. He dies . . . the airship dies with him. Is that what you want?"

"Wolf." Hermann. Even Hermann, his hand still palming his ribs.

Madness. "My brother hasn't the temperament to sit in my seat —he's certainly never shown any innate ability when it comes to machinery."

"What 'temperament' do you need to jerk on a stick?" Richard wanted to know. "What university degree? Oh, no, big brother. There is no great science to the operation of this device. It is simple, it is a snap to learn, and you have misgivings."

"Get out of my way." Wolf swatted them aside, boy and man,

reaching the ladder at the side of the apparatus, a gentle, loving hand pausing to touch the stretch of cloth at his right as he pulled himself up. The hand moved on to grip the rim of the seat in the well above, the wistful little smile on his face barely formed and immediately wiped away: there it was, that same joist, the one that Hermann hadn't fastened properly. "If I could have the screwdriver for just a minute—?"

"We don't have a minute." The screwdriver was retained in Richard's hand. The elder Kerner returned to the ground.

"It will come apart in midair," he said. The eyes locked.

"O ye of little faith." Pity, from both. For both. Minnie waited for the violence that would inevitably follow, but it didn't come. After the moment's challenge, Wolf wrenched his gaze and his body away from them all and let the night envelop him. No one had to follow him down to the shoreline: with escort or without he would be alone.

"Misgivings." Richard Kerner tossed the screwdriver to Ahrens and made his way to the bird.

■ "Low tide. Christ Almighty. Low tide."

Matthew Wyman couldn't get over it, how even the water itself was in Roosevelt's corner.

"No way would I ever agree to beach the *Molly G.* at high tide. You tarry one or two minutes too long and there you are, twenty, thirty feet up on the sand, stuck like a dying whale." Oh, yes. The Commissioner was one lucky man.

"Some nights." There had been others, when death was in the bedrooms, when wife and mother were both—

His eyes focused on the slope rising up to the plateau in the center of Captree Island. Those were voices he heard coming from there and, by God, it meant he'd figured it right. "Gentlemen!" T.R. barreled out of the pilothouse, waving at the officers on deck and those on the vessel adjacent, sugar in their palms for their nickering mounts. "Fall in, we're going ashore!"

They were right behind him as he leaped with surprising grace onto the sand. "No ignominious stumbles for Theodore Roosevelt at a time like this," Riis remarked in response to Hodges's reaction, watching the horse patrol slide a pair of four-by-eights from the deck to the shore: a ramp for their steeds.

Andrew Parker watched, too, shivering. There was saltwater in his shoes. Saltwater in his custom-made shoes.

"Our objective is the top of that slope," Teddy was telling the assembled platoon. "The first thing we want when we get there is my secretary, Miss Minnie Kelly. A prisoner." His finger flickered at a patrolman to his right. "What's your name, son?"

"Roth, sir. Milton Roth." Lindy's age. Scared. Brave.

"All right, Officer Roth. The minute we're on the high ground I want that girl freed, alive. Uninjured. I want her removed from harm's way, as fast as you can."

"Yes, sir." It would be his honor.

"*Ex*cellent." Now. "There's going to be a large, strange-looking object up there, an invention your opposition will be guarding with their lives. If my information is correct, it should look like an oversize dragonfly with muslin wings, two to a side. One in the rear, vertical."

"Isn't that what you were interviewed about in the paper?" Was the Commissioner saying that such a device actually existed? "A flying machine?"

"It exists. And whatever else happens up there, gentlemen," he emphasized, "it is not going to take to the air. We are not going to permit that, under no circumstance, no matter how fanatic the force facing us."

"You figure they won't exactly be welcoming us with open arms, do you?" The corrugated grin belonged to Captain Matthew Wyman, scratching the stubble on his chin with the business end of an old Civil War relic.

Mexican War, maybe.

"What I figure," T.R. said, "is that they're going to shoot the minute they sight us and we damn well better be ready to hold them off till the other boats show up. You five: you're Squad A, on the right. You five this side are B, on the left." They'd still try for the pincer, even with only half their intended number.

Roosevelt himself would take two men and go right up the

center on foot, "right through the front door." And, when he did, the men on horseback would have their cue.

"I want covering fire, boys. I want it two inches over our heads and I want it thick." Was Andrew coming along for the ride?

"Are you serious?" What kind of tactic was this? "I know you think you have to be up front at every parade, Theodore, but I don't play fife or drum and you forgot to bring a flag."

"Commissioner, it's hard to play 'Yankee Doodle' while you're crawling through the mud on your belly."

"My kind of strategy," Wyman declared. He reminded Riis of a rabid corgi he'd eluded once as a child, ridiculous and yet primevally fearsome. It was, in fact, the captain who began to lead the President of the Police Board up the indicated center, every inch a character out of Kipling: that pore benighted 'eathen who'd be the first-class fightin' man.

We gives you your certifikit . . .

"Behind me, sir?" Teddy assumed his rightful place at the front of the force, his own gun out and cocked. Good as the old-timer looked, Theodore Roosevelt looked better, the wide, upswept brim of his khaki hat adding height and stature. Even the *pince-nez* seemed more appropriate under these circumstances, steeling the eyes, drawing the whole body forward while at the same time giving the impression of an impenetrable shield.

"Sir?"

"Shh." Not that Roth's voice had been more than a whisper. But they had come thirty, perhaps as many as forty, zigzagging feet, too close to the enemy for anything but the lowest, most unobtrusive sounds.

The officer nodded, gesturing. T.R. could see something moving, coming toward them. One of the *Bund*, alone.

"Down," the Commissioner hissed, his men crouching, spreading out across the rushes in a ragged semicircle.

Moonlight illuminated the face of the figure moving past them down the incline, and Roosevelt stiffened, recognition all over his face, his stance, his breath. The man with the scar, Richard's brother, Wolf. The man who had laughed at his pursuer on the railing of the Brooklyn Bridge, who was audacious enough to chance a return engagement on the trellis behind the Hall house on West Thirty-seventh.

Here he was a soul distressed, his breath short and audible, his eyes watered with emotion.

What right, an angry Theodore Roosevelt had to wonder, what right had *he* to be in grief? This was a man who brought grief, even as he could never experience it. A man who sliced the throat of an old immigrant woman for a piece of paper, who would have in fact done the same to Teddy's niece had there been no interruption. It was an almost overwhelming temptation to just press the gun into the hollow at the back of the man's neck, to squeeze the trigger. To send the ball into the brain and watch what happened to the eyes.

He said as much when he rose up behind the outcast and cocked the pistol. Wolf froze, arms bent half up at the elbow, waiting as the Commissioner moved around to look him in the face. *"Herr* Kerner."

"Ah." The nameless had been named since last they'd met. "My brother warned me: you were resourceful. 'Do not underestimate him.' Perhaps I shouldn't have argued the point as much as I did." Rueful explanation for his presence here at the bottom of the hill.

Banishment?

He nodded. "Richard feels our group would be better served if its chief engineer spent the rest of the night patrolling our shores."

"While he flies the machine in your place."

"Someone who lives up to his reputation for intelligence," the elder of the Kerners murmured, impressed. "A rare commodity in this day and age."

"It wasn't just Richard who threw you out," Roosevelt was sure. "He couldn't have done it alone." They'd all turned on him: the Wolf at bay, shriveling inside at the thought of another set of hands on those cherished controls.

"Yes," the engineer admitted. "Doesn't that please you? My flying machine will be destroyed and you won't have to do anything but stand by and watch."

"I don't want it destroyed any more than you do, mister. I want it intact, improved—I want it to stay in this country where it can be developed for the transportation of people and freight and, yes, as a weapon of war."

"With its inventor permitted to go on with his work?"

T.R.'s mustache was proscenium for his teeth. *"Charles DeLacy* was—is—inventor of that machine, sir. Not you. Never you."

"Charles DeLacy." A slur, in the pronunciation itself. "Do you know anything about aerodynamics? Torque? Stability? Stress? If you did you'd know that those plans you're so hot to get your hands on don't work; Commissioner, believe me, your *wunderkind* wouldn't have flown his contraption two feet if he could have built it, not without Wolfgang Kerner to alter, to perfect—to fix. *I* created that instrument up there—based on what DeLacy proposed, granted—but mine, nonetheless."

"What rock did you crawl out from under?" Teddy asked, examining him like a specimen.

"The rock you have to look under if you want America to have the first honest-to-God fleet of airships in the world." Kerner drew himself up, proud as he had been at the edge of the Brooklyn Bridge. "She becomes the world-class power you've always wanted her to be, if . . ." If Roosevelt gave him amnesty. Looked the other way in the interest of progress and national pride. "It can't be done without me, you know that . . . unless you don't care if England beats you to the punch." Or Spain.

"Verräter!" Traitor—a shriek, ringing out from the tall grass on their left, hate-filled.

"Look out—!" Officer Roth fired as he shouted, the trajectory of his bullet intersecting the one from the weapon in Claus's hand. The snub-nosed German screamed and staggered up from his hiding place, gouts of blood pumping up from his chest even before he toppled over.

"Well done, sir, damned well," T.R. boomed, realizing as he spoke that the sound of the gunshots had to have carried up to the top of the hill, canceling the advantage of surprise. All the Commissioner could do was hurl the prisoner into Parker's custody, along with a set of handcuffs. "Guard this jackal, Andrew. You have a gun: get him to the boat. The rest of us will take care of the business with his friends."

Agitated figures could be seen on the height, gaining speed and purpose as they lunged for weapons and ammunition. Was that Richard there at the snout of the machine, wrestling with the propeller blade, cursing his brother's improvements to the engine when it refused to catch? The coil sparked, died, sparked again.

Died again.

"They heard the shots," Mayor Hodges was reporting below, as though he'd been the only one aware. "What do we do?" His hand tugged at Teddy's sleeve, rather endearingly. "Commissioner?"

"Do?" One second was all Teddy needed; he used it to pin the man with a scathing glance. "What else is there to do but"—and this was a direct order, to all—"*chaarge!*"

■ It was a bugle call all by itself, Riis wrote. There wasn't a man jack present who wasn't galvanized by the pitch of the command, the sheer propulsiveness of the call.

They charged. Exactly as directed, they charged, firing back when they were fired upon from above, advancing.

Had the defenders at the top of the slope been more alert, more on guard, the shots would have been more concentrated, more of a fusillade. But the speed of the assault meant that none of them were in position to meet the oncoming line. Each member of the company was on his own.

"They're coming up from the north, dammit," Ahrens could be heard yelling, sweeping around in a fevered attempt to rally his forces, to organize the hail of bullets which would keep the on-rushing police from the airship. Richard couldn't handle that assignment and get the engine going at the same time, the propeller blade only now beginning to turn, coughing up a cloud of gas. He squeezed off a shot as he spun around to grab Minnie and climb up into the bowels of the beast—two—but they were wild rounds adding to the din and his duty was to lose the machine in the clouds.

"Behind you," someone warned, a *Bundsman* named Schoen-

brun, firing southward despite Ahrens: more of the invaders were
coming, this time from the rear.

"How many are there?" Ahrens's pistol smoked and spat twice
more, three times, until one of the bullets whistling through the
predawn darkness struck him and spun him, crashing him to the
ground.

"More than you want to fight," Theodore Roosevelt told him,
looming mythologically against the streaks in the sky. By Godfrey, George Washington was right. Chinese Gordon was right.
Nothing could possibly be more exhilarating than battle, when
projectiles of all sizes and shapes blew wind through your hair
while they whizzed past your skull, leaving you upright and uninjured. Immortal. Nothing. Ever.

Schoenbrun emptied the chamber of his gun at the oncoming
apparition but the bullets which should have riddled the body did
no damage whatsoever, disappearing harmlessly into the night. A
click, a snap: the hammer of his weapon was striking the pin out
of reflex now; with the last shell gone, the man could only glance
this way and that, looking for a way out of the circle closing in on
him. Was that a hole over there, between those mounts on the
right? Could he take them by surprise with a feint in one direction
and then a sudden bolt in the other?

The entire scene was suddenly bathed in a red-orange glow: the
flare. The signal. The second pair of boats had come in from the
ocean, ten more officers landing on the beach.

"Reinforcements, sir!" Exultation, plain and simple, the Commissioner calling out to the members of the gang, those visible,
those not. "You will all drop your weapons, you are surrounded!
Now!"

Several guns thudded against the earth, some dropped, some
thrown. Several others were retained, shooting. Teddy crouched
and rolled, firing back as Officer Roth cried out beside him,
clutching a suddenly bloodied shoulder.

"Roth—?"

The fingers were hooking through the slash in the sleeve, rip-
ping it wider to expose the wound. "You know something, sir? I

always wanted a tattoo." His gun flashed. Someone yowled in the dark, a brief outcry trailing off as a gurgle.

"Two in a row: bully!" T.R. scrambled back onto his feet, man-handling Schoenbrun as he tossed him to another officer for cuff-ing, his eyes on the flying machine, the burr of its propeller. Where was Minnie? "Has anyone seen my secretary?"

More shots. A scream. Minnie. "There she is," Riis shouted, his finger cutting through the smoke.

"I see her." Roosevelt was already plunging forward, firing to make himself a right-of-way, heart thumping. Officer Kerner had her as a shield at the side of the airship, hostage, forearm locked around her neck from behind, gun to her head. Lindsay Hargate was in a coma because of that gun. A cabbie was dead.

"Clear the path for me," Richard rasped: Teddy's men were clustered at the top of the slope and they were going to be ordered aside, "or my fiancée will die, Commissioner. I cannot let her live in a world run by vermin."

■ "How many men does this creation of yours hold?" It was for verification, so that Andrew Parker could be sure he'd heard right there on the beach in front of the *Molly G.*, the weight of the gun in his fist uncomfortable. Unfamiliar. The smell of the powder in the wind coming down from the summit was unfamiliar, too.

"One," Wolf said, repeating for him as though this were a con-versation between businessmen over London broil at Lüchow's, so what if the wrists were manacled in front of him. The malevolence in his eyes was veiled by the dark and his custodian was a man more concerned with stray bullets and sharp sounds. "Theoreti-cally there'd be no limit to the size once the basic design were perfected: you and I could both live long enough to fly with sev-eral hundred other people from New York to London, in one day."

"That many that quick." The lips pursed.

"If I'd be allowed to do the work, yes. It'd be quite a windfall," the engineer added pointedly, "for people smart enough to see the profits just waiting to be made."

Parker laughed in his face. "You're the most deluded crackpot

I've ever met." Or the biggest snake oil salesman since Captain Billy Hostetter. Hundreds of people in one huge skeletal packing crate bouncing around the clouds, what kind of malarkey was that? "Nobody sane would ever set foot in something that dangerous; why, they get dizzy at the top of their ladders."

Profit in airships? There'd be more from Captain Billy's Kickapoo Elixir.

"Oh, no, sir: you're going to hang for your crimes." And mankind would muddle through with its feet on the ground, "as God intended."

There would have been more of the same except that the stray bullet the commissioner so feared chose that moment to pass by, calling to him as it sped on its way to a destination somewhere out in the middle of the Great South Bay. Theodore Roosevelt would have grinned to hear it: it was the one you didn't hear which had your name engraved on the shaft. Andrew Parker had never been within two feet of violent death before, however, and the experience curled him in on himself, hands wrapped over his head.

Wolf struck, driving the handcuffs into the hand holding the gun. It dropped to the ground and he snatched it up before Parker knew it was gone. "People will fly in my invention," he made a point of saying as he took the keys and freed himself. "They'll go from New York to London in *less* than a day and the only reason I'm not leaving you with a hole in your skull is I want you to live to see it." A kick to the old man's crotch and a blow to his uncovered temple. The commissioner fell, tasting the blood in his mouth as his prisoner ran back up the hill, snarling.

It was still not too late to save the airship, he had to believe that. He had to.

■ "Let her go," Teddy said.

"She doesn't want me to let her go." Richard looked around at her face, over Minnie's shoulder from behind her back. "Tell him," he urged. "We're of one mind now, aren't we." A twisted smile for their employer as he stepped the girl back into the shadow of the machine: it was not really necessary that she speak.

"Look at her, damn it." The whitened complexion, the quivering lips. "Is that your idea of 'willing'?"

The Commissioner's aide shifted his arm down from his fiancée's neck, hooking her waist and backing her farther into the vibrating heart of the airship, close enough to the wash of the rotating propeller to evoke an involuntary gasp, not only from Roosevelt, but from a good number of the officers clustered behind him, several mounted.

"Miss Kelly's made her peace with me, Mr. R. All the chalk in her cheek is your doing now, not mine: I didn't come here with a regiment on horseback, shooting." Supercilious pleasure colored the voice as Officer Kerner strained to keep Minnie snug in the operator's seat, simultaneously reaching for the old briefcase already tossed onto the lower wing at his right.

Brahms's present to Dvořák? It fit the description the composer gave, didn't it, and there was no real question as to what T.R. would find inside, either: DeLacy's drawings, the collected set, dog-eared and bloodstained.

"We're both scared to death," the patrolman added, lying and smiling. "Not for ourselves—for this machine." Didn't his benefactor understand? "Destroy it, intentionally or unintentionally, you know what you really destroy? The one thing human beings have developed that can finally deliver us from the beasts." Richard was not referring to the animals, no. These beasts were two-legged. "They're breeding us to death, litters of little hook-nosed mongrels who're seducing our women, contaminating our blood —that's how they intend to bring us down, but now we have the means to stop them." He'd attempted to explain that to the Commissioner's brother the previous August, "but too much crème de menthe: what can I say?"

"What day in August was that?"

"The fourteenth, of course." Of course: the day the Kerners had come to 102nd Street while Mrs. Evans was out shopping with the child.

"Elliott wouldn't tell you where he'd hidden DeLacy's sketches, would he." *Dear old beloved brother.* "The only argument you had left when it came down to it was murder."

Brief laughter, scornful. Teddy held himself in check as the officer adjusted the throttle, letting the engine grind.

"No one had to lift a finger against that lush," he wanted Roosevelt to know. "He fell against the corner of that radiator all by himself." You have to watch your feet when you're piss drunk and you start to give your guests the gate.

"After he'd heard all that good Bavarian philosophy?" *Good for Elliott.*

"On the contrary, Commissioner, your brother happens to have agreed with us on everything. He drank himself to death because of the Jews, for instance: did you know?"

"No. I didn't." The voice was flint.

"I'm not surprised," Richard said upon a moment's reflection, his hand resting against the grip at the end of a long metal rod. "You wouldn't have sent him to the sanitarium in Suresnes if you'd known it was operated by kikes—I hope not, anyway—and the same goes for that Hebrew quack in Illinois, what was his name . . . Keeley?"

"An Irish name," as far as T.R. could tell. "Close to 'Kelly,' isn't it."

"They *change* their names country to country, these 'chosen' people." How could a man as worldly as Teddy Roosevelt have such a gap in his education?

"All I know is you killed my brother, mister, and you killed Maurice Harbinger, too—not to save me from the knife you yourself threw down but because the person Mrs. Evans would have identified that night was you." One step forward, unobtrusive. Two . . .

The longer the exchange, the longer the airship would remain in place. The more opportunity to make a move.

One of Roosevelt's men was taking similar advantage of the confrontation, circling slowly around the periphery of the plateau. Roth? Wyman?

Wolf.

A pang burrowed through Teddy's gut. Where was Andrew? Alive? Dead? Had the engineer added a commissioner of police to his list of a servant, a Pinkerton, a little old lady and an innocent young inventor?

Had Officer Kerner seen the flick of the eyes behind the *pince-nez?*

No. Officer Kerner was too preoccupied with the success of the coup he'd pulled off in Harbinger's warehouse, the revelation of which brought glory to his name. Why shouldn't it be told, the equanimity of the *Wälsungen* under fire? "Crackerjack, Mr. R. How did you figure it out?"

What mistake had he made: Richard was dying to know. The hand moved away from the brake release, returning the engine to a steady idle.

"It had to have been small, right? Some minor little detail hardly anyone would spot . . . ?"

"As a matter of fact," T.R. said, "I can show it to you." His hand dug down into his pocket and he started forward toward the aircraft, openly. Only on the fourth step across the flat did his quarry remember to issue a warning, tightening up on Minnie as he did. Tightening up on the stick.

*"Un*armed, sir. Slowly."

"Absolutely." Roosevelt stopped, one hand still in his pocket, the other clutching his gun. He smiled, raising the weapon, displaying it to all and tossing it aside.

Gasps, even before Riis could reach out to catch it midarc. What protection was the Commissioner leaving himself, if any? What safe conduct could he expect from a renegade?

"This," he announced, holding something else up now: the mate to the ring on his secretary's finger. "My white flag." The eyes went to Richard's, locking them.

Minnie recognized the design immediately, even if her fiancé didn't. "They're identical," she whispered as Teddy reached the side of the machine, offering her the duplicate for comparison. "Where did you get it?"

He told her, keeping his gaze still fixed on Richard. "A real *Wälsung* would have been smart enough to make sure it wasn't one of a set before he gave it to a friend of mine."

"It never occurred to me," the fugitive had to confess, shrugging as he released the lever. The airship lurched forward at the top of the incline and began to roll. *"Auf Wiedersehen,* sir: the next time I take a ring from a dead man I'll remember that. Of course, you won't be around to make any comparisons, will you."

The gun was up in Kerner's hand, a final gift for a beloved mentor.

"No—Richard—!" Minnie lunged, her elbow jabbing sideward, sharply, directly into the ribs. The shot exploded from the chamber, deflected enough. Just enough. T.R. dove for cover under the flying machine, rolling, crying out even as he caught a glimpse of Richard's brother coming up from the other side.

"Minnie! Jump!" He could not wait to see what she did. He was in motion, his aide firing again. A spray of sand spouted at his feet, another furrowed through the dune on his right as he reached the rim of the hill, flinging himself over just as the squad from the second pair of boats converged at the summit, and Meeghan rode up, looking entirely out of place on a horse.

"Commissioner—"

"I'm commandeering that mount, Lieutenant: off!"

"Sir—?" Roosevelt yanked him out of the saddle, replacing him in one swift, free-flowing motion, Sioux.

"Hi yi *yi!"*

The animal beneath him broke into a gallop, gathering speed at the edge of the height as its new rider plucked the rifle out from the holster attached to the cinch, flipping it rightside up in midair and slamming the butt end tight to his shoulder. Were his target in the skidding airship not so entangled with Miss Minnie Gertrude Kelly it would have ended right there: Teddy was quite prepared to dispatch the officer with one shot. One single Annie Oakley shot.

But Minnie Gertrude Kelly was half in, half out of Richard's grasp, half on the lower of the wings, half in the seat. And Theodore Roosevelt on horseback was an even better target than Theodore Roosevelt on foot: the President of the Police Board had to duck down alongside the flanks of the onrushing steed, riding prone.

Richard cursed: it was impossible to get any of T.R. in his

sights at this angle. It was even more impossible now that the machine was bouncing up into the air in little arcs. Three feet. Five. Eight. Each time it came back down, wheels thudding, and the third of these jolts dislodged the gun from his fist. It clattered into the well beneath the seat, lodging there without dropping out of the aircraft itself.

"Now, Minnie—now!" The Commissioner dug his heels into the stallion, thundering forward alongside, leaning in at a precipitous angle to catch her as his aide let her go. Only for a moment: it would be only for a moment, till Officer Kerner retrieved his weapon. Three seconds.

It was more tumble than jump, but she did it and Roosevelt caught her, whirling her out from under the sweep of the machine, balancing her against the saddle and veering them away. His arm ached with the effort: the angle stretched the muscles of his shoulder and side to the tearing point and if they tore she would almost certainly fall beneath the spiking hooves, trampled.

"Someone catch her," he tried to cry, but his lungs were tearing, too, as they had on occasions like this, ever since he was four. Had anybody heard?

"I've got her, Commissioner—here!" Roth?

Riis.

Pencil and pad had been abandoned, flung into the dust as the journalist dashed out to gather Miss Kelly into the warmth and security of two good arms. He carried her to the shed: there were objects there that would shield them, and that met with T.R.'s approval. Elliott's brother was free to rise up in the stirrups now, to pursue the speeding machine down the slope and leap at the bottommost bracket on its side. He could close the fingers of one hand around the metal and let the acceleration pull him from one screaming beast to another.

▪ Richard fired at Teddy's face, the weapon back in his possession, the flash at the muzzle bright as the sun. Had Wolf's hand not at that moment closed down around his wrist, the engineer having clambered aboard from the other side, the slug would have gone straight through the Commissioner's left eye.

As it was, the wind came close enough to kiss his scalp.

"The plans, Commissioner," Wolf was gasping, struggling with his brother. "The briefcase!" Officer Kerner could die with this edition of the machine if that was his will, he could martyr himself for the cause. Fine.

So long as Wolfgang Freidrich had the sketches with which to construct the replacement.

They were suddenly airborne, higher than the trapeze at the top of Mr. Bailey's tent, the sensation driving Roosevelt's lungs up into his mouth. God's invisible palm was suffocating him, covering his mouth and his nose, pinching the nostrils.

Not now . . . !

With the last vestige of his strength he yanked at the leather-covered rectangle, trying to wrest it from Richard's control. The old clasps gave way with a metallic ping, the halves separating. A snowstorm of pages billowed up all around.

"You maniac," Wolf screamed, not at Teddy. Teddy was gone, having fallen backward out of the craft as it looped within three feet of the water off the shore of the island. Richard was the object of the malediction, Richard the fanatic whose zealotry was going to leave them with nothing—as the engineer had predicted from the start.

"This is 'nothing'?" This airship now gaining altitude, unheard-of altitude, nothing? The patrolman kicked out at his brother, flopping him against the crisscrossed struts which locked the engine in place. The crook of Wolf's knee hooked over a strut and Wolf dangled upside down, bucking as the giant insect caught a gust and kited higher.

"Catch me . . . !"

His leg was slipping, the calf muscle unable to maintain its grip on the rail. The engineer tried in desperation to swing himself horizontal: if he could do that he could grab hold of the cross-bar—

Richard kicked him again. The elder Kerner went sideways into the joist wired together by the *Bundsman* named Hermann, ducking as the tie gave way. As predicted, the wire whipped through the air, whipped across his brother's handsome face, slic-

ing it in half. It burst open, red and, under the red, blue, the
officer holding his head as though trying to glue the halves together again while, screaming, he fell.

Wolf didn't look down, he didn't have the time. He had to get
to the stick, to the pedal, to his rightful place in the heart of this
thing he'd given life to, the first of a species. "I'm here," he said,
laughing and crying and wiping his eyes on the back of his sleeve.
"I'm here." His fingers caressed the handle, stroking the circumference, and for a moment Theodore Roosevelt in the reeds at the
shore of the island below thought the airship was going to fly
away into the rising sun.

A groan from the beach distracted him: one of his troop,
wounded. T.R. splashed out of the surf, stumbling. "Andrew—?"

Parker looked up from the sand, not at his rival but beyond. "I
told him," he wanted his rescuer to know. "I told him it wouldn't
work." The arm was raised, one finger gesturing upward, shaking.
"Icarus, you see?"

It was spluttering up there, coughing and looping, and they
could hear Wolf at the stick, talking to it. "What did he do to you?
That bastard brother of mine, what did he do?"

No answer, no response. The creature went mute, midbreath,
all the life drained from the lever in the engineer's hand. He
pumped on the pedal, but no: they were going down. With increasing velocity they were going down.

"Mein Kind," he wailed, and then they smashed into the water,
the splash stretching skyward in an expanding arc lathered at the
crown. When the wave broke, it broke inward with tidal force, the
wood and muslin skin of the artificial bird folding in on the last of
Rupert Kerner's children, dragging him under.

After a while the surface of the bay regained its sheen, the gulls
circling above graceful and smug.

7 CHURCHILL

■ Afterward he and Riis went around the north face of the island, gathering what sketches had not been claimed by the bay and trying to ignore the damp in his clothes. "Ten, eleven . . . there's another one there, Jake."

"And one by that bush."

"You think there are enough pages left to rebuild?" Officer Roth spoke as he approached with several more sheets from the decimated collection.

Roosevelt shook his head as he ironed the crumples out of the "Uppermost Draft, Side View, Rudder Bar." "Not with Wolf out of the picture."

In a way, a relief. Which would have been more important to him had the engineer survived: justice for the dead at the end of a rope, or a fleet of flying machines guaranteed to catapult the United States into the ranks of the mighty? Exculpation was the condition, Richard's brother had minced no words, and the choice would have ripped Elliott's brother apart.

God had taken the matter out of his hands. Thank God.

"Then why are you bothering with them?" Roth was asking. "If we aren't going to be able to construct another airship, what difference does it make?"

"I don't know," the Commissioner had to admit. "For the rec-

ord, maybe, or maybe because somewhere down the line somebody might be able to take these drawings and do what we ourselves can't." He stuffed the newly retrieved pages into what was
left of Dvořák's old briefcase, looking up over his shoulder. "Is
that Minnie?"

She had told him she would be all right, that it was more important that he find as many of the DeLacy sketches as possible
before he took her home. She would sit by the shed at the top of
the hill and wait, and he was not to worry.

Of course it was Minnie, crying.

"I'll take her home, Theodore," Riis volunteered, but T.R.
shook his head, guilt stabbing him hard.

"My responsibility," he said. "I should have done it an hour
ago."

■ Her mother inhaled audibly at the sight of her. Her father
wanted to know if Mr. Roosevelt had an explanation for his
daughter's appearance.

It was forthcoming, in detail, once the girl was tucked safely
into her bed, he and the Kellys together downstairs in the kitchen.
"Richard," that was all the missus could say when he finished,
shaking her head. "Your own personal aide: how terrible for you."

"Not nearly as hard on me as it is on Minnie." Teddy wondered
whether it might be possible to prevail upon the young carpenter
who had previously asked for her hand: "His company might help
her through."

"Mr. Kenneth Boylan," Timothy Kelly informed him, "has left
our community; I hear he has taken the train to San Francisco. I
hear." His hands were busy with the salt shaker, with a glass, with
one of the forks in a mismatched set, straightening a tine bent
askew. They were chunky, powerful hands.

Roosevelt found himself wishing he still had the ranch. A
month in Dakota might not be quite as salubrious as the presence
of a Kenneth Boylan at Minnie's bedside but at least it would help
bring the bloom back to her cheeks: could that be bad? "I still
have friends in the territory," he wanted the couple to know. "It
could be arranged."

"How kind you are," Mrs. Kelly said, seizing his hand on impulse as her husband went to get the door. "How very kind."

Jacob Riis was standing on the threshold, introducing himself. "I had to find out how Minnie was doing," he said, off-duty. Charles Dana and the editors of the *Sun* had the scoop he'd telephoned in, the extra already on its way to the breathless newsboys gathered on Park Row. "As you see, no pad, no pencil. Just me."

If the Kellys didn't mind, he'd be happy to take the Commissioner's place at the kitchen table. Edith was alone on the other side of the river and Riis saw no reason to keep her waiting any longer . . . did Teddy?

A spray of laughter filled the air as Roosevelt made for the door. "Jake," he grinned, "you just might be better for that girl upstairs than Kenneth Boylan and the Dakota Territory put together."

He certainly was doing wonders for the marriage of Mr. and Mrs. Theodore Roosevelt.

■ His clothing was dry by the time he reached Sixty-second Street, but shrunk. "Ted'll be able to fit in that jacket now," Edith was sure, collecting it and the rest of the muddied outfit upstairs behind the closed door of their bedroom. Could that be why T.R. was glowering like that, because he'd ruined yet another coat and suit? No, that couldn't be it: "You're the only man I know who likes to go in swimming fully dressed."

It wasn't the clothes, of course. It was Richard; that the instinct he relied on could have been so wrong. So fundamentally wrong.

"I should have seen through him, Edith. The night I met him." A man on the up-and-up was just not to be found in Murphy's Saloon having drinks with Estes Hanrahan, "not at two in the afternoon, much less at two in the morning."

What made it worse was how eager he'd been to be gulled, to believe Richard the knight-errant of the Tenderloin, undercover on his own personal initiative.

"So the department isn't tarred if anything goes sour," the explanation went that night on Tenth Avenue, exciting the hell out of the newly appointed President of the Police Board. "No one could make up a story like that, I said. Not off the cuff at that time of night. It *had* to be true"—just as Elliott's repeated promises of abstinence had to be true. "Teedie wanted them to be, so they were." Until they were not.

"Hindsight is a perfect science," Edith countered, preceding him down the second-floor hall to check in on Officer Hargate, asleep on the bed in the guest room, the regular rise and fall of his bandaged rib cage reassuring.

T.R. joined his wife at the headboard, musing in a voice modulated so as not to wake the patient. "All right, I agree: I had no reason to think Richard wasn't the idealistic young man he pretended to be, not then." But later?

Were Theodore Roosevelt as observant as he liked to believe he was, he'd have noticed the ring on Eugene DeLacy's finger right there that afternoon at the Dakota, and he'd have remembered seeing another just like it on Officer Kerner, his recently selected aide.

"Shedding a whole new light on what Richard was and the real reason I found him with Estes Hanrahan in that bar." One thing would have been immediately clear: it had nothing to do with going undercover to "get the goods" on the leader of the West Side gangs.

"What did it have to do with, then?"

They looked down. Lindsay Hargate's eyes were open, the lids blinking to focus the pupils. Red veins fanned out across the whites, but the glaze was gone. Dr. Dietz would get a box of Cracker Jacks from Ethel and the boys and a hearty handshake from the head of the house.

"*Mis*ter Hargate." How was he feeling?

"Like I was shot." The rookie attempted a rueful little grin.

"You're supposed to be sleeping," Ethel admonished, motherly. Could she get him something?

"Just a finish to what the Commissioner was saying—why Kerner was in the bar with Hanrahan." The grin broadened. "I'm not going to even come close to falling asleep if I don't hear."

"Well." Teddy couldn't say for sure, "but I will bet my bottom dollar they were there to negotiate a deal for supplies and equipment. Building material."

"To make the flying machine."

"Precisely." What better than the black market when you want to avoid leaving a trail of receipts and bills of sale behind you, when you want to get a good discount on some damned expensive pieces of equipment—"and who ran the biggest black market in this city?"

Hanrahan, past tense. Walter Reed had called with the news from Staten Island the night before. The silent partner in the conspiracy had, ironically, succumbed at the same time as the Kerners, less a victim of the underwater altercation with the Police Commissioner than of his own greed.

"Richard wouldn't have answered that ad I put in the classified," T.R. was certain. "He wouldn't have had to: Wolf had the flying machine just about finished by then. But, of course, Estes didn't know that, did he."

Lindy propped himself up despite the resulting vertigo, his eyes glinting with interest. "So when he saw that ad in the paper, he figured if he acted fast enough he could get there first, buy those pages for a song—"

"—or take them, even better." The profit would have been sky's the limit, wouldn't it, his partners willing to give up their right arms to have every last sketch back in the set. "It wasn't going to be Hanrahan's day, even if we weren't waiting for him on the ferry." Roosevelt pressed the patrolman back down against the pillow. "Edith and I expect that you will now shut your eyes as the doctor instructed: we do not want to hear a peep out of you until tomorrow, late morning."

The loveliest of smiles transformed the youthful face. "Good night, Commissioner," he whispered. "Mrs. R."

"Good night, Lindy," even though the clock on the mantel said 1 P.M. "Sleep well."

"Yes, ma'am." Oh. "Sir? Miss Kelly: is she all right?"

"She is just fine," Teddy assured him, grinning at his wife when they were out in the hall and the door was closed. "With two new beaux she is going to be more than 'fine,' she is going to be belle of the ball!"

"*Two* new beaux?" Edith followed him back into their bedroom. "Officer Hargate and who else? Theodore?"

Would he stop smiling at her like that and talk?

■ "Bang!" said Kermit. "Bam! I don't care who you are, Mr. Theodore Roosevelt, you aren't getting onto this flying machine!"

"Don't bet on it, Kerner," came the retort, Ted having assumed the role of their father, his own rifle up, very realistic for a toy. "Pow! Pow!"

"Ahh, ya got me," his brother winced, clutching his clavicle and falling back between the four upturned chairs that served as a jury-rigged airship.

"And here I come!" The older of the boys scrambled up over the legs of the chair, boarding. "Told you I'd get on."

"If I knock you off, remember: it's a mile down now—we're a mile up in the air and you are going to go squish! Splat! All over the place."

Gun barrels clashed, the signal for the wrestling match which commenced. One of the chairs was sent spiraling across the waxed oak of the floor, halting only in collision with an armoire.

"Is this where this belongs?" Edith was standing next to the armoire, the tapping of her high-button shoes indicating parental displeasure.

Gulp, said Kermit's Adam's apple, the sound all too audible.

"We were playing Daddy and the Flying Machine," Ted felt obliged to add. "Mrs. Day didn't mind when we did it with her dining room chairs."

"That wasn't an airship." Kermit wanted to keep the record straight. "It was a fort."

"Who told you Mrs. Day 'didn't mind'?" their mother was curious to know. "Clarence?"

"Well." More would have been forthcoming—eventually—but Ted was tapping Kermit's ankle with the side of his shoe.

"Maybe we'd better put these chairs back in the dining room before Mother gets real mad at us . . . ?"

"Never," Edith declared, "have I heard you say anything so wise. Never." They scurried under her withering gaze, saved from further reproach by the thunder preceding their father, descending the stairs.

"So much noise." Disparagement mitigated by a wink. "No wonder the young man in the guest room is awake again." Neither Edith nor the children were to worry, however: "I heard his belly growling and I think that's the sound that actually got him up."

"He's hungry?" The kind of news that always brought relief to the face of the lady in charge of the sickroom.

"Ravenous," T.R. informed her, pecking at her mouth with puckered lips, deliberately tickling her with his mustache.

"Mr. Roosevelt!" In front of the children?

"Pancakes" was his only response. "Eggs. Three of each. Four rashers of bacon. Sautéed potatoes, what do you think?"

"For someone shot twice thirty-six hours ago?"

"Thirty-four." The statistician in Kermit felt bound to speak for the record.

"Porridge." Edith Roosevelt's prescription for the recovering patient. "Oatmeal. One soft-boiled egg on the side."

"Oatmeal?" Alice was joining them, followed by Ethel. "We're not having oatmeal for breakfast, are we?" Oatmeal was for babies like Archie. For people with buck teeth, like cousin Nell.

"And police officers with holes in them," her mother insisted. "Let's see what Officer Hargate can keep down before we shovel the pantry into his mouth."

Theodore could have the pancakes, if he wanted. He could have the bacon, the eggs, the sautéed potatoes and anything else they might have on hand. His own eighteen hours of sleep was fine, but now it was time to fuel the furnace and ward off the chill he'd no doubt break out with in the next few minutes.

"Give me your forehead."

"My forehead is fine." He avoided her palm and went for his coat. How could the light of his life be so cruel as to tempt him with a menu like that when she knew he had an early morning appointment downtown on Mulberry Street?

"You didn't mention it."

"Of course I did." Teddy distinctly remembered returning to their bedroom after making the phone call and . . . oh. "That's right. You were still wrapped up in the blanket."

First he'd shave, he'd thought. Then he'd tell her about the DeLacys.

"That's who you're meeting with? Doesn't this case ever end?" Hadn't T.R. come home telling her it was done with, finally done with?

"It is." Except for the return of a signet ring to the next of kin, it was finally done with.

■ He drew it out of the pocket on the lower right side of his jacket and passed it across the desk, struck by the way the morning sunlight from the window facing Houston Street beaded on the collet.

"Charles's ring," the old man whispered. "Look. Eugene." Trembling fingers brought it up for comparison, side by side, both rings, perfectly matched. "Aren't they beautiful?"

His body was racked by sudden sobs, but DeLacy refused to let either Roosevelt or his son reach out with a comforting hand.

"I expected I'd cry," he told them as he warded them off with the ragged handkerchief he'd fished up from his suit, working to regain his composure. "Maybe I'll go into soothsaying in my old age. The fulfillment of a lifelong ambition to run away with a carnival."

An improvement, perhaps, over the Wall Street office in which he'd finally found employment as second assistant bookkeeper.

"Between Pop's green eyeshade and my little changemaker on the Fourteenth Street Crosstown," Charles's brother revealed, "we're beginning to catch up on our debts, slowly."

"Not so slowly from here on in." The Commissioner's eyes twinkled behind the *pince-nez*.

"Excuse me?" Eugene spoke for his father as well as for himself.

"Without your help in this investigation those men would be on their way back to Germany, ready to start manufacturing God knows how many airships. I'd say that calls for a reward, don't you?" They could put the word "substantial" in front of the word "reward" if they liked.

"Mr. Roosevelt." Hushed. Awed. "What can we say?"

"Wait till I bring it up at the next meeting of the Board, tomorrow at three." Not that he anticipated any problems authorizing the funds—"Andrew Parker might very well want to be the one who hands you the voucher."

"Andrew Parker won't be there tomorrow at three—he and Freddie Grant had some fun yesterday, and rescheduled that meeting for right now." Jacob Riis stood at the top of the stairwell just outside Teddy's office, posing with an insouciant hand draped over the finial at the top of the banister.

" 'Now'?"

"Even as we speak." Something to do with abolishing the four-man reform board completely, replacing it with a kind of metropolitan kingpin answerable only to the legislature in Albany. " 'The legislature' is a real nice way of saying Boss Platt, don't you think?"

T.R. was already on the march, not having to think when he already knew. The DeLacys would be hearing from him, he promised, shooting a farewell over his shoulder as he sped down the stairs to the hearing room at the end of the hall below. "Andrew D. Parker and Frederick D. Grant are not selling this department out to the bosses," he wanted Jake to know as he strode through the double doors in his best mastiff manner. "I don't care what political party they belong to."

The men on the dais stood up in place, as though caught in the corncrib with a set of French postcards. "Theodore," said Grant. It sounded more like "Curses, foiled again."

Commissioner Parker also said "Theodore," in a voice more discommoded than surprised. He was in his element here, shoes dry, face stitched, and his characteristic aplomb could be only momentarily disturbed by their colleague's typically bombastic entrance. "Shouldn't you be sleeping in for the rest of the week?"

"And miss the party?" He took the President's chair and gavel, pounding it and beaming. "About this 'kingpin' proposal, now."

■ Not a bad session. Not a bad session at all, he reflected as he headed for the staircase two hours later. The DeLacy reward had been approved, three of the four board members voting yea, and by the same vote Boss Platt's takeover had been tabled, if only for the moment.

Good enough. All Teddy needed was time: he could lobby against the proposition very nicely, thank you.

"Commissioner." Sergeant Balter had a letter for him, hand-delivered. "The lady asked me to give it to you personal."

Lady?

"Yes, sir. I told her you'd be coming out of the board room any minute but she said it was all right, she had to take the boy shopping or something."

About four years old, maybe five, the sergeant estimated when asked, T.R. nodding as he examined the signature beneath the 'Most Sincerely' at the bottom of the page.

> *My Dear Mr. Roosevelt. It is with a feeling of overwhelming gratitude that I write to you, for seeing what no one else on two continents was able to see: that the death of my cousin, Mr. Charles DeLacy, was not the result of a random attack by mindless hooligans but, rather, a premeditated attempt to steal something unique and important not just from one man, but from all. What a shame it is that, for all the extraordinary effort you extended on his behalf, it was ultimately not possible to preserve the work which was meant to be Charles's legacy to the world.*
>
> *Even so, I believe with all my heart that his achievement will live because Mr. Theodore Roosevelt will insist upon it; that someday, somehow, some young inventor will be inspired by whatever pages of the plans are left. Perhaps it will not happen overnight, nor till after the turn of the century, but I am convinced that it will happen.*
>
> *A request, then, if you would be as kind as you already*

have been. When the time comes, it would make me the happiest woman in the world if you would see to it that my son, your brother's child, were present. To that end, I will try to keep you informed of our whereabouts—which will be, as of the first of this month, the Nation Boarding House on Fifteenth Street in Dayton, Ohio. I am told that Dayton is a wonderful city in which to raise a boy, and I am sure he will grow up tall and happy there.

How could he not? Mr. Tyrone Frank, the man to whom I am now betrothed, tells me that the home we will be moving into is located directly across the street from a bicycle shop.

Once more, thank you for privately proving that the public trust is not misplaced in you; I am sure your career will be nothing but blessed. For now and for ever I remain Yours, Most Sincerely . . .

Dayton.

A wonderful city in which to raise a boy, indeed. Small, tree-shaded, clean . . . Teddy approved. And what in blazes was Minnie Gertrude Kelly doing back at her desk?

"You're supposed to be taking a vacation," he reminded her as he walked into his office. "Sleep late, entertain a caller or two downstairs in the parlor—"

"I have," she said quietly. "Mr. Riis has been very solicitous, and Officer Hargate telephoned from his sickbed. I've slept, I've meditated; I've even mourned—not the Richard that was but the Richard I thought I knew—and after all of that I said to myself, 'What a close call. What a close, close call.' "

She could have been married to Officer Kerner; she could even have been carrying his child. What if it had taken that long for the truth to come out? What would she have done then?

"It scares me, the way it happened, but the truth is it could have come out a lot worse, a whole lot worse, and I'm feeling greatly relieved that I'm alive to get over it." If there were no objection, Minnie would seat herself at the Underwood "and fin-

ish all those letters I didn't get to because I left the office so early
the other day."

The Commissioner regarded her for one more moment and
then burst out with an ebullient "By George," *de*light radiating.
"I like that attitude. Forward, march!" Of course she could work
the emotions out at her typewriter. "To be honest with you, I was
beginning to have my doubts about how I was going to get along
here without you on the job."

Splendid!

"Get me Mr. Thomas Platt on the phone; we'll just go ahead
and start the day."

"Oh," his secretary said before he could move on into the inner
office. Did T.R. want her to do that even though his first appointment was already waiting behind the door?

It had been set some weeks previous, cablegrams having arrived
from London to inform Roosevelt and other prominent New
Yorkers that Second Lieutenant Winston Spencer Churchill, elder
son of the late Lord Randolph, would upon his graduation from
Sandhurst be stopping in the city—

"—On his way to Cuba, right. Right," Teddy whooped, the
drawers of the filing cabinets in his mind rolling open all at once.
"Correspondent for *The Daily Graphic* on Fleet Street, unless I'm
mistaken?"

The inquiry was put directly to the twenty-one-year-old now
standing in the open door, a slender subaltern in mufti: four-
button Savile Row jacket, single-breasted, wing collar, speckled
bow tie. The hat resting on the table adjacent was an elongated
bowler which, when worn, was designed to square a face rather
too round and at the same time hide a head of flaxen hair already
too thin.

"Indeed *The Daily Graphic*," young Churchill acknowledged,
the rumble of his voice not at all consonant with his appearance,
callow in spite of (or perhaps because of) the gargantuan cigar in
his hand. "They are hoping someone fresh will have the stomach
for a trip into the Sierra Maestra—an interview with Señor Martí.
Under fire, preferably."

"I wish I could go with you." It was the truth. The absolute truth. Roosevelt had been keeping his eye on Cuba, convinced that sooner or later the United States was going to get involved. "If Martí and Gómez can't do the job by themselves, we just might have to help them out. By George," he enthused. "It would be fun to send those Spaniards packing."

"You've been to war, sir?" Envy was unconcealed on Churchill's face. He envied anyone who had been to war, who knew the thrill of having been under fire, the ammunition live, potentially lethal. The high-pitched rattle of the Mauser was the real lure in Cuba, the fragrance of gunpowder.

History turned on such things. A single individual could make a difference, a tremendous difference, perhaps even with only one shot.

"Yes," the Commissioner had to agree, even if his war had so far been only a skirmish. It whetted the appetite, by God, and it was he who was the envious one, envious of the military upbringing, the professional training, the destination south. Into combat? Not yet.

"Come with me," Churchill urged, impulsive. "We've been promised an excursion to the front lines and I wouldn't be surprised if we saw some action; it would take only four or six weeks away from your desk." Easily managed for an official of Teddy's standing, he was sure.

"I'm tempted."

Parker would love it. And Boss Platt. "Go, by all means," they'd say, smiling. Smiling. "We'll come down to the station and see you off, in person."

When the campaign was over, T.R. would return to find his commissionership abolished, an ombudsman in his chair.

"Cuba is going to have to wait for me, I'm afraid." He gestured the Englishman's attention to the space between his ankle and the nearest leg of his desk. "You might not be able to see this with your eyes, but there is a chain there; I think it's made of Mr. Bessemer's steel." Only one thing could break it: "a declaration of war."

"Spain would actually have to make an overt move against the

United States for that to happen," in Churchill's opinion. "Do you think they'd be that stupid?"

"I have every confidence in the government of Spain," Roosevelt assured him, glancing up at the knock on the half-open door. "Miss Kelly?"

"Pardon the interruption, Commissioner," she said in a voice laced with urgency. "There's some kind of gun battle going on in the lobby of *The Morning Telegraph.* Anarchists, the man said."

" 'Man'?"

"He told me to tell you the name was Masterson and you knew him from out West."

"Bat? Bat Masterson's in town?" It was as though a torch had been applied to the executive's rump, as the subaltern later described it. "What the hell is he doing at the *Telegraph?"*

"Writing sports news," if Minnie had translated the gist of his remarks correctly. It had been hard to hear, "the gunshots were that loud."

"Bully!" the President of New York City's Police Board declared, chugging like one of Gottlieb Daimler's pistons, rounding Churchill up and running them both through the door into the hall. "Maybe we won't have to go all the way to Cuba to get into combat, after all!"

AFTERWORD

■ The feud between Theodore Roosevelt and Andrew Parker simmered for another year or so until, finally, in the spring of 1897, T.R. decided that it was time to return to Washington, the newly elected William McKinley offering him a position as Assistant Secretary of the Navy. He was serving in this capacity when the battleship *Maine* exploded in Havana harbor, almost immediately having himself appointed lieutenant colonel, second in command of the First U.S. Volunteer Cavalry. "Teddy's Terrors," the newspapers said in the beginning, changing that to "Teddy's Cowboy Contingent" and "Teddy's Riotous Rounders." It eventually became "Teddy's Rough 'Uns": the Rough Riders.

When he and his men returned from Cuba on August 15, 1898, the Republicans in Albany were ready to greet him with their party's gubernatorial nomination, which he promptly accepted. By January 1 he was in residence at the governor's mansion.

To get this disturbingly single-minded new governor off their backs, the bosses, Thomas C. Platt in the forefront, arranged the vice presidency at the first available opportunity, thinking that after March 4, 1901, Theodore Roosevelt would be, like Andrew Parker before him, consigned to the category of "whatever happened to him."

Neither boss reckoned with a man named Leon Czolgosz.

As for Mrs. Evans, it is not known whether she ever actually moved with her son to Dayton, nor whether she actually married again, Mr. Tyrone Frank or anyone else. There were several boys and young men present on the beach at Kitty Hawk on December 17, 1903, but the list of surnames published in the local newspaper that day included no Evans, Frank or Roosevelt.